Organs of Greed

A Novel By

A. A. Fowler MD

First Print Edition: July 2013

To Kathy, you've been my constant support, you never stopped believing.

Acknowledgements

Many thanks to members of the Richmond, Virginia SWAT team for their amazing suggestions that helped me create certain critical scenarios and scenes. Many thanks to Bobbie Christmas of Zebra Communications, Atlanta, Georgia for her masterful editing of the novel. Bobbie you made the words flow. Many many thanks to Amy Siders and Robert Reid and 52 Novels for their superb work formatting the manuscript for publication. Extreme thanks to Rebecca Swift for her amazing artwork and cover design. And finally, thanks to the Virginia Commonwealth University Department of Biochemistry and to the basic scientists who do amazing work in the laboratories of the Division of Pulmonary Disease and Critical Care Medicine at VCU. Your input and suggestions brought the entire novel together. And finally thanks to daughter Emily who thought up the sharp tagline for the cover when Dad couldn't get it together.

"It remains now to be seen how society will manage transplantation, the most recent product of its creativity and sponsorship"

—Thomas Starzl, MD
University of Pittsburgh

Where will it all end? What happens when the overheated medical market place of the 21st century drives runaway technology and rushed advances in drug development? Doctor Steven Fisher, a prominent heart transplant surgeon, gets a full dose of the possibilities as he races to crack open a secret conspiracy. Fighting for his life and fighting against time, Fisher confronts the treacherous scheme to save his close friends and to rescue the world of transplant medicine.

Organs of Greed

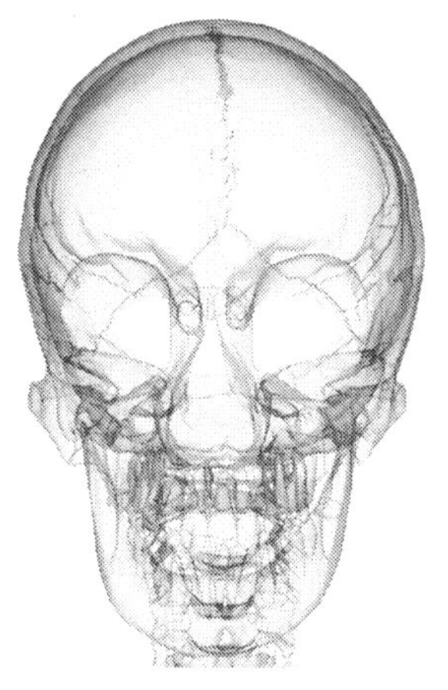

PROLOGUE

January 31

Cold fingers tugged on the stiffened shoe.

"Damn foot's going to fall off," the woman rasped.

A fissured face, cracked and weathered by the cold, raised from its perch. Tired eyes glanced about. The warmth and comfort brought by a bottle of wine had long since passed, and the woman had become offended by the odor of rain-soaked garbage littered around her cardboard house.

"Got to get some blood moving through that foot. Can't keep sitting here while the thing freezes."

Icy wind that howled past her makeshift shelter and the roar of the Caton River were the only sounds she heard. The city was quiet. Bitter cold kept it that way at night.

She gazed out at the city across the river. The few friends she knew would be searching for shelter. They, too, would find it tough to come by as the city turned the homeless away from overcrowded shelters. Many had sought safe haven in a vacant factory building down river, until a fire there had killed many.

She replayed her memory of that fire as wet walls sagged around her. She was in the old factory that night, seeking protection from the cold, hoping to find food. She had little recollection, recalling only her panicked dash away from the flames. Muffled cries of those trapped inside the blaze still haunted her.

Tears welled up as she stared through sleepless eyes. So many years she had struggled to free her mind of the voices, voices no one understood — sometimes friendly, sometimes comforting, sometimes maddening. Recently, they spoke more clearly. Still, none of her friends heard them.

Unexpectedly, her waterlogged box collapsed, folding in around her. She jerked back from her thoughts.

"Got to get my ass moving."

With much effort she stood, steadied herself against a gust of wind and reached for a small wire cart lying beside her. She then began hobbling towards the access road that led under the Ninth Street Bridge.

City lights illuminating a low cloud cover painted the night a ghostly orange-blue as she approached a sharp bend in the road. A few pin pricks of sensation gave a bit of assurance that her left foot wasn't completely frozen.

She struggled with the cart, towing it through the icy mud. Occasionally she paused and glanced up the access road, to keep her bearings as she ambled. Suddenly, though, she became aware of new images up ahead.

"What the hell is that?" she moaned to herself

She stared a moment, at first unconcerned. Strange things happened on the streets. She had seen many over the years. Turn your head, look the other way, and keep going, she told herself. She struggled on farther, glancing occasionally towards the city street.

The images had now become clearer. She stopped again. A sliver of fear crawled through her chest. The blurry silhouettes she'd seen before turned out to be three large men standing beside a darkened automobile.

There was silence for a moment — then a voice.

"That you, Mattie?"

The sound of the voice cut through the frigid air slicing into her brain.

Her heart pounded as sweat oozed onto her hands. She turned and headed back towards her cardboard home, her legs weakened by fear.

"Wrong way, Mattie."

That voice, it's familiar, she thought, as she struggled through the slush.

"We have a little deal to settle, don't we, Mattie?"

Fighting to keep panic from seizing her mind, she released the cart.

That voice. Why did she know that voice?

Fear loosened the cobwebs in her brain as she limped away from the figures. If she could make it to her campsite under the bridge, she would know where to hide.

"Don't wait too long," a voice whispered. "What's the range of that thing, anyway?"

Beside the whispering figure, a muted click was heard. The night scope atop the rifle splashed a milky-green light across a marksman's eyes as he aimed downrange. Through the sight, the woman's tattered clothing was sharp and clear. A wire cart was visible ten yards behind her.

"Stop your fucking chitchat and give me some space." The marksman elbowed the man next to him. "I'm accurate to at least a hundred yards."

The feeling in the woman's foot had not returned, but her gait had become more rhythmic. Her thoughts came easier as she approached the turn that led under the bridge. A plan formed as she examined her options. She would reach the camp, melt into the surrounding brush and escape down river. I'll be safe, she told herself.

Behind her, a soft thud rose above the wind. Her mind had only begun processing the noise, when the dart struck her at mid-thigh.

Searing pain filled her consciousness as the force of the impact threw her off balance. She fell forward into the slush, twisting her body to grope for the source of the pain. Her struggles were in vain. Powerful chemicals had entered her body.

Warmth, she thought. Warmth was everywhere. Her nightmare was put on hold as the powerful narcotic surged into her brain. Relax came the drug's directive.

For a few moments, calm flowed through her weathered body, and she floated.

Soon, however, fear jolted her mind again. My arm, she thought, ripping away from the short-lived trance. She struggled to a sitting position, her body growing heavier as the moments passed. She wanted to scream, but her voice wouldn't respond.

Heavy, so heavy. Can't anybody see I'm dying?

The paralytic agent completed its work, and she fell forward, her face striking the icy mud. She was down, motionless, paralyzed. The drugs produced a suspended animation, leaving her aware of her surroundings, yet unable to respond to them. She heard the rhythmic clicking sound and the approaching voices.

They are coming! That clicking! Why was it familiar?

The voice she recognized before she fled followed close behind the clicking. She tried to think as her mind teetered on the brink of unconsciousness. Her efforts were useless. She remembered no more as she succumbed.

"She's down."

A shadowy figure approached and knelt beside the woman lying still on the road. With a quick motion, a glove was removed, and fingers probed her neck.

"She's alive. She's bradycardic, but she'll do," he noted in guttural dialect.

"Don't talk that medical gibberish shit."

The voice came from ten feet away. The marksman was approaching. "Keep that crap to yourself."

"Her heart's beating slowly," the kneeling man remitted meekly. An almost imperceptible expression of scorn crossed his dark face. He knew the marksman would never see it.

"Idiots. Bring the car down, and be careful putting her in."

The rhythmic snapping sounded again as the kneeling man stood and headed for the car a hundred yards away.

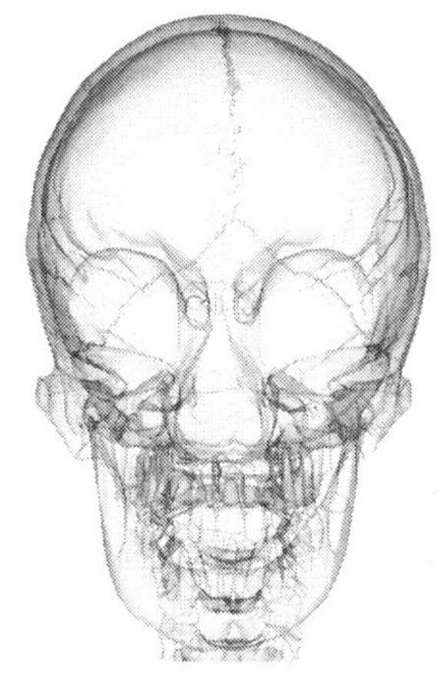

CHAPTER ONE

"Are we ready yet?"

No response.

In the near darkness of the room, the surgeon reached to the collar of his scrub shirt, felt the metal edges of the small microphone clipped there and adjusted it slightly.

"Are we ready yet?" The commanding tone reeked of impatience. "I don't have all day."

"Almost ready," a voice replied over the small speaker positioned behind the surgeon's shoulder. "Anesthesia induction is proceeding nicely."

"Then I can begin system initiation?" His voice still contained an impatient edge.

No reply.

"Shit," he whispered behind clinched teeth, careful not to be overheard. "What a fucking inconvenience, sitting here wasting my day off while . . . ."

"Okay to initiate," the voice crackled from the speaker.

"Fucking finally." He swiveled his chair toward a flat panel screen containing an array of lighted instrumentation.

In the center of the panel, two rows of pressure-sensitive icons glowed muted yellow. From where he sat, a transilluminated label TELEPRESENCE was visible on the monitor. With a light touch, he pushed icons starting with the top row from left to right. Pale yellow turned to bright green as he worked.

At once, a large disk drive emitted its familiar whine. Program initiation had begun.

Satisfied all programs had come online, the impatient surgeon rotated the chair toward a cubicle adjacent to the screen. The curious structure, suspended at waist height, measured nearly three feet on each side and opened on a single side. Its interior was dark. By reflex, he reached below the armrest, pressing two buttons that controlled preset adjustments. The seat and back inflated, molding the chair to his body. Slowly, the chair moved forward, inclining slightly to lift his feet off the carpet. He felt the pressure of footrests as they rose from the floor. Once the chair was fully adjusted, a familiar floating sensation surrounded him.

Lying directly in front of him on the surface of the enclosure, the virtual hood spilled its low intensity light. He picked it up and placed it on his head bringing two small viewing screens comfortably before his eyes. A continuous series of numbers and mathematical formulas associated with final system checks raced across the lower third of the screens. The flow of numbers and formulas were meaningless to the surgeon. As always he was there merely to operate. Within moments, a virtual surgical field appeared. He inspected it with the same critical eye he would apply if the patient was physically present.

"We're looking good from here." A more relaxed tone crept into his voice. Placing the hood on and seeing the surgical field before him always had a calming effect.

The voice flowed from the speaker. "Anesthesia is complete. I await your directions."

"Good. Move the nephrectomy frame into position and lock it into place."

The surgeon fidgeted as he waited for a response.

"Nephrectomy frame in place and secure," the voice replied.

"Very well." He slid his arms forward. They moved no more than four inches before his hands contacted the supple leather of the controller gloves, exactly where he had left them before. One at a time, he slipped on the gloves and adjusted his upper body in the molded chair until he was comfortable.

"Activate nephrectomy frame and power up the laser."

"Activated. You're online."

The surgeon moved the index finger of the right glove away from his other fingers. A virtual menu appeared suspended in the space above the cartoon-like surgical field before him. The menu listed an array of instruments from which he could choose. He reached forward in space, his index finger extended until he touched the third option: laser. The laser option flashed three times and the menu disappeared.

He spoke softly into the microphone. "Adjust the laser to cutting and coagulation at five hundred-fifty."

"Five hundred-fifty set."

Positioning the virtual laser beside the spine, the surgeon made a sweeping arc-like movement with his gloved hand. The right flank of the nameless individual sharing his virtual world opened in a bloodless manner, displaying the tissue below a small layer of adipose.

He worked quickly, virtually placing retractors to open the flank. A brief blunt dissection followed, and then he went back to the laser. Within ten minutes, the kidney came into view. The surgeon worked quickly, freeing the organ from its surrounding fat and anatomic structures. He placed vascular clips on the kidney's arterial and venous supply and severed them. Next, he clipped and cut the ureter. Another index finger movement, and the menu appeared again. He pointed to the choice: finger/grabber. Into the field appeared a mechanical hand. Using swift and certain movements with the controller glove, the surgeon saw the mechanical hand reach into the deep wound and retrieve the kidney. A pair of gloved hands appeared in the screen holding a green plastic bowl. The grabber gently released the kidney. Less than twenty minutes had passed.

The surgeon inspected the wound ensuring no bleeding sites had escaped his attention. Satisfied, he said, "Lay a sterile cover over the wound. Infuse fifty-thousand units of GrowStimulin now and again at eight hours. The client should be able to leave at that point."

"Yes sir," the voice replied. "All vital signs stable."

"Good."

He removed the gloves and hood and placed them down carefully. With his left hand, he located the chair's adjustment switch and pressed it. A muted hiss followed as the chair decompressed, loosening its grip on his torso. The surgeon turned to the panel and pressed a bright blue switch labeled auto-shutdown. The whine of the massive drive changed frequency as their RPMs fell.

He stood and looked at the faint glow of his wristwatch.

"Jesus." He was late for his scheduled tee-time at the club.

He was about to open the door to the small room when paused and returned to the console. He reached into his pocket and struggled to pull out a ring that held a number of keys. Identifying the one he wanted, he opened a drawer, took out a small ledger and shoved the drawer shut with his knee. He glanced at his watch again.

"Shit." He sat and hurriedly recorded the procedure. When he had finished, he stood and fumbled for the key ring once again but then stopped.

"Screw it."

He tossed the ledger on top of the console and quietly slipped out, locking the door behind.

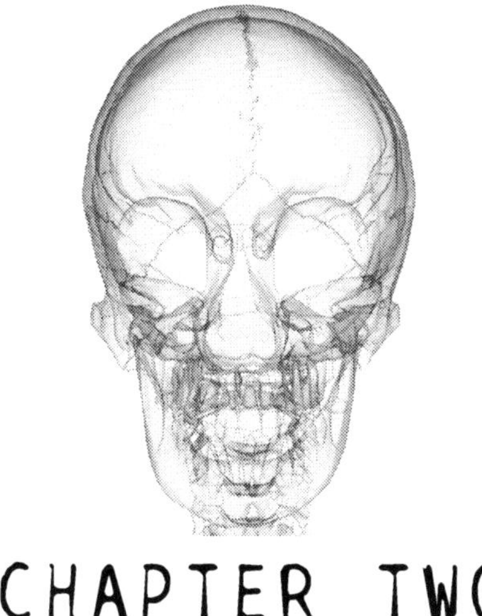

CHAPTER TWO

February 1

A brilliant sun lit the day. Fluorescent red and orange leaves loosened by gentle breezes journeyed towards earth. Rays of sunshine pierced through the fiery canopy of a large maple tree.

An attractive woman dressed in denim jeans kneeled to pluck stalks of clover.

"Wait, please wait. I'm coming," a voice pleaded.

The woman stood and glanced in the direction of the voice. Recognition crisscrossed her face with lines of worry.

She turned and walked away, passing under the canopy. Unexpectedly, a breeze whipped up fallen leaves, obscuring her departure.

Then it came — an annoying little sound. When it began it was far away, out of sight.

At first indistinct and out of the reaches of conscious thought, the noise soon became more distinct, an incessant chattering. It destroyed the moment, the pleasure of the breeze, the sky.

Chatter, chatter, chatter. The interruption spoiled the entire afternoon.

Wait. It was a ringing, not chattering.

Over and over the ringing became louder and more striking, each time the bells sounded.

Without warning, all remnants of the day were shattered, as if painted on a plate-glass canvas.

Then there was darkness — the peaceful day destroyed.

The noise didn't stop with the destruction of the day. The intrusive ringing broke the silence.

Ring! Ring!

Ring! Ring!

Doctor Steven Fisher sat bolt upright, disoriented, awakened from a deep sleep.

Ring! Ring!

Ring! Ring!

On a rickety table beside his bed, the telephone wailed.

His heart raced and his head pounded from the surprise. By automatic behavior, Fisher stroked his fingers through his hair. Beads of cold sweat were there.

Still only half oriented, he thrust his hand at the sound and groped. His hands trembled as he struggled in the darkness.

Finally, he secured the receiver with a death grip and hauled the instrument to his mouth.

"Hello." Fisher's response resembled a whisper.

"Is this Dr. Fisher?" The voice poured from the receiver.

He jerked the receiver away from his ear.

"Yes," Fisher responded, not completely awake.

"Dr. Fisher, this is the Medford University Hospital operator." The voice ascended and descended pitch like a pianist rolling up and down the scales of a piano.

"Dr. Binzemore in Medford Trauma would like to speak with you."

"Who wants me?" Fisher continued to struggle with who and where he was.

Ignoring Fisher's question, the hospital operator carried right on. "Dr. Fisher, shall I connect you?"

A long pause ensued. Fisher glanced around the bedroom of his apartment. Soft blue numbers on the bedside clock displayed the time as one 1:45 a.m. The clock display cast a pale blue light on a half empty bottle that, five hours earlier had been a fifth of Jack Daniels whiskey.

"Dr. Fisher, shall I connect you?" The voice was growing impatient.

Finally, Fisher pulled out of his disorientation and replied firmly, "No, I'll call back."

He replaced the telephone onto its receiver and rotated to a sitting position, his feet fumbling for the floor. His head and the knot of brown hair above it immediately sought the cradle of his hands. The reality of the situation was driving its way into his foggy mind.

He was Steven Fisher, Associate Professor of Surgery and a transplant surgeon, and he was hung over. His mouth was parched, and his head pounded.

The dream. Again, the same dream, he thought. It was not the first time he'd been troubled by his dreams. After Iraq, recurrent dreams drove him to the brink of insanity.

He picked up the receiver again. Feeling the key pad in the dark, he punched the last button on the top. The phone's speed-dial feature routed the call to Medford University Emergency Department.

"Medford Trauma," a youthful voice answered after a single ring.

Fisher fought to stay upright while holding the telephone to his ear. He spoke with his best effort. "Dr. Binzemore, please. Dr. Fisher returning his call."

Alan Binzemore, a fifth-year surgical resident, assigned to the Cardiac Transplant Service, was one of Medford University's finest.

After a brief delay, Binzemore came on the line. "Dr. Fisher?"

Binzemore's voice, though considerably softer than the operator's, resounded inside Fisher's hung-over brain.

"We've got a heart for Patricia Bingham. Medford Neurosurgery contacted OrganLink. They have an eighteen-year-old donor with a gunshot wound to the head. The parents consented to let his organs go. Father's a banker at one of Richland's big banks. He and the mother want it done quickly."

Binzemore halted his verbal bombardment momentarily and awaited a reply. When none was forthcoming, he continued. "The boy is out of surgery, but he's shocky. Dr. Nuncio from Neurosurgery said they almost lost him twice during exploratory craniotomy, but both times they got him back. Unofficially, the bullet tore into the left side of his head, massively damaging the left half of his brain. The neuro team's got vasopressors running, but his blood pressure's only hanging around one-hundred systolic. From what they're saying, we've got a small window of time to get in there and get the heart before his body goes, Dr. Fisher."

Binzemore's rapid-fire recitation slowly turned the cogwheels of Fisher's mind. Thinking was painful. "Did he get HIV tested and hepatitis screened?" was Fisher's first attempt at a relevant question.

"Yes. I think the neurosurgeons never expected the kid to survive. Organ donation was in the back of their minds from the start. HIV testing and hepatitis screening was done when the kid first landed at Medford Trauma. The tests are back. He's negatve for all."

"That's good."

"Look, I'm heading up to get him settled in the donor OR. When can we expect you?"

Fisher fought back the painful pulsations in his head. "I'll be there shortly, forty minutes, maybe."

"Dr. Fisher, you okay?"

"Fine, Alan," Fisher lied. "I'm fine. Just get up there before he dies. I'll be there soon. What's going to happen to the other organs? Going to be any takers?"

"Yeah, maybe, but the kid's so unstable the other transplant teams may not make it, unless they hurry. We're lucky Mrs. Bingham stayed in town. Transplant coordinator says she's on the way here. If she'd returned to Florida, the heart would most certainly have gone to Taggart Memorial. As it is, they've already called here claiming rights to the heart."

"Right." He replaced the phone in its cradle.

For a moment, Fisher sat in the quiet darkness of the apartment he had occupied for a month and a half. Six weeks since leaving Sharon, he thought. God, it felt like six years.

Although the fright produced by the phone call had passed, Fisher's head still pounded from his alcoholic depravity of the night before. He had not expected the early morning call. In fact, he had not planned to be at Medford the entire next day, but Fisher was the last Medford University surgeon performing heart transplantation, since Chip Carlton's unexpected departure six months earlier.

He stood, rickety and off balance, shielded his eyes, and reached to switch on the bedside light. The bedroom was a scene of chaos. Everywhere clothes were scattered in untidy piles. Boxes lay opened with articles hanging half in, half out. The bed resembled a battleground. Sheets and spread were knotted and no pillow was in sight.

With an unsteady gait, Fisher stepped towards the bathroom, where he flipped the wall switch.

The bathroom light further revealed a sparsely furnished bedroom. Perched atop a cheap wooden dresser along the opposite wall sat a framed photograph. The woman's long blond hair, pulled back tightly behind her head, framed high pink cheek bones, a sharp nose and blazingly blue eyes. Colorful fallen leaves littered the background. The woman, clad in denim jeans and an oversized sweatshirt emblazoned with a Stanford University logo, gazed upwards.

Adjacent to the bedroom, in the kitchen-living room area, counter tops and floors were littered with beer cans and pizza boxes. Unwashed plates filled the sink.

The living room, connected to the kitchen by an archway, contained a small flat screen television that sat on the floor next to a single chair. Past issues of the *American Journal of Surgery* and the *New England Journal of Medicine* were piled on the floor next to the chair. The stack appeared unsteady and ready to topple onto old copies of the *Richland Tribune* that lay nearby. A brass pharmacy light left burning all night stood beside the chair. Empty beer cans were scattered about.

Five minutes passed before Fisher moved his body out of the path of the stinging hot water. As the searing heat of the shower warmed him, he found the after effect of the booze hard to shake.

At forty-seven, Fisher's six-foot frame had remained well-muscled with little flab, despite a chronic lack of exercise and recent heavy alcohol use. Until six weeks earlier he had used early mornings for jogging. As bad as a surgeon's weekly hospital schedule was, Fisher had managed to stay well-conditioned. Leaving Sharon had changed that. He stopped running. Unwittingly, he recoiled inward. He spent more and more time alone in introspection. And, after years on the wagon, he picked up the booze again. He kept telling himself it wasn't like before. It was different, not like the months after Danny was killed.

Knowing he had to move, he finally grabbed the soap. Before leaving the shower, he swung the handle leftward. The cold blast proved to be the final boost he needed to snap his mind and body to full wakefulness.

Thank God, he thought climbing out.

At two fifteen, Fisher stepped out from the chaos of apartment number three and walked cautiously down the dimly lit sidewalk in front of the first floor apartments.

He almost stumbled, making the turn that led to the microscopic parking. This place is such cheap shit. Not a fucking light anywhere, he thought, realizing again how much he hated the place.

He had rented the apartment because of its proximity to Medford, expecting it to be temporary. As the arguments with Sharon became worse and her lies became more obvious, he had to leave. The night he left, there had been tears, anger and argument. She was trying to . . . .

Stop, he thought. As it always did, his mind put the brakes on. Can't think of this now, got to stay focused. "Got to operate," he muttered to himself.

The small, gravel parking area was dark. Although the night was cloudless, leafless giant oak trees shrouded the cluster of cars in front of Fisher's not-so-ritzy apartment complex. The whole situation left no light to navigate the area he had come to detest. Luckily, his car was close.

The Mazda rotary engine roared to life, and he swung the car out of the depressing complex. He headed for the winding road that hugged the Caton River as it traveled toward Richland. Turning onto River Path Drive, he momentarily broke out from under the thick grove of oak trees that covered the river bank. The half-light of a crescent moon glowed down onto nests of craggy boulders jutting up through the twisting river. River Path Drive was equally twisting, demanding careful coordination to navigate its course.

Fisher's vintage Mazda RX-7 sported a five-speed manual transmission and possessed significant power. Mix together a concoction of endless right and left turns sprinkled liberally with the bountiful gear changes needed to negotiate that section of road and one had a useful medicinal agent that could effectively treat any hangover. Up and down, switch back right, switch back left, the squeal of tires. As he drove, Fisher felt his arm and trunk muscles, tight from hours of inactivity, loosening. He loved the challenge of River Path's roller coaster ride.

Indian Promontory, the sign read, as Fisher approached one of the river's most turbulent sections. The road, mostly level as it ran along the river, climbed precipitously with about one hundred fifty yards of straight asphalt leading to the Promontory. Finally, it swung back right into a hairpin as it turned out of the trees.

Fisher drove to the shoulder of Indian Promontory and stopped. He opened the door, rose slowly out of the warmth, and walked near the precipice. He looked down at the boiling rapids of the Caton River three hundred feet below.

The cold of the February morning enveloped him as he watched the water dance in the moonlight. Within a few moments, Fisher started to shiver, but he lingered a bit longer. Stopping on the Promontory always helped clear his mind.

From where he stood, Richland's twinkling skyline was easily visible. He stared at the display. His head pounded less, but the constant aching and emptiness inside could not be shaken. His marriage of ten years had unraveled. He felt helpless and alone. He had left his comfortable house in the Richland suburbs for a rat hole apartment to cool off — to think things through. Six weeks had gone by and he was no closer to resolving his differences with Sharon than when he left.

"Shit," he uttered aloud. He turned and walked back to the Mazda. There wasn't time to think things out. There was never enough time. The tires squealed as he accelerated away from Indian Promontory.

The road soon became less demanding as the river approached Richland. Around a last sharp bend, the twinkling lights of the Richland skyline became visible again. The drive along River Path had produced its desired effect. The wheels of Fisher's mind were turning a bit faster. He had successfully suppressed painful thoughts of Sharon, but his attempts at mind control and concentration recently had been poor.

In support of the deficient concentration theory, Fisher's musings unpredictably changed gears. From out of the recesses of his mind thoughts of the Med bubbled to the surface. "The Med," he snorted out loud.

The Med, as Medford University was known by its devotees, was in trouble. Its lifeblood and that of virtually all sister medical universities was draining as American health care changed at an ever-quickening pace.

Like many surgeons, he worked long hours, at times going weeks without reading a newspaper or hearing the news. Like most doctors, Fisher was not politically savvy. But, the reasons for the Med's problems had become all too clear. Healthcare reform had devastated academic medicine. It had transformed the practice of medicine into a seething, heated, competitive market creating forces that dragged down American medical universities. Traditional medical schools like Medford University failed to compete for dollars with America's slick, for-profit hospitals. As medical schools struggled for survival, corporations like Health Pursuit, America's largest for-profit hospital corporation, spent hundreds of millions on acquisitions, mergers and persuasive advertising. Their dominance of the medical marketplace of the twenty-first century was, in essence, guaranteed.

The transmission whined loudly as Fisher shifted to lower gears to negotiate an approaching turn. The bridge over the Caton loomed ahead and River Path Drive was ending. After a sharp turn to swing onto the bridge, he headed over the rapids of Caton River toward Richland.

Such a coincidence, he mused as he completed the brief river crossing. "There it stands," he uttered, peering out the RX-7's window.

Taggart Memorial Hospital. America's sparkling monument to medical capitalism, he thought.

Standing out on the gentle slope that descended from the west down to Richland was the new sum and substance of America's healthcare system. Brightly lighted against the backdrop of a charcoal sky, Taggart Memorial Hospital was resplendent.

Taggart's got to be one of Health Pursuit's shining gems, Fisher quipped to himself. They've hired away more than a quarter of Medford University's doctors in the past five years.

He recalled a comment at a recent faculty meeting. Someone joked that Taggart was rapidly becoming "Medford West." He couldn't remember the author of that statement, but he vividly recalled that no one had chuckled when it was voiced.

Fisher didn't concentrate on the highly illuminated building as he rode by. He didn't care to give the place undue attention. Predictably though, the traffic light in front of Taggart Memorial turned red as he approached. For the better part of a minute, he was stuck sitting in front of the complex. As he waited, Fisher's thoughts jumped again. The image of Chip Carlton's face appeared in his mind.

"Why did you do it, Chip?" Fisher whispered.

He turned and looked at the brightly lighted group of buildings.

Chip Carlton, his friend and colleague for five years, had resigned his position on Medford's cardiac transplant team to go to Taggart Memorial. Carlton's absence was also part of his problem, he was convinced. Six months had passed since he had joined the heart transplant program at Taggart. Fisher's life had not been the same.

His gaze roved across the reflective glass atrium in front of Taggart's entry. Chip had left the Med for the identical reason given by other Medford faculty who had gone before him: money.

Somewhere in his belly a lead weight rolled over at the thought. Fisher stared straight ahead again. When the light changed, he gunned the Mazda and drove on. As he turned to downtown and Medford University he thought of the school. Despite its flaws, it still retained its greatness. It was revered across the globe for innovations and advancements in areas as diverse as transplantation and critical care. Among academic circles, Medford University ranked with Harvard and Yale. Fisher feared for the Med's survival, though. Scary things were happening. Either the powers that be had failed to recognize what was going on, or if they knew, they were helpless to respond to medicine's accelerating changes.

The aging buildings of the university came into view. Fisher recalled how he felt during the early years of his tenure at the Med. His nighttime trips to put in new hearts were unique. He was performing an unusual task accomplished largely in academic medical centers. That was ten years earlier. Myelopress had ended that.

The situation seemed clear to Fisher as he turned into the old parking deck beside the Med.

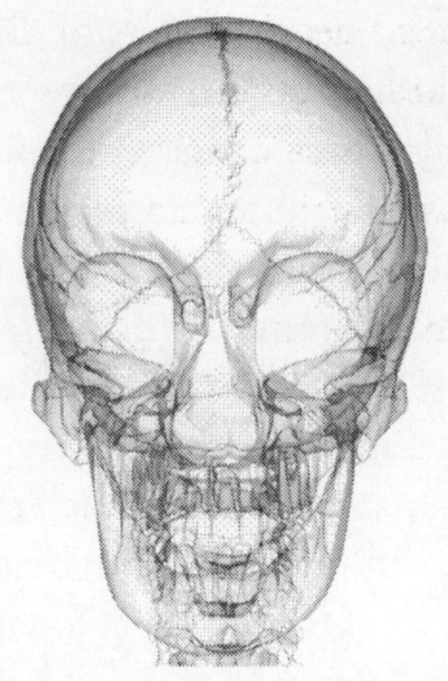

CHAPTER THREE

Three-twenty a.m.

The ORs at Medford University relentlessly pulsated. Much like a life force within the hospital's core — its heart throbbed — its vital flow never ceasing. In the womb of the benevolent beast, human suffering was alleviated. With its powerful instruments and perfectly milled cutting edges, the gentle creature renewed human life struck down by disease. There the beast also wept silently when forced to relinquish a life damaged beyond the powers of its healing magic.

On that February morning, within the breast of the beast, there would be sadness, and there would be joy. From the ashes of one ravaged life would rise the renewed life of others. Death and rebirth.

• • • • •

Rudy Smith's brain-dead body lay on the operating table in room sixteen. Large-bore infusion catheters and pressure monitoring devices entered internal jugular and subclavian veins through lily-white skin of the neck and upper chest. Out of translucent plastic bags, suspended above his body, flowed vasopressor agents, a stopgap measure to support a failing circulation — the result of dying brain centers. The shock, persistent over the last hours, had responded poorly. So had the body temperature, which stood at only eighty-nine degrees. A downward trend in temperature was present despite layers of OR blankets on top and a warming pad underneath his body.

A brief glance at the blood-soaked dressings that covered the boy's head explained his rapid deterioration. The missile had struck his head from point-blank range. White and gray brain matter oozed around bandages covering a gaping wound. Skull fragments were easily visible. Although the neurosurgeons made a valiant effort, there was never a chance of salvaging the brain blown apart by the impact. The boy lay still, unmoving, the criteria for brain death established. Rudy Smith had become a biomort — his brain was dead, his organs were alive.

• • • • •

Fisher struggled with tremulous hands and a pounding headache as he dragged a scrub brush across his arms. He stood at the scrub sink outside OR sixteen. It was the second time in as many hours he had prepared for surgery. The removal of Patricia Bingham's failed heart was proceeding without incident in OR fifteen. Fisher was thankful Alan Binzemore was performing the bulk of that procedure. Soon to be on cardiopulmonary bypass, she lay awaiting a new heart.

Fisher gazed through the window above the scrub sink inside room sixteen. A lone anesthesiologist was gowned and masked for the organ harvest. Fisher watched as he checked the digital displays on flat screen panels. He studied critical numbers on heart function, arterial pressure, body chemistry and blood oxygen levels. The data being gathered from indwelling sensors had been placed earlier to monitor the motionless body. Like a sentry standing watch over the final vestiges of life, Dr. Michael Ridgeway repeatedly scanned the biodata readouts. Fisher saw Ridgeway's eyes rove constantly, never pausing more than a few seconds. The intravenous tubing, the arterial lines, the endotracheal tube, the body's position, the mechanical ventilator, then back to the biodata displays. Fisher knew Ridgeway's mind. It rapidly processed information much like a pilot reading Stratoliner cockpit displays as his ship re-entered earth's atmosphere from low orbit.

Ridgeway's six-foot-four, two-hundred-and-forty-pound presence was impossible to overlook. From his days as an All-American running back at Boston College to his twenty-year tenure at Medford University, big Mike Ridgeway was essential, indispensable. He was *the* anesthesiologist at the Med, the one who surgeons demanded when the going was tough, and this night was tough. A brain-dead kid whose remains were rapidly dying was about to confer the gift of life to several strangers. The gift wasn't a given, however. It was dependent upon continued functioning of the body long enough to harvest its organs.

Ridgeway strained, his concentration maximally focused on holding those vital life threads together. Then, a digital readout flashed. The arterial pressure had fallen without warning. Beside that display, core temperature registered eighty-eight degrees. Ridgeway's reaction was propelled by reflex as he reached for the control panel. There he increased the flow of vasopressors and intravenous fluids.

Ridgeway was a wizard at pharmacology. He possessed extensive knowledge of the effects of hundreds of drugs on human physiology. But at the moment, red warning flags were waving. Vasopressors supported blood pressure by constricting arterial blood flow. Soon, the drugs would critically reduce blood flow to the very organs he struggled to preserve — a stage at which the organs would be useless.

"Steve, we gotta move," Ridgeway yelled. The hammer's coming down." Ridgeway's deep voice boomed across the operating room, commanding the attention of blue-clad OR staff who prepared for the harvest.

All activity stopped. The blanket-covered body, drenched by the white light from overhead discs, became the center of attention. Voices muted. OR background sounds, usually unnoticed, became intense, almost deafening. Air rushed from ventilation ducts overhead, the ventilator hissed its pneumatic sounds as air jetted into the lungs, infuser pumps bumped muted mechanical sounds, and the cardiac monitor give off sharp beeps with each of the heart's electrical excitations.

All present in the OR knew the urgency that existed — beating-heart donors yielded the best organs.

The swinging door opened as Fisher pushed his way into the room with a shoulder, his arms dripping from the scrub sink.

"Left ventricular function's still normal, Steve," Ridgeway said, studying ultrasound readouts obtained from a probe that rested in the esophagus. "Ejection fraction's at fifty percent, but it's falling. Heart rate and blood pressure are falling. I had to kick up the pressors."

Fisher was still dealing with his hangover. He wasn't quite ready to engage the reality the situation presented. He knew the biomort's deterioration signaled the start of the final phases of brain injury — herniation of the brain downward onto the spinal cord. Worsening shock and cardiac arrest were close at hand.

Fisher could feel the tremor in his hands and the weakness of his arms as he took a sterile towel from the circulating nurse. He blotted the water from his arms and hands hoping no one noticed the condition he was in. "Let's move," he said finally, feeling silent glances come to rest on him. He knew there was no choice. The organs would be lost if he didn't proceed with the harvest.

"Where are the other organs going?" Fisher asked as he prepped the chest and abdomen. He struggled to inject authority and enthusiasm into his voice.

"Kidneys will go to Philadelphia, the liver to Durham, the pancreas and small bowel to New York and the lungs to Pittsburgh," someone behind Fisher responded. "Corneas, ligaments and long bones will stay local."

Another voice, this time from the doorway, floated into the room. "The airport just called, Dr. Fisher. Procurement teams are on the ground."

"We're going, Mike." Fisher took the scalpel from the scrub nurse.

"The sooner, the better," Ridgeway thundered.

The wobbly feeling Fisher fought to hide was magnified as he placed the scalpel at the base of the neck and applied pressure to the blade. He hesitated as weakness and lassitude flowed through his body.

Moments passed.

"Steve, you all right?" Ridgeway stared down at him from his towering position above the anesthesia screen.

Saying nothing, Fisher simply nodded. He pulled the scalpel downward in a single clean stroke, producing a vertical incision down the length of the chest and abdomen. He followed the incision by cauterizing small bleeding points to prevent further blood loss. He then made a flank-to-flank incision to further expose the abdominal organs.

"Procurement teams are here, Dr. Fisher," a voice called.

Fisher said, "I'll need the liver team now."

"Right behind you, Dr. Fisher."

The voice was unfamiliar but as was often the case, Fisher didn't recognize the surgeon. Multiple organ procurements always brought unfamiliar faces to OR sixteen as hospitals across the country raced to procure organs. Other surgeons crowded into the room.

"The donor's become a category C." Fisher referred to the biomort's downward spiral in blood pressure and heart rate. "The hospital will do viability scanning on all harvested organs, if you'd like."

"That will be greatly appreciated," said the unfamiliar voice behind the mask.

A high-pitched whine erupted as Fisher switched on the sternal saw. He inserted the vibrating instrument at the top of the breast bone and applied downward pressure until he felt it cut through the bony plate. Within seconds the sternum was cut. Retractors then spread open the chest. A normal-sized, rapidly beating heart immediately came into view. The heart was flanked by two pink lungs intermittently inflating as Ridgeway's ventilator cycled a flow of air.

The window to the soul was open, Fisher thought momentarily staring into the chest. A transient, but familiar, chill raced through his body as he watched the heart struggle to keep the circulation operational.

"Looks pretty good, Steve," Ridgeway said, towering over the field.

"You're right," Fisher struggled out of his brief trance. He quickly inspected all visible organs looking for any unrecognized injury. "How are we, Mike?" Fisher looked at Ridgeway.

"Work fast if you want fresh organs, pal." Ridgeway's attention was directed to the biodata displays.

Fisher stepped back from the operating table to permit the proper sequence of organ preparation to begin.

With no words spoken, the liver harvest team approached the table to locate the blood supply to the liver and to free it from attachments to surrounding tissue. The task was accomplished within fifteen minutes.

Unnoticed by all others gathered in OR sixteen, Fisher breathed a sigh of relief during that quarter hour. The tremor in his hands had faded. He approached the table to prepare the heart for removal. His thoughts were clearer, the razor's edge returning.

Fisher worked quickly, opening the membrane that surrounded the heart. He next separated the heart's large vessels from each other, freeing them to be severed.

"Pressure's dropping." Ridgeway spoke quietly, but a tone of urgency was clearly present in his voice.

"Begin pre-cooling and heparinize the blood," Fisher fired back.

"There won't be much cooling needed." Ridgeway glanced at his readouts. "Body temp's hovering at eighty-seven degrees." Ridgeway reached down to the small green unit sitting at the head of the operating table and turned a knob to the off position. "Heating pad's off. I've got iced Ringer's Lactate and anti-coagulant infusing."

The team from Philadelphia next approached the table and performed dissections that would free the kidneys, small bowel and pancreas. The task was completed within ten minutes.

Preparations were almost complete, Fisher thought, glancing across an OR thick with blue movement. Those assembled were about to remove the internal organs of an eighteen-year-old boy, yet OR activity proceeded as if nothing were happening. Scrub nurses assisted at the table passing instruments; circulators and procurement teams conversed all around. An occasional burst of muted laughter floated on the air. He turned his attention back to the open body before him. All events from that point forward would be very mechanical. Organ removal had been culled to a science and for the most part, those involved in the process treated, it that way. Fisher had performed hundreds of organ harvests, but he always felt a catch in his chest as removal began.

Ridgeway boomed again, "Body temperature is at eighty degrees and we've got arrhythmias."

Fisher had heard the interruption in the heart's normal rhythm before Ridgeway announced it. The heart had responded to the rapidly falling temperature by entering a phase of erratic beats. The harvest had to begin.

"Are we ready with the cardioplegia solution?" Fisher asked.

"Iced and ready." The voice came from behind Fisher.

"Hang it," Fisher said, referring to the solution infused to preserve the heart.

Ridgeway took the bottle from the circulating nurse and hoisted it above the open chest. "It's hanging and ready."

With those words from Ridgeway, Fisher initiated the chain of events that would lead to the removal of all internal organs. Using two vascular clamps, Fisher stopped blood flow into the heart clamping shut the large entry vessels. He watched the contraction of the heart as it emptied itself within two beats. He then clamped the aorta.

Organ removal had begun.

The bloodless heart, simply a floppy bag, continued beating.

"Infuse cardioplegia solution." Fisher's confidence returned.

The iced solution, rich in electrolytes and essential sugars needed for muscle metabolism flowed into the coronary arteries. Within seconds, the heart ceased its rhythmic beating and quivered. Fisher next poured iced saline solution directly onto the heart to further cool it.

He then severed all vascular attachments to Rudy Smith's heart.

Room sixteen personnel were silent as Fisher slowly took the quivering young heart from the chest and inspected it.

"One life ends, several lives continue," Fisher said. He turned the muscle over in his hands several times. He looked back down at the chest then up at Ridgeway. "Good job, Mike."

"Thanks." The sharp edges in Ridgeway's voice had vanished.

Fisher turned and lowered the heart into an iced solution for transport to the next OR. He stepped back from the table. The other harvest teams began recovering the remaining organs.

A weight was lifted from Fisher's shoulders as he removed his gown and gloves. He walked out of OR sixteen carrying Rudy Smith's heart.

Four fifty-five a.m.

Fisher passed into the hallway, preoccupied by plans for implanting the heart he carried, unaware of anything unusual.

Medford University's ancient environmental systems never produced uniform temperatures. Medical personnel working the old ORs, either sweated or froze, and the temperatures did not necessarily depend on the weather outside. No one could recall a time when there weren't dramatic swings in temperature and humidity from OR to OR or hallways to ORs. That morning, the physical plant engineers had tried but failed to raise the temperature in the hallways. Consequently, most nurses wore sweaters or coats as they went about their tasks.

Fisher drew back from his thoughts as the eleven-degree temperature difference cooled his face. Any other time, Fisher would have proceeded about his business, but that morning, he stopped. At first, he couldn't explain why. An unseen force grabbed him, pulling him up short of the door to OR fifteen. Through an identical window above the scrub sink, he looked into the room. The scene before him was nothing out of the ordinary. Alan Binzemore, his back to the door, stood peering into Patricia

Bingham's opened chest cavity, numerous nurses residents and students standing around him. Her diseased heart had been removed. Binzemore waited at the table to begin the implantation of the heart Fisher carried.

Behind Binzemore, Fisher saw the rolling pumps of the cardiopulmonary bypass machine grinding away. The bypass technician cruised back and forth, fussing over the ancient machine, assuring Mrs. Bingham's blood remained well oxygenated. Unexpectedly, the scene before Fisher took on a surreal quality. He blinked several times as the lights dimmed and the noises around him muted.

Then, he heard it. "How does any Goddamn body do anything around this lousy place? My fingers are so fucking cold I can't operate."

Fisher gazed back into OR fifteen again. He didn't believe his ears. Chip Carlton was shouting complaints about the heating system just as he always did. For an instant, Fisher's mind played out a familiar scene as he looked at the back of Binzemore, but saw Carlton. There he was, Fisher thought, in all his glory, commanding the ship. Fisher snorted out a soft laugh as he recalled Carlton's penchant for control. He loved it.

Fisher continued to gaze at the illusion. Seconds turned into a minute. Fisher's mind drifted. He missed Chip.

"Dr. Fisher." The voice was accompanied by light pressure on his shoulder.

"Wha . . . What . . . ." Fisher snorted as he was yanked back to reality.

"They're ready for you, Dr. Fisher."

Fisher spun around, surprised out of his illusion, his pulse jumping.

"I didn't mean to startle you." The soft voice came from a masked nurse who wore a heavy woolen sweater. "Dr. Binzemore's ready to proceed."

"Thank you." Fisher turned and entered OR fifteen.

The temperature increased to a pleasant seventy degrees inside OR fifteen. His thoughts of Chip Carlton vaporized.

• • • • •

"Excellent, Alan," Fisher said as Binzemore completed the running suture line that secured the donor heart to Patricia Bingham's aorta. Rudy Smith's heart had been a perfect fit requiring minimal trimming.

The two surgeons stood back to inspect the implant.

"My third heart and it's damn good," Binzemore said softly.

"I'll have to agree with you on that." Fisher looked down at the bloodless heart lying still before them.

Binzemore aspirated the remaining air from the heart chambers. "Air's removed."

"I'm unclamping the aorta." Fisher eased open the jaws of the large vascular clamp. "Start rewarming."

"Rewarming beginning now, Dr. Fisher," the pump technician replied.

Fisher and Binzemore stood silent as warmed blood filled the young heart. Within seconds, the heart distended with blood from the bypass pump.

"Get going little buddy," Binzemore said, divulging the anxiety he fought back while awaiting signs of life from the implant.

OR fifteen fell silent. The implant lay still.

"It'll be fine, Alan." Fisher forced calm into his voice, but he felt his forehead becoming moist. Hearts from donors in shock always caused problems.

"There it goes," a scrub nurse whispered.

The heart began beating, irregularly at first, but soon it smoothed into a strong regular rhythm.

The cardiac anesthesiologist glanced across from his biodata displays. "Rate's one hundred-twenty, ejection fraction's fifty-six percent, blood pressure's one hundred-ten and stable."

Fisher said, "That's not bad. Infuse one hundred thousand units of Myelopress."

"Myleopress is coming, Dr. Fisher. We're drawing it up now."

Fisher turned toward the voice in time to see a blue-clad nurse drawing champagne-colored liquid from a glass vial into a large syringe.

"One hundred thousand units of Myelopress." She handed the syringe to the anesthesiologist who wasted no time infusing the anti-rejection drug.

Fisher turned his attention back to the newly implanted heart. Binzemore had attached a pacer wire to the surface of the implant. Even though the heart beat strongly and efficiently, the doctors would take no chances. The pacer wire would be temporary, but it would be insurance that the heart's rate could be increased, should it fall. Transplanted hearts dropped to dangerously slow rates in the first few days following implantation if the recipient rejected the new heart. Myelopress had eliminated that problem. Organ rejection was a problem of the past.

"Pacer's in," Binzemore noted.

Fisher turned to the bypass technician. "She's weaning from bypass nicely," the technician responded, reading Fisher's mind.

All systems go, Fisher said to himself. He was pleased.

"Okay, we'll pause. Alan, inspect all connection sites for leakage while weaning is completed." Fisher pointed to the places where Binzemore had sewn in the implanted heart. Fisher's mind relaxed. He watched as Binzemore examined the sites where he had stitched in the strong, young heart. Background conversation in OR fifteen increased as moods lightened. Fisher heard laughter break out as tension faded. He knew stories were being told, and plans were being made by the staff for after work activities.

When the telephone on the far wall of OR fifteen rang, no one paid particular attention. Within three rings, a circulating nurse answered the call.

"Well, I don't believe it," the nurse exclaimed, the volume of her voice audible above the background. A few seconds passed. She lowered her voice to engage in conversation with the caller. Then she placed her hand over the phone and turned. "Dr. Fisher, guess who I've got on the line?" She faced the OR table. "It's Dr. Carlton."

Fisher snapped his head toward the nurse.

"He wants to speak to you, Dr. Fisher."

No one in the OR saw behind Fisher's mask, but a large smile crept across his face. "Well, well," Fisher said as he backed away from the operating table, taking precautions not to break scrub. His mood lifted as he approached the telephone. He leaned an ear to the phone as the nurse held the receiver.

"Chip, it's great to hear from you. I got your message yesterday and was planning to return your call today, following this transplant." The message Carlton left on Fisher's answering machine had been short. It simply had said they needed to talk. The message was Carlton's first communication since his departure from the Med.

"I've got talk with you, Steve. Can you meet me at the College Inn today?"

A tightness surged through Fisher's body as Carlton spoke in a soft, almost whispering, tone, his usual cut-up demeanor absent. The tone in Carlton's voice had been similar on the answering machine.

"Sure, Chip," Fisher said, confused. "How's three-thirty sound?"

"That's fine. Please don't be late."

"Chip, I . . . ."

There was no answer. Carlton had hung up.

Fisher walked back to the table where Binzemore had completed the placement of chest tubes that, for the next two days, would rest alongside Patricia Bingham's new heart.

"We're ready to close, Dr. Fisher."

"That's fine, Alan," Fisher said, totally preoccupied. "Let's get her closed and out to recovery."

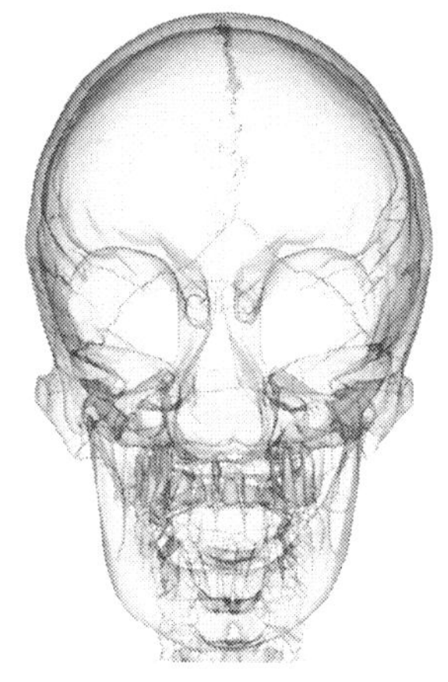

CHAPTER FOUR

At three o'clock Fisher left Medford University Hospital and headed for the Mazda. He was deep in thought as he crossed the elevated walkway to the old parking deck. Although usually numbed and exhausted after twelve hours of surgery, today Fisher was energized. The call to the OR from Carlton was a surprise, even though he had taken a similar message off his answering machine before diving into that bottle of Jack Daniels.

Six months with no contact and then two calls from Chip in less than twenty-four hours. Fisher wondered what was on his mind. He tried recalling the exact tone in Carlton's voice. It was stern and serious, his usual playfulness missing. Fisher smiled as a whimsical thought crossed his mind. "That son of a bitch," he uttered softly. "He's probably looking to come back to the Med and couldn't tell me over the phone." Fisher turned the key to start the engine.

Carlton loved the College Inn, he thought as he rolled out of the deck. The Inn was less than ten minutes from the hospital by foot, but Fisher didn't feel like walking. He turned onto University Drive, the main thoroughfare through the campus, and headed west.

The College Inn was a public establishment, but its clientele was almost exclusively Medford faculty. Taking a break at the "CI", as it was called, in the middle of a hard day served an important purpose. It gave Medford doctors a chance to relax and unwind in small groups.

Old Hunton Hall housed the Inn. From the turn of the century until around nineteen fifty, the structure served as a boarding facility for physicians coming to Medford University. The *Visiting Doctors Program* attracted physicians from across the world to study medical innovations. Medford University was renowned among American medical universities for its progressive practice of the medical sciences. During the heyday of the program, Hunton Hall was filled year-round. However, the program faded, and the building was eventually vacated, serving only as a storage facility — that is, until Dr. Wallace Shaklein renovated it and became the proprietor.

Customers new to the College Inn were amazed when they learned that Shaklein was the former chairman of the Biochemistry Department at Medford. After a decade in the chair, Shaklein decided he liked the food business more than the rigors of biochemistry research. "Wally," as he was called, surprised no one by his jump to the culinary sciences out of the world of gene splicing and protein chemistry. The *Richland Tribune* pronounced Shaklein "The Chef of Science" after learning of his penchant for creating masterpiece dinners in his laboratory.

The College Inn's renovation had occurred six years earlier. As a part of the renovation, a large, arching bay window was placed on the front wall of the building. The window provided unrestricted views of the Inn's circular driveway, and wrought iron fountain.

For years Fisher and Carlton insisted on sitting by that large bay window, and Shaklein catered to the two surgeons who three years earlier had successfully transplanted a new heart into Shaklein's wife Maria.

Fisher sat quietly at their favorite table, rotating a spoon in his second cup of coffee. He considered ordering a Jack Daniels on the rocks, but he knew he needed a clear mind for his discussion.

He gazed out the window, thinking. Carlton's departure six months earlier was heralded as a coup d'état for Health Pursuit. The company had put on a fraternity-style rush to convince Carlton to leave Medford and take up residence at Taggart Memorial. Taggart's one heart transplanter, Harry Talbott, told Carlton he was needed to "round out the program."

"Steve, they're tripling my salary, man," Carlton had revealed during one of their long conversations before he left.

Unknowingly, Carlton revealed how Taggart stalked its prey. Invite the targeted Medford doctor for a tour. Dazzle him with the facilities first, then pump him up with a description of Health Pursuit's vision of the future — one powerful network of health care facilities all headed by Health Pursuit. Finish up with an offer to more than triple a Medford salary and there was powerful one-two-three punch that left most rushees with swimming heads.

All Medford faculty who jumped to Taggart had surveyed the situation at the Med before making their decisions. They all concluded that there was no way but down for a medical university locked into a 1990's mindset to survive in the twenty-first century.

Fisher knew Carlton had decided to leave the Med from the very first time he mentioned meeting with Taggart officials. He realized Medford couldn't match salaries with a Health Pursuit hospital, and that the Med couldn't keep a bright surgeon like Chip if he wanted to leave. In Carlton's case, why not go for the best, Fisher mused. Organ transplantation wasn't the sole province of academic medical centers any longer. Myelopress had forever moved organ transplants out of the ivory towers of academia and into community hospitals, even the smallest of community hospitals.

Fisher's mind wandered. "Myelopress," he mumbled shaking his head. "How could one drug have changed organ transplantation so dramatically in such a short time?"

"Try these little sweethearts, Steve."

The voice pulled Fisher back to reality and the College Inn. He turned around and looked into the warm eyes and white bearded face of Wally Shaklein.

"Three-thirty. Hmmmm," Shaklein crooned as he sat a small plate of hot peach fritters in front of Fisher. "Just the thing to round out a hard day, eh, Steve?"

"Yeah, thanks, Wally," Fisher said, his mind drifting back to a point a hundred miles away.

Shaklein placed a hand on Fisher's shoulder and moved to the front of the Inn where more faculty members crowded in for afternoon drinks.

Fisher took a bite of the steaming fritter and drifted back into thought. Maybe Carlton was right to leave, he told himself. The Med was probably going down the tubes, and many people would be without jobs when the layoffs began.

Fisher's thoughts jumped to Carlton's two messages. Six months earlier, Carlton had promised things would not change between them. "We'll still meet at the CI for a snort after work," he said his last day. "I'll just be coming from across town." But the get-togethers never happened. Carlton shipped out to Taggart Memorial Hospital and stepped off the face of the earth — until the day before — when he left his first message on Fisher's answering machine.

He should have returned Chip's call then, but his day had taken a turn for the worse. Sharon had informed him through her scumbag lawyer that she was filing for divorce. To say that he was upset was an understatement. He brooded over the situation for a while at work and then decided to go home and get drunk.

No solutions were at hand and no amount of talking had resolved their problems. He wasn't sure he really wanted to salvage things. Her acid-laden remarks had made it easy for him to move out. He was convinced she was seeing someone else, but even that didn't seem to matter any longer.

As Fisher stared out the window, Carlton's late model BMW pulled up across University Drive. He snapped alert and thought of Carlton's brief conversation and urgent tone.

Carlton emerged from the automobile. He wore dark slacks and a light sport coat that added extra dimension to his broad shoulders and muscular arms. He crossed the thoroughfare with a fast-paced stride. Fisher had always likened Carlton's gait to that of a field marshal reviewing his troops. It was confident, sure-footed and bold.

Fisher turned away from the bay window and looked back into the building, to signal Wally to bring a fresh cup of coffee and more peach fritters. Fisher had consumed six fritters while his mind drifted. Carlton's favorite pastime at the CI was sipping coffee and putting away Wally's peach fritters. Fisher assumed that day would be no different.

However, Shaklein had moved to the back of the Inn where he was seating newly arrived faculty.

Fisher looked back at the circular drive. The winter sun produced a strobe-like effect on Carlton's face as he passed alternately between bright sunlight and the muted colors of lengthening shadows.

As Carlton walked by the frozen fountain, Fisher realized how much he had missed his friend's presence. During Carlton's five years at The Med, they had operated together, published together and become close friends. For Fisher, true friendships at the University had always come painfully hard. Self-interests and preoccupation with one's own corner of medicine was typical of physicians in academic medicine. Carlton had been different.

Fisher watched Carlton intently for a few more seconds before he turned again to find Shaklein. He was still in the rear of the restaurant with his newest arrivals engaged in a laughter-filled conversation. I'll just catch Wally when Chip arrives, Fisher thought, turning back to view Carlton's progress.

From Fisher's vantage point, the winter urban scenery outside the College Inn was picture perfect. Manicured grounds of the Inn complemented a pleasing backdrop of stark oak trees along University Drive and the green grass that covered the recently completed Downtown Park. In the extreme background of Fisher's winter landscape sat vacant office buildings soon scheduled for demolition.

The clear view afforded by his favorite window seat let Fisher witness the horror that unfolded next.

A glass pane below the level of the shrubbery burst, sending shards into the building. As if in a time warp, Carlton stopped and looked at the window. Then, in a sight Fisher would never forget, the right side of Carlton's neck exploded in a spray of blood, skin and bone. At the same time another pane exploded raining debris onto tables under the bay window. The sound of shattering glass was followed immediately by a clatter from the rear of the dining room.

Fisher was momentarily paralyzed as the high-velocity missile knocked Carlton forward. The short-lived spell ended as the second slug crashed through the bay window. Fisher plunged to the floor to avoid injury from flying glass. Although dulled by years of hospital duty since the Gulf War, Fisher's survival reflexes remained quick, the product of a bitter combat experience.

Fisher's mind suddenly went blank. Desert stench assaulted his nostrils. He was in Iraq again. He lay behind a troop carrier, intense gunfire flying overhead. Fisher buried his helmeted head in the sand. Vivid images came into sight then disappeared, the ones he had fought for so long to suppress. He looked around. Corporal Daniel Taylor crouched beside him.

Fisher's pulse raced. He and E company were preparing for the run to safety again. No, Fisher told himself, it can't be happening again. A throaty chop-chop-chop came from an obscure clearing as the helicopter engine idled behind them.

The war was drawing to a close and Steve Fisher, ranger medic, was part of E company's last patrol. Bullets whizzed overhead again, fire from remnants of the Republican Guard they had pursued. The fight had been intense. All but a few troops were gone.

"Let's go," yelled a young second lieutenant.

All twelve of the remaining men of E-company rose to crouched positions and sprinted to the waiting chopper. Corporal Daniel Taylor ran beside Fisher. Another volley of shots rang out and Danny went down.

Fisher stopped. Taylor's young body was covered with blood. The shot had killed him instantly.

The twenty year-old nightmare vaporized as Fisher became aware of his surroundings again in the College Inn. He eased to a half-standing position. With cat-like movements, he dodged between tables and faculty patrons quickly reaching the large oaken front door of the Inn. He glanced back, scanning for injured patrons. A bewildered Shaklein, frozen in his tracks, stood beside an iced tea urn, jetting a stream of brown liquid through a hole created by one of the slugs.

Fisher grasped a handle, cracked the door open and listened. There was nothing. He burst through the entrance door, sprinting to the end of the covered walkway. Carlton lay still, face down in a puddle of blood.

Fisher dropped to his knees, a wave of nausea jerking through him as he rolled his blood-soaked friend to his back. The major vasculature of Carlton's neck, the trachea and the cervical spine, were exposed and destroyed where the bullet had struck him.

Despite his tears, Fisher pulled back Carlton's jacket and ripped open his blood-drenched dress shirt, preparing for resuscitation. But he stopped. The bullet had exited through the upper sternum, leaving a three-inch gaping wound. Fisher fell back, speechless, overcome with nausea.

Chip Carlton was dead.

• • • • •

"Shit," the man muttered under his breath.

Two shots, he thought. He hated firing two shots. It was sloppy work.

"Fucking shadows." He took three steps forward from the interior of the room. Careful planning and observation almost down the toilet, because of fucking shadows.

The gunman transferred the Winchester 508 to his left hand, freeing the gloved right to close the six-inch opening in the window he had created earlier.

He returned to the open case, an ordinary piece of luggage indistinguishable from a briefcase, and removed the silencer. In less than twenty seconds, he broke down the rifle at the center point between stock and muzzle and placed the components in their proper places. He worked quickly and quietly, though there was no particular reason to suppress the noise. The building was vacant. Following Carlton's cellular call to the Medford OR, the gunman had thoroughly searched the building and found it satisfactory.

Once the attaché case was properly loaded, he took a small pouch from it and closed it. He took two additional steps, retrieved the shell casings and placed them in separate side pockets of the expensive, but understated, suit jacket to prevent jingling. He opened the pouch and sprinkled dust over all visible footprints as he backed out of the small front office. He continued covering prints that led to the office as he backed toward the stairwell across the hall. Then he adjusted his tie, straightened his suit and walked down the five flights he had ascended earlier. Appearing a typical Richland business type, he exited the rear, street-level door, walked the thirty-odd feet of the back alley and merged into the flow of pedestrian traffic.

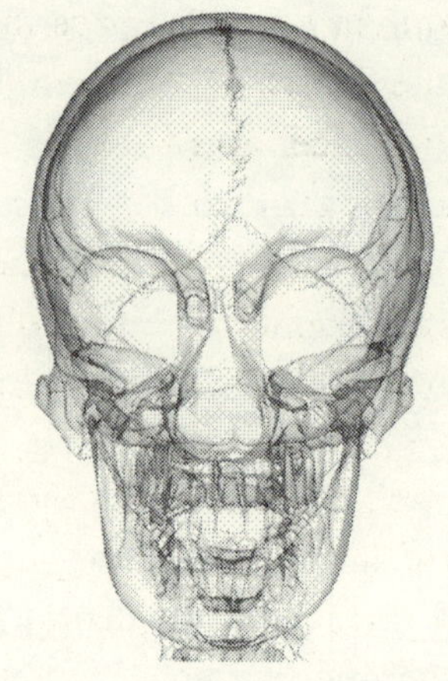

CHAPTER FIVE

Fisher was unaware of elapsed time. He sat staring at Chip Carlton's blood-soaked body. He shivered in the bitter cold, but it didn't matter. His mind was focused, but it wasn't. He was aware of his surroundings, but he wasn't. The wail of sirens filled the air, but he couldn't attach significance to the sound. His senses gathered and transmitted signals to his brain but they were rejected as background noise.

Intermittently, Fisher's mind jumped across vast stretches of time and space. Memories became fluid, flashing images which vaporized as rapidly as they had come.

FLASH: He saw Corporal Daniel Taylor sprawled, blood-covered, and unmoving in the desert sand.

FLASH: A conveyor belt rotated noisily as it delivered a wooden coffin holding Taylor's body into the belly of a green transport aircraft.

FLASH: Faces and bodies rushed past in succession, creating an imperceptible blur. Fisher recognized ten chairs pulled into a circle as blur became reality. Tortured memories of a VA hospital's substance abuse ward wedged into his thoughts. Endless hours spent recovering from alcohol addiction.

FLASH: Chip Carlton's face stood close at hand. In his gloved hands a human donor heart quivered as it was readied for implantation.

The rush of faces continued until they were only a blur. Dozens of times and places moved across the stage of Fisher's mind.

"Sir, please stand and move away from the body."

Fisher heard the unfamiliar voice call back in the reaches of his mind, but he couldn't process the words.

"Steve, Steve, do as the officer asks."

The second voice sounded familiar.

Wallace Shaklein's words pulled Fisher back from his trance. He glanced up to see a Richland police officer standing beside Shaklein.

For a moment, Fisher and Shaklein stared at each other. Their silent communication was clear. They shared sorrow, confusion and profound loss.

Finally, Fisher stood and moved away from the body. He shivered uncontrollably as the shadows of the late afternoon lengthened.

Around the College Inn, chaos mounted. EMS technicians rushed from rescue vehicles as the throaty sounds of fire trucks approached the scene. Richland police were everywhere.

Fisher glanced back at the Inn. Medford faculty crowded behind the bay window appeared as translucent shapes through the shattered glass.

EMS technicians couldn't conceal their expressions as they approached Carlton's body. No resuscitation was needed. One of the team members covered Carlton's body as the others headed inside to search for injuries.

Richland police dragged barriers into place to halt afternoon traffic. Two burly officers unrolled yellow tape while a third videoed the crime scene.

A loudspeaker blared from an unmarked vehicle sitting at the entrance to the circular drive. "All persons inside the building, come out immediately," a deep voice boomed. "Keep your hands visible at all times."

The front door opened as those inside filed out one by one. All were captured on video as they exited the Inn.

"Ladies and Gentlemen do not touch anything outside the building and do not leave the crime scene until detectives have spoken with you."

Fisher turned his head towards movement in his peripheral vision. An unmarked car pulled past the traffic barriers and stopped short of the entrance. The doors opened and two men wearing khaki overcoats stood and walked toward the officer holding the loudspeaker.

As Fisher watched the milling about continue, his mind began to clear. He slowly tested the reality around him.

This is the College Inn, he told himself. Chip Carlton is dead. Tears formed as he stared at Carlton's covered body.

Fisher raised his head to look away as the anguish of the moment overwhelmed him. He scanned the scene around him, limiting the things he lingered on. His overheated brain had to cool down.

The officer holding the microphone looked directly at Fisher and pointed. After a few more minutes of conversation the two over coated men walked across the drive. One of the two was obese and waddled as he walked towards Fisher. The other had an unremarkable build.

"Were you the person kneeling beside the victim as the police arrived?" asked the obese officer. His voice was abrupt and emotionless.

"Yes." Fisher's gaze drifted back to Carlton's body.

"I'm Lieutenant Benjamin Domao. This is Officer Martin Smith. Does the victim have family?"

Fisher continued staring.

Domao wrapped his lips around a soggy cigar butt, dragged it deeply, and exhaled a wheezy breath of smoke in Fisher's direction.

"He's got no immediate family," Fisher replied, unable to drag his eyes away from the blanket. "His mother and father are dead."

"Brothers or sisters?" The slender man snapped before Fisher finished speaking.

"No. No brothers or sisters."

"May I have your name?" The plump officer wiped at globs of sweat.

"Steven Fisher." Fisher's hand went for his wallet.

Domao took Fisher's identification card and studied it. He copied Fisher's name and University ID number and shoved the card back at Fisher.

"Doctor Fisher, could you come with us? We have a few questions."

"Okay," Fisher said, still a bit disoriented.

Men in brown coveralls with "Richland PD" embroidered across their shoulders kneeled by Carlton's body.

"What are they doing?" Fisher asked.

"Collecting crime scene material," Domao wheezed.

Fisher followed the detectives to their cruiser and sat down in back. He glanced at the Inn. There, behind the bay window, Wallace Shaklein stood alone, a prisoner of sadness.

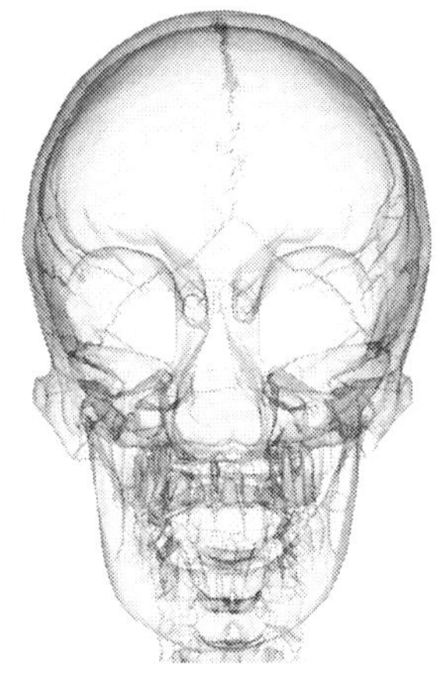

CHAPTER SIX

Fisher sat behind his desk, staring in numbed silence. The object of his gaze, the hospital parking deck, was virtually empty. Only cars belonging to the night shift remained. They were the people charged with keeping the beast alive until sun up. An occasional automobile dribbled out of the deck as the last of the day staff left for home.

Fisher had lost track of time, his mind absorbed by the day's events. When he returned from the killing he had seen, Mary Walker, his secretary and veteran of many years in the Surgery Department, was weeping quietly at her desk. She had heard the news. When she saw Fisher, she lost her composure and she cried openly. Tears flooded once again in Fisher's eyes as he tried to comfort her. Walker always held a special place for Carlton. During his years at the Med, she had treated him like a son. Fisher could hear her still sobbing as she ambled down the corridor that led out of the Surgery offices.

Time passed as Fisher stared out the window. The offices in the department were vacant and the hall was quiet. Images of Chip Carlton falling to an assassin's gunfire played over and over as did his encounter with the Richland Police Department.

Domao's swaggering gait and the roll of fat that bulged from his overcoat had repulsed Fisher. And the smell of that reeking cigar lingered in his mind.

"We would like you to answer some questions, Doctor," Domao had said tersely.

The questions came in rapid-fire succession.

"Why were you meeting Dr. Carlton at the College Inn?"

Fisher recalled the brief distraction before he answered that question. He turned to see members of a private removal service kneeling by Carlton's blanket-covered corpse. The sight added to the crushing weight on his shoulders. The men lifted Carlton's body onto a stretcher and placed it into a hearse.

Fisher looked back at the detective. Despite the bitter cold, sweat glistened as it rolled down Domao's rounded face.

"Dr. Carlton called me at the University earlier today and asked me to meet him here." The moment he said the words, Fisher had the feeling he became a suspect.

"Was Dr. Carlton upset or agitated when he spoke with you?" Domao exhaled noisily.

"No, but he insisted we meet today."

"Why, Doctor?" Domao fired back.

"I don't know why, Detective. He called yesterday and left a message. I wasn't able to get back to him. He called to the operating room this morning and insisted we meet here this afternoon."

"Why didn't you return his call yesterday, Doctor?"

Fisher recalled how the sharp tone of Domao's voice brought him to a boiling point.

"Detective, I will be answering any further questions in the presence of an attorney, if this inquisition continues."

Domao wiped the sweat from his forehead with the sleeve of his overcoat. After a short bout of wheezy coughs, the questioning continued. "Do you know any reason why Dr. Carlton would be the target of an assassination?"

Though he offered no apologies, Domao's voice was less accusatory.

"No, I don't," Fisher said, cooling slightly. "I have not seen Dr. Carlton since he left the University six months ago."

The questions continued, though less rapid-fire, until a uniformed officer approached the cruiser.

"Lieutenant," the officer said, sticking his head into the driver's side window, not bothering to pull Domao out of ear shot. "We've covered the grounds and the street out front. There's no trace of shell casings. Looks like sniper fire." The officer contorted his body slightly and pointed to the abandoned office buildings scheduled for demolition. "We've got some officers going through those buildings across the park."

"Thanks," Domao said curtly.

"Looks like a professional hit from the get-go, Lieutenant."

Domao reached into the pocket of his yellowed dress shirt, stretched taut by bulging fat. He fished out a nearly empty pack of cigarettes. He lit one, took a deep drag and puffed out a final statement. "Doctor, I think we're through for now. We'll get back with you if we need to discuss other matters. Notify us if you're going out of the area."

The meeting with the detectives and the shock of the murder had physically ended, but Fisher continued rewinding the events of the afternoon in his thoughts, like a prisoner to a nightmare that wouldn't end.

As he gazed into the night, his state of mind was similar to what he had experienced immediately following the shooting. He was aware, but he wasn't. He concentrated intensely, yet he was lost in the currents of his thoughts.

Fisher's mental turbulence caused the soft tapping on the office door to go unnoticed.

Tap, tap, tap — the knock came again and again he failed to hear it.

The sounds of his office doorknob turning also went unnoticed.

The door to the office opened slowly. Fisher's desk lamp partially illuminated his office, leaving the area near the door in shadows. A young woman's face came into view.

For a moment she said nothing, as if contemplating whether to interrupt.

"Doctor Fisher?" The voice was soft but firm.

Fisher jumped, startled by the intrusion into his private hell. He flailed about for a moment as he tried to regain his balance.

"Oh, I'm sorry." Seeing what had happened, the woman stepped forward from the shadows as if to catch Fisher before he fell. "Please forgive me, I didn't mean to . . . ."

Fisher recovered from his momentary loss of balance. "It's quite all right."

She stood about three feet from Fisher's desk. "Doctor Fisher, I didn't mean to frighten you," the young woman repeated.

"Who are you?" Fisher asked annoyed by the interruption.

"My name is Alli Shepard, Dr. Fisher. I'm in the fourth year medical school class."

Fisher studied her as she spoke. He judged her to be in her mid-thirties. She wore a knee-length clinic jacket over a stylish dress. Her chestnut hair hung in a ponytail over the collar of her coat. The desk light did not permit careful study of her features, but Fisher could see she was quite attractive.

Recovered from his fight with gravity and the chair, Fisher turned to face the woman. "Yes, what do you want?" he asked still a bit annoyed.

"I apologize for the hour, but I tried to reach you a few times today. I came here this morning, but Mrs. Walker said you were in surgery. She told me to come back this afternoon around four. When I got here at four, she told me you went to a meeting outside the hospital. Not long after that, I read the news about Dr. Carlton on my phone."

She paused a moment, then said, "The whole hospital is in shock."

Fisher's gaze drifted down to his desk. "I know. I was there. I saw the whole thing."

The room fell quiet.

"Dr. Fisher, I had no idea. I . . . ."

"That's all right. There's no way you could have known. Dr. Carlton and I were close friends. We were just grabbing a coffee at the College Inn." Fisher went silent to prevent a surge of emotion from breaking his voice.

After a few moments of silence, Fisher looked up at Alli.

"What do you want?"

"It's probably better for me to come back another time." She turned and stepped towards the door.

"No. It's all right," Fisher said. "Wait."

Alli had almost reached the office door to leave, but she stopped and turned. "Dr. Fisher, I can come back later. What I have to talk about is really out of place right now."

"No," Fisher reacted. "I need to think about something else. What happened today is ripping me apart."

Alli turned and approached the desk again. She stood for a moment then spoke.

"Two weeks of my third year surgery rotation last year I spent with Dr. Carlton. He talked a lot about a new drug being that completely blocks organ rejection."

"That would be Myelopress," Fisher uttered softly.

"It's been almost a year since then, but I think that's the drug he spoke of. He said it had modernized organ transplant all over the world."

"I'm sure he was speaking of Myelopress. It has changed the field of organ transplant. The US Food and Drug Administration rushed Myelopress into clinical use in the United States two years ago, because of the transplant results doctors were getting in Europe and Japan. But why does that bring you here?"

"Dr. Carlton told us that Myelopress was one of just a few drugs the FDA ever approved for use in the US from studies done in Europe, Scandinavia, and Japan. He said studies from overseas were so convincing that the FDA approved Myelopress without additional studies in the United States.

"That's correct."

"Doctor Carlton told us that U.S. studies of Myelopress needed to be performed, but in the years since the drug was released none had appeared."

"Right again, Miss Shepard. Where's this going?"

"During my time on the clerkship, Dr. Carlton and I found we shared mutual interests in computing and social media. Before starting medical school, I worked as a systems analyst at Darby Software here in Richland. He told me he had been an amateur hacker for years. He even gave me a tour through these offices one day showing me the intranet he'd created for the Surgery Department."

For the first time in twenty-four hours, Fisher smiled. He thought of Carlton's passion for computers and the iPad he always had with him. Fisher had often wondered why Carlton had landed in surgery and not at the helm of a firm leading the charge into cyberspace.

"Okay. I give up. Now I'm really lost."

Alli continued. "By the end of my clerkship, Dr. Carlton had cooked up an idea for a study using Medford University's transplant experience with Myelopress. He said it would be large enough for a credible study of the drug's effect and asked me if I would help him. He wanted to build a database of Medford transplant patients in the years before and after approval of Myelopress."

Fisher recalled Carlton mentioning a study in their conversations before he left the Med, though many months had passed since they'd discussed it.

"Look, Miss Shepard, it's getting late, and I've been awake since two o'clock this morning. Dr. Carlton is dead now, and it's obvious the study will never get done. I need to get home to get some sleep."

"Dr. Fisher." Alli stood fast in front of the desk, her face flushed in the half light. "Dr. Carlton offered me the chance to come work with him for a month of independent study this year. After a lot of hassle, I got permission from the Dean of Students to take the month of February off to work with Dr. Carlton to build the database for the study. I can't turn back at this late date."

"Miss Shepard." Anger mounted in Fisher's voice. "Chip Carlton was the computer genius. I know nothing about computers." Fisher rotated and pointed to the desktop computer sitting on the small table where his legs were propped when Alli had entered. "Using the Surgery Department's money, Dr. Carlton purchased and networked all these computers himself. He gave some of us computer illiterates beginner's lessons, but that's as far as it got. He left the university six months ago and that's probably the last time the machine was switched on. Besides that, we lost a transplant surgeon, and I'm the only one around to put hearts in."

She dropped her gaze. "I had no idea he had left the university. He never called to let me know."

After a few moments, Fisher spoke. "Doctor Carlton's decision to leave the University came out of the blue. It was a big surprise to us all. Over a week's time, he made up his mind, and in July of last year, he left. No one here can help you with this project."

"I see," the young woman said, her gaze glued to something on the desktop.

Again, the room fell quiet.

"Thanks, Dr. Fisher," Alli said finally. She turned toward the door. "I guess I'll be leaving."

Fisher watched her as she slowly walked out. He leaned back in his chair, resting his eyes for a moment. Images of Carlton's smiling face came into his thoughts. Helpless to stop it, Fisher was transported back to the College Inn. He again saw Carlton's mutilated body. Fisher opened his eyes to vaporize the spell and stood behind the desk.

"Yes," he said aloud, swinging around from behind the desk and heading for the door. "Miss Shepard, wait."

Alli was waiting for the elevator by the time she heard Fisher's voice.

"Miss Shepard," Fisher said as he approached. "I seem to remember that Chip put in many hours of work at his computer in the weeks before he left. He may have already begun to build that database. We'll never know, unless we try. You said you have prior computer experience."

"Yes." A smile cracked across her face.

"I'll call you in a couple of days. Doctor Carlton told me he used the University's computer system for all his work. Maybe he left files there. It would be a starting point."

A muted ring beside them indicated the elevator had arrived.

"What day should I come?" Alli asked as she stepped into the elevator car.

"I'll have my secretary call you. She'll have my schedule."

As the elevator doors closed, Fisher turned and walked back down the corridor to the Surgery offices. Before his mind could cycle into the torture mode again, his cell phone sounded in his right coat pocket. He hauled out the phone and placed it to his ear. "Hello."

"Dr. Fisher?" Binzemore's voice sounded on the line.

"Yes, Alan."

"I'm very sorry to hear the news of Dr. Carlton's death. Does anyone have any idea who would have killed him?"

"The police are working on it. That's all I can tell you. Why did you call?"

"I'm in the Medford Trauma Center and Dr. Garrett has just gone home ill. The attending list shows that you're tonight's back up. The Center needs an attending surgeon till midnight."

Fisher, still walking, stopped dead in his tracks and groaned audibly. He was tired. He flipped his wrist to stare at his watch. The last thing he wanted was to descend into the pits of hell, even if it was five hours. "Shit," he muttered softly. "Tell them I'll be right there."

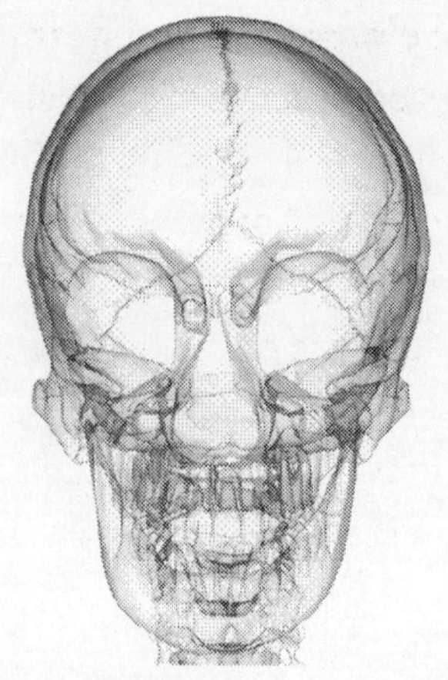

CHAPTER SEVEN

"Doctors, help. My husband's dying. Please help!"

The screeching came from a frail little woman standing outside exam room six. The scream instantly frayed nerves in the Medford University Trauma Center.

For a moment, no one moved, as all eyes searching to localize the cry for help. The next instant, trauma staff rushed toward the woman.

"Grab the cart!" shouted a nurse. "He's arrested."

From everywhere, bodies dressed in white coats and blue scrubs pounced on the lifeless black man in room six.

"What's happening here?" thundered Fisher, as he walked into the trauma center.

The question didn't go unnoticed, but it was lost in the flurry of activity surrounding the lifeless man. Cardiopulmonary resuscitation had started.

"Endotracheal tube is in place," called out an anesthesia resident as he successfully placed the airway. "I'll bag him. Somebody listen for breath sounds."

"Time your breaths with my chest compressions," called out the nurse already perched on the stretcher.

"What are you doing to my husband?"

The woman's withering voice was lost in the commotion.

The nurse delivering chest compressions yelled, "Can somebody take this lady to the triage area?"

A clerk standing at the nurse's station heard the command and raced to the woman's side. He took her hand and led her through the doors to the Center's triage area.

"Get me a twelve-lead EKG," ordered Fisher. "Alan, get a large line in. Somebody tell me about this guy."

Weary from the events of the never ending day, Fisher worked hard to snap back to alertness.

Binzemore had already gloved, anticipating the need for a central venous line. He quickly placed a large bore catheter in the patient's right internal jugular vein.

"EKG's running, Dr. Fisher," a nurse called.

"Stop compressions," Fisher commanded. "EKG's got electrical activity. Is there a pulse with that?" Fisher pointed to the patient's neck where the carotid artery should have been pulsating.

"No," was the immediate reply from one of ten or so people standing by the stretcher.

"Restart compressions," Fisher ordered. "EKG shows pulseless electrical activity. Give an amp of epinephrine."

Binzemore took the ampule of epinephrine from the resuscitation pharmacist. As he infused the drug, he recited the sketchy details.

"He's forty-two. He came in by ambulance about an hour ago from an accident. His car skidded off the road and struck a utility pole. His exam wasn't revealing, except for bruises across his chest and sternum. He just got back from X-Ray when this happened. I've haven't seen the films yet."

"Dr. Fisher, you better look at this."

Fisher turned to the voice. A young woman with a long brown pony tail and a tired face was standing by a large flat screen monitor across the room.

Fisher reached the monitor in a second. There the patient's chest x-rays glared on Medford's electronic imaging system.

Beside the stretcher, an ER technician studied the strips running off the cardiograph. "Dr. Fisher, that epinephrine tightened up his rhythm a little, but the QRS voltage is poor."

Fisher viewed the films on the oversized monitor. He scanned all parts of the film, muttering under his breath. "Lung fields are clear and there's no pneumothorax. The airways look good and there are no fractured ribs." His scanning eyes then focused on the heart.

Fisher again muttered under his breath. It was barely audible against the back drop of the commotion in the room. "The heart shadow is large." He pondered the news for less than a second. "Stop compression!" he ordered. "Is there a pulse?"

The room fell silent.

Binzemore, sleepless for twenty-four hours, his fatigued look was long gone as adrenaline surged through his tall, thin frame. He placed his fingers to check for pulsations through the lifeless man's carotid artery. "Nothing. There's nothing here."

"Start compressions again," Fisher ordered. "Let me see that EKG after the epi."

Fisher held the cardiogram in his left hand while standing by the monitor. He studied the electrical activity of the dying heart. Like a bolt of lightning that electrified his thinking, the solution came to him. He glanced again at the monitor. "The heart shadow on the film . . ."

The sentence went unfinished.

"Make a path." Fisher rushed to the stretcher. "Give me a large syringe with an eighteen-gauge spinal needle attached. Somebody get on the phone and call Cardiology and tell them we'll need their assistance in the cardiac cath lab immediately."

A nurse extended her hand towards Fisher. "Here's a sixty cc syringe with an eighteen-gauge spinal."

Fisher took the syringe and needle and inched toward the nurse who was delivering chest compressions. "What we've got ourselves here is a cardiac tamponade. He's got no pulse because his heart's pumping inside a tight bag of blood. That blow to the chest tore his pericardium, and the space around the heart filled with blood. All right, stop compressions."

Fisher swiped the chest with alcohol. With steady hands on the large syringe, he pierced the skin directly below the motionless, bruised breast bone, driving the four-inch needle in until barely a third of its original length remained visible.

"Keep that EKG running," he ordered.

Fisher pulled the syringe's plunger back. Dark red blood flowed easily into the syringe. "Give me a new syringe."

The new syringe pulled even more blood from around the heart.

"QRS voltage is increasing," the ER technician called, examining the strips coming off the machine.

"There's a strong pulse in the neck," Binzemore shouted.

The second syringe was almost full. "Okay that's over a hundred and twenty ccs. He's probably got more blood in there but it'll need to come out in the cath lab." Fisher pulled the syringe out of the man's chest.

Surprising to all, the man began thrashing about on the stretcher. The drainage had been lifesaving.

"Dr. Fisher," called a clerk from the nursing station. "The cath lab just called. Cardiology is finishing a case. They're on the way here now."

"Good call, Dr. Fisher," said Binzemore.

"Thanks, Alan." Fisher took off his latex gloves.

"They'll need to place a pigtail catheter in the pericardial space for several days to keep this from happening again."

• • • • •

"Dr. Fisher, you have a phone call." The clerk yelled above the commotion.

Fisher looked up from his chair in the cramped nursing station of the Medford Trauma Center. Two hours had passed since the first crisis had ended. With seeming endless interruptions, he was finally completing his notes in the patient's medical record. Fisher reached past a stack of registration forms and nudged one of the piles of paper that perpetually littered the counter top at the nursing station. As he picked up the receiver, he glanced around the cramped area. This space was never designed for humans to occupy, he thought.

"Hello, Dr. Fisher here."

"Dr. Fisher, this is Andrew Carter in the morgue. I'm calling for Dr. Roberts who is performing an autopsy. She would like for you to come over to the morgue."

Fisher looked at his watch. An odd hour for an autopsy to be in progress, he thought. He looked around the Trauma Center. Things were still active, but nothing that required his presence.

"Tell Dr. Roberts I'll be there soon."

Medford University was no different from most century-old American medical schools. Buildings and facilities added slowly over time and into available spaces had resulted in piecemeal expansion. The end result was the odd placement of various departments. The morgue was a classic example. It was in the basement of the University's old research building.

At night, the morgue was reached from the hospital only through underground tunnels. Fisher headed into the maze of winding tunnels, originally built as conduits for steam pipes. He walked cautiously, stooping occasionally to dodge pipes and large faucet handles that protruded down from the ceiling. The temperature of the cramped tunnel was always too warm, the result of small steam geysers hissing from the pipes.

Fisher exited the tunnel into a dimly lit corridor two floors below ground level. Double doors about forty yards from the tunnel marked the morgue's entry. Above them, a red light flashed inside a steel cage, indicating that an autopsy was in progress.

Hospital morgues were threatening places to clinicians, Fisher thought. They were places where death oozed from cracks in the walls and floors, a hallowed ground where Pathologists administered final doses of truth to a baffling mystery, unsolvable in life. Yes, morgues let clinicians gaze upon the demon that had taken the precious gift of life and returned death in trade.

Fisher pushed against the door and swung it inward. Before he could step inside, his eyes and nose began burning. He recognized the strong odor of formalin, the ubiquitous tissue preservative. Brilliant overhead fluorescent tubes caused Fisher to squint as he entered.

The old university morgue was rectangular, some thirty feet in its longest dimension. Four stainless steel tables, each supported by a single pedestal stood before him. The top surfaces of the tables had hundreds of perforations to permit fluids from body cavities, and the water used to rinse those cavities, to drain to a second surface below. The design permitted an unimpeded study of a corpse. An operating room style light was suspended above each table.

Along the wall opposite the tables were stainless steel doors that led to refrigeration chambers where corpses awaited autopsies. Ten feet from the entry, rows of yellow buckets held organs the Pathologists had removed and set aside for teaching and further study.

With his eyes finally accustomed to the light, Fisher scanned down the length of the room. At the last table stood Natalie Roberts and an assistant, presumably Andrew Carter. They were dressed in green scrub suits and waterproof surgical gowns. Fisher approached the table where the autopsy was in progress.

"Thank you for coming, Dr. Fisher," Roberts said, her voice muffled by a surgical mask. Medium-length blond hair, peppered by strands of gray, was pulled back tightly behind her head.

Roberts, about forty years of age, was an Associate Professor of Pathology. Fisher had not seen her in more than two years.

"Everyone was shocked to hear the horrible news of Chip Carlton's death, Steve. I know how hard you must be taking it."

"Thanks, Natalie." Renewed pain scattered across his gut. "I'm trying to get past it. I was surprised to hear from you. For some reason I thought you went to Taggart with Jacobson and several other Pathologists in the last year or so."

Roberts looked up, her eyes engaging Fisher's over the tightly fitted mask. "I did, for a while, but the work just wasn't for me."

"What do you mean?"

"Ho hum." Roberts looked back into the abdomen of the corpse lying on the stainless steel table. "Lots of uninteresting stuff, plus a ton of transplants. It's okay if you aren't used to the kinds of cases we see here. I missed the challenge."

"That's good to hear." Fisher smiled.

"Technically, I'm still a Taggart Memorial employee. Even with the four Medford Pathologists who joined the staff they're shorthanded. I told Jacobson I would stay on part-time to run the human tissue bank. I've been averaging two weekends a month."

"Natalie, it's almost midnight. Why are you here?"

Roberts' nose was back in the chest cavity of her corpse. "The Richland medical examiner, Tom McDonald, called me. He said they were overwhelmed with calls from the press about the Carlton shooting. CNN and CBS got into town first, and they're insisting on interviewing everyone. McDonald is expecting a pure media fest once the news wires start singing."

"I could have predicted that." A frown crossed Fisher's face.

"As for our Jane Doe here, she died in our Emergency Department earlier today. The state morgue told McDonald they wouldn't get to it for days and asked me if I could perform a medical examiner autopsy. I said yes and here we are. I've got a world of work tomorrow, and this was just the most convenient time to do it."

"Okay, Natalie what can I do for you?"

"I need your opinion."

Fisher walked around the stainless steel table. Other than the muted buzz of fluorescent lights, the trickling water was the only other sound in the underground morgue.

On the table lay the body of a woman, mid-forties, Fisher guessed. Her skin was weathered, most notably across the face, where it was badly wrinkled.

"She was found down on an access road under the Ninth Street Bridge. EMS brought her to Medford ER severely hypothermic. She died an hour later, during rewarming. She's got severe frostbite. These toes are necrotic and there's a demarcated line of early gangrene here." Roberts pointed to the corpse's left foot with a pair of forceps as she spoke.

Fisher leaned over for a closer look. All toes on the left foot were dark and swollen, changes consistent with gangrene. He stood and examined the remainder of the body. The abdomen and chest were opened. All internal organs were present indicating that Roberts had just begun her inspection. As Fisher studied the body, an item caught his eye. Tattooed in crude cursive across the left shoulder were the letters *M-a-t-t-i-e*.

"Steve, the most remarkable thing is here." Roberts pointed to the open abdomen. "Once we opened the abdomen, I felt for the organs in back of the abdomen, and I didn't feel a right kidney. Andrew, would you remove the intestines now, so Dr. Fisher can get a look?"

The morgue technician snipped away at the woman's stomach and intestines. In less than a minute, they were removed. Shortly after that, Carter removed the liver and spleen as well.

"Exactly as I thought." Roberts looked at the remaining organs behind the intestines. "As I palpated, I found a left kidney, but not a right one. All I could feel were metal clips on the right."

Fisher leaned forward to gain a better view of the abdomen. Organs in the extreme posterior region of the abdomen, the aorta, the pancreas and a single left kidney were all that remained. The most notable thing, as Roberts had predicted, was the absence of the right kidney, clipped in a clean surgical fashion. Numerous surgical clips were scattered about the empty space where the kidney had once been.

"Okay," Fisher commented, "the lady had a nephrectomy at some point in the past. Why is that so remarkable?"

"Well, it wouldn't be, if it weren't for one important thing," Roberts retorted. "Okay, Andrew, can you just roll her slightly to the left so Dr. Fisher can see her back?"

Carter reached across the morgue table and placed one hand on the woman's thigh and one on her shoulder. He gently rolled the body.

"Here." Roberts pointed to the woman's back. "Look at the right flank. Do you see any signs of a nephrectomy scar?"

Fisher circled around the table to where Roberts stood. He studied the body's right flank.

Fisher said, "She probably had the nephrectomy in early childhood and there's simply a remnant of a scar present. Did you look carefully for any defect on the skin?"

Roberts looked up at Carter. "Andrew, could you bring down the magnifier again?"

Carter steadied the body and then walked to the head of the table. He pulled down a small fluorescent lamp attached to the overhead surgical light. In its center was a large magnifying glass.

Roberts switched on the light and pulled it to the area just above the woman's right flank. "We've done that. Do you see any evidence of an old scar here?"

Fisher looked through the large lens. The skin of the flank was brilliantly lighted. With the exception of weathering of the skin, no scar tissue was evident.

Fisher stood. "I don't know what to make of this." A slight degree of irritation trickled into his voice. "The woman probably had a nephrectomy early in life, and she's one of the lucky people who didn't form a scar."

"Steve, I apologize for getting you down here on such short notice. I just needed another opinion. I'm still not convinced this occurred in as remote a time frame as you suggest. I'll prepare biopsy specimens from the sites around the kidney for light microscopy. Maybe they'll shed more light on the mystery."

"Come up with some convincing evidence, and you'll have a believer on your hands. Sorry, but you'll will have to excuse me. I'm not quite through with my shift in the trauma center. Then I've got to head home for some sleep."

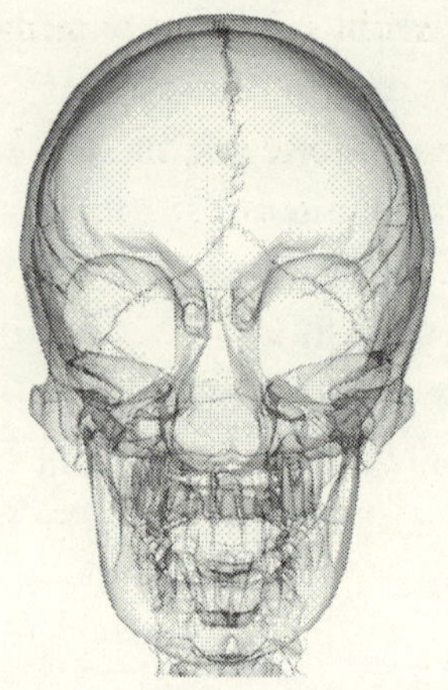

CHAPTER EIGHT

A lazy afternoon was coming to an end. Trade winds pranced gently overhead, producing a mesmerizing whisper as they buffeted the branches of an adjacent palm grove. Moving to and fro across the sands of a snow-white beach, crystalline blue water had become opaque, covered with liquid gold. The setting sun had begun its nightly dance.

Above the sands of the secluded beach, an elegant home sat nestled below the tree line, dense vegetation made it practically invisible from the beach.

A solitary figure sat quietly on a stone terrace. French doors leading into an opulent drawing room suite were open. The slender man, dressed in a swim suit, stroked his graying blond hair. His skin was bronzed from over-exposure to the tropical sun. For some time, he had stared transfixed by the shimmering gold water awaiting its evolution into deep firey red. He took a sip from the glass in his hand and then slid deeper into the cushion of the deck chair.

At that moment, the silence of the afternoon was broken by the chirping of a cell phone. The solitary man picked up the palm-sized phone. "Yes?"

"The target has been neutralized." The voice was flat and soft.

"Was the operation clean?"

"Surgical precision," the response came in an icy whisper.

The bronzed man stared at the reddening sun, a smile cracking subtly across his lips.

"Very nice. Our terms still stand. Your remaining compensation will arrive soon."

He clicked off the small phone and replaced it on the side table. For a while longer, he sipped from a glass, staring at the horizon.

He arose and walked a few paces toward the lagoon. Ice in the glass tinkled as he stopped and again brought the drink to his lips.

"Perfect," he said, whispering into the empty glass after he had drained its contents.

Fire ignited in the man's eyes as he turned to the water and gazed at the waning solar display.

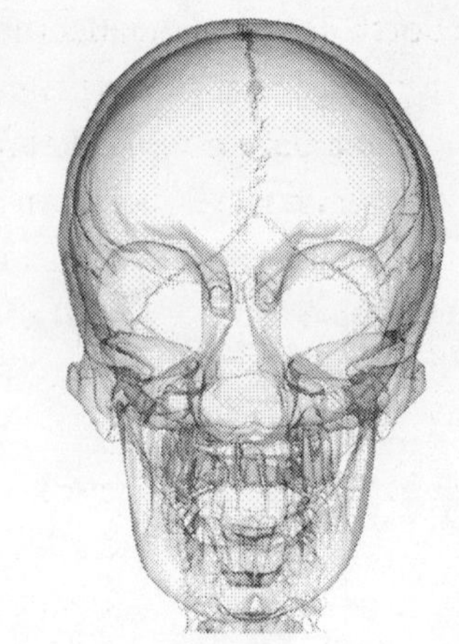

CHAPTER NINE

February 2

A few minutes had passed since Fisher entered the cardiac surgery ICU and walked to the bed where Patricia Bingham lay. If outward appearances were important, and at times they were in cardiac surgery, Mrs. Bingham's condition would be deemed excellent. She was sleeping comfortably, less than twenty-four hours following a heart transplant and she was slowly weaning off all cardiac support medications.

For Fisher, standing by her bed, things were different. His brain was fog bound and he struggled to get it jump-started for the day. On arriving home from his night shift in Medford Trauma, he hadn't simply gone to bed as he should have. He went straight for the bottle of Jack Daniels that sat unfinished from the night before. Without hesitation or forethought, he polished off the remainder of the bottle, eventually falling into a fitful sleep, plagued by a recurring dream. Unlike the night before, no calls came from the hospital.

Fisher was dealing with the whiskey's aftereffects. Important neurotransmitters that controlled conscious thought were not driving important impulses throughout in his brain. In other words, he was hung over.

Up to this point, Fisher couldn't understand the urge that was driving him back to the bottle. Maybe it was depression, he had told himself. For reasons he didn't understand, guilt loomed stronger every day.

He fumbled with the portable control panel that linked to the bedside monitor. The panel was supposed to give twenty-four hour graphical images of all cardiac performance data on Mrs. Bingham's new heart. The forty-eight hours after transplant were the most critical. Slight changes in left ventricular performance, cardiac output and mitochondrial oxygen consumption signaled acute rejection. Fisher and his other surgical colleagues had not had trouble with acute rejection since the release of Myelopress, but old practices die hard. Fisher still had Medford ICU nurses monitoring all the important parameters.

"Screw this damn thing," Fisher muttered softly as he tried to coax the hemodynamic panel to give up its graphical readouts. He hated computers. Ever since the hospital had installed continuous data monitors, his life had been hell. He had tried desperately to memorize the keystrokes that brought up the graphics, but his brain wouldn't cooperate. He had even written the commands on three-by-five cards, but they always got lost somewhere. Finally, he laid the small panel back on the monitor stand, totally frustrated. Computers would be his lifelong scourge.

Having no success with the monitor's keystrokes, he turned to the written nursing records — relics that were soon to be relegated to medical museums.

As he fumbled through the records, Fisher's thoughts drifted away from the ICU. Images of Sharon appeared in his mind. The letter he expected was in the mail slot when he had returned home. It explained in legal terms he didn't understand, that divorce was imminent.

Fisher turned and gazed out the window near Mrs. Bingham's bed. Organized thinking hurt him that morning, but he tried anyway. His troubles with Sharon couldn't account for everything. He and Sharon were having serious trouble for a while. Maybe it was the Med, he thought. The crazy medical marketplace was driving Medford University out of business. Downsizing had started, and layoffs would probably be forthcoming before long. The hospital was understaffed and . . . .

He paused.

His whole situation: Sharon, the hospital, Chip's leaving the University, was driving him back to what his therapists at the Houston VA Hospital called 'self-destructive behavior'. As he paused, he realized thought overload was coming on again. He turned away from the window and shuffled through the nursing flow sheets, pretending to be reading.

To top things off, he thought, the day before his closest friend had been killed. "Jesus," he whispered.

He had held things together pretty well until an image of Carlton's bloody, throatless body flooded into his thoughts. He gripped the chrome rails that surrounded the bed before him. He had to suppress the images or he would go crazy. He continued paging through the record occasionally glancing at his hands. They were trembling. He went back to flipping through the papers.

Fisher soon realized that shuffling papers wasn't doing any good. He couldn't get past the feeling that life was swirling out of control. He felt exposed, alone. The spiraling currents in his mind had gained velocity. It was like before when the maelstrom had trapped him in a vortex of hopelessness.

"You look like you need this," a gentle voice sounded to his right.

Fisher was startled as he turned. Jill Blaylock, Mrs. Bingham's cardiac nurse, stood beside him holding a cup of fresh coffee.

Fisher took the steaming drink from her.

"You're right. Thanks."

He put the coffee to his mouth and sipped. The stream of hot liquid worked its magic immediately.

For a moment, Fisher stood quietly. Blaylock was at the end of her shift tying up loose ends before leaving. She rounded the bed and readjusted the pillow to ensure her patient's comfort and then studied the myriad of intravenous lines and tubes protruding from Mrs. Bingham's chest. Finally, she gave an approving glance at the six bedside infuser pumps. All were set at different flow rates delivering inotropic drugs to stimulate the new heart.

Blaylock was mid-thirties, short in stature, probably not more than five-three. Her auburn hair was loose, producing a flow of brownish-red slightly longer than shoulder length. She was a vigilant nurse with keen intelligence. Fisher counted on her opinion and was glad to see her at Mrs. Bingham's beside when he entered the unit.

"She looks good," Fisher said finally, his mind starting to clear.

"She's doing fine," Blaylock noted. "Would you like to review the hemodynamic data?"

Blaylock was a ten-year veteran of the Medford Cardiac Surgery ICU, hiring on a year before Fisher joined the Medford faculty. She picked up the portable control panel from the monitor stand and accessed the numbers. Fisher's hatred of the control panel and its array of commands was a source of quiet amusement among Medford's cardiac nurses.

Blaylock and the regular cardiac nurses knew Fisher made no apologies. In fact, he kept his disdain of all computers no secret. In the old days when Fisher and Carlton made ICU rounds together, the nurses gathered quietly in the corner of the unit and snickered as Carlton tried to teach Fisher how to access the data stream off the bedside monitors.

"Go slowly, Jill, my brain is having trouble getting started this morning. I had a twenty-three-hour day yesterday." He didn't mention the half fifth of whiskey as he continued sipping the black coffee.

"Sure, Dr. Fisher." Blaylock entered the commands to display heart function. "Here's her eighteen-hour profile. It includes some data obtained in recovery immediately post-op."

Fisher and Blaylock looked at the twenty-inch flat screen suspended above the bed.

"Things have gone pretty much as expected. Cardiac index, left ventricular stroke work and ejection fractions all remained constant except for one period at about midnight when they dipped. I called Dr. Binzemore. He increased the Dintropin flow rate."

"That seems to have brought her back to predicted ventricular performance," Fisher noted. He counted heavily on Dintropin as the primary cardiac stimulator in his drug arsenal. It ensured performance of freshly transplanted hearts. Though infrequent, new hearts occasionally experienced periods of diminished output that required support.

"Yes, she responded well. Other than that, all animation values are at or above expected."

"Myelopress is infusing at one gram every twelve hours?" Fisher asked out of habit.

"Yes, she's getting her third post-op dose now."

Fisher nodded his approval, stepped to the bed and examined Mrs. Bingham. She was drowsy and vaguely aware of his presence. He removed the bandages from her sternum and inspected the incision running down the center of her chest. It was clean. The three tubes placed around the heart to signal bleeding were all free of any fresh blood. After donning gloves, Fisher clipped through the suture material holding the tubes in place and removed them. Mrs. Bingham winced briefly with pain. He finished his exam. He was satisfied with her progress.

"Jill, Alan Binzemore will be by later today to begin weaning the ventilator, if she makes it off the Dintropin this morning."

Fisher thanked Blaylock and turned to the double doors out of the cardiac unit.

As he was about to walk out of the unit, his cell phone rang softly in his lab coat pocket.

"Hello."

"Steve?" Mary Walker's frail voice was on the line.

"Just a minute, I've got to step out of the unit. It's a bit noisy in here."

He left the ICU and headed for the corridor outside. As he walked, he thought of asking Mary why she hadn't simply stayed home. Dealing with Chip's death was difficult enough for him. But after their encounter in the office the evening before, he knew she was taking Chip's death as hard as he was. He quickly discarded the stay-at-home idea as a viable one. Mary lived alone. Her husband, Tom, was killed in a tragic accident a few years back and though she had children, they were grown and lived away. Even if it was painful to be at work today, she had come in to avoid being alone. Her job was her life and the Med was her support system.

"Mary," Fisher spoke as he reached a quiet place. He conjured up images of her tear-filled eyes. He heard soft sobbing in the silence of the corridor.

"Are you okay?"

The sobbing continued a few seconds longer.

"I . . . I'm . . . okay, Steve. I'll be okay." A long sniffling sound flowed from the phone as she took a breath through swollen nasal passages.

Walker then spoke with a strengthened voice. "A Lieutenant Benjamin Domao from Richland Police Department called. He has more questions about yesterday and wants to know when he can meet with you."

Fisher looked at his calendar for the day. A cardiac pacemaker insertion was scheduled for ten o'clock, and there was one patient scheduled in the cardiac clinic afterwards.

"Let Lieutenant Domao know I can meet with him at one-thirty this afternoon? Tell him I'll come to the station."

"Sure." The familiar strength had returned to her voice. "Is there anything else?"

Fisher paused a moment, his thoughts coming smoother after the coffee.

"Yes, there is one other thing. Place a call to the Dean of Student Affairs. Get in touch with a medical student named Alli Shepard. Ask her to be in my office by ten o'clock Thursday morning."

• • • • •

At eleven-fifteen Fisher stepped out of the OR and headed to the Ambulatory Care Center. Things in the OR went exactly as he predicted. He ran a gauntlet of questions from the moment he arrived. Personnel in hospital operating rooms were a close-knit bunch. Like extended families, seeing the same faces day after day under life-and-death conditions bonded people. Chip Carlton was a member of the Medford OR family for five years.

Chip's call to OR fifteen during the Bingham operation spooked them, making the sense of loss all the more acute. From the moment Fisher stepped foot in OR receiving, he was swamped with questions about the shooting. He was suffering all over again.

He opened the door to the skywalk that connected the hospital to Ambulatory Care. A rush of frigid air greeted him as he entered the corridor. Environmental controls there like the OR had also been a sham. He looked down three stories to the street below as he walked. Everywhere people rushed to get out of the blustery February morning. The street sights below did not register, however. Bloody images flashed through Fisher's mind, images dredged up by the thoughtless inquisitors in the OR. In their eagerness to know the details of Carlton's murder, the OR staff had ripped open a fresh mental wound. He was thankful for a forty-five minute pacemaker insertion and not back-to-back transplants. He exited the bridge, resolving to keep the murder images out of his thoughts.

While awaiting the elevator, Fisher glanced at his watch. He made mental notes. Appointment at one-thirty to see Domao. He had allotted an hour for the outpatient. Pending no other disasters, he would make it.

The lift doors opened on the eighth floor, and Fisher made his way to the Cardiac Outpatient Offices. He was greeted by clinic staff who, unlike the OR family, said nothing about the prior day's events. He was thankful not to sift through the rubble of his thoughts again.

The clinic offices had a light schedule, no other doctors were present. Fisher was directed to room four where a blank Medford outpatient folder and referral medical records sat nestled in a plastic pouch on the door. The medical records had come from a Richland Cardiologist. Fisher took the records and reached for the doorknob. He stopped short of entering the room, however, when he read the name: *Thomas Winston*. Fisher took the papers and sat down at the desk in an adjacent room. On top of the copied material sat a letter from Jonathan Kepner, the Richland Cardiologist. The letter confirmed Fisher's suspicions as to the identity of his new patient. Thomas Winston was indeed a member of Richland's most notable family.

Fisher reflected a moment on the name. He recalled a recent article in the *Richland Tribune* concerning the family and its patriarch, Spencer Winston. The details of the article were fuzzy, but he remembered Winston had built a financial empire manufacturing fiber-optic cable for long distance data transmission. He was an engineer by trade but a genius as an entrepreneur. Spencer Winston recognized early the potential importance of fiber-optic technology for high-speed data transmission. The article disclosed he held many important patents for digital data transmission and signal boosting.

Winston's company, Fiberwire, had its headquarters in Richland, the article had said, but five other manufacturing sites were in operation in the U.S. and overseas struggling to meet global demand for its cable. Fiberwire's sales the previous year had exceeded eleven billion, and Spencer Winston's personal wealth was some ridiculous figure like six billion dollars. The *Tribune* piece had also mentioned that Winston's son, Thomas, age twenty five, had completed an MBA from Harvard Business and was to become vice president of Fiberwire's Richland operations. The author hinted that Thomas was being groomed to take over the company.

Fisher read Kepner's letter dated January twenty-eight. It outlined the basics of a sad story and gave details that were missing from the *Trib* story. Shortly after starting work, young Winston had fallen ill. Kepner first saw him four months earlier for complaints of breathlessness, and diagnosed heart failure from a viral injury to the heart. Kepner treated Winston for heart failure but he was deteriorating. By all indications, he would soon need heart transplantation. The rest of the letter simply gave the details of Kepner's medical evaluation and the results of various tests. The findings were clear: Thomas Winston was headed for a heart transplant.

The referral from Kepner was surprising. He usually referred patients for heart transplant evaluation who had no medical insurance.

Fisher opened the blank Medford outpatient folder and placed Kepner's letter inside. He walked to the door leading into room four and knocked. As he entered he saw two people bearing stark resemblance to each other. The older of the two stood. The elder Winston wore a dark three-piece suit with muted pin stripes. The tailor-fit garment covered a thin, wiry frame held overly erect. Closely cropped gray hair surrounded a hardened face covered by prominent worry lines. A short, gracefully pointed nose sat between eyes that resembled chips of black coal. They pinned Fisher with a disquieting stare.

The younger Winston had a pasty complexion that contrasted sharply in tone to his nose, identical in shape to the elder Winston's. Thomas had a blue tint to his nose, a sign of advanced heart failure. Young Winston wore a sport coat, unmatched pants and an open-collar shirt. He was visibly breathless, leaning on an elbow for support. His forehead oozed a fine skim of sweat. He made no effort to stand, only briefly making eye contact.

Fisher surmised his walk to the clinic had been physically taxing. "Good morning Mr. Winston, I'm Dr. Fisher." Fisher offered his hand to the elder Winston. Iron grip, continued stare. Spencer Winston, clearly sizing up Fisher, was slow to respond to Fisher's greeting.

Fisher turned to Thomas Winston and offered his hand. "Good morning, Thomas."

"Uh. . . morning, Doctor." The voice was weak, his handshake listless, barely perceptible.

Spencer Winston spoke, "Dr. Fisher, as you may know, Dr. Harrowood and I attended undergraduate school together at MIT. I spoke with him just yesterday, and he has assured me that your team will be managing Thomas's case."

Before Fisher could respond to the name dropping of Medford University's president, Winston spoke again, this time with a condescending undertone. "I should tell you, quite frankly, that Doctor Kepner encouraged us to seek help from specialists at Taggart Memorial or even the Mayo Clinic, but out of respect for Dr. Harrowood, we came here first."

Winston's words reverberated inside Fisher's head. It hadn't been spelled out, but the message was clear: Medford was second rate, not the first choice on the list, maybe even the last. He was doing Harrowood a favor coming by to look.

Fisher sensed the tension in his jaw and knew his blood pressure and pulse had risen as his blood heated up. Why, you son of a . . . .

Pause.

No. Fisher stopped himself from saying aloud the thoughts that burned through his mind. No angry words, he told himself, no angry words. Control, he thought. Don't dignify that remark with a hasty reply.

"Well," Fisher responded. "We'll certainly give Thomas the best care possible."

"That's good to hear you say, Dr. Fisher."

Fisher turned to the ill-appearing young man then back to a glaring Spencer Winston. His words were slow and deliberate: "Would you excuse us, please? I will need to examine Thomas."

"I think I'll just remain in . . . ."

"In the waiting room," Fisher said, interrupting Spencer Winston before he could finish.

Fisher pulled open a drawer and held an examination gown in his hand. He met the chief executive's icy stare with a look that let Winston know he would not back down. Without speaking again, the elder Winston leaned over and picked up his black woolen top coat. He walked to door and let himself out.

"You'll have to forgive my father, Dr. Fisher. He's used to having his way with everything."

"I can see that, Thomas."

Thomas Winston removed his shirt slowly but became breathless and more deeply blue-tinted in the process. Fisher helped the young man onto the exam table. He was wheezing and sweating by the time he got into position for the exam.

Fisher worked quickly: Pulse, 125; blood pressure, 88/45; respirations, 26 breaths per minute. The skin was blue toned and sweaty. Winston's hands and feet were icy cold. Glancing at the young man's neck, Fisher saw distended veins, a sign of advanced heart failure. With his stethoscope, he examined the lungs. They were wet and congested. The heartbeat was weak and rapid. Murmurs of valvular leakage and abnormal additional heart sounds were present. The abdomen was distended, and the liver enlarged and pulsating. A final inspection of the legs revealed them to be tight and swollen.

As Fisher helped Winston to a sitting position, he summarized the findings as consistent with severe heart failure.

"Dr. Kepner's diagnosis is correct, Thomas. The exam fits with advanced heart failure."

"Do you think I'll need a transplant?"

Fisher stared at Winston. "It's a good bet, Thomas. To confirm my exam, we'll need an additional test or two."

"Thanks," he said, his breath audible. "I guess you should let my father know."

Fisher opened the exam room door and stepped out to the waiting room. "Mr. Winston?"

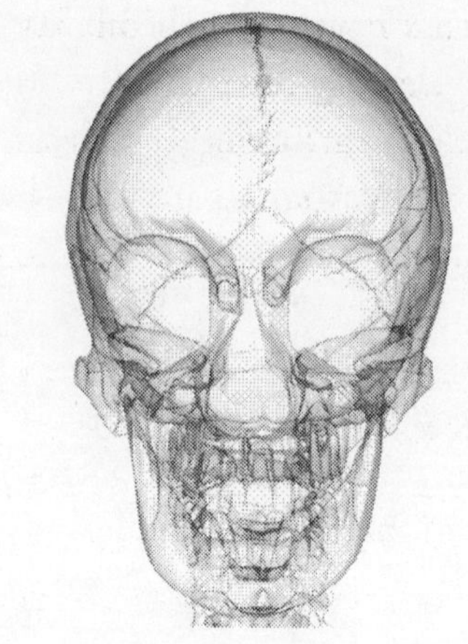

CHAPTER TEN

Fisher finished his discussion with the Winstons and scheduled several tests, including a ventricular photon imaging scan. A VPI scan, the last important study of Winston's heart, would give a near-final assessment of the urgency for heart transplantation by measuring the metabolic stability of Winston's heart. It would predict with accuracy the time that remained until cardiac arrest. Spencer Winston's facial expression denoted satisfaction with Fisher's plan for additional studies, at least for the time being. Fisher knew things would heat up again between him and Spencer Winston.

Before departing, he checked with Mary. She had contacted Alli, who said she would wait to hear from Fisher concerning her project.

Fisher estimated the drive to Richland's Police Department would take fifteen minutes. He glanced at the digital clock as he descended into the Mazda's leather seat. He would arrive on time for his one thirty appointment with Lieutenant Domao, no sweat. The engine caught on the first try, and he pulled out of the deck.

Fisher sped across the campus avoiding University Drive. He had struggled all day to suppress the horrible images of the previous day's events. Riding past the College Inn would have torn open his fragile mental wounds again.

The traffic across downtown was light, and Fisher approached his destination with ten minutes to spare. He turned off Tuckman Avenue, one of Richland's main thoroughfares, onto Twentieth Street. Fisher parked in a small meter lot across from the station. Icy winds whipped down Twentieth as he crossed the busy roadway.

The Richland Police Department sat across the street from City Hall, and was a five-story brick structure, circa nineteen-thirties, Fisher guessed, as he hurried up the front steps and entered the station through a heavy wooden door.

The door, scuffed from years of abuse, opened into a large atrium. A gust of frigid air entering with Fisher dispersed, increasing quickly to the inside temperature. As his nose warmed, the pungent aroma of stale body odor mixed with cheap perfume and fresh coffee flooded his senses.

The station's entry room was dark and dungeon-like. Along the perimeter of the room sat several worn benches reserved for the public.

Fisher noticed a lone man lying on a bench at the far end of the room. He was thin and weathered, his clothes unkempt. A lengthy beard obscured most of his face as he lay sleeping. The heavy door closed with a resounding thud, reverberating throughout the room, but the man remained still.

On the wall opposite the entry, a counter traversed half the room's length. Fisher saw feverish activity in an adjoining space behind the counter where blue uniforms and plain-clothes officers milled about. From behind the counter, a stiff-backed young officer dressed in a heavily starched blue uniform studied Fisher as he approached.

"Good afternoon. I'm Dr. Steven Fisher. I have an appointment with Lieutenant Domao. Could you direct me to his office?"

Striking blue eyes under heavy blond eyebrows stared out over a short, rounded nose. At first, he said nothing. Finally, the taut, fair skin across the young man's face bent upwards toward close-cropped hair. A subtle grin broke out on the officer's face. "Sure, Doctor. You'll find Lieutenant Domao's office in . . . ."

"Okay, John, here's the bag lunch you asked for. Who gets it?"

The grin on the young officer's face faded as his attention was diverted. He turned as a female officer approached. The young black woman, also wearing a blue uniform, carried a brown paper bag.

"Over there, Linda." The blond officer pointed to the bearded man asleep on the bench. "Wake him up, feed him and get him moving along."

"What's he up to? He using us as a way-station to get out of the cold?" she asked.

"Nah, he's looking for his girlfriend. 'Says she disappeared a couple of days ago. Didn't look like he'd eaten in a week, so I told him to wait while I got him a lunch. He fell asleep. The Missing Persons officer spoke with him to get a description, but so far, nothing."

"So, how do you want to handle this?" the young woman asked.

"Just wake him up and let him eat. You might give him a cup of that coffee you just brewed."

"Yes, your highness." The young woman stared a moment then burst into a grin.

"Thanks, Linda."

The officer turned back to Fisher. "Sorry, Doc. You'll find the Lieutenant in Homicide on the third floor."

The young officer glanced over his shoulder at the clock. It was precisely one thirty.

"The stairs will be the fastest. Elevators are ancient and get jammed up all the time."

He pointed to a door to Fisher's left.

"Just take the stairs to the third floor. Domao's office will be on the right about halfway down. It's room three twelve. I'll call him to tell him you're here."

Fisher thanked the officer and headed for the stairwell.

The female officer stood at the bench as Fisher reached the door leading to the stairs. She had placed a hand on the sleeping derelict's shoulder and was shaking him. "Okay, friend, time to wake up."

"Wha. . . wha. . .?"

Fisher was entering the stairwell when he saw the street-weary man sit bolt upright and grip the young woman's uniform shirt. "D'you find my Mattie Officer?" Fisher heard him ask as he climbed the steps. The frail voice was interrupted by a spasm of loud coughing still audible halfway up the stairs to the second floor. The conversation became muffled as the door to the stairwell closed.

Fisher exited the stairs onto the third floor. Like the entrance to the station, the Homicide section was old and unrenovated, probably since the building was originally opened. Low intensity fluorescent tubes overhead combined with dark tiled floors to give a gloomy effect. Doors leading into offices were half wood, half densely frosted glass. Room numbers were painted in the center of the glass on each door. Fisher found room three hundred twelve and knocked.

"It's open."

The stink of stale cigar smoke hit Fisher the moment he entered Domao's office. Domao stood behind his desk and the two men shook hands.

Without the khaki trench coat, Domao's short, fleshy body stood out more clearly. His dress shirt stretched tight over a bulging belly that flopped forward completely hiding his belt.

"Have a seat, Dr. Fisher." Domao pointed to the chair directly in front of the desk.

A moment of silence followed as Fisher settled into a tired-looking Naugahyde chair. Domao gazed at Fisher from behind a desktop in chaos. Small mountains of paper were stacked in random directions. Atop the tallest sat an ashtray filled with cigar butts.

"I have been formally assigned to the Carlton case, Dr. Fisher."

A stabbing pain ripped through Fisher the second he heard his dead friend referred to as a case. "I see," Fisher said softly.

"Okay, Doctor, why don't we get down to business? I'm sure you're a busy man."

Fisher didn't reply.

"First thing is to inform you that you are no longer a suspect in the killing of Dr. Charles Carlton."

Fisher didn't speak, but alarm bells rang inside his brain. Why would they suspect me, he asked himself, still saying nothing.

Domao leaned away from the desk. Wheezy coughs Fisher had heard the day before rolled out. He then swiveled his fat body back toward Fisher, his rounded face blood red.

"Your story has checked out so far, but I've got a couple of questions. The cellular phone service Dr. Carlton used checked its call logs for us and confirmed that he did, in fact, call you yesterday, not vice versa. We spoke with the OR nurse who worked your operation yesterday, and she corroborates your story about Dr. Carlton's phone call to the OR. And Dr. Shaklein, the proprietor at the College Inn, substantiates your claim that you and Dr. Carlton were long-time friends."

"We were."

"Doctor, I'm not going to beat around the bush with what's worrying me. You and your wife are having marital problems, are you not?"

Fisher was startled. "Just exactly what do you mean by that question, Lieutenant?"

"Do you have any reason to suspect that your wife and Dr. Carlton were romantically involved?"

For a moment Fisher was speechless, his stomach grinding into knots. "No. They were friends only."

"Are you sure, Doctor?"

The inference angered Fisher. He could see how jumbles of unrelated facts thrown down like tarot cards could tell any tale someone wanted to hear.

"As sure as I can be. Dr. Carlton and my wife were not having an affair. Our troubles did not relate to Dr. Carlton."

"Did you know that your house in Rosewood is vacant, Doctor?"

The bottom dropped out of Fisher's chest. "My house, empty? What do you mean? My wife is living there."

"You gave your residence yesterday as an apartment on the west side, yet you have a house in Rosewood."

"Yes." Fisher's face flushed with a mix of anger and embarrassment. "I'm living in an apartment. My wife and I are temporarily separated."

Another series of coughs. "Do you know where your wife has gone?"

"I have no idea. My wife and I haven't spoken in about a month. Our separation had nothing to do with Dr. Carlton. If my house in Rosewood is vacant, that probably means she has returned to her father's home near Arlington."

"Good enough. I'll need that address before you leave. As I said before, your story checks out for now, and it looks like you're clean. Just be informed that we still want to talk with your wife."

"Would it be inappropriate of me to ask if you have any other leads, or have you just been trying to incriminate me?"

Domao's brow furrowed deeply as he scowled at Fisher. "We're just following standard procedure, Doctor. We always suspect everyone. As for other facts, it's early in the investigation, but we have obtained some information. Probably enough to know Dr. Carlton was likely the target, not anyone else in the restaurant. Fourteen people besides you were in the Inn during the time of the assault, including the proprietor, Dr.

Shaklein. Overnight background checks were performed on all those present. Three professors from the History Department were there. Two were emeritus professors who are drawing pensions. None of them have outstanding debt and all have stable long-term marriages. One of the three is still working and has two college-age children whose tuition is funded by trusts. There were two primary care physicians, a husband and wife. They have no excessive debt, they own a house, have children, and there are no reports of extramarital affairs. The last one of note is the former head of the Neurology Department in the medical school who has just completed a substance-abuse program for prescription drugs. Dr. Shaklein and his staff were questioned at great length. There's nothing there."

"Then, if that leaves Dr. Carlton, the question is why would anyone want to kill him?"

"We don't know yet, Doctor. Yesterday's shooting has the trappings of a contract hit."

"But why?" Fisher asked.

"That's one of the reasons I asked you to come here today. We need additional information which you can probably provide. Did Dr. Carlton visit prostitutes?"

"I don't know."

"Did Dr. Carlton have a drug problem?"

"Now just a goddamn minute. Dr. Carlton was a talented, accomplished surgeon highly respected by all his colleagues. It's an insult to his memory to link him to underworld dealings."

A long series of coughs ensued, taking Domao close to the point of vomiting. He recomposed himself.

"Dr. Fisher, a man has been killed. I have to determine whether anyone had a reason to kill him. You were his closest personal friend and the one in the best position to know. My forensics team has determined that the slugs came from a high-powered weapon. Wake up. The murder was a professional hit. The killer knew who his target was. Now, I need your cooperation. I'm just doing my job. So I'll ask you again, Doctor. Do you know whether Dr. Carlton had a habit of using illegal drugs?"

"No, I don't."

"There are no prior arrest records. We have no evidence he ever attempted to purchase drugs. A check of his DEA license shows no citations for abuse of prescription drugs."

Fisher felt ill. He realized the questions had to be asked, but the whole process was disgusting. "Where does that leave things?"

"Without much at present, Doctor," Domao said, his breathing labored. "That's all I have. Before you leave, someone else would like a word with you."

"Concerning?"

"Dr. Carlton's iPad."

"I know nothing about computers, Lieutenant."

Domao stood revealing his lard-like abdomen. He waddled around the desk to the office door.

"We found the iPad in Dr. Carlton's car. It contains encrypted files. Brad Hinton, our in-house technician, has tried since yesterday to break the password without success. Before we call the Apple Store, we thought you might be able to help us with educated guesses. He's waiting for you in forensics."

Fisher followed behind Domao, smelling the pungent odor of cigar emanating from his clothing as he shuffled down the third floor.

As he approached the stairs, Domao said, "Forensics is down on two. We'll use the stairs."

On the second floor, just as they emerged from the stairwell, a thin young man dressed in old jeans and a sweatshirt stopped them.

"Lieutenant, I've been out to Carlton's house and . . . ."

"Excuse me a moment, Doctor," Domao rasped.

The two men stepped about five feet away and restarted their conversation audible simply as mumbling.

"Right, we'll go out today," Domao said, walking back to Fisher.

They continued their walk down the length of the hallway. The second floor wasn't as dark as the third. The overhead lights were more intense and the floor tile lighter, making it less gloomy. The office doors were still composed of the same half-wood, half-frosted glass arrangement Fisher had seen on the third floor.

Domao stopped in front of room two hundred forty-five. A small placard on the wall beside the door read: "SPECIAL PROCEDURES."

Domao knocked.

"Yes, come in," a voice behind the frosted glass said clearly.

"Morning, Brad," Domao panted as he stuck his head in the office. "I've got Dr. Fisher with me. Now a good time?"

"Sure."

Fisher and Domao entered. The office of special procedures was small and dark. At a third the size of Domao's office, the dungeon-like space was lighted by a single low-intensity incandescent lamp. Behind the desk, a large flat screen monitor mounted on a small table cast an eerie glow onto the man facing the screen.

The whole scene was surrealistic, Fisher thought.

Domao spoke, "Dr. Fisher, this is Bradley Hinton, director of RPD's Cyber Crimes Section."

The man seated at the monitor stood and shook hands with Fisher.

Hinton was somewhat taller than Fisher and exceedingly thin. Long hair, pulled back into a short pony tail, lay on the open collar of a casual plaid shirt. Sharp features of a kind face were obscured by heavy black-rimmed glasses. Thick lenses strangely refracted his eyes.

"I can take it from here, Lieutenant," Hinton said. "Will you need Dr. Fisher after we're through?"

"No." Domao closed the door as he left.

"Thank you for coming, Dr. Fisher. Have a seat."

Hinton pulled a set of keys from his pocket and sat down behind the desk. He unlocked the top right-hand drawer of the desk and pulled out a shiny black object.

Fisher immediately recognized Carlton's iPad.

"Dr. Carlton used a password to prevent unauthorized entry. I've used all the usual guesses from the biographical data sheet Homicide brought down on Dr. Carlton. Birthdays, nicknames, parent's birthdays, college name, his profession, his hospital. Nothing."

Hinton held the thin device with his hands. The machine consisted of a shiny glass front and metal backing. Hinton pressed a small button on the side and the small screen lit up.

"Apple computers and other companies who manufacture tablets these days use very sophisticated encryption software. If I can't come up with the password, I'll have to go to rapid sequence decoding which throws tens of thousands of passwords at the machine to crack it, but that could take days or even weeks to accomplish."

"How can I help you, Mr. Hinton?"

"The Lieutenant says that you and Dr. Carlton were good friends. Did the two of you share a mutual interest, some activity, some sport, some favorite book, an author, anything really?"

"We worked together at the University for about five years. We had many shared interests, but they were exclusively medical. Six months ago he left the University and began working at Taggart Memorial."

"Does any single incident stick out in your mind?"

"No, not really," Fisher said, thinking back. "The day he bought that iPad, he came to our house for dinner. I remember it, because he spent the entire evening totally locked into the screen."

Hinton said, "Are there any facts about Dr. Carlton's day-to-day life that stand out in your mind?"

"He used to have a house cat named Rosebud."

Hinton fed in the seven digits of the cat's name. No luck.

"His home was in the Chaparral development."

Hinton said, "I thought of that, but virtually all Apple machines these days will require a ten character or larger password."

"Nothing's immediately popping out, Mr. Hinton. I'm sorry."

Hinton readjusted the heavy frames that supported the thick lenses, pushing them up the bridge of his nose. "Just think about it, Dr. Fisher, if you will. If you come up with something, give me a call."

Fisher took Hinton's business card and left the office, entering the stairwell for the trip to the first floor. As he descended, he heard sobbing. He passed through the heavy door leading to the large entry hall. The street-weary, homeless man who had awakened earlier sat on the wooden bench, bent at the waist, holding his bearded face in his hands. To the man's right, a half-eaten sandwich sat on a crumpled lunch bag. To his left, the officer named Linda sat on the bench, her arm across his shoulder, attempting to console him.

"My Mattie, my Mattie," his weak voice sobbed pitifully.

"There there, Mister Worley," The female officer said. "We'll find Mattie. Don't you worry."

Fisher passed the two, buttoning his coat as he walked by.

Outside the weather had deteriorated. The sky was gray and overcast. Small snowflakes had begun flying on the icy wind. A winter storm was predicted by early evening.

As he pulled out of the lot and onto Twentieth, Fisher was deep in thought.

Ninety-five percent of the time passwords are predictable if you know an individual's habits, Hinton had said. Did you and Dr. Carlton have shared interests or activities?

Fisher drove on. Outside of work, he and Carlton had not really had shared interests. Besides work, the other activity Carlton pursued with a passion was eating. Many was the time Sharon had complained that there was never enough food for Chip when he came to the house to eat. Chip raved to the OR nurses that Sharon Fisher was a great cook, particularly with her desserts.

Fisher slowed for the light at Twentieth and Tuckman. The night Carlton came to dinner with his new iPad went back almost a year. Fisher remembered it, because he and Sharon had an argument before Carlton arrived. He pressed his mind for details as to why they were arguing, but nothing came to light.

Fisher turned onto Tuckman and drove on. Binzemore wanted to start afternoon rounds at four o'clock and Fisher needed to get back to the Med. He slowed the Mazda as he approached a light at Tuckman and Harrison. The hospital, usually in view at that point, was obscured by the approaching weather. The light turned red, and Fisher stopped.

As he waited for the light to turn, he gazed absentmindedly at the urban landscape. Around the intersection stood a branch of the Tri-State Bank, Hamilton's Jewelers and another one of Richland's ever-present Rainbow Donut shops.

It was three-thirty-five and traffic into the Rainbow was sparse. Fisher could see two or three patrons sitting at the counter, sipping coffee and eating donuts. For no particular reason, his gaze migrated from the customers to a large hand-painted banner in the front window of the shop. WE HAVE FRESH HOMEMADE FRITTERS.

Fisher directed his attention back to the traffic light. It was shift change at one of the east-end mills, and the intersection was crowded with vehicles, causing Fisher to miss the light.

That's okay, he thought, glancing at his watch. He had the time. He glanced back at the Rainbow and smiled at the banner. Carlton's favorite dessert above all others was fritters. Apple, peach, pear, you name it. Fritters, he thought.

"Jesus." Fisher yelled inside the airtight Mazda, but no one heard him. That's it! Chip Carlton loved fritters.

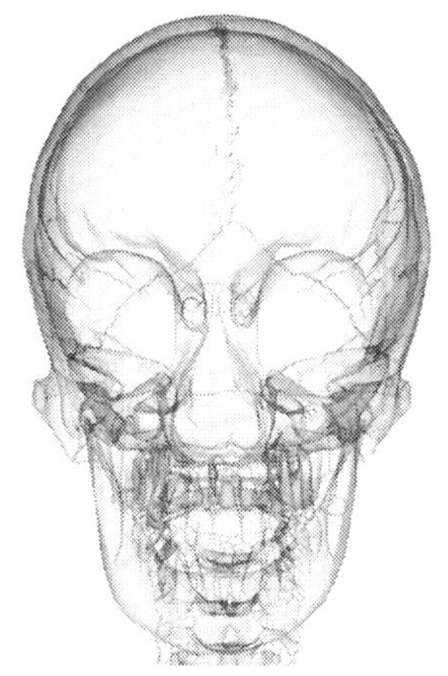

CHAPTER ELEVEN

Fisher was back on the second floor of the RPD heading to Bradley Hinton's office in less than ten minutes. He bounded up the steps to the second floor two at the time. Though he glanced as he passed through the station's entry hall, he noticed the bench formerly occupied by the homeless man and the female officer was vacant.

Bradley Hinton stood outside his office, engaged in a conversation with a uniformed officer. He turned as Fisher approached. "Forget something, Dr. Fisher?"

"No, I uh, had a thought as I was driving away." Fisher glanced at Hinton then at the officer next to him. His breathing had quickened from the sprint.

Hinton looked first at the officer, then at Fisher. "Shall we go into my office, Doctor?"

The two walked into Hinton's minute, little office.

Fisher sat in the same seat he had occupied minutes earlier. His wind was returning. "I may have come up with something. My wife and I frequently invited Dr. Carlton to the house to eat. He was a gourmand of sorts, eating virtually everything; but his favorite food was fritters."

Hinton stared from behind Coca-Cola bottle lenses. "I'm afraid I don't understand."

"Chip Carlton loved fritters. They are a sweet dessert created by frying fruit surrounded by batter."

Fisher's cell phone chirped. He pulled the phone from his coat pocket.

"Dr. Fisher," Binzemore's familiar voice said immediately.

"Yes, Alan." Fisher looked at his watch.

"We are ready to begin afternoon rounds any time you are."

"Alan, I'm afraid I won't make it this afternoon. Could you take the team through rounds?"

"Sure," Binzemore said without hesitation.

"Everyone's stable. We're set to discharge Mister Royster this afternoon."

"Fine, I'll be in touch later." He jammed the phone into his pocket.

Fisher looked at Hinton. "On the way back, I remembered that the night Dr. Carlton bought this iPad, Sharon prepared apple fritters, but only after some coaxing from both Dr. Carlton and me."

Hinton said, "Oooookay. That's a little bizarre. But hey, if it works, who's complaining?" Hinton retrieved the tablet out of the top drawer of the desk and switched it on.

He keyed in the letters: F-R-I-T-T-E-R-S into password field.

Fisher waited anxiously.

"Bingo!" Hinton said. "That's a nice piece of work, Doc."

Hinton turned the screen toward Fisher. It read:

FILE ENCRYPTION SEQUENCE SOLVED: DO YOU WISH TO ENTER? (Y/N), Apple Software, Inc.

Hinton pressed Y. Another screen appeared showing all the usual Apple icons. One of the icons, unfamiliar to Hinton was present. It read: **Carlton Files**. Hinton pressed the icon and a new screen appeared.

4 files present select number:

(1) >> NOS

(2) >> OpComp

(3) >> ToDo

(4) >> MedNetRt

Hinton pressed 1. It contained a spreadsheet file entitled: NUMBERS

Numbers		
1	DEA number #	AC8524937
2	Pharmacy Control Board #	VY-23-455-3
3	Dr. #: T M H	8510

4	TMH Info Systems sign on code/password	CHPR/AORTA3 TMH.com/dr/ra/access
5	State Board of Medicine License #	6657T45-015
6	Driver's License #	T134-45-7823
7	Spartan Health Club Membership #	4568
8	MasterCard #	5217 5660 2482 4983

Both Fisher and Hinton were silent. Each man stared at the screen. Under normal circumstances, the types of items listed would not have heightened anyone's level of interest. In view of recent events, any information, even the mundane, might be significant.

Hinton said, "From the looks of things, the list of numbers was incomplete."

"What makes you say that?"

"The table has two empty rows. Tables are usually just large enough to contain a complete data set. The blank spaces here suggest that more numbers were set to be entered."

Fisher said nothing.

"What's item three?"

"It appears to be Dr. Carlton's doctor identification number. Virtually all hospitals require them now to be on orders for laboratory tests, imaging services, medications and other services like dictations. Eight-five-one-zero would have to have been on all orders written by Dr. Carlton at Taggart Memorial Hospital."

"I see."

"Can you explain item four?"

"Item four is a password to Taggart Memorial Hospital's electronic medical record. The letters C-H-P-R represent a personal log-on code chosen directly by the computer. He told me that Taggart Memorial's log-on codes permitted stage one access. The letter sequence AORTA3 I guess was Dr. Carlton's personally chosen password."

"And TMH.com/dr/ra/access?" Fisher asked.

"That's Taggart Memorial's website. It must allow the user to gain access from a remote computer. Dr. Carlton would have used this, for example, if he were communicating with Taggart's electronic medical record from a desktop computer at home or from this iPad, for that matter. Did Dr. Carlton keep a computer outside of work?"

"Yes," Fisher said. "Dr. Carlton took pride in owning the latest computer technology. On several occasions during the time he worked at Medford, he purchased new pieces of equipment for home. He was the hands down guru for the Cardiothoracic Division."

While Hinton hit more keys, Fisher took out a small note pad and jotted down Carlton's doctor identification number, his personal log on/password sequence and the TMH doctor remote access. It seemed like the right thing to do.

Hinton opened file two entitled OPComp. Another table appeared.

>> OpComp

OP/Post Op Complications (6/30 - 1/30)			
	Name	**Med Rec**	**Comp.**
1	Alice Timlawn	5376645	Sternal dehiscence
2	David Smith	2334378	Post-operative sepsis
3	Enrique Swarez	3259801	Recurrent V-tach
4	Thomas Blanton	3235613	Cerebrovascular accident
5	Hans Smallwood	4625557	Recurrent V-tach

Hinton again nudged the heavy glasses back up the bridge of his nose as he raised his eyes off the screen and gave Fisher a questioning look. "What is this?"

"Dr. Carlton was obviously keeping a record of unanticipated complications after open-heart surgery. Most surgeons keep lists like that. If it's the complete list, the number and type of complications he's shown here are small, compared to most active cardiac surgeons. Dr. Carlton always kept careful records of his complications."

Both men again directed their attention to the screen as Hinton closed the second file and entered file three named ToDo.

>> ToDo

Calls: January 31	
Cliff Stryker	Done
Steve Fisher	Done
Harry Talbott	———

Silence again fell on the small Special Operations office. Fisher looked at the names. The two other than his own were familiar. Cliff Striker was Taggart Memorial's megalomaniac administrator and chief "hit man" for physician hiring. The Medford faculty who ultimately hired on to Taggart Memorial had gotten the high pressure rush from Cliff Striker. In Carlton's case, Striker had needed help from Taggart's chief cardiac surgeon, Harry Talbott.

The ancient wooden desk chair creaked as Fisher leaned back. Fisher had disliked Talbott the first time they'd met. Talbott was arrogant and condescending and, in Fisher's opinion, of questionable skill. Before Talbott began practicing at Taggart, he had worked in a small Midwestern hospital. Fisher had seen Talbott's surprisingly small résumé while Carlton was being rushed for the Taggart job. He remembered thinking Talbott had no basis for his patronizing attitude.

"You know these two, Dr. Fisher?"

"Yes. Striker is the Taggart administrator, and Talbott is their chief of Transplantation."

"Wonder why those two men and you were on Dr. Carlton's to-do list."

Fisher shrugged.

Hinton keyed in the command for the last file entitled: MedNedRt. Fisher saw that it contained a website that was a word soup of letters and symbols.

>> MedNetRt

HTTM//www.MedNet@Jade.ucil.edu

It was Fisher's turn to look up with a questioning expression.

Hinton said, "This is an Internet routing sequence for a site named MedNet. Jade's the name of their server and ucil is the abbreviation for the University of Illinois. The .edu indicates it's an educational institution.

This is gibberish, Fisher thought, reaffirming the notion that he despised computers but was being dragged whether he liked it or not into 21st century technology.

Hinton's office door opened and the two men turned to see the blob-like figure of Benjamin Domao. With a loud whistle in his breath, he exhaled cigar smoke into the small office.

"Doctor, you're still here. Good. Could you come with me please?"

"Where?" Fisher asked.

"Dr. Carlton's house has been ransacked and we need your assistance."

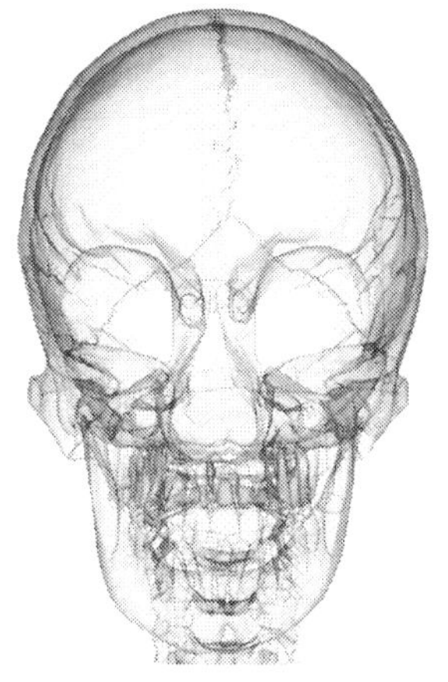

CHAPTER TWELVE

The interior of Domao's unmarked cruiser was littered with flotsam jettisoned by an early-century professional whose life was on a collision course with disaster. Styrofoam coffee cups, fast-food wrappers, empty bottles of non-aspirin pain relievers and antacid bottles were strewn across the seats and floorboards. The cruiser had the same acrid cigar odor Fisher smelled in Domao's office. An ashtray crammed full of chewed cigar butts drizzled ash onto the cruiser's carpet as Fisher opened the door of the vehicle. Styrofoam cups in the passenger's foot well crunched as Fisher pulled his feet into the cruiser.

The twenty-five minute drive to the Chaparral area west of Richland was miserable. As they left the office, Fisher was convinced that Domao intended to light a burned out stogy from the filthy ashtray. He had not, but Fisher and Domao rode mostly in silence except for Domao's coughing. At predictable intervals, Domao rattled off torrents of wheezy coughs.

Following one particularly heavy tussive series, Domao turned to Fisher and initiated conversation. "At the station, you said you and your wife helped Dr. Carlton locate this house."

"My wife did."

"Oh. . . . your wife did?"

Domao nervously glanced at Fisher as he drove. "And?" he squawked, implying that Fisher needed to continue.

"And what?" Fisher turned to face Domao.

"And I want to know some of the details." Domao finished with another dreadful staccato of coughs.

"Details of what, Lieutenant?"

"The details of how your wife helped the doctor locate a house."

"Why is that important?"

"It just is."

"Look, it's not what you're trying to make it out to be. When Dr. Carlton first arrived at Medford, I told him my wife worked in real estate. He contacted her, and she helped him locate the house in Chaparral."

"Why Chaparral?" Domao asked.

"I couldn't begin to tell you why Dr. Carlton chose a house out here. Knowing Dr. Carlton, I would say it was because he wanted a home with an exclusive address."

"Humph." Domao mumbled his disapproval under his wheezy breath.

As the car fell quiet, Fisher guessed his answer was largely correct. Chip had liked expensive things: clothes, cars, houses. In fact, Fisher knew it was personal taste that eventually landed Carlton at Taggart Memorial. His University salary wasn't able to support the lifestyle he wanted. The house in Chaparral had come at a hefty price. Sharon had never mentioned the exact amount, but Fisher knew it was high.

"So she works in real estate, huh?"

"Yes, she does. She's helped many faculty members locate homes, not just Dr. Carlton. So you can dispense with the notion that Dr. Carlton and my wife were having an affair, Lieutenant. That was more than five years ago. My moving to an apartment six weeks ago was pure coincidence and had nothing to do with any relationship my wife was having with Dr. Carlton."

"Can't leave any stone unturned, Doctor," Domao said. "Can't leave any stone unturned."

As Fisher had feared, the biological time-bomb reached for the ashtray, secured a previously gnawed cigar butt and placed it between his teeth. A lighter appeared in Domao's left hand and, before Fisher could object, a plume of smoke burst from his mouth.

Disgusting, Fisher thought as he turned to appraise the road and the lay of the land. Snowflakes still flew, but the overcast was less impenetrable. A bend in the road gave the first glimpse of the Caton River. Its water was somber gray, blended with shades of white where the rapids surged over the rocks.

Another turn and the road inclined sharply. They passed by two large granite columns, each bearing a thick brass placard imprinted with the word, Chaparral. The cruiser ascended into a stand of oak and evergreen. Though the oaks were leafless, the density of the hardwoods and evergreens permitted only glimpses of Chaparral's secluded villas, mostly positioned at the end of graceful, winding drives. Fisher had been there a dozen or more times and was familiar with the development. Carlton's place was in the back at a slightly higher elevation than the other homes. The road passed by finely manicured properties accented by a dusting of snow. At the rear of the Chaparral, the road leveled out. Domao turned left off Chaparral's main thoroughfare into the drive that led to Carlton's house. A familiar pain welled up in Fisher's gut, followed immediately by heaviness in his chest. The narrow, paved lane weaved its way through dense leafless oak trees. Fisher trembled slightly as the house came into sight — only twenty-four hours after the brutal murder of his closest friend. The passage of months or years might lessen the sting of Chip's death but Fisher would never accept his absence.

Domao nosed the unmarked cruiser alongside two other police cruisers, a black and white with the familiar RPD logo and another, identical to Domao's. Close by stood a large navy blue van. Discreet white lettering on the side read Richland Police Department Crime Scene Investigations Unit.

"Looks like Forensics is here," Domao said pulling a deep drag off the smelly stogy. With a harsh croak, he exhaled the smoke into Fisher's airspace.

Fisher said nothing. He simply opened the cruiser's right front door and stood up. A gentle breeze stung his face with fresh, frigid air. Fisher inhaled, desperate to clear the cigar fumes from his lungs. He turned and watched the beefy detective struggle out of the car.

You're a shit-head, Domao, Fisher thought.

A screen door leading to the house's back entrance opened, and a gaunt middle-aged man approached the cruiser. He wore navy pants and an undersized plaid sport coat that he or someone else had slept in the night before. He was scantily clad for such a cold day, but he didn't seem to be affected by it.

"Afraid they got here ahead of us, Lieutenant."

Domao seemed preoccupied with extracting the remains of the stogy from between his front teeth, digging in with a fingernail previously chewed to the quick.

Fisher spoke up. "What do you mean?"

The man in the wrinkled coat turned and looked at Fisher as if he had not previously noticed his presence.

"Who's this, Lieutenant?"

Finished with his makeshift dental surgery, Domao produced two perfunctory wheezy coughs and shut the cruiser's front door. "This is Dr. Steven Fisher. He and Dr. Carlton worked together at Medford University. I asked him to come with me. Figured he could tell us whether anything had been removed from the house."

As if forced to perform the formalities, Domao turned to Fisher. "Doctor, this is Detective Hamilton Miller, Richland PD."

"You expected the house to be ransacked, Domao?" Miller said quizzically.

"Yeah."

For a moment, Miller trained his dark eyes on Domao, then looked away.

Fisher followed closely as the two detectives walked to the screened door Miller had come through moments earlier.

Miller said, "Whoever these guys were, they knew their stuff. The house wasn't forcibly entered. The lock here has been picked."

Miller pulled out a pen light and shined it on the back door dead bolt lock. Fresh scrapes and cuts were visible on the lock's surface. Miller looked at Domao. "The alarm company that monitors the house didn't detect an entry, so whoever it was either knew the disarm code or knew how to shut the system off. Forensics has dusted for prints here and in the house. So far, nothing."

Domao and Miller entered the house. Fisher followed.

Miller spoke again. "The house is torn up everywhere. They were looking pretty hard for something."

The rear entrance of Carlton's house led into a kitchen. Fisher was immediately alarmed by what he saw. All drawers and cabinets had been pulled open and the contents poured out onto the floor.

"Jesus, what a mess." Domao barked a cough as he looked around the kitchen.

Miller shook his head. "This is what you can expect from the rest of the house."

The detectives walked out of the kitchen. Fisher followed, suppressing feelings of disbelief and anger.

Carlton's home was unusual in its design, containing few partitions and mostly wide open space. Besides the wall separating the kitchen from the rest of the house, the other dividing structure was the partition leading into Carlton's bedroom. It was possible to look across most of the house's interior, once out of the kitchen. What Fisher saw on entering the dining area dismayed him. Everywhere, there was complete devastation. Six other men, two in RPD uniforms, stood at various locations throughout the main body of the house sifting through the debris of what formerly had been an elegant home. Furniture was overturned, upholstery ripped. Oriental rugs were pulled up and lying in heaps. Pictures and artwork had been pulled from the walls, their backs ripped off. Fisher looked across the open space. The search had been thorough. All electrical outlet covers and switch covers had been removed from the walls and the contents pulled out.

A seventh man, a uniformed officer, came through the door leading to Carlton's bedroom and walked to where Domao, Miller and Fisher stood. "Professional job, Lieutenant, all the way down to drain covers and goose neck pipes in the kitchen and bathroom. Somebody really wanted to find something."

Domao turned to Fisher and threw out a command. "Doctor, look around please." He then turned to the uniformed officer and spoke with a volume so low it sounded like mumbling.

Fisher moved around rubble, attempting to reconstruct how the scattered furniture, books and magazines used to look. The last time Fisher visited Carlton's home was more than seven months earlier. He found the reconstruction job a formidable task.

He made his way down three steps to a sunken sitting area next to large windows that looked out over the cliffs and down onto the Caton River's crashing rapids. That had been Fisher's favorite place. He and Carlton often sat for hours drinking in the magnificent view while talking. The conversation pit was chaos. Carlton's leather sofas were overturned, their cushions ripped open. Two six-foot hi-fi speakers lay on their sides, their backs removed. The electronic equipment that drove the speakers had been ripped out of the in wall cabinet.

Fisher hurt inside as he surveyed the ruins across the other areas of Carlton's home. He tried to stay objective, but it was difficult. He turned and walked to the bedroom. There, too, was chaos: drawers emptied, dressers overturned, mattress and bedding ripped up and pulled onto the floor, pictures pulled off the wall, closets emptied. So far, nothing screamed out as missing, though. Fisher peered into Carlton's opulent bathroom that revolved around a pedestal-mounted Jacuzzi. All controls along the Jacuzzi's rim, including the pipe space panel at its base, had been removed. Nothing was left unsearched.

Fisher turned and surveyed the shambles of Carlton's bedroom. His roving eyes stopped at the pocket door that led to Carlton's study. Sidestepping the wreckage, Fisher crossed the room and pulled the sliding door open. Interestingly, the study had been spared. Oak-grained shelves filled mostly with medical and surgical textbooks covered the walls. They had not been disturbed. Cabinet doors were opened but not looted. At the end of the study stood a desk. Atop the desk sat Carlton's personal computer.

Fisher walked to the desk and studied the area carefully. Nothing had been disturbed. He started to sit down.

"Please don't sit in the chair or touch anything, Doctor."

Startled by the voice, Fisher reflexively stood erect.

Hamilton Miller walked into the study. "I'm very sorry to have frightened you. The crime scene must be preserved at all costs."

"Thanks for reminding me. I was concentrating on Chip's computer."

"Anything look disturbed?"

"Actually, I know nothing about computers, so it's hard to say exactly but. . . ."

"Yes?" Miller walked across the study to stand by Fisher at the computer.

"Well, I was only in here once, but I recall there was a container of brightly colored plastic items which he called jump drives. They were piled into a clear container. I remember them because of the different colors. I don't see them now. Have your guys taken them?"

"Got me, Doc. Let me get a forensics guy in here. Maybe one of them'll know."

Miller stuck his head out the door of the study and called into the great room. A few moments later, a member of the forensics team dressed in black coveralls appeared in the study. He was a frail man. His gray hair placed him in his late fifties, early sixties.

"Bob, Dr. Fisher here thinks something is missing."

Fisher described the multicolored objects he remembered as accurately as possible to the feeble-appearing forensics specialist.

"Sounds like jump drives to me," the man said, looking over the desk and computer.

"What's that?"

"People use 'em to store data. They store large amounts of digital data and they are pretty secure. You insert them here." He pointed to an empty slot on the computer's processor box. "Most people these days are using cloud services mostly to store data rather than using jump drives. Guess Dr. Carlton used both."

Together, the three men began a systematic search of the study for the container. No drives fitting Fisher's description were found.

"Cute, very cute," Miller said. "They removed backup material." Miller looked around a few more moments and turned to Fisher. "You have been a great assistance, Doctor. Thank you."

From the next room, the three men could hear a staccato of wheezy coughs. Seconds later, handkerchief in hand, Domao ambled through the doorway into the study. Although Carlton's house was uncomfortably chilly, Domao sweated profusely. He wiped across his cheeks and neck. The recessed incandescent lighting pouring down from overhead produced a glistening effect over Domao's face.

"Lieutenant, Dr. Fisher discovered that a library of backup computer drives is missing."

Domao stuffed the handkerchief in the side pocket of his sport coat and walked across to the desk where the men stood.

"Have you searched Dr. Carlton's hospital office? Could the drives Dr. Fisher described have ended up in that office?"

"I don't think so, Ben. That office was searched last night, only hours after the killing. Nothing like what Dr. Fisher here is describing was found."

With a jerky, almost impatient, motion, Domao reached inside his jacket and pulled out a small flip pad and jotted a few notes.

"Bob," Domao wheezed. "Once all the computer equipment is dusted, make sure it gets down to Hinton. Doctor, I think we're done here. I'll drop you back downtown."

Fisher and Miller followed Domao back through the chaos of the house to the driveway.

"Ben, I've got two men searching the grounds and going door to door, speaking with the neighbors."

"That's fine," snapped Domao. "Keep me informed. Doctor?"

Fisher reluctantly returned to the cruiser, pushing rubbish aside as he had earlier. He dreaded the drive back to Richland.

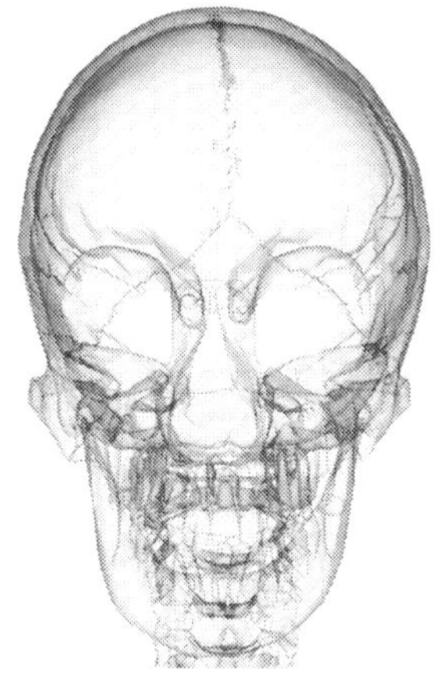

CHAPTER THIRTEEN

Doctor Natalie Roberts stared through the microscope's high-powered lens, studying the same slides for the fifth time in four hours. At the start of the day, she had dozens of things to do, all of them important, and none of them related to the Jane Doe she had autopsied the night before. But since the autopsy, she had been troubled.

Roberts had made her usual morning trip by the coffee pot on arriving in the Pathology Department at seven in the morning. She had just finished stirring sugar substitute into her coffee when Cynthia Jennings entered, carrying an empty coffee cup. Jennings was the senior histologic technologist responsible for processing all tissues taken from autopsies performed at Medford. After the two greeted each other, Jennings roadblocked the doorway out of the tiny room which smelled of chocolate hazelnut coffee.

Jennings wore an impish smile. "Dr. Roberts, weren't you on autopsy call last night?"

Roberts pulled a long, slow sip from the steaming coffee mug and swallowed. She had counted on her 'Morning Elixir,' as she called it, to snap her to alertness.

"Yes, Andrew and I did a Jane Doe for the ME's office last night."

"You must be a little anxious to see the material," Jennings prodded as she poured a cup of steaming hot coffee.

"Why do you ask, Cynthia?"

"Well, I must say that in my twelve years in Medford Pathology, I don't recall a single instance when the tissue processor was started after six at night for autopsy material. The processor timer indicates a start time of one forty-five in the morning."

Roberts must have blushed, though she managed to maintain her usual controlled composure. "Well, maybe I'm. . . ."

"Gotcha!" Jennings laughed. "You must have had a long night."

Jennings was right. After completing the Jane Doe autopsy, it was after one in the morning. She and Andrew Carter had pared down all the tissues removed at autopsy to fit into plastic processor cassettes. The cassettes held the tissue firmly in the processor while they were fixed for later cutting and mounting on glass slides.

Roberts had arrived home after two, but struggled to fall asleep. The autopsy, as mundane to the casual observer as it was, had left her puzzled. She lay awake, sifting through the results in her mind until well after four. With an unusual level of energy, she bounded out of the bed when the alarm sounded, eager to continue her examination of the Jane Doe material.

Before Jennings and Roberts parted company at the coffee urn, Jennings promised to section, mount and stain the autopsy tissue ASAP. Roberts knew that a request for immediate turnaround of autopsy material was unusual. Without exception, tissues from autopsies were always shoved behind surgical specimens coming from the ORs. Delays of two to three weeks were common.

Roberts' task list, so masterfully constructed the day before, had gone down the tubes, along with the rest of her appointments for the day. Until Cynthia Jennings delivered the freshly mounted autopsy slides around eleven, all Roberts had managed to do was stare out across the Medford campus at lightly blowing snow, puzzling over the Jane Doe findings. The thing that perplexed her most was not the woman's death. Hypothermia deaths were common among the homeless, especially when alcohol was involved. Blood taken from the woman in Medford Emergency just before her death had revealed a moderate blood alcohol level. The vexing question was simple: How had the Jane Doe undergone surgical removal of her right kidney with no evidence of a surgical wound?

Roberts thought back to the autopsy. Following Fisher's departure from the morgue, she carefully dissected the tissue planes of the woman's right flank, exactly where the incision for a nephrectomy would be expected. She had found nothing. The tissues were perfectly intact. However, no one could refute the presence of the surgical clips on the remnants of the renal artery and vein, the kidney's vital blood supply.

She had carefully sampled all tissue from around the site of the absent kidney, taking care to obtain pieces of overlying muscle and skin. The left kidney was normal to Roberts' exam and she removed identical tissues from the area that surrounded it. She tentatively rejected Fisher's nephrectomy-at-birth theory, convinced that Fisher, shocked by Carlton's brutal killing, couldn't have delivered a rational explanation. It was Roberts' opinion that no matter how old the woman had been when her kidney was removed, a nephrectomy scar across the right flank would have been present.

• • • • •

From the moment Cynthia Jennings laid the slide carriers of freshly mounted tissue sections on her desk, Roberts confronted a rare event for an experienced Pathologist. Specifically, she was observing a new biological phenomenon.

She started with the tissue from the woman's left foot. At autopsy, the foot showed signs of severe frostbite injury. Under the microscope, she saw broad bands of necrosis. Signs of cell death were everywhere in the foot. In view of the foot's physical appearance, that was not surprising.

Next, she systematically inspected the organs she had removed from the Jane Doe. In her exam of the lungs, she found early emphysema and an area teeming with bacteria. Heart, bowel, skeletal muscle, and spleen tissue were normal, as was the woman's one remaining kidney. The liver and pancreas showed changes of heavy and prolonged alcohol consumption. Roberts concluded, as would most pathologists, that her Jane Doe was a heavy-smoking, heavy-drinking homeless woman who likely died from exposure. She had severe frostbite covering her entire left foot along with a developing pneumonia in her left chest. At first glance, those were not earth-shattering findings.

The amazing part came when Roberts examined the tissues removed from the woman's right flank. The findings were astounding. Every microscopic field showed evidence of massive cell division, changes indicative of rapidly growing tissue. In some areas, cell growth appeared virtually out of control. The identical tissue taken from the woman's left flank showed no evidence of those changes.

She leaned back in her chair. Her eyes burned from prolonged exposure to the microscope's high-intensity light. She rubbed her eyes gently, and then gazed out across the winter landscape again. Her intuition had been correct. Something highly unusual had occurred in Jane Doe's body.

Roberts looked down at her wrist watch. It was two thirty. She had other things to attend to, but they would have to wait. She had to prove her theory beyond a doubt.

• • • • •

The clock showed the time to be after eight. A fidgety Natalie Roberts opened the cover shrouding the vertical electrophoresis chamber on her laboratory bench.

"Shit," she uttered, staring at the two ten-inch sheets of glass illuminated by an ultraviolet light. "What the hell is taking you so long? If this goddamn place could just keep up with technology, I'd have my results by now," she hissed, checking her watch again.

As she spoke, the chamber's electrical supply drove samples of the homeless woman's DNA across the final length of an acrylamide gel. The electrophoresis display was old and slow but would eventually yield the information she needed.

By compulsion, Roberts had spent seven hours subjecting the Jane Doe flank tissue to quantitative realtime PCR. The powerful molecular diagnostic study would measure the extent of growth gene expression from the tissue and either support or refute her theory. For another thirty minutes, she fidgeted nervously around the laboratory.

Finally the gene analysis from the PCR run was complete enough for Roberts to get the information she wanted. She shut off the electrical current and removed the cover from the chamber. The wafer-thin gel trapped between two sheets of glass had separated the DNA samples by their molecular size.

Roberts removed the glass sheets and walked to the other side of her laboratory, where she carefully inserted the sandwich into an ultraviolet light chamber. If her hunch was correct, the carefully prepared DNA samples would light up brilliantly.

It took a few minutes for the old gel imaging system to acquire the ultraviolet image. Once acquired, a picture would be transferred onto a thermal printer beside Roberts' bench-top computer. She might then have confirmation of her hunch.

The light flashed indicating an image had been transferred and was about to be produced.

"My god," Roberts whispered under her breath as the complete print appeared on the printer.

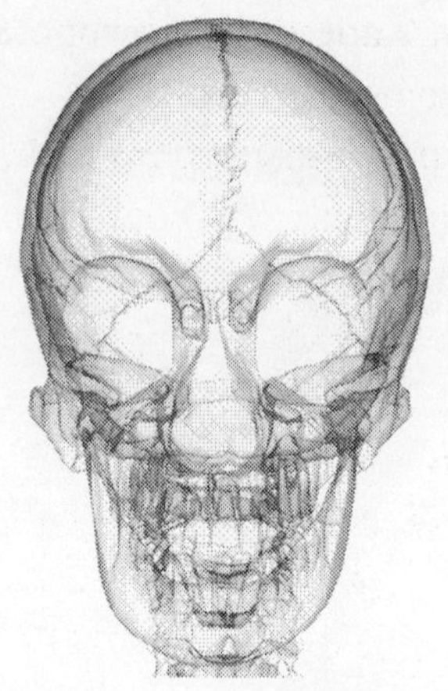

CHAPTER FOURTEEN

February 3

An icy wind rushed down from the mountains and swept across the treeless, grassy knoll. Fisher stood shivering. He had pulled the collar of his overcoat tighter around his neck to lessen the heat loss from his body, but the attempt wasn't helping. The small cemetery where the town had buried its dead for almost a century was completely exposed to the weather coming off the adjacent mountain chain. That day was no exception. Blue sky and tree-covered mountains provided a backdrop to the quaint little village, but stinging cold prevented a full appreciation of the beauty.

Fisher stood apart from the knot of mourners gathered on the windy hillside, but he studied their faces. They, like him, were expressionless in their grief as they awaited the burial of Dr. Charles W. Carlton, one of the town's favorite sons.

The pastor of the small church Carlton attended as a boy had delivered a moving eulogy. He reminisced of a little boy he knew long before who's greatest desire was to become a doctor. "That little boy," the pastor said, "followed his dream. He became a doctor, bringing honor to his town and to his profession."

At the funeral, the Carlton family was represented by aunts, uncles and cousins. Chip Carlton had no brothers or sisters. His parents had both died in their sixties. Carlton's body would rest beside his parents on the windy hill that overlooked the town.

Outside the cemetery, an honor guard from Arbor Military College, Carlton's alma mater, had assembled. Young men wearing taut, blue uniforms and white caps formed two columns.

A scarcely audible command, all but hidden by the icy wind, drifted toward the mourners, starting the slow procession. Two at a time, straight-backed cadets passed under the gray granite archway that led into the cemetery. At the rear of the procession, eight cadet pallbearers carried a graceful wooden casket.

Fisher's face flushed hot, though the wind blew numbing cold. He struggled to hold back tears as the procession neared the freshly dug grave. With ease, the eight cadets maneuvered Carlton's coffin into position for burial. They then stood at attention as the mourners, led by the pastor, gathered closer.

The pastor, his face reddened by biting cold, said a final prayer.

Beside the other mourners, Fisher stood motionless looking down at the casket unaware of his stinging face. His mind raced back in time. His thoughts fell on Lance Corporal Daniel Taylor. Once again there was the breathless, labored sprint he endured, bearing the weight of Taylor's blood-soaked body. The thumping Huey blades were a football field away, an endless distance carrying the lifeless weight on his shoulders. But he arrived, stumbling through the desert sand. He was drenched by sweat and blood as he placed his friend on a stretcher in the waiting helicopter. He collapsed beside the body as they became airborne.

As he had done in his dreams and flashbacks often for many years, Fisher turned to look at the lifeless body without a chest. Taylor was dead, his body mutilated by a high-speed missile. He could still see it clearly.

At that moment, the pain began that plagued him for years. Fisher shivered on the windswept hill. The unseen enemy that kicked him in his gut and gripped his throat was the dreaded combatant, returned after so many years to inflict pain once again. The morning that a flag-draped casket holding Taylor's corpse rolled up a conveyor belt and into the military transport, the pain was identical.

Tears cascaded down Fisher's cheeks. Crippling memories had surged out of a black hole in his brain where they had remained dormant for years. In Iraq, psychic pain led to uncontrollable drinking and deep depression after Taylor's death. With Danny Taylor at his side, Ranger Medic Steven Fisher had functioned well. For eighteen months, he had cared for the wounded, assisted surgeons as they put shredded GIs back together, and retrieved body parts from the field of battle. After Danny's death, something in Fisher's brain snapped. Because it eased the pain, alcohol became his friend. He tried to drown the nightmares, but he failed.

"The nightmares. They're always the same," he told the doctors. "Over and over, Danny Taylor keeps dying in my arms." Finally a MED-EVAC hospital in Kuwait had issued a medical furlough. Fisher later landed in a VA hospital outside of Houston where he spent a year in rehabilitation.

They were memories, he thought, that . . . .

Crack!

Rifle fire filled Fisher's senses, bringing him back from the memories he had spent years trying to repress. Standing in front of him, eight cadets remained stiff at full attention as Carlton's casket was lowered slowly into the waiting grave. Fisher looked toward the crest of the hill. Seven cadets held rifles aimed at the distant mountains. Another muffled command, another volley of shots rang out. Then another. Twenty-one shots were fired in final tribute to former cadet Charles W. Carlton.

Their salute complete, the cadets remained motionless a few moments. A muffled command reformed the honor guard, and they marched from the small cemetery. Pastor and mourners followed.

Fisher remained.

He stared as two men in gray coveralls moved freshly dug soil back into the rectangular opening. Working quickly, they filled the grave and left. A short time later, Fisher also left.

• • • • •

As Fisher left town, he anticipated his driving time to be about three hours. He maneuvered out of the small town and, before long, the Mazda swept along, quietly gliding down the country byway that led to the interstate some fifty miles away. Fisher's actions behind the wheel became automatic as his thoughts fell immediately back to Carlton.

The funeral closed Chip Carlton's life, but for Fisher the memory of his friend's murder remained. The war in Iraq had prevented Fisher from witnessing Danny Taylor's burial. Twenty-five years later, he saw how painful memories emerged when resolution was incomplete. The trip this day was emotionally draining, but Fisher hoped it would aid in healing the fresh wounds he suffered at the loss of another friend. For three days, he had not been able to focus without reliving the scene over and over, much the same as he had done during the war, years before.

"Goddamn." Fisher placed a death grip on the steering wheel.

Helpless, he thought. Just helpless. Carlton had fallen face down into a pool of blood thirty feet outside the College Inn, and he was helpless to stop it. Just like before.

As Fisher sped along, he found it impossible to control his thoughts. Feelings of rage tore at his brain as images of both scenes burned in his consciousness.

He became aware of his clenched jaw and his strangle hold on the steering wheel, consciously trying to relax, struggling to clear his mind. He had to have a break.

The opportunity came ten minutes later as the byway finally intersected the interstate. He pulled into a convenience store, shut off the engine and went in for coffee.

Few patrons were present in the roadside station, and he was served without delay.

With coffee in hand, he turned to the sitting area. Several tables were scattered about in the front of the store. One other patron occupied a table. Fisher seated himself near a large window and looked west. Radials of red-orange sunlight projected above a cloudless horizon as the sun neared the end of its shortened trip across a winter sky.

For a few minutes, Fisher parked his brain in neutral, sipping the black liquid, allowing his mind to unwind.

Thoughts flowed as he sorted through the events of the two previous days. He first thought of his phone call to the Medical Examiner's office before leaving Richland for the funeral. He had spoken briefly with the new assistant chief, Melissa Greene. She was fresh out of a forensics residency in New York City and had been on the job for a couple of months. Fisher had heard she had rough edges and that she followed procedures by the book, but his encounter had been slightly different.

"Dr. Fisher," the assistant chief had said when Fisher finally got her on the phone, "you know it's against state law to reveal postmortem results before the final report is reviewed by the Chief Medical Examiner."

"Look, uh . . . Dr. Carlton was a friend and colleague. Can't you just give me some . . . . I'm . . . I'm trying to deal with this the best way I can and it would help if you . . . ."

"I'm going to do this as a favor, because I understand your circumstances. I'm new here, and I don't want to get started off on the wrong foot with doctors in the area, but let me tell you, if it comes back to me, I'm going to know where the source is, and you will never get a thing from me in the future. A police reporter from the *Tribune* has hounded me incessantly for two days. If the press found out I gave you the information and withheld it from them, they'd do their best to lynch me."

Greene then described the gory details of her autopsy. It sickened Fisher to hear them, but it confirmed his observations the day of the shooting. The bullet had penetrated at an angle about thirty degrees above horizontal into the posterior surface of the right neck. The soft tissue and cervical vertebrae had exploded on impact. Carlton's death had come quickly, due to complete severing of the carotid artery, the internal jugular vein, and a two-inch section of the cervical spinal cord. The bullet then tracked through the neck destroying the trachea and the larynx as it exited anteriorly. The bullet then penetrated the bay window, traveling through the iced tea urn coming to rest in the rear wall where investigators had removed it. She also noted that ballistics tentatively identified the slug as originating from a Bushmaster, a high-powered rifle employed occasionally by snipers.

"Thirty degrees above horizontal with a Bushmaster. A sniper's rifle," Fisher whispered into the steaming cup before he took a sip.

"What the hell does it all mean?" he mumbled, exhaling vapor from the swallow of coffee. He continued laying down the pieces of the puzzle in his mind, building a framework for his thoughts. Domao's inquisitional questions concerning illegal drug use and prostitutes suggested he thought Carlton placed himself in harm's way by having a connection with Richland's underworld.

But there was more. Carlton's home had been thoroughly ransacked and searched. His killers were looking for something, and Fisher was convinced they took the missing back-up disks.

Fisher confronted the reality of the situation. Carlton was killed by an assassin's bullet. Information from several sources supported that conclusion. Why? What had Chip gotten himself into? Why had he called the OR? Why, after having no communications for six months, had he suddenly decided twenty-four hours before his death, it was important to talk? Fisher lightly tapped the cup he held in his right hand. Did Chip know he was in danger?

Fisher lowered the half-empty cup onto the bright Formica surface and put his head in his hands. His eyes closed, but his mind raced.

After a few minutes, Fisher looked up. The last vestiges of winter sunset were gone; the sky was dark.

He discarded remnants of the coffee and headed out to check his gas gauge.

Soon he was back on the road. Night had fallen and stars were visible as he motored on.

The remainder of the drive was uneventful, but also unnerving. As he neared Richland, the image of Carlton lying face down outside the large bay window surged into his thoughts. Then, as quickly as it had come, it vaporized.

Fisher realized the experience had left him numbed and exhausted. Three days of riding an emotional roller coaster had taken its toll. Probably the worst part, he thought, was not having anyone to talk to. It compounded the misery.

He took his hand off the steering wheel and reached for the console between the front seats. Finding the ashtray by feel, he pulled it open in search of a roll of Lifesavers he had left there some time back. As the ashtray came open, the soft display light revealed a crumpled package of Newport cigarettes.

They were Sharon's.

Fisher extracted the empty package and held it above the steering wheel as he sped eastward. Sharon always promised to give up smoking, but like most of her promises, she had broken it.

"God, how life gets screwed up," Fisher uttered. During their six-week separation, they had lived apart as if their marriage had never taken place. She had not called, nor had he — until the night before.

Fisher called the house in Rosewood, but there was no answer. Figuring her first stopping off place would be her father's house, Fisher called Darren Fitzpatrick. She had gone home in the past, when they had disagreements. Darren was cordial but cool. He and Fisher had developed a reasonably close relationship over ten years, but Sharon's father would definitely side with Sharon when it came to matters as serious as separation and divorce. Sharon wasn't there, or at least her father said she wasn't.

The city lights of Richland became visible in the distance, brilliant like a string of diamonds. Fisher was sleep-deprived and exhausted. He would be home soon, and he knew he would need help easing the pain.

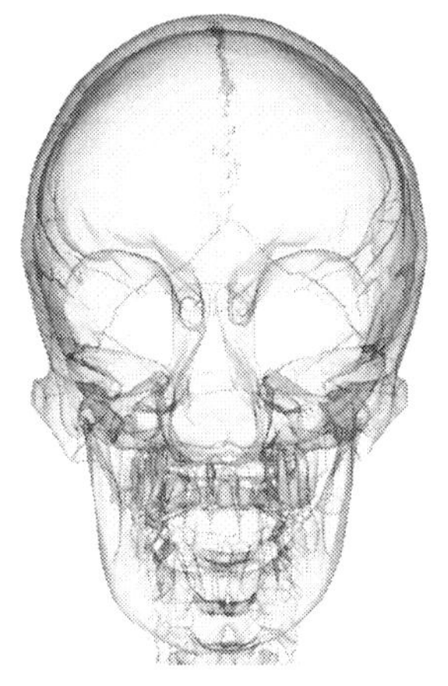

CHAPTER FIFTEEN

February 4

Fisher walked slowly down the hallway leading to the Cardiac Surgery offices. He took extra care not to aggravate the pounding in his head. His current situation was in small part due to fatigue, but mostly booze.

Binzemore's call to Fisher's cell phone had caught him on the outskirts of Richland the night before. Twenty minutes later, he and Binzemore were in the Medford OR, repairing a dissecting aortic aneurysm. The operation went smoothly and he'd arrived home by ten. Five minutes later he had polished off the first of many shots from a new fifth of Jack Daniels. By one in the morning, the fifth was gone and Fisher's tortured mind rested in an alcohol stupor.

Like many mornings around that time, he took the winding route down River Path Drive into Richland, hoping for a pick-me-up. That morning, though, fatigue and hangover prevented the crooked roadway from working its magic.

"Good morning, Steve," Mary Walker said as Fisher walked slowly by her desk.

Fisher grunted an unintelligible response and entered his office. He went straight for his desk and sat down slowly glancing around for messages. Satisfied that there were none, he closed his eyes and rubbed lightly.

Earlier they'd looked bloodshot in the bathroom mirror, now they merely burned. Rubbing them didn't help much.

A few moments later, Mary entered the office and placed a fresh cup of hot coffee on the desk in front of him. "How was your trip?" Walker carefully controlled the volume of her voice.

"Sad, very sad." On smelling the coffee's aroma, he opened his eyes. "Thanks."

Fisher took the steaming cup, eased back in his chair and sipped slowly. He didn't want to talk about the funeral.

"Are you okay?"

"I'm okay," Fisher said, still sipping, though he knew he wasn't. He appreciated her concern, and he knew he needed time off, but it wasn't in the plan. Not then anyway.

Mary walked to the door but stopped and wheeled around, just before crossing the threshold.

"Don't forget, Alli Shepard is scheduled at ten to discuss the research project."

Fisher looked down at his watch. It was nine-fifty. He took a deep gulp from the cup and extended the cup toward Walker. "Could you please bring me another?" he asked, beginning to see clearly through the haze of his hangover.

"Sure." She took the empty mug and left.

Fisher swiveled in his chair and stared out the window as Walker left his office. He knew she was worried about him. Her concern was evident weeks before Carlton's death. She had said nothing directly, but her silence spoke volumes. In the nine years Walker had worked in the Cardiac Division, Fisher had never known her to hold back her opinions. In one respect, he was thankful she chose not to confront him about late arrivals, wrinkled shirts and mood swings. On the other hand, Fisher knew he was edging closer to the brink. The week before, under Walker's silent but inquiring gaze, he mentioned he and Sharon were having trouble. She had said nothing, asked no questions.

"Dr. Fisher?"

Jostled from his thoughts, Fisher turned to see Alli Shepard standing at the door.

Fisher stood slowly. Although improved, the throbbing had not fully disappeared. "Come in, Miss Shepard."

"Please call me Alli, Dr. Fisher." The young woman walked to the chair in front of Fisher's desk.

Alli was a slender woman of medium height. She wore a knee-length white clinic coat over a dark green dress. Her chestnut hair was pulled back tightly behind her head to a pony tail that draped across her collar.

"Thank you very much for agreeing to help me with the project."

"Would you like coffee?"

"No, thank you."

Walker entered carrying a second cup of hot coffee. "Oh. Good morning, Alli. I didn't see you come in." She handed the coffee to Fisher. "Can I get you a cup of coffee?"

"No. I'm fine, thanks. Dr. Fisher just offered."

"Very well." She turned to Fisher. "Steve, can I get you anything before I leave?"

"Nothing else. Thanks, Mary."

As Walker left, Alli spoke, "I apologize again for interrupting you the night Dr. Carlton was killed. I had no idea you and he were close friends."

"Don't worry about it, Alli. There's no way you could have known."

Fisher took a long pull of coffee from the cup. His head was improving. The second cup would definitely help it along. "I've been busy for the last three days and haven't had an opportunity to think more about our conversation. Perhaps you could tell me more about the discussions you and Dr. Carlton had during your surgical clerkship."

"Really, they weren't very detailed. Dr. Carlton was convinced that Medford University was well positioned to publish the first U.S. study on the effectiveness of Myelopress at combating organ rejection."

"If this is intended to be a one-month study, I presume it's a medical-records review."

"Yes," Alli replied. "Dr. Carlton estimated that the various transplant teams at Medford had performed about four-hundred transplants during the three-year period."

"That's quite a task. Do you think you can pull data from that many medical records in a month? It's already the fourth, and February is a short month."

"After Mrs. Walker called, I spoke to the Medical Records Department and told them I'd be working with you on the project and that Dr.

Carlton had originally suggested that the research needed to be done. After they heard that, they assured me that forty charts per day would be available from the electronic medical record."

"Still, that's quite a bit of data to accumulate and keep straight."

"Really, Dr. Fisher, I'm used to it. Grabbing and archiving data was what I did in my other life. Before starting medical school, I worked for almost five years at Darby Software. Are you familiar with Darby?"

"No. It doesn't sound familiar." Fisher leaned closer. "Tell me about it."

"Darby is based in Richland. The company writes educational programs for children and learning-impaired adults. My division was information management. We were charged with capture and storage of computer code sent over the Internet from independent writers and artists. Darby out-sourced a great deal of their work within a three-state region."

"Sounds like interesting work." Fisher drained the last few drops of coffee. The pounding in his head had lessened considerably. "You mentioned Monday night that you wouldn't need any outside help with the computer. Now I understand why."

"Once you decide what data to obtain from the patient records, I'll use the online programs available through Academic Computing to construct a database and begin entry."

When Alli mentioned constructing a database, Fisher concealed the momentary chill that raced up his spine. Deep inside, he knew he was avoiding the inevitable. Someday he knew he would have to overcome computer phobia. "Maybe you could give me some beginning instruction this month." Fisher couldn't believe those words had come from his mouth. He despised the thought of sitting down at a keyboard, but maybe with Alli tutoring him, things would be different.

"Sure. No problem."

"What else needs to be worked out?"

"There's the problem of where I'm going to work. My brother and I have a computer at home, but I think I'll need access to a desk here at the Med for data entry. The student computer labs are always packed. A secretary in Academic Computing told me they couldn't guarantee me any space. She said winter semester is their busiest, and the demand for work stations is heavy."

Fisher swiveled, extended his arm and placed his hand on top of the desk top computer that had rested under a dust cover for six months.

"It shouldn't be a problem. You can do your work right here. Dr. Carlton set this up before he left the Med. I've never used it. He told me it was connected to the Med's main computer, wherever that is."

"Great. I won't get in the way if I am connected to the electronic medical record will I?

"No, I don't really spend much time in the office, anyway. I'm usually here either early or late."

"Okay. That gets what I wanted to cover out of the way. My last question relates to Myelopress. The drug is so new; there isn't much information about it in the medical literature. Could you tell me more about it?"

Fisher was thankful his hangover symptoms had finally gone. His thoughts were fluid, no longer painful. "The Myelopress story's an interesting one," Fisher began. "The drug was discovered by two scientists, Drs. Timothy Thornley and Harold Sarnes, working in an outpost laboratory in Brazil in the early two thousands. Their lab was funded by Katsumi Pharmaceuticals, a Japanese pharmaceutical giant.

"Thornley and Sarnes isolated the Myelopress compound from the root of a small fruit tree, the Octus Saliensis. It grows wild in the rain forest there.

"Thornley is actually being credited with the Myelopress discovery. Although he's a chemist by training, his hobby is anthropology. In the months prior to the discovery, Thornley, in his time off, had studied a small tribe living along the banks of the Amazon."

Fisher continued. "In an interview with CNN, he told how he visited the tribe over a period of several months, finally establishing a few friendships among the tribal members. During his trips, Thornley told how he kept noticing that many adults had an oval-shaped discoloration of the skin on the outer surface of their right arms, just below the shoulder. When he studied it, he determined it to be a patch of skin about an inch long." Fisher pointed to the upper part of his right arm for emphasis.

"Thornley said it was curious because all who had the patch had skin tones that were distinctly different from the patch. When Thornley asked the significance of the patch, he was ignored. None of the members of the tribe would answer his questions. He asked many times, but he never got a response."

"Just a patch on the arm?" Alli asked.

"Right. One night some weeks later, a male tribesman he had befriended showed up at the lab after he was in bed and rousted him out. Thornley couldn't speak the man's language, but with hand signals, the man got across that he wanted Thornley to follow. Together Thornley and the tribesman left the laboratory and walked into the rain forest. He feared for his life, but he followed the man. After walking for what seemed like miles they came upon a clearing in the forest where three torches were burning. Several members of the tribe were gathered around the corpse of a middle-aged woman. One man about her same age sat next to her, chanting. Thornley later learned the woman was the chanting man's wife. Among the people gathered in the clearing, Thornley recognized the tribal chief."

"A funeral ritual?"

"Yes, of sorts," Fisher replied. "Following his arrival, Thornley said the chief stood and removed an odd-shaped metal instrument from a sack. As the chief approached the man sitting beside the corpse, the husband held up his right arm. With practiced skill and blinding speed, the tribal chief used the instrument to remove that same type of oval patch of skin from the husband's right arm. The chief then turned to the corpse and removed an oval patch of skin from the same location. The chief exchanged the pieces of skin and laid the deceased wife's skin over the husband's wound. After speaking a few words, the chief turned to the corpse and performed an identical ritual, laying the husband's live skin across the site where the woman's skin had been removed. Without further ado, Thornley was escorted back to the laboratory."

"That's one of the weirdest things I've ever heard."

"The story gets more interesting." Fisher smiled. "Over the coming days and weeks, Thornley took particular notice of the man who had received the skin patch from his deceased wife. At first, the site was covered by a leather bandage, but soon it was removed. To Thornley's amazement, the woman's skin had perfectly engrafted on the husband's arm."

"Incredible."

"Thornley's training was primarily chemistry, but he knew a substantial amount of immunology. He knew the wife's skin should have been rejected and sloughed off, but it hadn't. He was mystified by his observation. Over the next few weeks he studied the tribe members carefully.

At first he considered the possibility that the tribe had evolved in such a way that their bodies had lost the ability to reject tissue from a fellow human. He quickly discarded that idea and began searching for a logical explanation. He soon found it."

"The fruit tree," Alli exclaimed.

"Exactly." Fisher grinned. "Thornley noticed that virtually all adult tribal members continually munched on the small bitter berries of an indigenous tree, the Octus Saliensis. It grows in abundance in the area. He took the berries and samples of the tree root back to his laboratory for testing. In the next few months, Thornley and Sarnes isolated dozens of compounds from the root and defined their chemical structures. Over the next few years, working with doctors at medical universities in Japan and France, Thornley and Sarnes showed that one of the original compounds isolated from the root of the tree completely suppressed skin-to-skin transplant rejection in human volunteers. Within months of that finding, the first dose of the compound by then named Myelopress was given to recipients of organ transplants. The effects of the drug were dramatic. Further studies were undertaken and, two years later, the drug was released worldwide. Organ rejection was eliminated, and transplantation was forever changed."

"That is an amazing story," Alli said with an inquisitive look. "But how does the drug work?"

"I have a few papers published by the company partially detailing the drug's pharmacology, but Katsumi Pharmaceuticals has demanded secrecy. What the company will say is that Myelopress, unlike other drugs that fight rejection, works completely on the transplanted organ, not on the recipient or host. Most scientists believe Myelopress transforms the donor organ immunologically so that the patient's body doesn't recognize the organ as a foreign body and therefore won't reject it."

Alli looked up from her notepad to ask another question when Walker walked into Fisher's office.

"Steve, I'm sorry to interrupt, but at eleven-thirty you're due in the Ambulatory Care Center for a follow-up visit with Thomas Winston. It's eleven-twenty now."

"Thanks, Mary."

He turned to Alli. "Why don't you get started? The office is yours. I'll be back. I have a patient to examine."

"Fine," Alli said.

Before leaving for his encounter with the Winstons, Fisher rummaged through his desk and dragged out a small slip of paper that laid forgotten and undisturbed since Carlton had given it to him six months earlier. It held Fisher's account information and password to Medford's computer server. He turned it over to Alli to use until her account was established.

Fisher stood, pulled on his clinic coat and left the office.

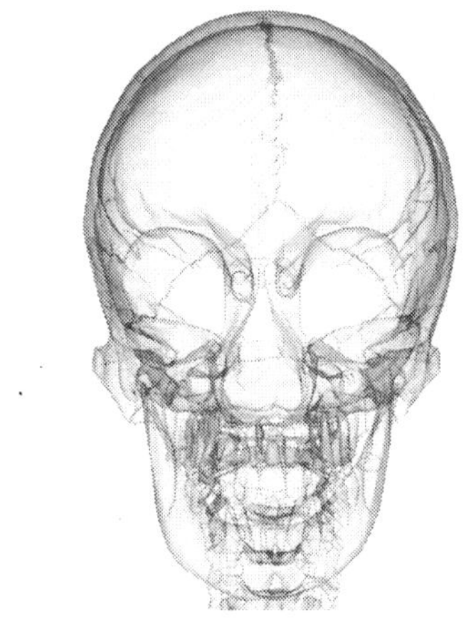

CHAPTER SIXTEEN

The elevator doors opened on the eighth floor of Ambulatory Care. Unlike before, the surgery waiting room was crowded. Fisher briefly scanned the room as he passed through. All seats were taken.

Wendy Martin, the nurse manager, frowned at Fisher as he walked into the office. She intercepted him as he headed for the coffee pot. "Dr. Fisher, you don't have time for that. Do you know what time it is?"

Fisher glanced at his watch then looked back at Wendy Martin. "I'm late."

"That's right. Thomas Winston's father began looking for you at eleven-twenty-five. He's already quite upset."

Fisher dropped the unused coffee cup back on the column of inverted cups and walked to the exam room. His gut sunk merely thinking of another encounter with Spencer Winston.

"One second, Dr. Fisher."

Before grasping the exam room doorknob, Fisher looked back. Martin hurried down the hallway from the nurses' station carrying a manila folder.

"These just arrived by campus mail," she said.

The folder contained Thomas Winston's test results. As Fisher leafed through the pages, he was saddened. The echocardiogram report stated that all chambers of Winston's heart were severely enlarged and functioned poorly. There was severe regurgitation of blood through two of the four valves. The Iridium circulation studies were next. The report stated that all coronary arteries were patent and circulated adequate amounts of blood to Winston's enlarged heart. He flipped to the last report, the Ventricular Photon Imaging study. The news was bad. His worst fears were confirmed as he read the report:

> **Interpretation:** Axial photon images of left ventricular myocardium were acquired immediately following injection of one-hundred milliliters of bio-scintillation medium number six. Incorporation of the imaging agent was extremely poor (< 5%). Little or no bioluminescence was observed during a thirty-minute period of observation indicating poor to minimal mitochondrial metabolic activity.
>
> **Impression:** The lack of incorporation of bio-scintillate is consistent with a terminal myocardium within thirty to forty days.

He closed the folder and entered the examination room.

The patient smiled weakly as Fisher entered the room. He was pale and breathless. Even though he wore the nasal oxygen Fisher had prescribed, his nose was blue and a fine film of sweat was visible on his forehead. Both were signs of a severely failing heart.

"Hello, Thomas." Fisher crossed the room and shook the frail young man's hand, then turned to greet the elder Winston, who sat in a chair.

"Good morning," Spencer Winston replied in a preoccupied tone. He gazed out the window, rather than engaging eye contact with Fisher.

Fisher turned back to the younger Winston.

"Thomas, has the oxygen made you more comfortable?"

Winston cracked a weak smile. "Yes. It has . . . helped me . . . to sleep but . . . ."

"Look, Dr. Fisher," Spencer Winston interrupted. "We can dispense with the small talk. Just tell us what the tests showed and what your plans are."

A few moments ticked by as Fisher locked his gaze onto Spencer Winston's, refusing to blink.

You son-of-a-bitch, Fisher thought to himself, gritting his teeth to the point of pain. He said nothing aloud. He was determined to maintain a dignified interaction with Spencer Winston, though, at the moment, he struggled to suppress the urge to flatten his nose.

Fisher seated himself behind the desk and opened the folder. "Thomas, I'm afraid I have bad news. The echocardiogram and the VPI scan clearly show that your heart is dying."

Thomas Winston fumbled with his hands for a few moments. Then he asked, his question fragmented by breathlessness, "Am I . . . in . . . immediate danger . . ., Dr. Fisher?"

Fisher responded with warmth in his voice. "The photon imaging study shows that your heart's metabolic activity is critically low. If something isn't done within a month, severe heart rhythm disturbances will begin, and cardiac arrest will follow shortly after that."

The younger Winston became paler. He silently dropped his head and stared at the floor.

Spencer Winston snapped, "Well, that cinches it then, doesn't it? He needs a new heart."

"That's the short of it, yes, but hearts are no longer available on an emergency basis. We have sixty-five or seventy patients in the same crisis as Thomas. Everyone goes on a waiting list. Hearts are transplanted into patients on the list as they become available."

"What does that mean for my son, Doctor? He has to have a heart now."

"It means a few months wait, Mr. Winston."

"Does . . . that . . . mean I will . . . die before . . . I . . . I get a heart?" Thomas Winston struggled to say.

Fisher turned to the younger Winston. "No, Thomas, but a ventricular assist device will need to be inserted until we can find you a heart. It's a small pump that will support your heart."

The elder Winston shot up from his chair and stomped to the desk where Fisher sat. His face flushed crimson and his eyelids drew tight, producing two narrow slits. He leaned over and stared down at Fisher, reeking hostility and loathing. "Now wait just a fucking minute. You're telling me my son has terminal heart failure that will take his life in one month, and you're going to stick him on some goddamn waiting list? Are you crazy? Do you know who you're dealing with? Do you know I personally bailed Gene Harrowood, the president of your University, out of hot water by giving him half the money to build this stinking clinic?"

Fisher stood and looked the older Winston squarely in the face. He then turned to Thomas. The young man's face had flushed red at his father's outburst. "Thomas, your father and I are going to step outside for a moment."

Fisher pointed to the door. "If you will, Mr. Winston."

In the hallway, Fisher turned to the man. "Mr. Winston, I don't care if you gave every penny to build the clinic. If you yell at me like that again, I will have security remove you from the building."

Spencer Winston, his face still deeply red, opened his mouth to speak, but Fisher cut him off. "I take it from your outburst, Mr. Winston, that you feel that position, wealth and power determine the worth of one human life over another. Well, that's not the way we operate at Medford University. The cardiac transplant program operates by strict rules which will not be broken while I'm the director. If you want to impose the philosophy of life according to Spencer Winston, you will have to find some other institution. And I suggest you do it promptly because the added stress you've just heaped upon your son's shoulder has likely shaved several days from his life."

Fisher did not disengage his icy stare.

"Dr. Kepner was right," Winston hissed. "This place is half-assed."

Winston turned to open the exam room door but then stopped. He rotated on his heel and faced Fisher once again. "My son will get his heart, Dr. Fisher. While you're over here playing your little games, my son will get his heart."

Wendy Martin had started down the hall from the nurses' station but stopped when she saw the two men standing in the hall. Winston caught sight of her and called to her.

"Nurse, bring me a wheelchair." Winston said. "My son and I will be leaving."

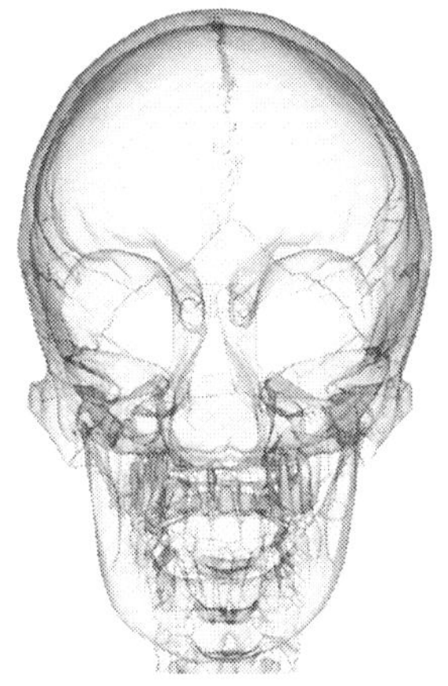

CHAPTER SEVENTEEN

Fisher walked the entire distance from the Ambulatory Care Center with his jaws and fists tightened. He fumed as he approached the Cardiac Surgery offices. Spencer Winston's arrogance, combined with his willingness to use his son as a pawn in a high-stakes game of life and death, galled him. His anger wasn't directed totally at the billionaire, however. During his encounter with the Winstons, he saw with painful clarity that Medford University Medical Center failed to provide comprehensive medical care.

Five years earlier, Fisher thought as he tried to loosen his jaw muscles, patients like Thomas Winston would not have landed on a waiting list at the Med. Hearts were available then for category-one patients. Two years after the release of Myelopress, everything had changed. Virtually every hospital, regardless of size, either had a transplant program or had one on the drawing board. The avalanche began when Congress hurriedly passed the Barton-Hagens act that prevented institutions such as Medford University from exercising a seniority advantage when it came to organ procurement. Thus, the bane of his existence, the organ lottery, was born. Under lottery rules, a small community hospital had the same shot at organs that an established institution like Medford University had.

As Fisher passed through the outer office, he noticed that Mary was out. He looked at his watch. She must have gone for lunch and the mail, he thought. He turned to enter his office.

"Dr. Fisher!" Alli's voice surprised Fisher.

She jumped up and was standing by Fisher's computer as he entered the room. The monitor was switched on for the first time since Carlton had left.

Alli looked excited. "Did you know you have mail from Dr. Carlton?"

Fisher was still preoccupied by his run-in with the Winstons. At the mention of Carlton's name he froze in his tracks.

"What do you mean I have mail from Dr. Carlton? Is this some kind of a joke?"

"It's no joke."

"I haven't received a thing from Dr. Carlton. I told you he left here six months ago, and that's the last contact we . . . ."

"No, you don't understand!" Alli interrupted, unable to contain her excitement. "He sent you email through to your Medford University email address. I would never have known had I not signed on under your name and password."

All the hassles Fisher had wrestled with vaporized. He pulled a chair next to Alli as she sat down to the keyboard he had never used. Fisher was quiet as Alli clicked rapid-fire key strokes. When she had finished, a confusing list of seventeen e-mail messages flowed down the screen.

```
TO:SFisher@MedU.surg.edu.From:ASpeir@MedU.IT.edu-06/02/14 re: New Accnt.
TO:SFisher@MedU.surg.edu.From:ASpeir@MedU.IT.edu.-06/19/14 re: Accnt usage.
TO:SFisher@MedU.surg.edu.From:ASpeir@MedU.IT.edu.-06/30/14 re: menu mod.
TO:SFisher@MedU.surg.edu.From:ASpeir@MedU.IT.edu.-07/19/14 re: Accnt usage.
TO:SFisher@MedU.surg.edu.From:HKamen@MedU.SMed.edu.-08/03/14 re: Faculty Mtg.
TO:SFisher@MedU.surg.edu.From:CCarlton@TMH.com.-08/10/14 re: Hello.
TO:SFisher@MedU.surg.edu.From:ASpeir@MedU.IT.edu.-08/19/14 re: Accnt usage.
TO:SFisher@MedU.surg.edu.From:ASpeir@MedU.IT.edu.-09/19/14 re: Accnt usage.
```

```
TO:SFisher@MedU.surg.edu.From:CCarlton@TMH.com.-
10/08/14 re: Ventriculostomy.
TO:SFisher@MedU.surg.edu.From:ASpeir@MedU.
IT.edu.-10/19/14 re: Accnt usage.
TO:SFisher@MedU.surg.edu.From:CCarlton@TMH.com.-
11/04/14 re: Write Back.
TO:SFisher@MedU.surg.edu.From:ASpeir@MedU.
IT.edu.-11/19/14 re: Accnt usage.
TO:SFisher@MedU.surg.edu.From:ASpeir@MedU.
IT.edu.-12/19/14 re: Accnt usage.
TO:SFisher@MedU.surg.edu.From:ASpeir@MedU.
IT.edu.-12/19/14 re: Accnt usage.
TO:SFisher@MedU.surg.edu.From:ASpeir@MedU.
IT.edu.-01/19/15 re: Accnt usage.
TO:SFisher@MedU.surg.edu.From:CCarlton@Mednet.org.-
01/30/15 re: Trouble.
TO:SFisher@MedU.surg.edu.From:CCarlton@Mednet.org.-
01/31/15 re: X#$%&#.
```

Fisher said, "Okay, I'm lost. Tell me what we're reading."

"I'm sorry, Dr. Fisher. The list is written in email syntax." She pointed to the screen. "That's your e-mail address at Medford University Department of Surgery. All these messages are written to your address and are from individuals who also have their return addresses displayed. To the uninitiated, it's confusing."

Fisher stared at the list. He wasn't about to tell her what he was thinking at that moment.

"All right," Alli said, starting to go through the messages. "You have eleven messages from an ASpeir in the University Information Technology department. Those are probably related to your account. They will give you the amount of time you spend and the dates using the University's facility. Information Technology facilities in American universities don't charge for online time."

She went on, "Then there is one message from HKamen concerning a faculty meeting on August third."

"Hinson Kaman is the Dean of the School of Medicine at Medford University," Fisher said. "That letter would have concerned the yearly school-wide faculty meeting that usually takes place in August." Fisher lowered his voice, "Lately that's been the place where faculty position cuts have been announced."

A moment passed.

"Go on, Alli." A rising sense of urgency filled Fisher's mind.

"There are five messages listed from CCarlton." She paused for a moment, staring intently at the screen. "That's interesting. Dr. Carlton sent you three messages from TMH.COM, which is probably from his Taggart Memorial Hospital account. Internet mail addresses will end in COM if the site is a commercial entity. But two messages are here which were sent over MedNet."

"What's MedNet?"

"I don't know very much about MedNet," Alli said. "It stands for Medicine Network. It was started about five years ago by the National Institutes of Health. I heard about it when I was a second-year student. I don't remember a lot about it. It was designed as a non-profit organization for physicians throughout the United States. It's out there on the Internet with its own website. It was started to keep doctors up to date on things like health-care reform, new treatments and therapies for various diseases. It also keeps doctors in touch with each other. If Dr. Carlton had an account on the MedNet, he would have been able to send messages to your account here at Medford from any remote site, say from his home. It's a social network for healthcare professionals kind of like Facebook.

"Chip Carlton definitely had a computer at home. Alli, can you bring up those messages?"

"I'll show you the keystrokes, and you can read your mail in private."

"No. There's no reason for you to leave."

Alli clicked the keyboard lightly. Carlton's first message appeared.

```
TO: SFisher@MedU.edu
From: CCarlton@TMH.com
Date: 08/10/14
```

RE: Hello

```
   Hi, Steve. I've just gotten my account set up
here at TMH. Unfortunately, the server here at
Taggart is nothing compared to the Med's, but it
```

will make it easy to send messages back and forth. Hopefully we will be able to communicate regularly. Don't forget to keep checking your email like I showed you. Things here at Taggart are going great. Harry Talbott and I transplanted a heart last night and I have two bypasses scheduled for today. Hope to hear from you soon.

Sincerely, Chip

Fisher said nothing as Alli clicked in commands for the next message from Chip Carlton. The next message came up.

To: SFisher@MedU.edu
From: CCarlton@TMH.com
Date: 10/08/14
RE: Ventriculostomy

Hey, Steve. You need to start checking you email, buddy. Yesterday Harry Talbott showed me a secret technique of his to bleed air from a transplanted left ventricle. He makes a small ventriculostomy just below the suture line and massages the ventricle gently. It works great. Things continue to go great here.

Sincerely, Chip

Alli issued more key strokes. The third message dated November fourth read:

To: SFisher@MedU.edu
From: CCarlton@TMH.com
Date: 11/04/14
RE: Write back

Steve. What's the matter? Aren't you going to respond to my messages? I have a sneaking suspicion you lost that crinkly slip of paper you used the day you jotted down the instructions I gave you. After all that trouble I went to getting your account set up. If I don't hear from you in the next couple of days I'm going to give you a call. Let's try to meet at the CI. I'm ready for some of Wally's fritters. Things continue to go well here. I can't believe how many hearts we have transplanted in the last three and a half months.

Sincerely, Chip

"Jesus," Fisher uttered under his breath. "If I had only known he was communicating through email."

Alli typed in a fourth set of commands.

To: SFisher@MedU.edu
From: CCarlton@MedNet.org
Date: 01/30/15
RE: Trouble

Steve, I know now there's no way that you are checking your email. And I know you will probably not get this message. I should have called you in November but I got distracted by some things going on here at Taggart. I need to talk to you ASAP. If you don't answer this message, I will call and leave a message on your answering machine. I prefer we meet somewhere we can be alone.

Sincerely, Chip

Alli turned to look at Fisher, who stared at the screen. She broke the silence. "I'm surprised that with Dr. Carlton only being across town he wouldn't just call."

"Let's look at the last message," Fisher said with determination.

Alli again ran her fingers across the keyboard to display the message.

TO: SFisher@MedU.edu
From: CCarlton@MedNet.org
Date: 1/31/15
RE: X#$%&#.
--Begin IES Message, Version: 9.05--

pghhhak24jjjpop09978mmngnkJCuTMaNQEmPMDweEtH-
hpaanxzZhglLWdinglstkhhieosLeKh14vheoOshchEld-
heiOtsOth+DeeosyeEdhdoANfotyWeno[ndion]kdonsh-
todhDKRi2diDgi+c3Bt4pgAAKku9D8whJCJN8j[+kd0dth-
DEoAnANdkoy1+2Nf3NtKwlQuK9TEBLygDkRi2diDgi+c#Bt-
4kTfNbg2xYKpghhhak24jjjpop09978mmngnkJCuTMaNQEmP-
MDweEtHhpaanxzZhglLWdinglstkhhieosLeKh14vheoOsh-
chEldheiOtsOthDeeosyeEdhdoANfotyWeno[ndion]
kdonshtodhDKRi2diDgi+c3Bt4pgAAKku9D8whJCJN8j[+kd0dth-
DEoAnANdkoy1+2Nf3NtKwlQuK9TEBLygDkRi2diDgi+c#Bt-
4kTfNbg=2xYKd0dthDEoAnANdkoy1+2Nf3NtKwlQuK9TEB-
ygDkRi2diDgi+c#Bt4kTfNbg2xYKpghhhak24jjjpop-
09978mmngnkJCuTMaNQEmPMDweEtHhpaanxzZh-
glLWdinglstkhhieosLeKh14vheoOshchEld-
heiOtsOthDeeosyeEdhdoANfotyWeno[ndion]
kdonshtodhDKRi2diDgi+c3Bt4pgAAKku9D8whJCJN-
8j[+kd0dthDEoAnANdkoy1+2Nf3NtKwlQuK9TEBLygDkRi-
2diDgi+c#Bt4kTfNbg=2xYK1+2Nf3NtKwlQuK9TEBLyg-
DkRi2diDgi+c#t4kTfNbg2xYKpghhhak24jjjpop-
09978mmngnkJCuTMaNQEmPMDweEtHhpaanxzZhglL-
WdinglstkhhieosLeKh14vheoOshchEldhei-
OtsOthDeeosyeEdhdoANfotyWeno[ndion]
kdonshtodhDKRi2diDgi+c3Bt4pgAAKku9D8whJCJN-
8j[+kd0dthDEoAnANdkoy1+2Nf3NtKwlQuK9TEBLygDkRi-
2diDgi+c#Bt4kTfNbg=2xYK

--End IES Message--

In stunned silence, Fisher and Alli stared at the screen.

He was the first to speak. "Alli, what in hell is that?"

Alli's voice had a clearly discernible tremor present. "Dr. Carlton's last email message dated 1/31/15 was sent encrypted."

"You mean this alphabet soup is a message?"

"Yes."

"But why?"

"Look, Dr. Fisher, something is seriously wrong here. I think you need to show this to the police."

"Wait a minute. You're telling me that Dr. Carlton's last message was sent in code? Is there any way this can be de-coded so we can read it?"

Alli pointed to the screen.

"See the line, IES message, Version 9.05."

"Yes."

"That's an abbreviation for Internet Encryption System. It's a consensus program available to Internet users to ensure privacy, if it's needed. Back in the dark ages, when I worked for Darby Software, our outsourcers writing code for educational software encrypted all transfers over the Internet using IES protocols. It used to be the industry standard."

"Then you can break the code?" Fisher said hurriedly.

"Not without a key, Dr. Fisher. When Dr. Carlton encrypted the file, he established a key unique to that file. Without that key, the file can't be opened."

A note of anxiety entered Fisher's voice, "What's your next suggestion?"

"I would take it to the police. They probably have an expert who could at least get it started."

Bradley Hinton and his tortoise-shell glasses immediately appeared in Fisher's mind. "Yes, there's a guy at the RPD who may be able to decode the file. How do I get it to him?"

"We can send him a copy. Do you know his email address?"

"No."

"Then I'll make you a copy. I have a small jump drive I use that I can lend you. All you have to do is take it to him."

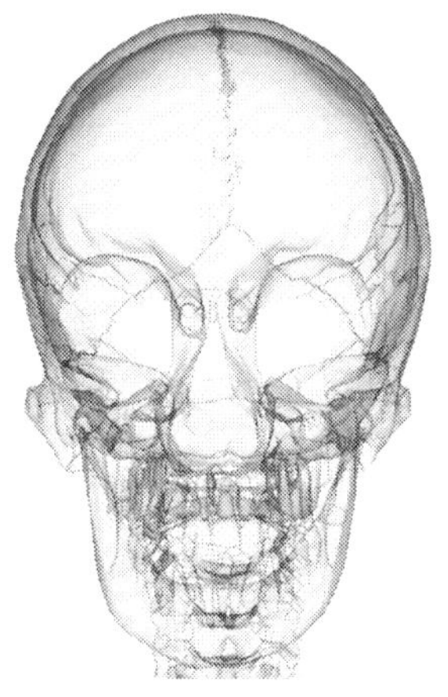

CHAPTER EIGHTEEN

The winter sun had dropped low in the sky by the time Fisher left Medford's aging hospital building. Shadows from campus buildings and other structures had lengthened considerably. The cold February afternoon stung Fisher's face as he walked with a quick stride. His destination, the Department of Pathology, required a brisk walk across a large courtyard. Plans were on the drawing board to connect the Pathology Department to the hospital by an elevated walkway, but the Med's budget crisis had placed those plans on indefinite hold. The access to the building was either through the steam tunnels below the streets as he had done three nights earlier, or across the courtyard.

The courtyard was the quickest route. Fisher was in a hurry. Over the previous two hours, someone in the department of Pathology had paged him three times. He had ignored it the first two times. Persistence paid off for the unknown caller, because Fisher finally answered the third page. Natalie Roberts wanted Fisher to come by her laboratory before he left the hospital for the day. He promised he would.

As he walked, Fisher glanced at his watch. Almost an hour had passed since he had spoken with Roberts. When the pages came through, he had been staring at his monitor, lost in thought, still reeling from the messages Alli had discovered. He was totally confused, processing the information. His closest friend leaves the University to work at a busy city hospital. The friend wants to communicate but never does, by conventional means, that is. All the while he is sending email messages over the Internet. His last readable message says trouble is brewing, but he won't say what the trouble is. Finally, he sends an encrypted message that can't be read. The day he sends the encrypted message he's gunned down coming to a meeting, presumably to discuss the trouble.

Fisher felt stonewalled. What was the trouble? What cost Carlton his life? Fisher knew he didn't have a clue. If Carlton's death was a puzzle, it had so many missing pieces that the picture was totally obscured.

He reached the Pathology building and climbed the flight of stone steps leading to the entrance. As he pulled open the heavy metal-and-glass door, he recalled the tone of Roberts' voice when he returned the third page. She was excited which was a bit unusual. Roberts' usual demeanor was calm and collected, not eager. As he walked to the elevators, he wondered what was on her mind.

The doors of the ancient elevator opened on the fourth floor. Using Roberts' directions, he turned left and followed the room numbers until he came to four hundred twenty-three. The door was closed. To the right of the threshold a placard read Natalie Roberts, MD, Molecular Pathology

Fisher tapped on the door and entered. Once inside, he glanced around Roberts' laboratory. The center of the room was crowded with laboratory benches that supported numerous pieces of equipment. Wooden shelves held glass bottles with orange or blue screw caps. The bottles contained multicolored liquids. The room had a pronounced chemical odor.

At first glance, Fisher saw no one present in the laboratory. He knew the hour was late for research personnel to be working. Perhaps Roberts had left. Finally, he caught sight of her. She stood in the corner of the laboratory staring at a photograph.

"Natalie," Fisher called as he approached her.

Roberts jumped in surprise but recovered quickly. "Thanks for coming, Steve. I'm sorry to page you the way I did, but I wanted to show you something very interesting."

"Sure," Fisher said. "What's it concerning?"

"It's the Jane Doe I autopsied three nights ago."

Fisher's face was expressionless. He didn't want to disappoint Roberts, but his thoughts were a thousand miles away. The encrypted message had been etched permanently in his brain, and he couldn't get it out of his thoughts. Frankly, learning anything else about a homeless woman who had a kidney removed as a child and had no nephrectomy scar was of no interest to him whatsoever. Roberts was probably going to tell him she had applied an advanced molecular diagnostic test that confirmed Fisher had been right.

"After the other night," Roberts was saying, as Fisher resurfaced from his thoughts, "I couldn't stop wondering how the woman's right kidney had been removed, yet no surgical incision was present. To learn more about it, I performed some molecular testing on tissue I removed at the time of autopsy."

As he had predicted, Fisher thought, continuing to look blankly at her, so he would not let on that he had more important things to do — like speaking to Richland PD about the encrypted file he carried in his coat pocket.

"I have three things to show you." Roberts walked to her microscope. She motioned for him to follow. They both sat down to her teaching microscope, an odd contraption with three viewing heads. She opened a small box that contained the slides she had already examined extensively. From the box, the first slide she removed was labeled "left flank." She related the initial findings as she had discovered them. The tissue specimen removed from Jane Doe's left flank was nothing out of the ordinary. There were spirals of connective tissue interspersed with slips of muscle, all falling into their proper anatomical location. The cell shapes and sizes were all what Fisher would have considered normal.

Next she pulled a slide from the box labeled "right flank." Fisher considered glancing at his watch to insinuate that he was working on a tight schedule.

Roberts showed Fisher how the tissue removed from the Jane Doe's right flank, the site over the absent kidney, contained cells that were dividing at a dramatic rate. As Fisher looked through the lenses, he saw tissue distributed across the field in a chaotic fashion. He could discern no organization in the tissue. The differences were not subtle. Even an untrained eye would have had no trouble identifying the features Roberts pointed out.

"This shows," Roberts said, "that the woman's flank tissue was growing at an extraordinarily high rate at the time she died. It's a similar growth rate to that usually associated with young children. It's not what you'd expect from a sickly, malnourished, alcoholic woman living on the streets."

Fisher's mind did a double-take.

"Now look at this picture." Roberts picked up the black-and-white photograph she was studying earlier. There were vertical columns with black hatch marks superimposed on a white background. Each column contained two to three hatch marks, each about one-fourth of an inch long. Some hatch marks displayed a greater darkness on the white background than others.

"I'm afraid you'll have to tell me what we're looking at, Natalie."

"This is a photograph of a quantitative real-time PCR analysis or qPCR. It's a sensitive way to study how the genes inside tissue cells are functioning. In using the microscope to study the appearance of the tissue from the right flank, you would predict that the cells in the tissue would be growing at an alarmingly high rate. QPCR can tell just how fast a tissue is growing by measuring the rate at which certain genes are transcribing or working."

Roberts held the photograph as she continued. "To perform the study, I purified RNA from the tissue of the right and left flank areas. In this test, RNA is the starting point. It's the part of the cell that can tell us exactly how much a gene has been turned on and how fast it's working. The RNA from the flank tissue is placed in separate small tubes and treated with a special enzyme called reverse transcriptase that changes RNA to DNA. If the genes in the right flank tissue are working abnormally fast, a lot more RNA will be present there that will in turn produce more DNA after enzyme treatment."

Roberts stood and walked to one of the laboratory benches not far from where she and Fisher were sitting. She laid her right hand on a piece of equipment the size of a shoe box. "Once the enzyme has converted the RNA to DNA, we use this machine, a thermocycler." She gently patted the machine as she talked. "After adding several more chemicals to the tubes, they are placed in here where they undergo thermocycling. This means the tubes are heated and cooled over a period of several hours, which increases the amount of DNA in each of the tubes at the same rate. After thermocycling, all samples are subjected to electrophoresis, which separates the pieces of DNA by their size. The columns of hatch marks you see here are pieces of DNA of varying sizes."

Roberts reached into her tightly coiled hair, removed a pencil from its perch and pointed to the photograph. "In these columns are the samples taken from the right flank. The hatch marks are significantly brighter on the photograph than the left flank columns here. The analysis shows that the tissue from the woman's right flank was growing at an alarming rate. From my estimation, the tissue from Jane Doe's right flank shows at least a six-hundred percent increase in growth-gene activity over the left flank tissue."

Fisher continued to look at the photograph. He finally spoke. "So for reasons not clear from the autopsy, the woman's kidney was removed recently. Not when she was a child, as I initially suggested the night of the autopsy."

"Exactly."

The conversation again stopped as Fisher stared intently at the photograph. He continued thinking aloud. "The findings from your studies indicate that after the nephrectomy, something happened to the surgical wound where the kidney was removed. The woman's tissue underwent a wild increase of growth-gene expression, which accelerated tissue repair. And unlike the typical situation, her repairing tissue left no physical evidence of surgery."

For a moment, Fisher's thoughts had veered away from the events of the previous three days. His mind raced along a different road, clean and challenging. Ideas and potential scenarios entered his conscious thinking and vaporized instantly, as he and Roberts stood in silence.

Roberts plunged the pencil back into her hair.

Fisher asked, "Is it possible to determine from these findings when surgery was performed? Was it days, weeks, months?"

"Hours to days," Roberts responded without hesitation. "The repair probably took place less than forty-eight hours before autopsy."

They looked at each other.

"The question is why?" Roberts said. The tone in her voice showed frustration. "The woman was clearly homeless. Maybe she developed a serious infection in the kidney that necessitated its removal."

Fisher asked, "Did you find any evidence of infection when you performed the post-mortem exam?"

"That's the problem with that theory. There was no evidence of kidney infection anywhere. If an infection had caused the kidney to come out, there would certainly have been . . . ."

CHIRP, CHIRP. CHIRP, CHIRP. Fisher's cell phone rang in his coat pocket. He put the small phone to his ear. "Dr. Fisher, it's Alan Binzemore. Sorry to interrupt you. Are you still in the hospital?"

"Yes. What's happening, Alan?"

"It's the patient with the aortic dissection we repaired last night."

"Yes?"

"He has suddenly begun having chest pain. I've just run an EKG. He's in the middle of a heart attack."

"Have Cardiology see him and I'll be right there."

Fisher clicked off the phone and dropped it back into his pocket. "Natalie, I have to run. I've got a patient who is probably having a heart attack. Sorry, but we'll have to postpone our discussion."

"I understand." Roberts' couldn't conceal her disappointment as she spoke.

Fisher turned abruptly and left the laboratory.

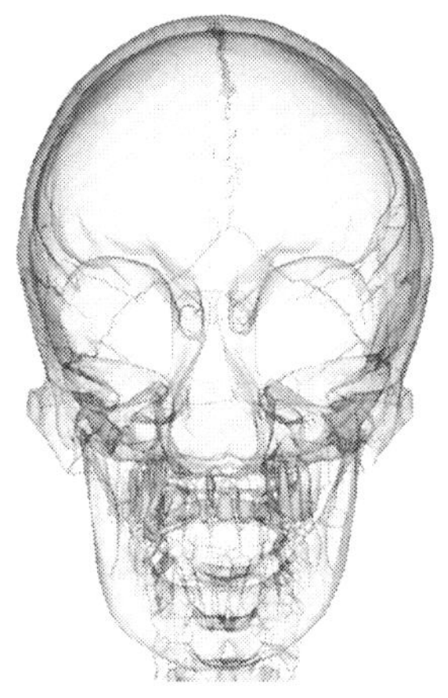

CHAPTER NINTEEN

To the pedestrians walking past the lone park bench, Alexi Ibanov appeared listless and disengaged. His dark wiry hair hung chaotically above thick bushy eyebrows and prominent white cheekbones. Anyone studying his features for a moment might accurately identify Ibanov's Russian lineage.

He sat motionless, gazing across Midtown Park, his eyes tear-laden and reddened. The frigid winter air burned as it moved rhythmically in and out of his chest through a mouth hanging partially open. Ibanov was intoxicated again, and like other nights, he ignored the worsening chill and the burning sensation the cold produced under his breast bone as he stared at the ice hanging from the frozen fountain.

The wool jacket, gathered tightly around him, fell six inches short of covering his chest. A soiled dress shirt, easily visible underneath the gap in front, was too light in weight to provide any protection from the cold. His plaid trousers, taken from a give-away bin in front of the soup kitchen he frequented, were torn, the result of a struggle with two would-be muggers the night before.

Oblivious to passersby, Ibanov reached down to the cold, wooden bench slats, encircled the top of a thin paper bag, raised it toward his mouth, but then stopped. With a trembling hand, he folded back the loose brown paper to reveal the glass mouth of a vodka bottle. He lifted the paper-shrouded vessel to his mouth and drank deeply for a few seconds, happy with the burning sensation the vodka produced as it went down. He shivered as he pulled the flask from his lips and looked around.

Across from the park, the Security Savings Bank's digital thermometer had documented falling temperatures degree by degree. Ibanov didn't care. His mind swirled from the alcohol as tears fell onto his filthy pants. He had prayed that the vodka would relieve his pain, but the agony inside remained as he thought of the letter in his pocket. As if taking his cue from an unseen force, he pulled out the crumpled sheet of paper, folded exactly as the sender had intended.

For a moment he stared at it. Finally he unfolded it. In the winter twilight, he reread the letter.

January 20th
Minsk

Dear Alexi,

It is time you gave up the charade you are playing in the United States and return home. Your two years there have been a failure, and you must admit it. Elena and the children have been home in Minsk for months. Elena says she will never return to the nightmare of living on American welfare again. Things are better here now. You may not be able to find work as an engineer, but there will be work for you.

I tell you, Alexi, you have caused your mother and me needless pain and embarrassment. Come back home. Admit you have failed. Please do not bring additional disgrace on our house.

Your Father,
Dimitri

Since its arrival, Ibanov had crumpled the letter a dozen times and shoved it back into the pocket of his tattered jacket, pulling it out to refold it after his anger had subsided. He crumpled it again and threw the small wad at the frozen fountain.

"He will not rule my life any more, not one minute," Ibanov said in Russian, his voice breaking with emotion. He stood in front of the bench, wobbled slightly, but then regained his balance. He walked to the park's exit.

The work day was ending, and the sidewalks were crowded. Ibanov stepped into the crowd and made his way down the business streets glancing briefly at the well-dressed pedestrians. He was careful never to make eye contact. It caused him too much pain to look at them. He knew most of them were headed for their commute to the suburbs and their comfortable homes.

His gut cramped again, augmenting the pain that had been present for weeks. He had wanted that life. More than anything, he had wanted that life. He had come, bringing Elena and the children to seek that life, in America.

He had given up their small apartment in Minsk and his dead-end job as an engineer for the government ministry. With their meager possessions and all their savings, they had arrived full of hope and excitement. Like all immigrants, they were starting a new life, but nothing went as they had planned. Alexi Ibanov did not find work. Within a few months of arriving in Richland, their savings were gone. At first, they managed to keep their apartment, subsisting on a monthly stipend from Ibanov's father, but with the arrival of each check, Dimitri Ibanov demanded that they return home. Ibanov persisted in his search for work, ignoring his father's demands. When at last the checks stopped coming from Minsk, Ibanov and his family were evicted from their small apartment. For months after that, they lived in a series of homeless shelters, surviving on occasional public assistance and handouts. Elena Ibanov finally took the children and returned to Minsk.

Ibanov walked west, away from the financial district. Within several blocks, the streets narrowed and street lights became sparse. The sidewalks sloped downward as he approached the warehouse district along the basin leading to the Caton River. It was well past twilight as he approached a dimly lighted pub sandwiched between two dark warehouses. Ibanov did not hesitate as he climbed the four steps to the entrance of the small bar.

A single low-wattage bulb hanging under a rusted metal lampshade lit the top of the platform. Ibanov peered through the grimy window to the left of the entrance door. Inside he saw four, maybe five people, all men, either milling around or seated. He strained his eyes searching the small space. On the right, a rough wooden bar with stools scattered in front traveled the length of the room. A man, presumably the bartender, slouched in conversation with a single customer. Ibanov was about to turn away when he noticed one final individual seated at a small table in the rear. The man faced the entrance, a fair distance from the window. Ibanov recognized the man he had met two nights earlier outside a soup kitchen. His pulse quickened as he grasped the rusting doorknob and entered.

The stench of stale beer and human despair was pervasive as Ibanov pulled the door closed behind him. Not one of the patrons noticed him as he made his way to the rear, his gait still wobbly.

As Ibanov approached, the lone figure stood.

"I see you had no trouble finding the place."

For a moment the two men looked at each other, saying nothing. They were a study in contrast — Ibanov, broken and destitute; the man, confident, self-assured.

Ibanov was the first to sit down, eyeing the tall, well-groomed man suspiciously. Occasional strands of gray peppered out of a black, neatly trimmed, mustache. A suit of expensive, yet understated, cloth was visible under his heavy overcoat.

The man raised his hand to signal the bartender, then seated himself across from Ibanov.

The bartender begrudgingly left his conversation and walked to where the men were seated.

"Vodka, my friend?" The man focused his dark eyes on Ibanov.

Ibanov nodded his reply.

"Two double vodkas. Absolut, on the rocks."

The sullen bartender left to retrieve their drinks.

"Well, Mr. Ibanov," the man said, a confident tone in his voice. "Have you considered my offer?"

Ibanov stared at the man without saying a word. He struggled to arrange his thoughts in a logical flow, but the vodka he had consumed earlier impaired his efforts. At least the vodka had given him the courage to come. He wrung his hands together under the table, out of sight. They were cold from the walk and wet from the fear of what he was about to do.

"It has been a few days," Ibanov said, his voice shaking almost imperceptibly. "Please, you will told me again what my signature it will bring."

The man leaned forward against the table, his eyes black in the subdued light of the small barroom. He locked his gaze directly on Ibanov's eyes before he spoke. He lowered his voice. "The deal is very simple, Mr. Ibanov. You sign the agreement, and we'll place thirty thousand dollars American into any account you wish to be used by anyone you designate."

The bartender returned with the two tall vodkas. The man handed the bartender cash and moments later, they were alone again.

Ibanov lifted the drink to his mouth and consumed it with the same urgency he had earlier drained the paper-shrouded bottle. The burning double shot made its way down. He knew instantly the grade of alcohol was higher than the bottle in his pocket.

For a few moments, Ibanov held the tall glass end up, taking care to suck the vodka from around each cube of ice before lowering the empty glass onto the table. There was a rush from the drink almost before the glass left his lips. He was calm, emboldened. The drink had worked its magic. As a final gesture, he took a satisfying swipe at the residual moisture covering his lips, using the sleeve of the ragged coat.

He looked across the table with renewed confidence. "The money you can put so my wife Elena she can get?"

"Yes."

"Thirty thousand dollars," Ibanov said, his muted voice causing the man across the table to strain to hear his words.

The vodka flowed freely through Ibanov's veins. His hands were warm and dry. The courage that had spurred him to seek a new life in America filled his chest once again. He had always been a pioneer, one willing to venture into the unknown. It was in his Russian blood.

His mind relaxed and floated free. He thought of Elena and the children. They were waving final good-byes as they entered the jet way, flying home to Minsk on tickets bought by Ibanov's father.

"I will sign," Ibanov said without further hesitation.

From under the dark overcoat, the well-groomed man pulled a simple form printed in small English typeface that Ibanov wasn't even going to attempt to read. He knew what he had to do. With the heavy ball-point pen the man provided, he stroked boldly across the bottom of the agreement. The image of his father, so onerous in his thoughts these last few weeks suddenly was shattered. He was free.

"We will notify you when you are needed," the man said, standing. He signaled the bartender again. "Another double Absolut, here."

Ibanov and the man stared at each other again. As if reading Ibanov's mind, the man reached into the pocket of his overcoat and pulled out a wad of bills.

"Get some good food to eat. We need you healthy."

He stuffed the money into the pocket of Ibanov's coat and quietly left the pub.

Ibanov patiently waited.

"Double tall Absolut," the bartender said, placing the drink on the table.

Ibanov grasped the large glass and raised it to his lips. He knew he would have no trouble releasing the pain that night.

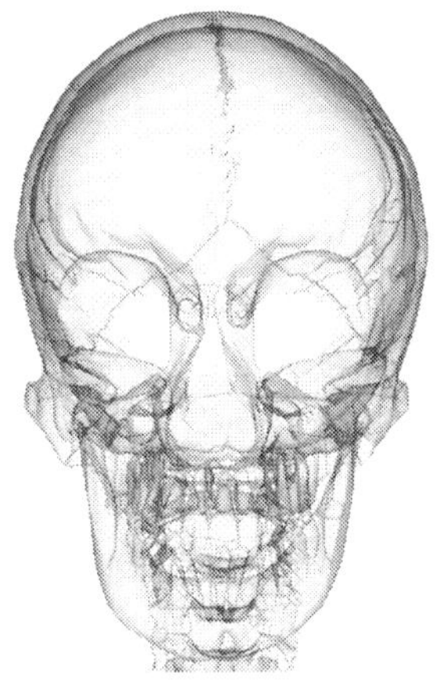

CHAPTER TWENTY

Well after dark, Fisher walked out of the Cardiac Cath lab and headed for the Cardiac Surgery offices. The post-op patient was rushed to cath where Cardiologists placed a stent to re-establish the heart's blood flow. The patient was safely back in the ICU where he would be monitored for the next several days.

When Fisher arrived in the Surgery offices, all was dark except for the overhead fluorescents in his office. From across the room, he could see the yellow post-it note Alli had stuck to the monitor screen.

> Dr. Fisher,
>
> I studied the encrypted file several times. I don't have a clue to what it says. To find out its contents, you will have to have a key or consult with someone who has file encryption experience. I made a couple of extra copies besides the one I gave you.

Fisher probed for the disk in his coat pocket. It was still right where he had left it.

The note continued:

> I found the file on Medford's electronic medical record that holds all the records Dr. Carlton

```
initially set up for the transplant study. I will
start placing the information in a database to-
morrow. Good luck with the encrypted file. Sorry I
don't know anyone who could help.
   Sincerely, AS
```

Fisher placed a call to Binzmore before he left. He was informed that nothing new had developed with their patient. He hung up the phone, again tapped the copy of the file in his pocket, and walked out of the office.

• • • • •

Within fifteen minutes, Fisher parked his car in the lot across the street from the Richland Police Department.

The RPD was alive with activity. The large receiving room was thick with people, many being attended to by uniformed officers. With the level of confusion high, no one noticed Fisher as he skirted the room and entered the stairwell. He bounded up the flights two steps at the time to the second floor, but as he emerged from the stairwell, he stopped. The second floor hallway was dark. He saw no offices lighted as he had seen a few days earlier. Disappointed, Fisher turned to retrace his steps but hesitated. His eyes were becoming accustomed to the hallway, and he thought he detected a faint difference in tint to one of the office's frosted glass windows on Hinton's side of the hall. Fisher walked toward to the light. It became increasingly visible as he approached. "Yes," he whispered softly.

The soft light radiated from Bradley Hinton's office. He approached the door and knocked gently on the glass.

"Come in," the familiar voice responded.

Fisher opened the door. There in the Special Operations office was Hinton sitting in front of his computer. Hinton's monitor, the small room's single light source, produced weak but eerie illumination.

Hinton looked up as Fisher walked into the room.

"Dr. Fisher." Hinton spoke like one who had suddenly been pulled away from deep concentration. "D'you forget something?"

Fisher closed the door.

"Brad, I realize it's late, but I discovered something this afternoon you may be able to help me with."

Hinton slid his heavy lenses back up his nose. "Sure, Doc, no problem."

Fisher told Hinton the story of his discovery then reached into his side coat pocket, pulled out the jump drive and handed it to Hinton.

"Did you mention this to Lt. Domao?" Hinton stared hard at Fisher.

"No, I haven't. Since Special Operations is your area, I figured the Lieutenant would just turn around and hand the drive off to you, anyway. I came straight here from the hospital and didn't think he would be around this time of night."

"Sometimes he is when he's not working his second job."

"Lt. Domao works two jobs?"

"Yeah, he works as a part-time security cop somewhere in Richland." Hinton inserted the drive into his computer's USB port. "Okay, let's see what we have here."

Fisher could hear a high-pitched whine as the computer's drive recognized the drive. Finally, Hinton's screen displayed the contents of the drive, a single file Alli had aptly named Encrypt.doc.

Hinton turned to Fisher. "First, I'll simply open the file through some word processing software to get a look at what we are dealing with."

Fisher sat in a chair off to Hinton's left, anxiously waiting as Hinton clicked the keys of his keyboard in rapid succession. Finally, the encrypted file Fisher had seen six hours earlier appeared on the screen.

```
TO: SFisher@MedU.edu
From: CCarlton@MedNet.org
Date: 1/31/15
RE: X#$%&#.
--Begin IES Message, Version: 9.05--

   pghhhak24jjjpop09978mmngnkJCuTMaNQEmPMDweEtH-
hpaanxzZhglLWdinglstkhhieosLeKh. . . .
```

"Oh, Internet Encryption Systems," Hinton said. "This could be tough."

Hinton studied the message for a few minutes. Fisher watched his gaze through the thick glasses as it jumped wildly from corner to corner of the screen. With the exception of the muted hum of Hinton's computer, the silence in the office was deafening. Fisher was surprised that one floor above the crowded intake area, Hinton's office was so quiet.

Fisher finally spoke, "Can you glean information from just studying the characters of the file?"

"Sometimes," Hinton said, his attention still glued to the screen. "Depending on the complexity of the cryptosystems used to encrypt a file, letter patterns may emerge that give tips to decryption. Uncomplicated systems simply rely on letter substitutions where, for example, the letter A becomes D or B becomes E, and so on. Another technique, referred to as a transposition cipher, changes the order of the letters but not the letters themselves. Certain letters appear quite frequently in written and spoken English, and at times, careful study of the cipher will suggest one of these simpler systems. If an experienced cryptologist can recognize these or other ciphers that don't employ keys, the encryption method will be discovered and the file cracked."

"A key?"

"Yes, a key. It's a bit pattern recognized by the encryption software. Practically all complex cryptosystems use one, sometimes two keys. The software will encrypt or decrypt according to the key's bit pattern."

"I'm sorry to be so naive." Fisher said, his frustration increasing. "But where does the key come from?"

"Hey, don't tear yourself up over this, Doc," Hinton said with a snort. "The complexity of this stuff is nothing compared to what you do every day. Look, a key is usually derived from a password like you and I were dealing with a couple of days ago. Dr. Carlton's iPad had a single key encryption program referred to as an XOR cipher. Once we discovered the key, the file was decrypted, and we gained access. Fortunately you correctly guessed the password. If you hadn't, even that one would have been hard to crack. This one's going to be different, though. I seem to remember reading about IES sometime back. Its program developed from a two-key system written especially for keeping Internet email secure. The original program it came from was called PGP, which stood for Pretty Good Privacy. PGP was a first-generation encryption program published in the early nineties. By the turn of the century, the scum that surfed the net broke the code. IES was developed out of a need to keep the Internet secure although with all the hacking that's going on recently even IES is up for grabs."

Hinton went on, "If IES is like its predecessor, it used a public key for encryption and a private key for decryption. First the user, in this case it was Dr. Carlton, chooses two large, random prime numbers. Those are numbers divisible by themselves or by one. The larger the numbers the better. The numbers are then multiplied together to produce the public key. That number can be freely distributed to anyone who wanted to send Dr. Carlton email. To decrypt the file, the two prime numbers have to be known. That's the private-key part."

"Okay. Maybe this will become clearer if I think about it further. What you're saying is that to decrypt the file, we have to know Dr. Carlton's private key, which will likely be two very large prime numbers."

"That's the beauty of two-key systems, they are virtually unsolvable. But we may have a chance. Back during the Clinton administration, the National Security Agency began the Clipper Chip Project. The Clipper Chip, subsequently known as the Key Escrow Chip, was supposed to provide a new two-key system the government would distribute freely to anyone who needed airtight security. Almost from the beginning, though, people complained because written into the chip was a back door to breaking code that government agencies and law enforcement could use to decrypt any file. Clipper's popularity didn't last long, but some popular programs subsequently adapted Clipper Chip technology. I just can't remember whether IES was one of those."

Hinton's said nothing further as his fingers flew across the keyboard. The monitor screen went dark. Seconds later, the screen became polar white. In the center of the screen was emblazoned the seals of the United States Justice Department and the National Security Agency. Under the agency seals, several lines of text read:

Warning
Key Escrow Chip (formerly Clipper Chip)
decryption software

For use by:
Authorized law enforcement
And intelligence agencies only
[Unauthorized use punishable by fines and imprisonment]

"Maybe this will do." Hinton spoke softly to himself as he became less aware of his surroundings and more a part of cyberspace. "Okay, first I'm going to pull you into clipper and run you through some skipjack algorithms."

Fisher didn't make any effort to understand. He simply watched Hinton work.

As Hinton clicked across the keyboard, Carlton's encrypted file disappeared and reappeared several times. Over the next three quarters of an hour, Hinton subjected the file to repeated attempts at decryption, using the Key Escrow program and others, but to no avail. All failed.

Finally, without taking his eyes off the monitor screen, Hinton pointed to the encrypted file. "This IES is a bad one, Dr. Fisher. It has absolutely no Clipper Chip elements. This Dr. Carlton buddy of yours was really something. Not just anybody has a program like that. The software is out there on the Internet, but it's damn hard to get. You almost have to sell your soul for it, and here he's got it."

"Chip was a pretty smart guy all right," Fisher said, thinking about Carlton.

"I'm the only cryptologist RPD's got, and I've just exhausted all our firepower. I doubt we'll find the private key for this file. It probably went down with Dr. Carlton. That's the problem with two-key encryption. You lose the private key, the file's history. It'll never be decrypted without it."

"So a specific private key is the only way to decrypt the file?"

"Pretty much," Hinton said, exiting the last decryption program. "Without a private key, the only way we're going to crack it is to hand it over to the FBI cryptologists at Quantico. They've got some major firepower there, but it could still take them weeks or months."

The two men became quiet, the air heavy with frustration.

Hinton said, "In the morning I'll . . . ."

Before he could go further, the door to the Special Operations office opened. Fisher looked at Hinton before turning and saw Hinton's surprised expression.

Blocking what little light came in from the hallway; Domao's fleshy silhouette looked more massive than usual. As before, Fisher's senses were immediately assailed by Domao's presence. The officer coughed loudly and stunk of stale cigar smoke.

"Dr. Fisher, what the hell are you doing here?"

Hinton responded first. "Ben, come in. Dr. Fisher's made a discovery that may be important to the Carlton killing."

Domao slowly entered the room and closed the door.

Hinton pushed back from his computer, readjusting his glasses, which by that time had migrated back down the bridge of his nose.

"Why wasn't I freakin called about this, Hinton? Do you think you're heading up the investigation now?"

"Ben, the Doc just got here about an hour ago. Shit, it was late when he got here. I had no idea you were still here."

Domao spewed venom. "So now, besides doing my job, I got to watch my back, eh?"

Fisher spoke up, "Lieutenant, I'm sure you would have handed off the information to Officer Hinton. It's a message Dr. Carlton sent me before he was killed. The message was intended for me, but it's in a code we can't break."

Domao's demeanor changed completely. He tugged at his frayed sport coat and straightened his tie. A plastic grin spread across his face. "Okay, thanks a lot for bringing this new information to light, Dr. Fisher. I'm sure you and Officer Hinton have made plans for the next step."

"Next step's Quantico, Ben. I'm going to call them first thing tomorrow morning. The file's tough. I've got a few tricks left, but for the most part, I've thrown all RPD's heavy artillery at it."

"Good," said Domao, reeking of sarcasm. Turning to Fisher he announced curtly, "That will be all, Dr. Fisher."

• • • • •

Hinton rubbed his eyes. After his workout with Fisher and his nasty encounter with Domao, he was ready to call it a night. Even though the IES encrypted file was tough, he had not totally given up hope. Once the office became quiet again, he went back to work on the file. He made little progress.

Two hours had passed since Domao stormed out of his office. His eyes were shot from staring at the screen and his back cramped from long hours of sitting. It was time to head for home.

Hinton's old Dodge Valiant moaned and groaned when he turned the ignition key. He pumped the accelerator several times after the first unsuccessful try and let it sit a few seconds. The car was a temperamental old bitch that never liked to start in temperatures below twenty degrees.

Finally, the engine caught.

Hinton rubbed his hands together to warm them. The Valiant's steering wheel was like ice and one could even feel the cold through gloves. He could expect the heater to take a while to kick in. The old Valiant sputtered as he coaxed it up Twentieth Street. At Main Street, he turned and headed east.

With luck and cooperating traffic, he would reach home in twenty minutes, going the back way. His modest house wasn't too far from Richland Municipal Airport and was a ten-minute jump from the RPD, if he were willing to pay the insane seventy-cent toll on the downtown expressway.

No sir, Bradley Hinton was not lining the pockets of the city with his seventy cents, he told himself. The downside, however, was that the back way took him through one of Richland's crime-ridden sections.

Main Street, like Tuckman, was one of Richland's major thoroughfares, but of the two, Main carried far less traffic. As he traveled east, Hinton was pleased that traffic had thinned nicely.

I just might make it for the Sci-Fi midnight movie, he thought, regaining a bit of energy.

He had driven the Main Street route so frequently that automatic behavior would lead him home, freeing his mind for higher-ordered thinking. Dozens of police matters, along with Fisher's IES file revolved in his head. Because of his fast-paced, complex thinking, Hinton failed to notice a car that followed him almost from the moment he left the RPD, maintaining a gap of about one quarter of a mile. That gap narrowed as traffic thinned out through a particularly bad section known as Everyready Park. The Park was empty.

Hinton pulled up to the traffic light at Main and Forty-third. As he idled at the light, he realized he had forgotten to buckle his seat belt. Locating the door-half of the seat belt was always a struggle, so he shifted to park and began the search.

During those few seconds, Hinton didn't notice a set of headlights approach the Valiant and swing into the right hand lane beside him, but by that point, evasive action was impossible.

The driver's window of the car dropped and the silenced barrel of a nine millimeter pistol projected toward the Valiant's passenger window. The driver, poorly visible in the shadows, aimed quickly. A soft thump sounded as the muffled shot left the barrel, followed instantly by the sound of splintering glass as the bullet penetrated the Valiant.

Unaware of anything but the sound of splintering glass, Hinton had no chance of reacting before the speeding bullet struck his head. Hinton slumped forward.

The driver-side window ascended in the car adjacent to the idling Valiant, sealing the vehicle once again. As the light at Main and Forty-Third changed, the driver slowly pulled away.

The Valiant remained at the intersection, idling. Blood had sprayed across the window from the large exit wound in Hinton's head.

On the dark second floor of the Richland Police Department in the office of Special Operations, a desk light was switched on. A key was inserted into the locked drawer below the computer. The drawer opened quietly, and a jump drive containing an encrypted email file was removed.

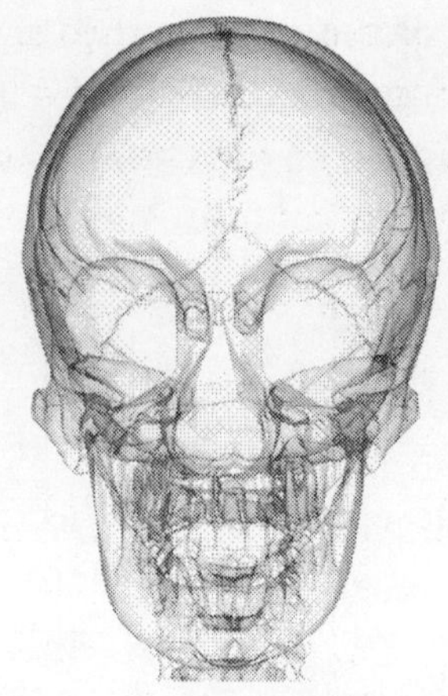

CHAPTER TWENTY-ONE

February 5

At seven-thirty in the morning, Fisher's mind was crisp and unclouded as he walked between two rows of tables in the Medford Hospital cafeteria. He took care not to spill the hot coffee he carried while fumbling to open a morning copy of the *Richland Tribune.* As he sipped the rich black liquid, a fleeting but important thought, nonetheless, entered his mind — *no booze.* For the first time in weeks, he had not needed a drink for sleep. He had returned to his apartment following his meeting with Hinton with his mind full of thoughts and questions, but as he lay in bed, sleep came naturally from fatigue, not from alcohol. In a similar, but important way, that morning was different from virtually all others of late. He had not needed to search for a morning fix to clear a hung-over brain before starting his day. As he brought the steaming cup to his mouth for another sip, he also noticed something else that pleased him — his hands were steady. The tremors, also a result of the alcohol, were gone.

As Fisher approached the table where Binzemore and several surgical residents and medical students were sitting for breakfast, the thought occurred to him, as it often had, that the traditions of medical education which The Med still carried on were in danger of extinction. The rise of the medical marketplace and the expansion of proprietary hospital corporations like Health Pursuit had pushed medical education into the back seat. Like the Med, university hospitals all over the United States had changed their mission as they struggled to survive against the corporate giants of the twenty-first century. They had jerked away from medical education.

"Morning, Dr. Fisher."

"Good morning, Alan. Good morning to all." Fisher realized he sounded a little too enthusiastic.

A communal grumbling of the word morning came from the remainder of those seated at the table.

Fisher looked around. Unkempt hair, glassy eyes and unshaven faces spoke volumes about what that particular surgical team had done during the night.

"Busy night, Alan?" Fisher asked.

"No, not really. Little things kept the residents and students going all night. The ORs were quiet for a change last night."

"Good," Fisher said, thinking he was grateful for a complete night's sleep. "I don't recall seeing anything on the schedule for today."

"No, the schedule's clean so far," Binzemore said.

Fisher sat back in his chair, took another sip from his coffee and picked up the *Tribune*. Above the fold, the headlines announced more troubles in the waters that separated Taiwan and mainland China. A smaller headline concerned the vice-president's open-heart surgery being performed at Bethesda Naval Hospital, following the chest pain he developed on a good will tour to Brazil. He was rushed back to the States for cardiac catheterization and surgery.

"Morning." Mike Ridgeway cheerfully issued the greeting as his massive frame glided by. He carried four doughnuts and a giant cup of coffee.

"Hi, Mike. Think that'll hold you `til lunch?"

"Hey," Ridgeway boomed back as he exited the cafeteria, "I'm a growing boy."

Fisher watched Ridgeway leave the cafeteria. He then directed his attention back to the paper. As he scanned down, his attention became riveted to the lower front page. His palms grew moist, his pulse quickened. A small headline read:

Richland Police Officer Murdered

Officer Bradley Hinton, a deciphering technician in charge of Special Operations for the Richland Police Department, was shot once in the head while stopped at a traffic light at Main Street and Forty-Third. The killing occurred around 11:45 p.m. Wednesday night. The officer was declared dead at the scene by Richland EMS. The body was taken to the State Medical Examiner for autopsy.

The spot near Everready Park where the murder occurred is the identical area where three Richland youths were murdered in a dispute between warring gangs two weeks ago.

Officer Hinton is survived by a brother and a sister who live in the victim's home of Dallas, Texas. A formal police funeral procession for the fallen officer will be held Saturday.

The article ended with a statement by the RPD Chief of Police that the murder was under investigation.

Pressure in Fisher's throat increased as his muscles contracted. His heart raced, and he felt light-headed.

"Are you all right, Dr. Fisher?" a fatigued-appearing female resident asked.

"I'm . . . I'm . . . okay," Fisher struggled to say, finally feeling the air caught in his chest flow out. "I've just read some bad news. I'll be back in a few minutes."

Fisher stood and walked shakily out of the cafeteria, leaving his half-drunk cup of coffee behind.

Still severely upset, Fisher found himself in the main thoroughfare outside the cafeteria. For a moment, he simply stood amid the rush of morning activity. People clad in white and green, some he knew, some he didn't, hurried by. A crying child, a security guard giving directions, wheelchairs being pushed by aides, all added to the cacophony that erupted in Fisher's brain.

His gaze roved until he spotted the atrium. The glass enclosed structure with its scattered seating served as a waiting area for the Medford

ORs. The waiting area was not occupied. Fisher entered and picked a seat in the far corner. He pulled his cellular phone from the large pocket of his clinic coat and dialed the Richland Police Department.

"Domao," the raspy voice answered without inflection.

"Lieutenant, this is Dr. Steven Fisher. I've just seen the *Richland Tribune*. I am so sorry to learn of Brad Hinton's death. What do you think happened?"

"It's pretty straightforward to me, Dr. Fisher," Domao said. "We live in a violent city. Hinton lived on the wrong side of it, and it finally caught up with him."

That's a hell of an attitude for a police detective to have, especially towards a colleague he worked with every day, Fisher thought. "Well, I guess it's just acute for me at the moment, especially after having been with Officer Hinton not twelve hours ago."

Domao didn't reply.

"Is there any possibility that the encrypted file from Dr. Carlton played a role in Officer Hinton's death?"

"That's impossible," Domao replied. "Officer Hinton was killed while driving home. He had stopped his car at an intersection near one of the city's most drug-infested areas."

"Were there any witnesses? Did he attempt to defend himself?"

"Doctor Fisher, the matter is under investigation."

The remainder of the conversation with Domao was frustrating. The officer acted as if the previous night never happened, Fisher thought. In the end, Domao gave Fisher no real hope that the file would be sent to Quantico. Fisher didn't push it, and Domao was unwilling to offer it.

Fisher severed the call and replaced the phone in his pocket. He continued sitting in the still-silent waiting area, thinking. He was thankful for an alert, unclouded brain.

Fisher closed his eyes for a moment, attempting to reset his brain. Physicians often have to perform mental reset maneuvers to gain new perspective in solving problems. Frequently surgical operations took unexpected turns and required quick re-appraisals that ultimately demanded completely different solutions to certain situations. This was one of those times.

Fisher started his re-appraisal by making the assumption that the contents of the encrypted file was of a critical nature. If so, one could assume that two people were dead because of the file's contents. Chip Carlton was killed because he discovered something someone wanted kept secret. Cryptography was Hinton's specialty, so it was logical for someone to assume he might break the code and view the contents of the file.

Who? No one but Domao knew Fisher was with Hinton the night before. Had someone else followed him to the station? It was a chilling thought.

If I was followed, Fisher thought, why had that someone not tried to kill me, knowing I had the Carlton file? The single logical answer is that I didn't have the ability to decipher the file, and Hinton did.

Different approach again, Fisher thought, as other chilling revelations popped into his rapidly spinning mind. If one assumes that no one followed me to the station, that leaves one person besides Hinton who knew I was at the station — Domao. Could this have been an inside job? Could Domao have alerted the killer that Hinton had the file?

Chilling thoughts continued. Does this mean someone, besides Alli and me, has read my e-mail? I can't possibly crack that file, but, exclusive of the encrypted file, Carlton said there was trouble. Where was the trouble? At Taggart Memorial Hospital? If someone read my email, does that person think I'm suspicious that something at Taggart Memorial caused Chip's death?

God, he thought, there are too many Questions.

"Dr. Fisher? Are you ready for rounds?"

Fisher looked up, startled out of his deep analysis.

"Would you like to start rounds now?" Binzemore asked a second time.

For a moment, Fisher's mind was still tethered to his thoughts. He stared blankly.

Binzemore looked down at Fisher. "Dr. Peters has asked me to scrub with him on an aortic valve repair today. We have ten post-ops to see. No one is critical."

"Yes, Alan, I'm ready." Fisher rose out of the deeply cushioned chair.

Fisher and Binzemore were walking toward the knot of surgery residents and medical students when Fisher stopped.

Not quite back to reality, in his last vestige of the netherworld, one more thought flashed. "Sharon," he muttered softly under his breath. He shook his head. "Why was she important?"

He continued walking.

Sharon, Sharon. He had lost the next logical progression of his thinking. He followed behind the group headed to the Cardiac Surgery floor. Then it hit him. Not Sharon, Darren. Yes, Darren Fitzpatrick. Fisher stopped a moment, his mind racing. Darren Fitzpatrick, Sharon's father, could crack that file.

"Dr. Fisher, we're going up," Binzemore called back.

Fisher looked up. His group was on the elevator ready to ascend. He boarded the lift. He had the beginnings of a plan.

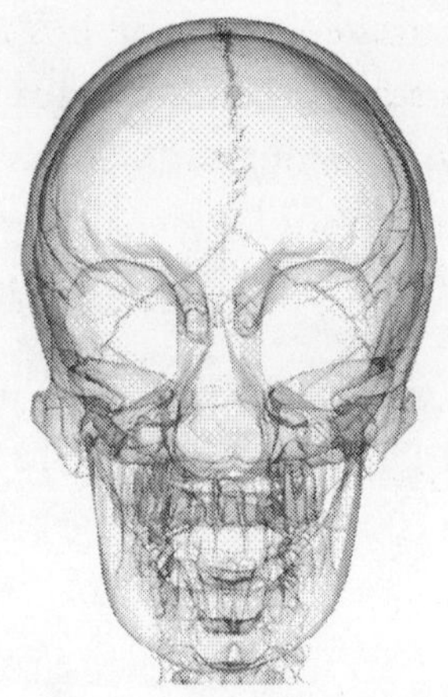

CHAPTER TWENTY-TWO

Darren Fitzpatrick could not mask the surprise in his voice when an agency assistant put Fisher's call through. Fitzpatrick's phone number was not present on any document, official or unofficial, civilian or military. Fisher found the number scribbled on a yellowed slip of paper that had been folded in his wallet for nine years.

"Darren, I need to see you, and I can't tell you what it's concerning," Fisher said.

There was a pause, when neither man spoke. Then Fitzpatrick asked the question Fisher expected, "Steve, is this concerning Sharon?"

"No, Darren. It's not. Will you have some time today when I can see you?"

"Yes, but very little," came the sharp reply.

Fisher returned to ward rounds, but he was preoccupied thinking over his analysis of the last five days. He was convinced that his movements were being monitored, if not before, they were certain to be that day.

Following rounds, he took an indirect route back to his office, where he informed Mary and Alli that he would be out of the office for the remainder of the day. He provided no explanations. "If there's an emergency, contact me by cell phone."

While Mary and Alli conversed at Mary's desk, he slipped into his office and removed another copy of the encrypted file Alli had made, taking care not to be seen. He next caught Alan Binzemore by pager as he was going into surgery and gave him the same instructions. Finally,

Fisher took a circuitous route out of the hospital to the parking deck. He walked all around the deck level where his car was parked before he approached his car. He saw no one suspicious.

He drove around the city until satisfied he wasn't being followed and then headed to Washington, DC, and Georgetown. The drive would take about two hours.

For the duration of the trip, the Mazda hummed along, Fisher was lost in thought. He continued thinking of his conversation with Domao. His indifference to Brad Hinton's murder was unexpected and it worried him. Cops usually protected cops, no matter what. That included the memory of cops. He couldn't recall a single time ever when the killing of a law enforcement agent wasn't a big deal, especially to the members of a downed agent's own police force.

Fisher changed lanes as traffic near Washington's beltway slowed. He had not made the drive in several years, but recalled a bitter taste in his mouth every time he found himself caught in the gridlock.

He fell back into thought. The other thing that struck Fisher as odd was Domao's response to Fisher's discovery of the encrypted file and his meeting with Hinton. Instead of viewing the file as a possible break in the Carlton murder case, he had become infuriated by the information. He was too interested in hustling Fisher out of the building the night before to ask the first question about Fisher's email or how he had found it.

Fisher's attention returned to the road as he discovered the reason traffic had slowed. A fender bender involving two late-model cars had tied up a lane. The owners had left their vehicles and stood by them, engaged in hand waving and finger pointing. No law enforcement had arrived, and traffic struggled to get by the two cars. Once Fisher passed the mishap, he immediately returned to his thoughts and images of Domao's sweaty face.

Anger, he thought — anger. He repeated the word several times to himself. Anger was an emotion that frequently emerged in response to a loss of control. Sometimes it was an expression of fear, the fear of losing something or fear of the unknown. From his observations, Domao was somewhat of a control freak, but the administrative hierarchy answered directly to him. So loss of control should not be that big an issue for him, Fisher thought.

Traffic flow increased, easing the driving conditions as he turned onto the George Washington Parkway.

What about fear? Why would Domao be afraid of the discovery of the encrypted message, Fisher asked himself. He pondered that thought as he entered the Parkway's weaving path. Is Domao afraid that the file might expose something he wants kept secret? Fisher continued to raise question after question, but he was convinced Domao had a purpose to his actions, and he was resolved to find out more.

The directions to the address on K Street had been perfect. He had found it without difficulty.

Fisher's mind still burst with questions as he pulled up to a gate and an adjacent wrought iron door, the sole openings through a high stucco wall at the address he had been given. The winter morning sun shone bright and clear, though changing weather conditions were predicted for later in the afternoon. Fisher did not plan to linger.

Within seconds, a young man came through the door and signaled for Fisher to roll down his window. "Good morning. I'm Agent Timmons. May I ask what your business is, Sir?" His broad shoulders filled his dark suit. Winter-white skin contrasted sharply with short, straight black hair. His face was partially obscured by dark sunglasses. Fisher guessed Agent Timmons to be in his late twenties.

"I'm Dr. Steven Fisher. Mr. Fitzpatrick is expecting me."

"Yes, Sir," Timmons responded. "May I see your driver's license, please?"

Fisher produced his recently renewed driver's license. The agent studied it carefully, looking alternately at Fisher and the license.

"Excuse me a moment, Sir," the agent said and disappeared through the wrought iron door.

Within two to three minutes, Agent Timmons returned carrying the driver's license and a clipboard. He handed Fisher the clipboard that held a blank sheet of paper, but held back the license.

"Would you please sign your name as it appears on the license, Sir?"

Fisher signed his name. The agent studied the signature.

"Do you have any weapons in the car, sir?" Timmons stared straight at Fisher through dark glasses.

Fisher thought of his glove box, where he used to carry a .38 caliber handgun, but he had removed it long before, because Sharon had complained. "I have no weapons."

"Could you step out of the car, Sir?"

The agent performed a quick, but thorough, frisk of Fisher's body, following which he engaged in a moderately thorough search of the Mazda.

"You can return to your car, Sir," the young agent said as Fisher reseated himself in his still-running car.

Timmons pulled his coat aside and grasped a rectangular transmitter hanging from his belt. Fisher could see a pistol hanging from the agent's shoulder strap.

Timmons mumbled a few words, and the heavy iron gate opened. "Pull your car over to the far right side of the parking lot, please."

As Fisher drove into the small parking lot inside the high stucco wall, his mind churned again. If there were a way to decrypt the email file, Fisher thought, Fitzpatrick would have the resource.

Fisher had never known the extent of Fitzpatrick's job. He knew what Sharon had told him, and that wasn't much. Probably because she never knew much. From the bits and pieces he had gleaned from her, he knew Fitzpatrick worked for a shadowy branch of the FBI that involved domestic US intelligence, but that was the extent of it. If Fisher's calculations were correct, Fitzpatrick would be planning retirement in the near future.

Agent Timmons stood at the end of the parking lot, which contained six or seven other cars, as Fisher got out of the Mazda. Together they walked to the brick sidewalk that led to the entrance of the classic Georgetown home. Between the high wall and the house were a huge variety of trees and shrubs. Even with its surrounding wall, the house did not stand out particularly from others along K Street. As he crossed the threshold, Fisher looked up to see a small surveillance camera, the size of a cigarette pack.

"Please hang this from your lapel and follow me, Sir."

Fisher took the laminated visitor's tag and snapped it to his lapel. He and Timmons walked down the central hallway of the Georgetown home converted to security outpost. Fisher followed straight back past a staircase with a closed door at the top of the steps. As they walked, Fisher could see former living spaces converted into offices. Computers sat on desks; copiers and Fax machines were in evidence everywhere. Men and women concentrated on their assigned tasks, not looking up as he and Agent Timmons walked past. At the end of the central hallway, Timmons stopped and knocked on a closed door.

"Come in," said a muffled voice.

Timmons inserted himself halfway through the doorway. "Sir, Dr. Fisher has arrived." Timmons then turned to Fisher and made a space for him to pass.

Sitting behind a neatly ordered desk examining an open folder was Darren Fitzpatrick. As he stood, Fisher instantly recalled always thinking that Fitzpatrick looked younger than his actual age. Nearing retirement, he looked like a man rounding into his early fifties. He was tall and slender with broad shoulders. His hair, a silvery mixture, was short, parted high over his left temple and swept to the right.

Fisher and Fitzpatrick shook hands, but the shake was short and not as engaging as past encounters had been.

"I guess you know Sharon's living with me at present." Fitzpatrick didn't take his eyes off Fisher.

"I indirectly found out last week that she vacated the house. I presumed she'd come to stay with you. She never bothered to call me." Fisher glanced briefly at the floor. "Darren, I . . . really didn't come to talk about Sharon, as I said when I called. Things have been bad between us for a long time and you and I really should talk sometime about what drove us apart. But I have an extremely pressing matter I've come to you with."

Fitzpatrick's expression didn't change.

Over the next forty minutes, Fisher filled Fitzpatrick in on the details of the last few days. In the midst of Fisher's monologue, Fitzpatrick took a pipe from its resting place on the desk and stuffed it full of tobacco. He gently applied the flame from a small lighter then rocked back, dragging on the pipe, producing small puffs of smoke.

"Darren, I suspect the information in this file played a large part in Chip Carlton's murder." Fisher reached into his coat pocket and pulled out the drive. Leaning over the desk, he handed the file to Fitzpatrick.

With the pipe clinched between his teeth, Fitzpatrick took the jump drive from Fisher. He dragged on the pipe again and exhaled a small puff of aromatic smoke into the room. He fixed his eyes on Fisher. "Steve, do you feel you're personally in danger?"

Fisher had not anticipated the question. He thought for a moment. "I don't know."

Fitzpatrick tapped the drive against his index finger eyeing Fisher a moment, then spoke. "Cryptography is a tough science. Decrypting a file like this with no key is many times virtually impossible. If Officer Hinton tried skipjack algorithms and was unsuccessful, that means the program IES doesn't incorporate Clipper Chip technology."

Fisher could feel his muscles tightened. Chip Carlton was murdered because of something he knew, something he cleverly locked inside a damn computer file that may never come to light.

"Without more to go on than you've given me, I'm afraid I can't help you."

"Wait a minute." Fisher heard the volume of his voice go up. "I've given you a great deal of information. Two men are dead now, possibly because of what's in that file."

"You have no hard proof of that. It's simply your speculation. You told me yourself Lt. Domao stated flatly that Officer Hinton lived in a crime-riddled section of Richland."

Warm blood rose into Fisher's face. "I know it sounds like speculation, but it's more than that. I have a strong gut feeling. I've been involved with this for the last few days and it's a strong feeling. Couldn't you place a few agents in Richland? Something?"

"The FBI and Central Intelligence got hit with huge budget cuts because of the budget sequester congress passed. The country's got no idea what shoestring operations we're all running because of those cuts. I think about it every day. I'm thankful to be retiring, and I look forward to it. I can guarantee that my position will be eliminated when I leave. This office will likely be closed. Besides all that, it's illegal for me to have our staff decrypt the file on this drive, when the agency's not directly involved with the case."

Fitzpatrick leaned forward, placing the pipe in a small ashtray. His eyes were focused on Fisher. "I'll hand this disk over to cryptography at Quantico with the understanding that Federal law enforcement will get involved if its contents had anything to do with Chip Carlton's murder. If the file is decrypted and it's non-specific, as I suspect it is — that is, it doesn't really put the finger on the killer — we can't intervene. The bottom line is you need solid proof, solid evidence to jump over the heads of the law enforcement in your own area."

Then Fitzpatrick stood, Fisher knew the meeting was over. The two men walked to the front door of the Georgetown outpost. Fitzpatrick shook Fisher's hand. "If you find further hard evidence, you can call me. It might change things."

While returning in the afternoon, Fisher received a call from Binzemore. He was completely lost in thought until the cell phone splintered the white noise the engine imparted.

As Fisher hung up, he was glad to be heading back to the Med for a chest trauma case. With disappointment again slapping him in the face, he knew he would find the booze in his apartment easy to return to.

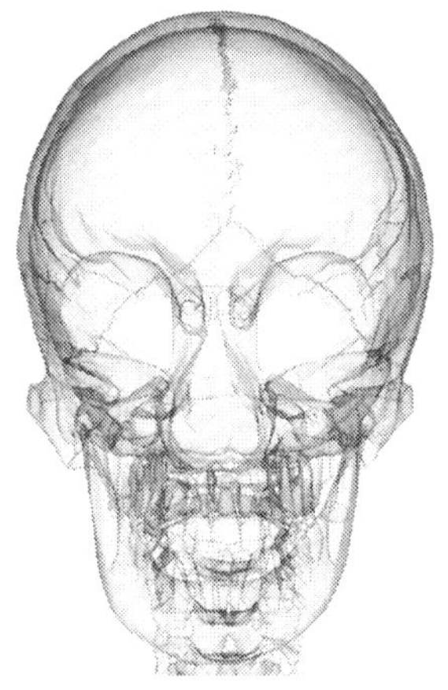

CHAPTER TWENTY-THREE

Fisher walked down the covered front walk that led to the College Inn's circular drive. Sharp images of Carlton's blood-soaked body flooded into his mind as he passed the intersection of the walkway and the drive. He stopped. Pigment from Carlton's blood was still visible. The recent events spiraled in his mind at high velocity as he stared at the place where his friend had fallen.

Fisher lingered a moment lost in thought. Finally, chilled from the damp night air, he headed for the Mazda which he had left in the lot beside the Inn. As he walked he realized his sorrow was still acute, but his pain was diminishing. Shaklein, on the other hand, remained in a state of shock. Carlton was Shaklein's favorite, his adopted son, they used to joke. He would be forever saddened.

The cold leather of the seat bit into Fisher's legs as he started the car and waited for the engine to settle into its sewing-machine rhythm. Richland weather, though cold and clear during the day, had deteriorated. The sky had become overcast and a misty fog had set in during his visit to the Inn.

The clock on the dash showed the time to be after nine. Following a possibly fruitless drive to Georgetown, he had returned to six hours of emergency open-heart surgery. He was exhausted and had trouble focusing his thoughts.

As the car warmed, Fisher looked at an envelope Shaklein had handed him before he left. "You must have dropped this the other day, Steve.

We found it during clean up today," Shaklein had said. The envelope simply had Fisher's name typed on the outside. His fatigued brain didn't remember the envelope, but anything was possible. He tossed it on the passenger seat and massaged his eyes to stop the stinging.

With the engine running smoothly, he turned onto University Drive and headed across the Caton River. Fisher realized he was leaving for home earlier than usual. Something always came up to keep him late. That night all was quiet and he had called it an early night.

In a no-contest decision, Fisher chose Talton Avenue instead of River Path Drive for the trip home. Talton flowed with few turns and required no huge expenditure of mental or physical energy. It was the more attractive option in his weary state.

Talton turned out to be hazardous. The fog and mist of the approaching storm system slowed traffic. Fisher traveled at about half his usual speed, which extended the commute to forty minutes.

His turnoff finally came into view, and he made his way carefully off Talton and navigated the two turns over dark residential streets to arrive at the lousy apartment complex he called home.

"Shit!" Fisher cursed as he came to a stop. The wash of the headlights showed the cramped, unlighted parking lot to be full.

"One space per customer, Doctor, guaranteed." He recalled the hissing words that came from Junior Broadus' beet-red, obese face the day he signed the lease. He had long since stopped calling the jerk, because none of his calls were ever returned. He was tempted to hire a lawyer to scare the worthless landlord, but it was too much trouble.

Fisher paused. His headlights glared across the lot as the Mazda engine idled. If he had ever struggled with the thought of moving back to Rosewood and letting this rat's nest go his mind was made up. The last filled space meant that the little sweetheart up in number four was having her boyfriend in for another sleep over.

"Inconsiderate shit," Fisher mumbled as he backed out of the lot and parked at the curb along the street.

He was angry, but was also exhausted. He needed sleep desperately.

He walked through the parking lot feeling his way to the middle of the three cars that faced the apartments, finally locating the sloping cement walk that inclined from the parking lot to the porch. Faint light was visible through the curtain-covered windows of two of the three second-floor apartments. Fisher's apartment, number three, at the end on the bottom right, was best accessible in darkness and inclimate weather by the front walkway directly up to the strip of porch. The porch was actually a sidewalk about five feet wide that ran in front of the first floor apartments ending just beyond Fisher's apartment. All the downstairs apartments and the walkway were in complete darkness.

Fisher headed down the porch to his apartment. As he approached number three, he reached into his pocket, retrieved his keys and sorted by feel for the proper one. Always returning at night, Fisher had developed a sense of spatial relationship where key and lock should engage. He turned to face the door and extended the key. Instead of the metallic feel of the dead bolt, he encountered empty space.

Fisher froze.

Was the door to his apartment open? He couldn't be certain. His pulse quickened, and his hands moistened.

He extended his arm an inch further, and the key encountered the wood of door.

It was open!

The contact only moved the door slightly, but caused the rusted hinges to squawk.

Almost immediately, Fisher heard rustling inside. Empty beer cans he had left on the floor of the apartment clanged together. He instantly moved to the left of the door frame. That same instinctual movement had driven him to the floor days earlier when bullets penetrated the College Inn.

An ear-splitting crash hit two feet from Fisher's right shoulder. Debris flew around him and onto the sidewalk, as the door exploded. He clung to the door frame as he jerked back further from the threshold, his mind momentarily stunned.

Beer cans clanged once again inside the apartment.

Fisher turned and sprinted down the walkway.

He had traveled less than ten feet when he heard the squawking hinges again.

Logical thoughts raced through his mind. If a bullet had blown away part of the door, another shot would soon follow, once the shooter reached the porch.

His plan of flight took shape as he ran. He could not see the sidewalk, but he knew the end was approaching and it would be his path for escape. He would jump from the porch and cut around the back of building. There he could sink into the blackness and later make it to his car.

The plan terminated before it began.

As Fisher approached the end of the porch at full sprint, his foot struck a planter pot by apartment number one. He tripped and fell forward into the blackness. The distance to the ground was a couple of feet, but it felt like an endless free fall.

"Oomph." The air rushed from his chest as he sprawled on the ground.

Thump. Thump.

Muffled noises arose from the direction of the porch followed by two loud pops overhead as two slugs impacted the magnolia tree a few feet above his body. Fisher stayed still and flattened against the ground near the tree.

The pot had saved his life, he thought as he took stock of his injuries. Although a bed of waxy leaves lay under the magnolia, he had sustained abrasions when he fell. His hands and knees were on fire and he quietly spit dirt. His mouth had also contacted the ground.

Fisher raised his head enough to see what lay around him. The side of the apartment building was pitch black. He was thankful it lay close to the street. He instantly discarded the idea of rushing to the back of the building. It would be a dead end.

He looked to the street where he had parked his car. The Mazda was a ghostly image some forty feet away. Fisher considered alternatives as he listened for footsteps that would indicate the shooter's approach.

No sound. No movement.

He settled on plan B, to make it to his car. That would be his last chance. Shifting his weight slightly, he became aware of a new problem. The bed of dry magnolia leaves that cushioned his fall also made noise when he moved. It was a problem he was pondering when the silence was broken.

The door to apartment number four upstairs opened. Heavy footsteps sounded overhead.

"Who the fuck's out there?"

It was the voice of number four's boyfriend. The son of a bitch who took the last parking spot sauntered noisily out onto the upstairs walkway and leaned over the railing.

Fisher knew he had to move now. He jumped to his feet, trying not to rustle the magnolia leaves, but that was impossible. As he ran to the parking lot, everywhere he stepped, leaves cracked loudly.

"Who's there, goddamn it?" the male voice boomed from above. "I'm coming down there, you little shit."

Fisher's heart raced as he sprinted down the small strip of lawn to the parking lot, where his feet crunched on pea-sized gravel.

From the sidewalk in front of his apartment, new shots thumped from the would-be killer's weapon.

Three feet from Fisher's shoulder, the windshield of a parked car shattered as the bullet slammed into it.

"Hey, that's my goddamn car." Number four's boyfriend shrieked as he heard the glass shatter.

Fisher ran at full speed. The faint image of the Mazda was a few feet ahead.

Thump. Thump.

More shots, but no impact. Fisher figured the shots had gone wild.

Breathless, he reached the Mazda. In his right hand, he still gripped the key originally intended for his dead bolt. He crouched, fumbling for the key hole below the car's door handle. But it took an eternity.

"Shit," he whispered.

Finally, he stabbed the key into the lock, turned it and fell into the still-warm interior.

In seconds, he had the engine started. Tires squealed and the engine gave a throaty whine as he accelerated away from the apartments.

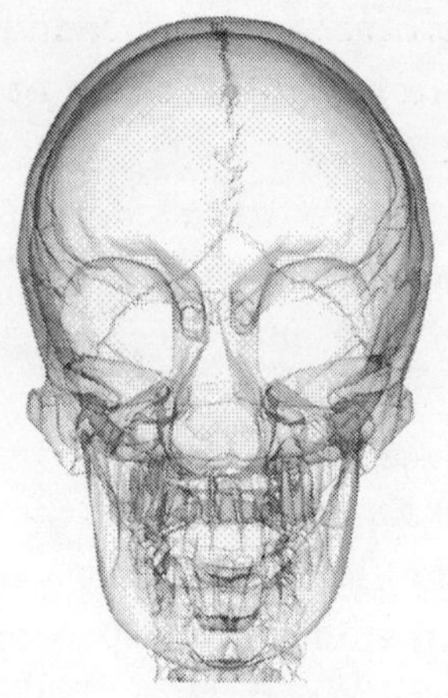

CHAPTER TWENTY-FOUR

Exhaustion, a doctor's constant adversary, had driven Fisher home to sleep, but that had vanished completely. His mind was fully alert as he raced away from the apartments.

He headed toward River Path Drive, putting as much distance as possible between himself and the intruder.

"Jesus," Fisher screamed above the engine sounds, realizing how close he had come to death. Whoever he surprised had not expected him to return at such an early hour, and using a silenced pistol definitely took the break-in out of the cat-burglar category.

A maze of residential streets bordered River Path Drive requiring frequent turns and slow speeds, which made Fisher nervous. However, the road was not the top item on his thinking agenda. His mind searched for answers.

Who, he asked himself, as he maneuvered the Mazda.

Who would know my usual schedule, and who would want to search that dump? Who would want to shoot at me? Kill me?

Headlights burst into the rearview mirror, causing Fisher to squint. The mirror then went dark again as Fisher negotiated a familiar, lazy turn around one of the old grandiose estates that dotted the landscape along the river. The turn signaled the final approach to River Path Drive.

The high beams reappeared. Fisher glanced briefly at the mirror again. The gap between the two cars had closed as the car behind him approached at high speed. A splinter of fear sneaked into Fisher's mind as the unknown car approached. The upcoming intersection with River Path Drive demanded that he brake. Under the circumstances, he had no choice but to reduce his speed.

If any question existed as to who was in the rapidly approaching car, it vaporized as Fisher slowed for the turn.

Crash! The right half of the rear windshield exploded.

Fisher ducked involuntarily as glass fragments flew into the car. The Mazda swerved right as Fisher lowered his head. He looked up from his hunched-over position in time to yank the steering wheel hard to the left, barely avoiding a collision with the embankment.

Fisher's heart raced. His hands moistened as adrenaline surged through his body.

He downshifted and punched hard on the accelerator, the powerful engine never sputtering as it surged onto the tortuous roadway. As he moved away from the intersection, Fisher saw through the broken glass that the car had pulled onto River Path Drive.

Cold, wet air rushed in through the hole in the rear windshield. The car's rapidly cooling interior added to Fisher's worry and fright, but he kept his attention riveted on the road. He knew River Path Drive well, but the roadway was treacherous at night. Matters were made worse as the headlights reflected off the mist and fog, reducing the already poor visibility.

The Mazda howled as he shifted down to enter an upcoming turn. Sensing a new light, Fisher glanced in the rearview mirror and froze for a second. The car behind him had approached so fast that its headlights filled the mirror, briefly blinding him.

Fisher directed his attention back to the road. Halfway into the turn, the chase car crashed into his rear bumper, pushing him wide. Fisher pulled hard on the steering wheel to stay on the road.

Another nervous glance into the rearview mirror. Fisher saw for the first time the vague outline of the car pursuing him. Though he only captured a glimpse, the car appeared to be a large, late model.

He shifted quickly and accelerated away from the turn.

The car pursued closely.

The old road twisted sharply right then switched back left again as it clung to the rugged landscape created by the Caton River which rushed along its crooked path more than one hundred feet below.

During the day, given clear visibility, a race down River Path Drive would be more frightening, by the view of what waited below. In places, the riverbed was a straight descent off the roadway, with only cables strung between wooden posts to prevent a car from descending the hillside to the water below. That night mist and fog limited visibility to a few feet beyond the headlights, but Fisher knew what was out there.

Another turn and another bone-jarring impact from the chase car. Luck and extreme effort kept Fisher's car from flying out of control.

He downshifted and crushed the accelerator to the floor. His wet hands shook from fear. He went through three more sharp turns. Each time he decelerated to turn, the high-beam lights surged behind him, filling his rearview mirror. Then the collision would come.

As Fisher frantically negotiated another corner, a thought bubbled into his consciousness. No shots had been fired since the first turn onto River Path Drive. The driver must be alone, Fisher thought, and is as preoccupied with the turns on the roadway as I am. If there were a passenger in the car, he would have been firing.

As Fisher continued twisting and turning down River Path Drive, a horrifying thought emerged. A straight road meant renewed firing. He cringed at the thought. The roadway would soon straighten as it flowed into Richland. He would become an easy target.

He was running out of time.

There were three turns left before Indian Promontory. The road became tame after the Promontory, and his chances of escaping would drop to nil.

Fisher's mind raced as he struggled to formulate some plan of escape. He knew the road well. That was his sole advantage. But what could he do?

He shifted down and pulled the steering wheel hard to negotiate the next turn.

"Left hand turn, right hand turn, left hand turn," he mumbled aloud, thinking over the road that remained before Indian Promontory.

Crash. The Mazda sustained another serious blow. The driver had surged forward, striking the right half of the rear bumper as Fisher went to exit the turn.

Fisher glanced at his hands. He didn't need illumination to know that his knuckles were white. He gripped the steering wheel so tightly there could not have been an ounce of blood in his fingers.

Two turns remained: one right, one left. Then a one-hundred-fifty to two-hundred yard straight-away to Indian Promontory. The Promontory was the last and sharpest turn of River Path Drive.

"The sharpest turn," Fisher uttered aloud.

Indian Promontory was a virtual hairpin, one-hundred-eighty degrees. It was the highest point of the roadway.

Fisher knew it was his last chance.

He slowed and shifted down again as he went through the right hand turn ahead of his pursuer. He accelerated out of the turn before the trailing car had a chance to smash him again.

This was it, Fisher thought. One left hand turn and then the Promontory. His mind sped along as he peered through the foggy mist.

The kernel of a plan began to form. Fisher knew he had to do something radically different. He had to throw the driver off balance. He needed a distraction.

The last turn approached fast as Fisher kept his distance from the car. He pushed the clutch in and down-shifted to start the turn.

Out of the recesses of his mind a voice called: *You're too far away.*

In the middle of the turn, with the pursuer's car bearing down from behind, Fisher did the unexpected. He jammed hard on the brakes, bringing the car to a near stop. The tires gave a low-pitched squeal on the damp pavement.

Fisher pressed himself firmly into the head rest and awaited the crash.

The driver was unprepared. As Fisher had hoped, the large car crashed directly into the rear end of the Mazda.

Fisher was shaken, but not stunned by the anticipated blow.

Totally focused, Fisher released the battered sports car's clutch. With power yet untapped, the Mazda raced out of the turn.

Glancing in the rearview mirror, Fisher saw the chase car roll out of the turn slowly. He hoped the unexpected crash had angered the chaser. He counted on that anger to train the driver's mind on his prey. He wanted his tail lights to command the assailant's total attention.

The road approaching the Promontory was the longest straight-away of River Path Drive up to that point. The roadway was deceptive, however. The single indication of the upcoming hairpin turn was a small rectangular sign sunk into the hillside off to the right.

The sign, to Fisher's relief, was partially obscured by branches from overhanging trees limbs.

Fisher accelerated hard, pushing the engine up through the gears; a crescendo of sound burst forth at each stage.

For the turn at the Promontory, Fisher planned to slow his car by down-shifting. Touching the brake pedal would ignite the brake lights, tipping off the driver rushing up behind him.

The Promontory approached.

Fisher could feel the hair on his neck bristle long before he reached the danger zone.

There it was! The start of the turn was barely twenty yards away.

At the last possible second, Fisher punched the clutch and wrenched the small car down into first gear. The transmission emitted a loud grinding noise, but the synchronizers engaged. He pulled right on the steering wheel as he released the clutch. The chase car's headlights approached the back of the Mazda at high speed as Fisher decelerated.

The plan was working.

The rearview mirror, ablaze from the pursuer's headlights, was the last thing Fisher saw before he skidded clockwise on the wet pavement.

Fisher's car rotated about two hundred-seventy degrees sliding off the road and onto the thin shoulder of gravel before coming to a stop just short of plunging over the side. His engine stalled.

All was quiet.

His headlights, still blazing, pointed back in the direction of the hairpin curve.

Fisher still held the steering wheel with a death grip, waiting for the car to appear in the headlights. There was no one.

Nothing.

Finally, he loosened his grip and slowly opened the door. His heart pounded as he stood. The abrasion on his knee burned as he straightened his leg.

There was no car. The only sounds he heard were those coming up from the Caton River as it flowed below.

Fisher walked to the pavement in the middle of the hairpin turn. He saw no skid marks. An eerie feeling came over him as he inspected the area bathed in a strange half illumination produced by the mist.

Then, out of the corner of his eye, he saw it. He walked onto the narrow gravel shoulder. Just beyond the edge, a section of the cabling was torn loose.

Fisher stood quietly for a moment, staring at the break in the barrier. He walked to the edge of the black abyss, the sounds of the river and the mist flooded his senses. There were no signs of a car and no fire. No other sounds besides the rushing water of the Caton could be heard.

When a cold, wet breeze whipped across the Promontory, Fisher turned and walked back to the Mazda sitting quietly half off the pavement. He inspected the rear of the car. The old Mazda had survived, but it looked a wreck. The bumper and trunk had been smashed badly by the repeated bashings and the rear windshield had a one-foot hole above the trunk on the far right side.

He turned and looked back at the hairpin turn of Indian Promontory. Since he had stopped there to pull himself from the jaws of a hangover a few days earlier, a great deal had occurred.

Fisher glanced at his watch. It was eleven-thirty. He had been awake for more that twenty-one hours. At the outset of the evening, he had been tired, but after the two-hour ordeal, all signs of fatigue had evaporated.

He started to sit down in the Mazda but stopped. An object in the driver side foot well caught his attention. It was the envelope Shaklein had given him during his stop by the College Inn. The blast of air from the hole in the rear windshield had blown it from its resting place on the passenger seat. Fisher reached down and hauled the envelope up. Earlier, intense fatigue had caused him to ignore it. He tore it open.

Every muscle in Fisher's body froze. He stood motionless and silent unaware of the icy wind flowing across the Promontory.

"My god," he said, his voice muffled by the wind.

In the half-light Fisher held a jump drive. He slowly raised it to get a better look.

"This is what they wanted."

"Chip, you son-of-a-bitch! You son-of-a-bitch!"

Fisher stuffed the drive into his pocket and ran to the rear of the car. He inserted the key in the trunk, but opening it took some doing.

Finally, though badly out of shape, the trunk lid opened with a crack. Fisher reached in and grabbed his briefcase. He stooped to the ground, opened the hard shelled case and took out a small spiral pad. He closed the brief case, placed it back in the trunk and slammed the warped lid almost shut. It would need work, if it were ever to close right again, he thought.

Fisher walked around the car in front of the headlights and opened the spiral notebook to the first page where he had copied important numbers.

He stepped back into the automobile and pulled the cell phone from his coat. He punched the keypad seven times and waited. After five or six rings, a male voice answered. "Hello," the voice said.

"May I speak to Alli Shepard?"

"Uh, sure."

"Alli, phone."

Alli's voice came on the line. "Hello?"

"This is Steve Fisher. I've got some new information. Could we get together?"

There was a pause.

"Uh, okay. Shall I meet you, Dr. Fisher?"

"No. Didn't you say you had a computer at home?"

"Well, sure. Isn't it awfully late?"

Fisher was quiet.

"Oh, I'm sorry," she broke in before he could reply. "Sure you can come over. My address is . . . ."

"No," Fisher stopped her. "Don't give it to me now. I will call you back."

"Well, uh, okay," said a bewildered Alli.

Fisher clicked off the cell phone and placed it on the seat beside him.

He started the car, pulled it back onto the roadway and headed toward Richland.

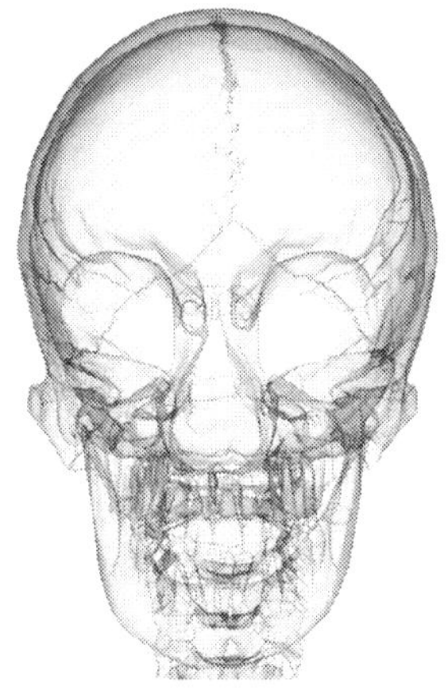

CHAPTER TWENTY-FIVE

Fisher drove the remaining leg of River Path Drive at legal speed, but found himself glancing into the rearview mirror searching for signs of headlights coming out of the black mist. There were none. He found a pay phone outside an all-night market and called Binzemore to inform him he would be away for a few days.

"But, what if I need . . . ."

"Dr. Peters will handle any problems while I'm gone. Just tell him I have a family problem," Fisher lied.

"Whatever you say, Dr. Fisher," a confused Binzemore said on the other end of the line.

Fisher dialed Alli for directions. He hung up and walked into the market.

Preoccupied by a replay of the last two hours, Fisher failed to notice the questioning glances from the check-out clerk and two patrons as they looked at his torn clothing. He poured black coffee, paid and headed for the east side of Richland, following Alli's directions.

After midnight, Fisher drove past Alli's address without stopping. Two blocks away, he parallel parked between a car and an old delivery truck along a dark section without a street light.

As he walked away he turned and looked at his car in the subdued light. The Mazda had taken a beating. He stepped onto the sidewalk and walked briskly.

Alli lived in a row house typical of those found on the east end of Richland. Early in the twentieth century, neighborhoods had sprung up around three fabric mills on the city's east side. The area remained populated mostly by blue collar workers. The neighborhood around Alli's residence was clean and the houses well kept. The area's location more than twenty blocks away from hot spots for illegal drug sales probably made it safe.

The house was small, one story and boxy. A postage stamp yard rose up about five feet off street level.

Fisher climbed the steps into the yard. Within a moment after he rang the doorbell, a young man appeared behind the door's cloth-covered oval window.

"Yes?" the young man said.

"I'm Steven Fisher. Alli Shepard is expecting me."

Alli walked up behind the young man. "This is Dr. Fisher, Gary. It's okay."

The young man turned three dead bolt locks in succession and opened the door.

Fisher spoke first. "I'm sorry for coming so late. I . . . ."

Alli interrupted. "Dr. Fisher, what happened? Are you all right?" Alli's gaze traveled the length of Fisher's torso.

For the first time since leaving the College Inn, Fisher looked down at his clothing. The right lapel of his sport coat was torn and soiled. His right pant leg had a one-inch tear at the knee.

She pointed to a scrape on Fisher's right cheek. "Your face. Are you hurt?"

Fisher glanced up from his brief inspection and for a moment stood without speaking. His mind ticked forward.

Finally, he made up his mind.

"Alli, I've got to speak with you. I apologize again for the hour of my visit."

"It's no problem, Dr. Fisher. This was a late night for us anyway."

Fisher turned to look at the young man standing next to Alli.

"Oh. Please forgive me." Alli stepped back and placed her hand on the young man's shoulder. "This is my brother, Gary Shepard."

Gary was an inch taller than his sister. He had an athletic physique with a broad chest and defined muscular arms that filled his faded T-shirt.

His blue eyes were covered by wire-rim glasses and a shock of blond hair stuck out in random directions.

Gary immediately stuck out his hand and shook Fisher's with a firm grip.

"Gary's in his second year at Medford University undergraduate."

"That's great, Gary," Fisher said. "Things are going well, I hope?"

"Yes, they are, thank you." The young man spoke softly.

Alli said, "I've told Gary your position at the University, and he knows you and I have been working together."

Gary excused himself, saying he would be in the basement for a while before going to bed.

"Would you care to wash off your face?" Alli asked.

"Thanks, but no."

"You look exhausted. Please come inside." She motioned to the overstuffed chair in the corner of the small living room.

Fisher eased into the chair. For the first time that night he realized how tired he was.

"Gary and I live here alone. Mother died three years ago and now it's just the two of us."

"I'm very sorry. And your father?"

"He died when I was ten. Gary was a year old at the time. We don't remember much about him. Mother always told us he wanted to be a doctor, but he never made it."

Silence followed as Fisher gathered his thoughts. He slowly surveyed the modestly furnished front room. Sparse furniture surrounded a small fireplace with gray ashes from a previous fire. On the mantel, an antique clock ticked softly. Beside the clock stood a photograph of Alli and her brother, both much younger. Standing between them was an attractive woman with blond hair, presumably their mother. The woman had her arms draped across the shoulders of the two children. Fisher studied the photograph, then he looked directly into Alli's eyes. He did not speak immediately. He was struggling with the advisability of revealing potentially dangerous information. He didn't want to pull her into the maelstrom that was escalating around him.

Finally, Fisher broke the silence. "Alli, someone tried to kill me tonight."

Alli's face paled. She looked mystified. "Why? Is this concerning Dr. Carlton's email file?"

He was relieved to have someone to talk to. Over the next half hour, he described what had happened after they discovered the encrypted file.

Alli was speechless.

Fisher leaned back in the chair, a feeling of relief flooding through his body. He closed his eyes, which burned from lack of sleep. Not two weeks ago he would have looked for a stiff drink during a crisis like this, but swigging booze was the farthest thing from his mind. Got to stay clear-headed he thought.

Nothing had changed as a result of his half hour monologue. In fact, the level of danger was probably higher. He turned back to look at Alli. She stared intently at the floor. For the first time, he was struck by her beauty. Her wavy chestnut colored hair usually pulled back straight and tight, hung loose and unbrushed, draping down her back and shoulders. Her figure, usually obscured by a white clinic coat and loose-fitting dresses, was accentuated by tight-fitting jeans and a sweater. The scent of perfume was present.

He rested his head back.

"I . . ., I don't know what to say," she said, breaking the silence.

Fisher's eyes, stinging from loss of sleep, had closed momentarily. He opened them, straightened himself in the chair and snapped alert. Virtually all of his work as a surgeon demanded that sleep come as a secondary consideration, behind the business at hand. He had long since become accustomed to sleep deprivation.

"Who else in the Richland Police Department do you know? If you suspect Lt. Domao is behind some of this, then where can we go for help?"

Fisher instantly caught Alli's use of the word "*we*." He turned and faced her as she sat up from her slumped position. Her deep blue eyes focused on his.

"Alli you can't get involved with this. Someone tried to kill me tonight, and it's for damn well sure there'll be others before I can get to the proper authorities. It's too risky. You and your brother could be killed. Somebody out there thinks I've got damaging information, and they're going to do anything they can to stop me from revealing it."

"I understand but, right now you need help. From what you just told me, do you think it's safe to return to the hospital, to your apartment? Do you feel safe even going to the Richland police station? If you think Lt. Domao is somehow involved with this, could there be others in the Richland Police Department who are involved in whatever this is?"

Fisher closed his stinging eyes again.

"What about your father-in-law?"

His forehead wrinkled before he started massaging it.

"Darren and I used to get along great while things were going right with Sharon, but over the past year, he's become distant. My visit to Washington was no exception. I'm sure Sharon's filled his brain with lies to support the illusion that I was the reason the marriage fell apart."

Fisher looked at Alli through tired, reddened eyes. Again, a few moments passed with no words spoken.

"Alli, I'm sorry to have told you all this, but I needed to tell someone. I have got to think things through."

"It's okay." She placed her hand lightly on his forearm.

The antique clock over the fireplace made a muted sound as it ticked, and then it chimed twice.

Fisher reached into his coat pocket. "This jump drive probably explains a lot about what's been happening. If I were a gambler, I'd bet it's the key to Chip Carlton's encrypted email file."

Alli's face lit up with surprise. "What's that?"

"This may tell us why Chip was killed. Wallace Shaklein handed it to me earlier saying it was found at the College Inn. It was in an envelope with my name typed on a label.

Alli shifted nervously on the sofa.

"You said you had a home computer." Fisher closed his eyes and leaned back. He desperately wanted to know the contents of the unmarked jump drive, but he was exhausted.

Alli smiled. "Yes, we have a computer."

She stood and glanced at the kitchen, where Gary had disappeared an hour earlier.

"Dr. Fisher, don't you think . . .?" Alli stopped mid-sentence as she looked back at Fisher. He had fallen asleep. She covered him with a knitted afghan from the sofa and switched off the table lamp. The drive would have to wait.

•••••

February 6

The delicate arms on the clock face displayed the time at seven-thirty. Gray light filtered into the living room through drawn curtains. As he sat upright in the chair, Fisher rubbed his eyes. The burning had gone, but he was not yet fully awake. The aroma of freshly perked coffee filled the living room. Looking through the small dining room to the kitchen, he could see Alli at work.

She caught sight of him, and then disappeared, returning moments later carrying a cup. "How are you feeling?" Alli handed him the cup.

"Thanks." Fisher ran his fingers through his unkempt hair and sipped the hot, black liquid. Its effects were almost immediate. "I'm fine. Sorry I crashed on you."

"It's quite all right, Dr. Fisher. You were in no shape to go anywhere."

Fisher looked up at Alli. She had returned her hair to the familiar tight pony tail that fully displayed her fair complexion. She wore a bulky blue sweater over faded jeans.

"Do you think you could call me Steve?"

"Why . . . sure," Alli said, not really sounding sure. "If you're hungry, I fixed some breakfast."

"That sounds really good right now."

"I hope you don't mind, but Gary pulled your car into our garage shortly after you fell asleep. I was afraid it would draw attention. This neighborhood is very tight-knit and someone would call the police. You were right. It's in awful shape."

Fisher smiled, feeling a growing admiration for the woman's intelligence and beauty.

"Thanks. I haven't seen it in the daylight, but I can imagine how it looks." Fisher stood.

After breakfast, he showered and shaved with a disposable razor Gary provided. He felt human again as he walked back into the living room where Alli and Gary sat reading the Saturday morning paper. A gray morning had come in the wake of rainy conditions the night before. The living room curtains were drawn and the room required a table light.

Alli looked up as Fisher entered the room. "I thought it better to leave the curtains drawn to keep prying eyes out."

Fisher had become greatly impressed by Alli's intuition, almost since their first meeting the night of Carlton's murder. He headed for his tattered sport coat, where he retrieved the unmarked jump drive. "You said last night you had a computer here. Could you examine this drive?"

Alli exchanged glances with her brother. They both grinned.

Alli said, "Let's go down to the basement."

Fisher followed them through the kitchen and down a flight of steps that led by the garage, where he presumed his beat-up Mazda was housed, and into the basement. The basement was unfinished and was much cooler than the first floor. It spanned the entire length and width of the house. Brick columns stationed at frequent intervals broke up the space, giving a partitioned effect. A washer, dryer and utility sink sat adjacent to an old workbench on the left as they walked through. Fisher followed a few steps behind Alli as they came into an open area. A thick oriental rug was on the floor. An old sofa sat a comfortable distance from a large flat screen TV. As he scanned the area, Fisher gulped in amazement.

Gary was seating himself at a large table loaded with a sophisticated array of computer hardware. Fisher looked at Alli.

"I guess you do have a home computer," he said sheepishly.

Alli looked at her brother and smiled. "Gary is majoring in computer sciences at Medford, but he's been a computer geek for years. In computerese, Gary would be considered a serious chip head."

Gary turned from the monitor screen with a grin. "Hey — Sis I resent that remark."

Alli retorted, "It was meant as a compliment, Gary. Besides, how many nineteen-year olds have over 350 friends on Facebook?"

"I'll be twenty next week," Gary corrected.

Alli pointed to several metallic boxes on the floor by the table. Each box measured about ten inches in thickness and two feet in depth rising about three feet off the floor. Cables of differing thicknesses and lengths interconnected virtually everything in sight. "Gary, want to tell Dr. Fisher about your project?"

"Sure. I'm created my own social media site. It's called The Richland Express. It's small by Facebook standards, but I've only had it going for about a year. All calls come into my network by way of these three main nodes." He pointed to the gray boxes. "I have four phone lines dedicated to The Express. The Express runs twenty-four hours a day. I've got about four thousand subscribers from around the region who regularly use The Express."

"I guess this is a real cyberspace family," Fisher said, grinning.

Gary reached up. "Let's see what you've got, Dr. Fisher."

Fisher handed him the drive.

The young man examined it. "Twenty megabyte drive," he mumbled as he pushed the drive into a USB port in one of the gray boxes.

No more than ten seconds passed, but to Fisher it crawled by like hours. His pulse quickened in anticipation. Finally a window appeared on the screen. Fisher could feel his hands becoming cool and moist.

"There are two files on the drive," Gary said. "There's a small one entitled Readme, and a large program file named IES.EXE."

Fisher's mouth suddenly turned dry. He looked at Alli. Her gaze was glued to the screen. She showed the same excitement and fear.

"Is it the program Chip Carlton used to encrypt the email file?" Fisher asked nervously.

Gary shook his head. "I don't understand which email file you are referring to, but . . . ."

"It'll get clearer as we go along," Alli said. She turned to Fisher. "Is that okay?"

"We need his help. Please continue, Gary."

Gary still looked confused as he clicked on the icon entitled "Readme." For a moment, the monitor screen went blank, then became white again. A single line of text appeared on the screen

Chief's Date of Hire and First Heart

Everyone studied the text.

Alli asked, "Is that all there is or are there other pages in the file?"

"No," Gary responded, "There's nothing else."

Fisher racked his brain. What could he be telling me, he asked himself as frustration crept in? He stared at the text. The only sound in the chilly basement came from the large hard disk drives whining inside Gary's computers.

Fisher stepped back and walked the space between the old sofa and the computer hardware. He always paced when he worked through problems with no clear answers. An image of Carlton's impish smile passed fleetingly through his mind.

No, Fisher told himself. No, I can't think of Chip. I can only think of why Chip had sent this message, this statement. Why?

After several more paces, Fisher stopped. He turned and faced Alli and Gary. "I may have an idea." He walked back to the table. "Chip was making two statements, not one."

Gary had a question mark written across his face and was obviously confused, but he said nothing.

Fisher continued. "Brad Hinton told me the IES program was tough to crack because of its design. He said it took two keys. One key encrypted the message, and the second key decrypted it."

Gary spoke. "Actually, several people who subscribe to the Richland Express have asked whether I'd consider using a program to permit users to encrypt their messages. I've been reluctant to do it, but, on the Internet, it's pretty common. About a year ago, I looked at what was out there. The two-key system you're referring to has become the most popular. Alli, what program did Darby Software use?"

"It was a two-key system. Our downloaded files were immediately decrypted, so we didn't know the keys, but I think Darby used a number sequence."

"Wait! That's it, that's it!" Fisher said. "Brad Hinton said most two-key systems were based on prime numbers. One number, the product of two secret numbers, was public knowledge. The public number let people encrypt a message. The two secret numbers would decrypt the message."

Three sets of eyes returned to the single line of text on the monitor screen.

"Date of hire. They're dates," said Gary. "And they're expressed as prime numbers. But who is chief?"

"It's me," Fisher said. "I was Chip Carlton's chief for five years before he left Medford University."

Alli turned to Fisher, "Then he's referring to the date you hired on at the Med?"

"Chip Carlton always poked fun at what he called my double jinx."

Both Alli and Gary looked lost.

"During training in cardiac transplant, I performed my first solo transplant on Friday, the thirteenth of July, nineteen ninety-nine. Two years later on Friday, the thirteenth of July, 2001, I became a faculty member at Medford University.

"That would put the two numbers as 71399 and 71301." Alli's voice carried a tone of excitement.

"Let's try it," Gary burst out. "I'll load the program file from the drive. Does anyone have the encrypted file?"

"There's a copy of the email file in my briefcase. It was in the trunk of my car," Fisher said.

Fisher went with Alli to the garage. When they returned, Gary had opened the IES program. The monitor screen displayed a simple message.

Insert Private Keys:

1) ___________

2) ___________

Gary took the drive containing the encrypted file from Fisher and placed it in another USB port. He typed the numbers 71399 and 71301 into the spaces. All were tense as the program next asked for the file to be decrypted. Gary indicated the file Fisher had given him. Within seconds, what had formerly been a mass of chaotic symbols became a clear message.

Dear Steve — I'm writing this note from my lap top uplinked by trans-star to the MedNet. If you have deciphered the note it means the key successfully made it to Wally. I will drop it into the mail as soon as I'm finished. I am doing this because I've recently gotten threats and I wanted to make sure the information makes it intact to someone in case something happens to me.

I suspected things were funny at Taggart back in November when the number of transplants we were doing was staying extremely high. You know how seasonal organ supply can be, and there's an inevitable down turn after the warmer months are over. We did 46 hearts from Sept first until Thanksgiving. What's more, I never saw OrganLink personnel around. Not one single time.

"What's OrganLink?" asked Gary.

"It's the regional organ procurement organization. They allocate organs according to lottery priority," Fisher said.

"I see. Does that mean all hospitals have to get their organs through OrganLink?"

"Exactly. Across the U.S., there are about one hundred-fifty agencies like OrganLink. They all work under a parent organization called UNOS, the United Network for Organ Sharing."

Gary turned back to the screen and clicked "page down." The three read on:

I asked other transplant surgeons if they thought the numbers were high, but they just smiled, slapped me on the back and told me to lay back and enjoy it. I asked Harry Talbott why there were never any procurement representatives from OrganLink around. He said that Health Pursuit had removed the burden of paperwork from the docs and for me not to worry.

One night after finishing a transplant, I was walking out to the doctor's parking lot when I noticed a large number of vans and other utility vehicles parked in front of the outpatient surgery center. I still had my scrubs on, so I went over to check it out. I followed two guys I had never seen before down to the doctor's locker room. I slipped into a utility closet and listened. The two men were talking about transporting the week's shipment. One guy said his cargo had to go quickly because it came in from overseas. The other guy laughed, saying his cargo was taken locally and he wasn't in a hurry.

Then one of the TMH security guards came into the locker room and rushed them out, telling them

> they had to prepare for security clearance before they could leave the building. I was worried about being seen, so I left the locker room and looked for a back entrance. A fat guy chewing a cigar caught sight of me. I turned the corner and ran to the back of the building, but I couldn't find an exit.
>
> At the far end of the building, I came to a dead end but saw a room labeled No Admittance. It had a card slide lock. I used my TMH Doctor's card, and my TMH Doctor's ID#, and the door opened. I got in just in time to hear voices. It was the fat guy. I could hear him wheezing. Cigar smoke came under the door.

"Domao," Fisher said. "The night I worked with Hinton, the night he was killed, he said Domao had two jobs. Now we know which company he works security for. Taggart Memorial Hospital."

He resumed reading.

> After the voices left, I flipped on the light. It was a small room, and it was weird. There was a large console with multicolored buttons. Next to the console was some sort of chamber that held a pair of gloves and a hood. Coming off the hood and the gloves were some connecting wires. The console was dark, but I could see the word telepresence on two rows of four buttons. I waited awhile, listening outside to be sure the voices had gone. I was just about to leave when I noticed a green ledger book on top of the console. Inside were one hundred eighty names or partial names with listings of various organs (pancreas, liver, kidney, skin, lung). I took the ledger, opened the door and slipped out. I finally found a back way out. I hid the ledger at the house. I don't know what all this means, but I plan to speak with Harry Talbott about the ledger today – Sincerely, Chip

Fisher stared silently at the last portion of the message. Gary fidgeted in his chair but said nothing. The deciphered email message was the last communication from a murder victim. Finally, Alli turned to Fisher. "Steve, this has got to go to the police. What Dr. Carlton stumbled onto at Taggart Memorial was probably the reason he was murdered."

"This can't go to the Richland police. It's right there in Chip's message — Lt. Domao of the Richland police is involved with whatever is going on over there. That description of the cigar smoking security cop. It's Domao. If Domao's involved, there may be others. Going to the Richland police would be too risky."

"Your father-in-law, then."

"He said they needed solid proof before they could do anything. They can't just roll into town and raid Taggart Memorial Hospital on the basis of an email message. We need proof and a good start would be that ledger Chip found."

"From Dr. Carlton's house?"

"Yes."

"But you said the house was searched. Ransacked."

"It was. The house was a wreck, but I've got to search it again. Maybe they didn't find the ledger."

"Well," Gary said, wearing his sly smile, "Maybe I can help. If Taggart Memorial has its own central computer intranet, maybe I should slip in and take a look around. Never can tell what we might run across."

"Is there a chance you'll get caught?" Fisher asked.

Gary grinned again and simply said, "My friends call me the invisible man."

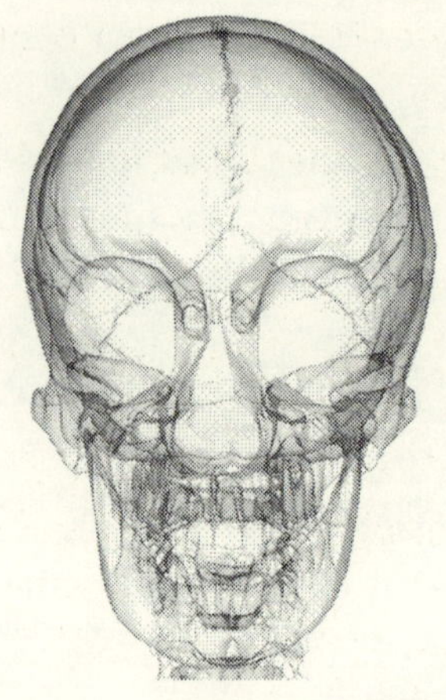

CHAPTER TWENTY-SIX

February 7

Practically since leaving Richland's east side, Fisher had wrestled with the heater in Alli's old Chevy Cavalier. The defroster refused to share warm air with the floor vents, which meant that a clear windshield came at the expense of ice cold feet. Struggling behind the wheel, Alli didn't seem to notice the chill as she concentrated on the road, but Fisher did. He finally gave up, took the shoe off his foot and rubbed it for warmth. As he rubbed, his mind sifted through the events of the last few hours. In the basement of the Shepard house, further discussion had occurred after the email file was deciphered. Gary heard the entire story from the beginning. He asked intelligent questions and it was clear he understood the danger of the situation. Like his sister, he was quick to join the effort to solve the mystery of Chip Carlton's death. Fisher hadn't asked Gary what he meant by the invisible man comment, but he could guess.

The windshield wipers beat like two enormous metronomes as they swept aside the wet snow that had been falling since the trip began. Heavy salting by city trucks and temperatures that stopped dropping at the freezing point had prevented significant accumulation, but Alli complained that driving was treacherous. From the passenger side of the car, Fisher agreed. Twice on the way to the Chaparral development, the small car had fish-tailed, almost skidding out of control. Alli's quick response had avoided an accident.

Fisher flipped on the flashlight and looked at his watch. It was after midnight. He expected the roads to worsen, despite the salting, but he had no choice — he had to find the ledger Chip Carlton had found. Fisher was convinced of its importance. That same conviction had sent them out in deteriorating weather to search for it.

"Is that the entrance?" Alli's words pulled Fisher out of his thoughts.

Fisher looked through the blowing white flakes that reflected off the Cavalier's headlights. Two imposing brick columns that stood at the entrance to the development had come into view.

"Yes." Fisher pulled his shoe back on. The rubbing had done nothing to warm his foot.

As the Cavalier passed into Chaparral, Fisher pondered the best way to approach Carlton's house. He considered the possibility that Domao had the house under surveillance, and the thought worried him.

"Turn right," Fisher said, "The perimeter road that skirts the development might be our best choice."

Alli maintained a slow speed. The snowfall had diminished, but she was taking no chances. She could see no evidence that Chaparral's roads had been salted.

"There are about eight hundred homes here," Fisher said, recalling the master plan Sharon had shown him at the time Carlton built his house. "Chaparral's basically laid out as a large rectangle with winding roads and cul de sacs in the interior. This road borders the subdivision and will bring us around to Chip's house from the north."

Carlton's house was stuck off the back of Chaparral where the density of homes was far less. The entrance road would have been a more direct path. It ran directly to the rear of the huge tract of land, and it was the route Domao had chosen the day Fisher had accompanied him. Fisher hoped anyone watching the house would have chosen that direction for access. If so, Alli's car approaching from the north would come headlight-to-headlight with any parked surveillance car. Anyone with evil intent would have difficulty identifying Alli's license plate.

"Are you okay?" Fisher asked.

"I'm fine." Alli steered carefully. "I'm just a little worried about this."

"We'll be okay." Fisher reached over and patted her shoulder.

Richland's most prestigious development had no street lights. With the exception of an occasional security light, all the houses were dark. The darkness, combined with treacherous streets slowed travel to a crawl. A single curve remained before the entrance to Carlton's winding driveway came into view.

Fisher was anxious as he recognized familiar landmarks lit by the Cavalier's headlights. Even in the slop of a winter season, the occasional view afforded by the car's headlights confirmed that Chaparral's inhabitants spent enormous sums of money on landscaping and exterior maintenance.

Fisher's pulse quickened as the headlights bathed a portion of the road in front the Carlton property. Parked across the road, in front of an undeveloped lot, was an unmarked cruiser. Its lights were off, and it was pulled half-off the pavement onto the apron.

"Damn," Fisher said. "I thought this was going to happen."

"Do you recognize the car?" Alli's voice showed concern.

"Yeah. It's the same make and model I rode in the day Domao brought me here."

"I'll just drive past it," Alli said.

"That's probably best. But keep your speed the same, if you can. We don't want to attract attention."

As they rolled by, it was obvious the cruiser had been standing for some time. Wet snow completely covered the car's windows and no tire tracks were visible on the road behind it.

"There's no one in it," Alli said, finally letting herself breathe.

Fisher did not respond immediately. He knew his big idea of rolling out and searching Carlton's house was simplistic and foolish. "Pull in here," he directed about a quarter mile beyond Carlton's driveway.

Alli turned left off the perimeter. "Are we turning around?"

"No," Fisher said. "I'm thinking. This is a cul-de-sac with no houses. I spotted it the day I came here with Domao. Pull around the curve and shut off the engine. We should be safe here."

Alli guided her car to the end, turned off the lights and switched off the ignition.

For a moment they sat in silence. As their eyes adjusted, they saw the area around them was not pitch black. Rather, it was bathed in a ghostly half-light that probably originated miles away in the city. Objects and shapes slowly came into view.

Fisher covered the lens of the flashlight with one hand and switched it on with the other. A sliver of light cut between his index and middle fingers, illuminating his wrist watch.

"One-fifteen," he said, pausing briefly. He turned to Alli. In the low light, he could see her silhouette. "Alli, I think you should stay with the car and let me go at this alone. I won't be . . . ."

"No, Steve," she interrupted. "I'm going with you."

"You saw the cruiser sitting out there. Domao may just be trying to pull a fast one, or there may really be someone watching the property."

"I don't care. I'm going with you."

"Okay," he shrugged. "Let's go."

The Cavalier was nothing more than a black shape sitting at the end of the vacant cul-de-sac. As they walked to the road, all was silent save for a faint squeak as their feet compressed the snow. The outline of the roadway became clearer as their eyes grew more accustomed to the light.

All was quiet. Snow had continued falling but was not visible. Before they stepped out onto the roadway, Fisher turned to Alli. Not taking a chance on being heard, he cupped his hands around her ear before speaking. In a barely audible voice, he said, "There is an unpaved service road onto the property. It was cut through when Chip installed a swimming pool. The entrance to the road is about fifty yards this side of the driveway. It'll bring us up to the back of the property. Chip kept a spare back door key in the little cabana beside the pool."

They turned to the right and walked toward the main driveway entrance and the parked cruiser. Fisher looked for the service road. In the years since the pool was installed, Carlton had purposefully let the brush around the road grow. Fisher was worried he would miss the entrance in such low light. But to his surprise, the break in the brush was visible. They turned left and headed into the dense oak forest that surrounded Carlton's property.

The service access turned out to be nothing more than an overgrown path. Years of rainfall had eroded the surface, filling it with deep fissures. Long tentacles of untrimmed brush sagged under the weight of fresh snow and hung down. Fisher grasped Alli's gloved hand as they walked up the uneven surface.

Within fifty yards, the road inclined sharply as it led to the house. Though it wasn't deep, the fresh snow made progress difficult. On two occasions, they slipped, as they struggled up the incline. The oak trees, though leafless, reduced the reflected light, making the path practically black. They had to carefully think about each step before making them.

In the midst of struggling, Fisher stopped. The silence had been broken. He could hear a continuous, barely audible, mechanical sound.

Alli stopped also.

Fisher strained to hear.

He whispered, "The sound seems to be coming from the pool. Let's keep going."

She squeezed Fisher's hand to signify that she understood, and they proceeded.

As they approached, the noise grew in intensity, taking on a humming quality as it drifted across the snowy landscape.

It was indeed coming from the pool. Someone had left the filter running. The increased intensity meant they were drawing closer to the house.

The service road took a sharp turn to the left as they came out from under the cover of the scrub oak and stepped back into the half-light.

Looming ahead of them, the black mass of a small poolside cabana became visible.

He reached toward the cabana, his hand contacting the structure's clapboard exterior. Fisher slowly worked his way to the left. Alli stayed close, still clasping his hand.

On reaching the back corner, Fisher looked around from the cabana's back side out in the direction of the swimming pool. The outline of the small body of water, provided by a snow-covered concrete deck, was barely visible. The main house was about one hundred feet away and could not be seen.

Fisher scanned the pool area. He saw nothing beyond its ghostly outline. He was anxious about this moment from the start, wondering whether someone was watching the house. Had Domao put that car out front to scare off would-be visitors, or was someone hidden in the shadows, watching the house? The thought sent pin pricks up the back of his neck.

He leaned against the cabana's clapboard surface. An image of Benjamin Domao flashed through his mind. Domao was a slob, he thought, but what kind of policeman was he? Fisher realized he had no knowledge of how sly or cunning he was. Was he an incompetent slob or was his demeanor simply smoke and mirrors that obscured a highly effective police detective?

Fisher finally decided to go with his first instincts about Domao. He had to assume the cruiser had an owner who was probably hidden in the shadows of Carlton's property.

He pulled Alli close. "I think Domao's got someone here watching the place. If we get the key and go waltzing up to the back door, we may run into trouble."

"How will you know?"

"The scrub oak grove completely surrounds the house. It'll provide the cover I need to have a look at the house from all sides. That's the best I can do, under these conditions."

"Please be careful," Alli said softly, her face inches from his.

Fisher stared at the dark image before him. He moved his face toward her silhouette. Her lips were warm on his, the scent of her perfume subtle. For a few moments, they were far away as they kissed.

Fisher drew back slowly, still looking into her face.

"Please be careful," she said again.

"I will. Stay back here behind the cabana."

Fisher walked a short way down the service road and entered the dense scrub oak, pervasive on the land near the Caton River. Once in the grove, it was back to darkness. Fisher made his way slowly to the edge of the grove taking care to remain deep in the shadows. Carlton's house soon became visible through the trees because of its contrast with the pale white of the fallen snow.

At the time that Carlton built the house, he cleared a large area of the scrub oak. When construction was finished, a forty-foot strip of cleared area around the house remained.

Concealed just inside the oak grove, Fisher viewed the cleared area. He had an unobstructed view of the house and its grounds. He moved slowly around the house, studying the snowy area as well as he could.

Progress was slow. Each step required concentration to ensure his feet were set down quietly. His thighs screamed with pain as he moved in a crouched position through the shadows of the snowy grove. When he had traveled about a third of the distance around the house, he came to the black-topped driveway that ran from the perimeter road to the back entrance of the house. He had seen no one and was encouraged as he stopped short of stepping out onto the driveway.

Then, he froze.

A single trail of footprints led up from the perimeter road and disappeared in the direction of the house.

Fisher's heart raced and his hands moistened inside his heavy gloves as fear and panic gripped him. He turned away from the driveway and moved back into the grove, being careful to remain concealed.

Crouching in the grove away from the driveway, Fisher's senses were on full alert as he struggled to get his mind back under control. His heart pounded, his breathing was rapid and shallow. Another image of Domao flashed across his mind.

"You shit head," Fisher said softly, as he looked back through the trees at the cabana. He thought of Alli standing behind the little building. He doubted anyone else knew of the old road's existence. She would be safe.

He had to continue.

Fisher returned to the driveway's edge and studied the footprints again. Only a single set was visible. He crossed the driveway and melted into the grove on the opposite side. From his vantage point inside the dense stand of trees, Fisher could see the rear entrance to the house. Interestingly, the trail of prints did not lead to the back entrance. They led off the driveway around the property to the river side of the house. He continued moving, following the trail of prints. The roar of the river, barely audible at first, increased as he moved around the corner to the far side of the house.

As he arrived there, he saw what he had prayed not to see. Barely visible, the dark figure of a man stood motionless on the concrete deck that led off the living room by the large bay window of Carlton's house.

Fisher fought feelings of helplessness. He searched the pockets of his bulky overcoat. In the right pocket, the metal handle of the flashlight filled his grip. It would be no match for the type of weapon the man standing on the deck probably carried.

He crouched in the cold of the oak grove, struggling with his next move. For a few moments, he considered retracing his steps to the cabana, grabbing Alli and getting the hell out.

No, he thought. Discovering the reasons for Carlton's murder hinged on getting that ledger. There's a way to take out the watchman. I've just have to figure it out.

Before Fisher could work out any strategy, the figure on the deck turned and walked to the steps leading down to the snow-covered grass. He was coming straight at Fisher.

Having no other choice, Fisher slowly pulled the heavy black flashlight out of his pocket and squeezed its grip.

Chirp Chirp! Chirp Chirp!

A cellular phone's harsh ring filled the air. The figure stopped at the top of the stairs and opened his coat with a loud zip. "Yeah," he said in muffled tones as he turned and walked back to where he had been standing.

The wind, ever present along the elevated bluffs of the Chaparral, blew the sound back in Fisher's direction. The conversation was soft but audible.

"Listen, you tell that son-of-a-bitch that the price for traipsing around this empty fuckin' house is set and there ain't no . . . . I don't give a shit what he says. The price stays the same."

Fisher knew he had to act. He would get no second chance. He shed the overcoat and moved to the base of the stairs. The wind stung his face and hands. He shivered, but he didn't notice. His heart raced and his palms were damp as he climbed the four steps that led up to the deck.

Moving with a cat-like glide, Fisher edged toward the figure ten or twelve feet away. He needed only ten seconds.

"Fuck him," the man said. "Hell no. You tell that asshole I'll come by the station in the morning."

The man snapped off the cell phone. He started to place the phone in his pocket just as the shaft of Fisher's flashlight crashed onto the crown of his head. Without a word, he crumpled, unconscious, onto the deck.

• • • • •

As the beam from the flashlight swept across the living room of Carlton's house, it revealed the scene of chaos Fisher had remembered.

Furniture was overturned; area rugs were pulled up into heaps, magazines littered across the floor.

He and Alli had located the house key hanging inside the cabana door and entered through the kitchen, where similar chaos existed.

Fisher went to the bay window and looked out onto the deck. Barely visible was a black heap at the deck railing. The watchman still lay where Fisher had left him ten minutes earlier. A quick search of the man's pockets had yielded a Glock nine millimeter pistol and three loaded clips. He carried no police identification.

"We don't have much time," Fisher said, turning away from the window. "He'll be waking up soon, and I want us out of here. He won't find his pistol or his cellular phone, but he could cause trouble."

"Where do we start?" Alli stood amid the rubble of fine furniture.

"Chip's office. It's back through the bedroom."

They made their way through the wreckage of the once elegant home, passing through the bedroom and into the office. They searched it completely.

"Whoever rummaged through the house missed this room," Alli said. "It still looks neat."

"Yeah, the same thought occurred to me the day I was here. Domao's colleague brought me straight to this room and specifically asked me whether anything was missing. I noticed that Chip's box of jump drives was gone. Shortly after that we left."

Fisher looked down at Carlton's desk. Nothing had been moved, he thought. It was exactly as it was the other day.

Finally Fisher looked up and said, "There's nothing in this office, Alli. They searched it just like they searched the rest of the house. But, for some reason they didn't wreck it." He stopped, again sweeping the flashlight. He was deep in thought.

"That's it," Fisher said finally, anger seething from his lips. "Shit! It was a set up and I couldn't see it. That bastard brought me out here just so I could notice the files were gone. That way, I'd conclude that whoever searched the place found what they were after. That son-of-a-bitch even had the crime scene squad buying into it."

"Where do we look then?"

"Hell. It could be anywhere. This is turning out to be tougher than I thought. Let's take one room at the time. We'll start with the bedroom and bath and make our way to the rest of the house."

They passed into Carlton's bedroom. Mattress and box springs were off the bed frame on the floor. Drawers were pulled open and the contents dumped. The closets were emptied.

Fisher scanned the large walk-in closet. There was nothing but tangled clothing.

"This is a disaster zone." Alli grabbed a mattress corner and looked underneath with a pen light. The light was dim, with insufficient brightness to see under the bed. "Steve, can you bring the flashlight here for a moment?"

"Sure. Be there in just a second," Fisher responded, his voice coming from the master bathroom.

As the flashlight shined across the bathroom, he examined each detail carefully. The door to the shower had been ripped off its supports and lay on the floor next to the pedestal that supported the green marble Jacuzzi. The medicine cabinet contents were strewn across the room and the toilet lid ripped off and smashed.

There's something here, he told himself. There's something. But what?

"Steve," Alli called again. "Give me just a little light under the bed."

"Oh." He moved into the bedroom and handed the light down to Alli.

"There's nothing here either." She handed the light back.

"Okay. Let's go to the living room. We've got to wrap this up."

As they walked to the bedroom door, Fisher stopped. "Let's go back to the bathroom for a second."

Fisher re-entered the large bathroom and swept the light across the room again. He couldn't shake the feeling that settled into his chest. "Alli, there's something here. I can't describe it. It's just a feeling."

He turned the flashlight beam into the shower then back down onto the Jacuzzi. Fisher approached the large tub. Debris ripped from the walls was piled into the bottom of the tub.

"Nothing here," Fisher said.

He looked at the pedestal. A rectangular panel that gave access to the Jacuzzi controls had been ripped off. Fisher looked inside. Nothing.

He had just begun looking in the corner of the bathroom away from the Jacuzzi when he stopped.

"Did you find something?" Alli stepped behind him.

"It's a smaller panel. It may have been missed because of its location next to the wall."

The panel was difficult to see. Fisher tried opening it with his fingers, but it wouldn't budge.

"Try this." Alli handed him a large dagger-like shard from the smashed toilet lid.

Fisher inserted the small point into the panel's seam and used it in a crowbar-like fashion. "That's got it," Fisher said as the panel snapped open.

He shined the light through the opening in the pedestal.

"There's nothing here." Fisher sat back on the floor, frustration in his voice. "It looks like old Dr. Carlton has outdone himself this time."

Fisher was about to stand, but he stopped. He stared at the opening in the base of the Jacuzzi.

"One last spot has to be checked." He handed the flashlight to Alli and inserted the palm of his hand into the pedestal, feeling the inside surface above the opening. Nothing. Fisher next inserted his entire right arm into the pedestal and explored the area with a sweeping motion. His probing fingertips touched the edge of a three-inch wide piece of adhesive tape.

In the low light, Alli could see Fisher's face break into a huge grin. He ripped up the tape and an object tumbled to the floor inside the base of the tub. Fisher reached down and brought out a small, hardback ledger. "We're in business," he said.

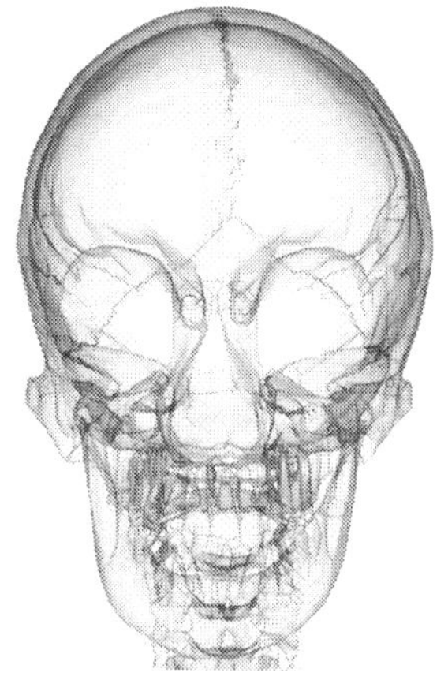

CHAPTER TWENTY-SEVEN

Snaps and wheezes arose from the living room, the fire place sounds overshadowing the mantel clock's rhythmic ticking. The crackling fire had warmed the room and dissipated the chill in Fisher's body, but he was unaware of its passing. His attention was focused on the small ledger book recovered from Carlton's plundered house.

Alli walked into the living room carrying two mugs of hot coffee. She placed one of them on the end table next to Fisher and sat down on the sofa. She stared at the noisy fire, taking occasional sips from the mug.

Fisher looked up from the ledger. "Alli, there are a total of one hundred eighty entries, exactly as Chip noted. Only four columns of the ledger have been used. The first column consists of dates spanning an eighteen-month period prior to January thirty-first of this year."

Fisher dragged a finger down the first column, examining the dates as he turned the pages. "The entries seem to average two per week. Some weeks more, some less."

"So whatever Dr. Carlton stumbled onto had been in progress for a year and a half," Alli observed.

"That sounds right." Fisher continued paging through the ledger. "The second column is strange. It's a listing of names. The entries aren't complete, though. They're full names recorded for some dates and single names recorded for others. A few entries have no name recorded."

Fisher paused as if contemplating his words then continued. "In the third column, a seven digit number is recorded by each date. That column has no omissions." Fisher completed his scan of the third column turning through the pages of the ledger.

"Identification numbers maybe?" Alli said, thinking out loud.

"Possibly." Fisher continued flipping through the pages to confirm the accuracy of his statement. "No two entries are in any numerical sequence," he said after a few seconds.

"How do hospitals assign patient identification numbers?"

"By numerical order." Fisher became silent. He studied the column of numbers again, looking up from the book frequently to rest his eyes.

The sounds from the fireplace, though muted now as the fire had burned down, became more noticeable as they pondered the significance of the column of numbers.

Alli turned away from the glowing fire and looked at Fisher. "If those numbers represent patient identification numbers, wouldn't that mean each entry represents new patients admitted and assigned ID numbers at different times? No two patients would have been admitted at the same time on the same day, or the numbers would have been in sequence."

"That's right. But how does that jibe with the fourth column? The fourth column simply lists operative organ removal procedures." Fisher read from the column. "Here's partial hepatectomy, nephrectomy, partial pancreatectomy, partial and complete pneumonectomy. There's a listing for nearly every visceral organ except the heart. I'm afraid I don't understand why an operative ledger listing those procedures, poorly recorded in the first place, was in the day surgery center away from the main hospital. What was so important that Chip lost his life for it?"

Fisher continued flipping through the fifteen pages of entries. Fatigue was wearing him down. His thoughts were becoming confused. Alli had closed her eyes, but fought to stay awake. The trip to Chaparral had drained them both.

For a moment, Fisher looked away from the ledger and pinched his burning eyes, attempting to clear the haze. He reopened his eyes and read through the ledger's pages a final time. His gaze drifted down the page following his finger. At the last entry, dated January 31, 2015, he stopped. An invisible hand gripped his throat. His pulse jumped and his head pounded as he looked at the entry.

With his repeated scans through the ledger, Fisher hadn't noticed the last entry. Recorded in column two of the ledger's last line a single named entry screamed off the page at him.

It simply read, Mattie.

Fisher was silent. Fatigue melted as adrenaline surged, propelling his heart rate upward and clearing his brain.

As if moving at the speed of light, Fisher's reality was yanked back seven days in time.

Why is this happening? he asked. His conscious mind was no longer in control. This was not by my intention, he told himself, as he was dragged to an unknown destination. He was alarmed at his lack of control.

With blinding speed, immediate answers came to his questions. Fisher saw a blood-splattered, stainless steel surface. He was standing by a morgue table, deep inside Medford University. On the table lay the nude corpse of a white woman. Fisher looked at her lifeless, weather-beaten face. Her half-opened eyes cast a distant stare at the fluorescent lights overhead. Although his brain produced a still-life shot of the scene, Fisher could see Natalie Roberts and Andrew Carter as they bent over the corpse opened by a long vertical incision.

The Jane Doe who died of hypothermia, he thought.

But why am I here, Fisher asked himself again. Hypothermia is a common problem among the homeless in winter. The lady was clearly homeless.

Oh yes, this was the lady Natalie got worked up over, when she found the surgical clips and no right kidney. He walked closer to the autopsy, propelled by unseen forces. He looked down on the dead woman. He saw her wrinkled skin; greasy, disheveled hair, and loosened, decayed teeth.

His mind, thoroughly in control, prompted him to scan down from the face onto the skin of the neck and out onto the lifeless musculature of her left shoulder.

There.

He saw it clearly. Across the shoulder, tattooed in single color crude cursive, were the six letters he had seen before.

M-a-t-t-i-e!

Fisher gasped.

As quickly as it came, the flashback ended. He became aware of the warmth of the room, the soft crackles of the dying fire, and Alli dozing on the sofa beside him.

Fisher looked down at the ledger still open in his lap. He yanked up the book and searched for the final entry. Locating the name Mattie, he scanned to the fourth column.

His insides twisted into a knotted mess as he read the entry.

Right Nephrectomy.

For a moment, he simply stared down at the ledger. His throat was parched and gritty, his hands damp and trembling.

"Goddamn," he hissed softly under his breath. "Goddamn. Those sons-of-bitches."

The volume in his voice awakened Alli.

"What is it?"

"Those sons of bitches!"

"What's the matter? What's wrong?"

"That's what's wrong." He shoved the ledger into Alli's lap.

"Those bastards at Taggart Memorial killed Carlton because he discovered their nasty little secret."

"I don't understand," Alli said, surprised by the rage in Fisher's voice. "What nasty little secret?"

"That ledger is a record of one hundred eighty organ removals."

"Yes, well I thought we established that earlier."

"No, no. Those organs weren't removed because they were diseased. That's a list of organ donors. Those were organ harvests!"

"Steve, what proof do you have of that?"

Fisher stood and walked to the ebbing fire. He placed his hand onto the mantel and stared into the glowing orange coals.

"Jesus. How could I have been so stupid? It was all there right before my eyes."

"Okay, okay. I'm out of the loop here. Why don't you just sit back down and press restart, so I can understand."

Fisher returned to the overstuffed chair. He shaped his fingers into a steeple in front his mouth and began talking.

He told her how Roberts had called him to the morgue the night Carlton was killed. "She wanted an opinion concerning an autopsy she was performing on a woman who died from hypothermia. Richland

EMS found her and brought her in. From her physical appearance, she'd probably come from the streets. When I looked into her opened abdomen, I saw a large fatty liver, but that wasn't unusual. Street people are always in the Medford ER. At first glance, she was just another wino who died from exposure."

"I'm listening."

Fisher went on. "But she wasn't just another dead wino to Natalie. She'd found that the woman was missing a right kidney and had questions about it."

"That wouldn't be unusual. Three to five percent of the U.S. population will have one congenitally absent kidney."

"The woman's right kidney wasn't absent from birth," Fisher responded. "It had been removed. There were surgical clips present on the renal artery and vein."

"That's still not unusual, is it?"

"It wouldn't have been except that no scar was present over the right flank, no evidence that a surgical wound had ever been created. She'd called me to ask if someone could undergo a nephrectomy without having evidence of a surgical wound."

Alli was silent, her full attention directed toward Fisher.

Fisher went on. "A couple of nights later Natalie called me again. I went to her laboratory where she informed me that molecular studies she'd done on the right flank tissue showed the tissue to be in the midst of accelerated wound repair."

"What about tissue from the woman's left flank?" Alli's eyes were opened wide as she consumed the bizarre story.

"Excellent question. The tissue removed from the woman's left flank showed no evidence of exaggerated growth."

"Okay," Alli said an air of puzzlement in her voice. "Let me see if I get this. Dr. Roberts performs some molecular diagnostic studies on the woman's tissues and determines that the tissue over the removed kidney, though it appeared normal, actually wasn't. It actually was a wound in the process of repair."

"That's right."

"I'm afraid I don't see the connection between the woman, Dr. Roberts' findings, and the ledger."

Fisher shifted his body, leaning on the arm of the chair, bringing his face closer to Alli's.

"There's a final piece to the puzzle I haven't told you yet."

"Okay. What's that?"

"While studying the woman's body, I saw a crude tattoo on her shoulder that spelled the name Mattie."

Alli wrinkled her forehead, but Fisher spoke quickly before she could puzzle over the name further.

"Look at the ledger's last entry."

Alli pulled the ledger into the light cast by the end table's lamp and studied the ledger. Fisher saw her normally rosy cheeks turn pale.

"It's the name Mattie," she said, her voice quivering. "Then you think the others had their organs taken the way Mattie did?"

"It's looking that way." Fisher sat forward, his expression deadly serious. "If I let my imagination go conjuring up the wildest possible scenario, it would conclude that this ledger is a listing of the homeless, the street-weary, and the poor of Richland. The nasty secret Chip stumbled upon was that Taggart Memorial is taking the organs it needs to support its transplant program."

"Oh, Jesus," she whispered. "Do you think Dr. Carlton knew the real significance of the ledger?"

"I can't be sure. The last thing he wrote in the message was that he was headed to speak with Harry Talbott. We'll never know. But the big picture is falling into place now. The encrypted message Chip sent. He commented on how the numbers of transplants at Taggart were staying high. No expected seasonal lag, he said. He also mentioned that he got approving pats on the back when he asked about it. I have to assume that all the transplant surgeons including Harry Talbott knew what's was going on. I'll also bet Harry Talbott was instrumental in seeing that OrganLink personnel were never around."

"Steve, we've got to go to the police."

"Alli, I know how you feel, but going to the police is out. I've already tried that. Brad Hinton is dead because I tried to get help from the RPD. It was by sheer luck I wasn't killed too. Right now, the answer is still no. We need solid proof. At the moment, the only thing we have is a mysterious ledger that could have come from anywhere and emails from a dead surgeon who thought the ledger was significant. We need proof."

It was just before dawn, and Alli's living room had been silent for a while. Fisher sat holding a fresh cup of coffee between both hands staring at the last vestiges of the fire. He was fatigued, but his mind was churning. He examined every detail of the past seven days.

Alli returned from the basement with a smile. "Gary's asleep in front of the computer. He probably worked on getting into Taggart's system until he fell asleep. I left your note beside the monitor."

"I wish I had remembered to give him Chip's doctor number earlier. It'll make his job a lot easier."

Fisher returned to his thoughts. Mattie, Mattie, he repeated. Where else had he heard the name spoken? He just couldn't call it up. Fatigue finally beat him down as he dozed off.

"Anybody hungry?"

The voice broke the silence, awakening Fisher from his nap. Involuntarily he stood and gazed across the room, momentarily disoriented as sleep evaporated.

It was Gary. He had awakened following his early morning snooze and was searching the kitchen for food.

"What did you say, Gary?" Fisher's mind became crisp as he turned toward the younger Shepard.

"I asked whether anybody was hungry."

Fisher snapped his finger. "Homeless, hungry. Gary you did it!"

Gary turned toward the living room, a stalk of celery hanging from his mouth.

The volume of Fisher's voice increased. "The female officer at the police station offered the homeless man food."

"What homeless man?"

"The day after Chip was killed. I went for a meeting with Domao. While the desk officer was giving me directions to Domao's office, a female officer walked up with a sack lunch. The desk sergeant pointed to a bearded man asleep on one of the benches. When she awakened him with the offer of food, the man sat up and asked if they had found Mattie."

"Any idea where he was from?" asked Alli.

"I don't know. At the time the name Mattie wasn't significant. I didn't pay attention. He was a poor, homeless man in need."

Gary walked into the room carrying a large sandwich and a glass of milk.

"How can you think of food this time of the morning?" Alli asked.

"Did I hear you say homeless, Dr. Fisher?" Gary asked, ignoring Alli's remark.

"Yes." Fisher explained the significance of his revelation.

Gary held the sandwich poised to enter his mouth, but stopped. "My Urban Studies professor, Dr. Klemmer, says homeless people flock together in small groups of ten to fifteen when they're on the streets."

"What do you mean?" Fisher asked.

"It's a matter of safety, protection in numbers, Dr. Klemmer says."

Fisher glanced at Alli. By the look on their faces, they shared identical thoughts.

The words rolled from Alli's mouth first. "The rescue squad that brought Mattie into the ER the night she died."

"Where was she found?" Fisher blurted out the next logical Question.

Fisher reached into the pocket of his jacket and pulled out his cell phone. He dialed Medford Trauma.

"Trauma, this is Jane," a female voice replied.

Jane Dalton was the nurse manager who worked permanent nights in Medford Trauma. Fisher had come to know her from his early morning visits to the Trauma Center.

"Jane, this is Dr. Steve Fisher."

"Good morning, Dr. Fisher. Did someone page you?"

"No. I'm calling with a question."

"Sure. What's the question?"

"Seven or eight days ago, a homeless maybe forties year-old woman was brought in severely hypothermic. She was coded in the ER but died. Do you remember her?"

Fisher waited.

"Dr. Fisher, many people have crashed in here off the streets since the weather turned cold. It doesn't sound familiar."

Undaunted, Fisher pressed on. "She was middle age, maybe in her forties. Her left foot was severely frostbitten."

"Excuse me, Dr. Fisher." She turned away from the phone to give someone directions. "Just put that patient in room nine. Vascular Surgery knows about him. They should be here in the next few minutes. Anna, could you get vitals on the new patient in nine?"

Fisher waited patiently while Dalton directed early morning activities in Medford Trauma.

"Sorry, Dr. Fisher, EMTs are bringing a patient in."

"That's quite all right."

"We've been so busy lately, I'm afraid I don't remember the lady, Dr. Fisher. The last ten days are a blur."

Fisher had been afraid that would happen. Medford Trauma was the busiest ER in Richland, and it was no surprise that a nameless soul dying quietly of hypothermia would not be remembered. Fisher was disappointed.

"Wait a second, Dr. Fisher," Dalton said. "Let me ask the guys from Richland EMS. They've just brought a patient in."

Dalton turned away from the phone once again and called out to someone nearby. "Johnson, did you guys bring in a code off the streets about ten days ago? A lady, mid-forties, found down, hypothermic?"

"Yeah, Jane, you remember that." The male voice was clearly audible over the phone. "The lady we found in the large cardboard box."

"God, how could I forget that?" Dalton chastised herself as she returned to the phone. "Dr. Fisher, one of the Richland EMTs remembers the case."

"Could you ask him where she was found?"

Dalton hesitated a moment. "I'm going to put the EMT who brought her in on the line."

"Johnson, this is Dr. Fisher from Transplant Surgery," Fisher could hear her say.

"This is Johnson from Richland EMT, Dr. Fisher." The deep male voice boomed out of the phone. "What's up?"

"The lady you brought in about seven days ago who arrested in the ER. Where was she found?"

"Oh yeah, Doc, she was the lady we pulled out of a box under the Ninth Street Bridge.

"Under the Ninth Street Bridge?"

"Yeah. It's a mess back under there, but that's where she was lying. Just barely alive when we picked her up."

"Were there others around when you got there?" Fisher asked.

"There was no one around, but you could tell from all the trash and garbage scattered about the area it was a gathering site. And there were those boxes too."

"Boxes?" asked Fisher.

"Yeah, old boxes, large ones, like you'd use to ship appliances. Looked to me like people had been living in them. Makeshift housing, sort of."

"You've been a big help, Johnson. Thank you very much," Fisher said as he clicked off the phone.

Fisher glanced at the clock. It was five-fifteen.

"Looks like our mystery lady was found down under the Ninth Street Bridge."

Alli spoke, "If you think the bearded man knew her that sounds like the place to start looking."

"Yes." Fisher looked down at the ledger lying open in his lap. The last entry screamed off the page at him. "But there's one person we need to talk with first."

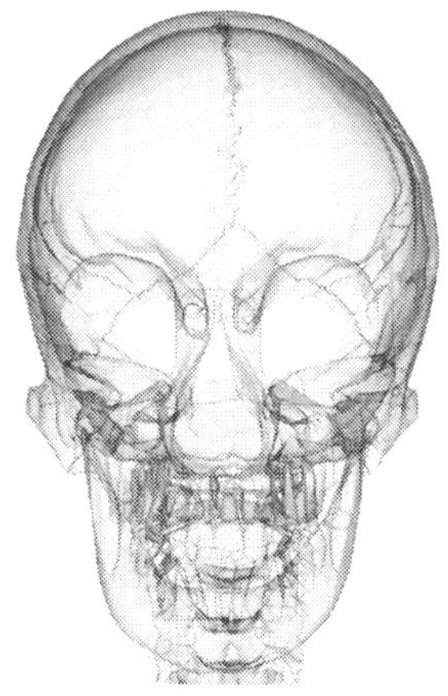

CHAPTER TWENTY-EIGHT

Cigarette smoke choked the air in the small room, but the regulars who gathered at Risarti's Restaurant and Bar showed no outward signs they cared. The small Italian kitchen, popular with Richland's east-end blue-collar set, was practically full. Two tables near the front of the restaurant were vacant, but those would fill in a hurry at the rate people were arriving.

Risarti's was Old World with simple accommodations, but it oozed a bistro-like atmosphere, with dimmed lighting and an Italian tenor that poured from corner-mounted speakers. From Fisher's vantage point in the rear of the restaurant, he could see the patrons as they arrived. Small candles in colored-glass burned on each table providing meager tabletop illumination.

That faint light cast muted shadows across Alli's face as she sat across from Fisher, her back to the restaurant entrance. "Do you think she'll come?"

"I'm not sure," Fisher responded, an unmistakable tone of doubt in his voice. He had paged Natalie Roberts to a pay phone outside a convenience store in Alli's neighborhood. Street noise in the background during their conversation had made it difficult to hear Roberts.

She was surprised to hear from Fisher. "I've been trying to get hold of you for a couple of days. Is your pager working?"

"I've had it turned off."

With those few words spoken, Roberts sensed something was different.

"Steve, is everything all right?"

"Are you in the lab?" Fisher ignored the Question.

"Yes, but do you . . .?"

"There's a pay phone in the lobby of the Pathology Building. Please call me back immediately from that phone at the number that just displayed on your pager."

Fisher stood by the phone outside the convenience store stomping his feet and rubbing the sleeves of his sport coat to keep warm while he waited. When the phone rang, he had jerked the receiver off its hook. A bewildered Roberts had returned his call in less than five minutes.

"Steve, what's going on?"

"I can't talk now but I need to see you."

Roberts didn't respond immediately. Fisher could hear conversation coming through the receiver. Thirty or forty seconds passed before she spoke again.

"Sorry, some of the path techs were leaving, and I turned away. It looks a bit strange for me to be using a pay phone down here in the lobby."

"There's a small restaurant on the east end at Forty-Third and Steward named Risarti's. Meet me there at nine. Come alone."

Fisher ended the conversation abruptly, not giving Roberts a chance to ask further questions.

The crowd in Risarti's was building. At the front end of the restaurant, five or six people stood waiting for tables. Fisher looked at his watch. It was nine-thirty. He and Alli had arrived fifteen minutes ahead of schedule and occupied a table in the rear of the restaurant for forty-five minutes. Two glasses of water sat untouched as they waited. They had not ordered.

"I sense our waiter is growing impatient," Alli said. "He keeps glancing in our direction and looking at his watch."

"Yes, I saw him do that, too. We'll give Natalie five more minutes and then split."

Fisher glanced back at the knot of patrons crowding into the front of the restaurant. He considered going for a closer look when he saw Roberts. She was standing alone near the cash register, wedged behind three young women.

"She's here." Fisher rose and stepped to the front of the restaurant.

Fisher looked around. Every table was occupied and every stool at the bar taken. Waiters scurried from table to table. The volume of background chatter and conversation had risen and drowned out the Italian tenor blaring from the speakers. This was exactly what he had in mind for the meeting with Natalie — a noisy, public gathering. Fisher rescued Roberts and escorted her to the table where Alli was seated.

"Natalie, may I introduce Alli Shepard, a member of the fourth-year class at the Med?"

The two women shook hands. Roberts took a seat next to Alli while Fisher faced the front of the restaurant. Before saying anything further, he glanced at the entrance studying the crowd for a few moments. Satisfied that nothing appeared out of the ordinary, he turned to Roberts.

Roberts spoke first, "Could you tell me what's going on?"

Fisher guessed Roberts had come directly from work. He remembered seeing her dark blue business suit under her lab coat the day he visited her laboratory. As always, her hair was pulled up tightly into a bun with a thin line of graying blond framing her sharp facial features. A pair of small wire-rim spectacles straddled the bridge of her nose.

"Natalie, forgive me for getting you here under such obscure circumstances."

Roberts kept silent, staring at Fisher over her wire rims.

"I've got to tell you that . . .," Fisher stopped and glanced out into the room again. He then glanced at Alli.

Without taking her eyes off Fisher, Alli gently nodded.

Fisher looked back into Roberts' eyes.

"I have to tell you that your Jane Doe theory was totally correct."

Roberts cocked her head and wrinkled her brow. Her confused expression lasted only a few seconds, however. The wrinkle smoothed as her eyes opened to double their usual width. Roberts whispered, controlling the volume of her voice. "You what . . .? How did you . . .?"

"Uh, excuse me folks. I . . . uh . . . need to take yous orda, okay?"

Fisher and the two women turned to see the impatient waiter from earlier.

"I see the last memba of ya party has arrived. I hate ta rush yous along, but they's backed up to the street."

"Sure." Fisher snapped open the menu. "Uh, ladies would a round of steamed mussels be good as a starter?"

Heads across the table nodded and the waiter disappeared.

Over the next quarter of an hour, Fisher watched Roberts' expression change from surprise to conviction as he set out the details.

In the midst of Fisher's monologue, their nervous waiter placed a mountain of steaming mussels on the table. The aroma was superb. Fisher ended his account with a description of their trip to the Chaparral and the recovery of the ledger.

"I remember that tattoo," Roberts exclaimed, as Fisher described the last ledger entry. "It was on her left shoulder, handmade, crude, probably fashioned with a sewing needle dipped in ink."

"Exactly." Fisher glanced at Alli. Their eyes met briefly, but they both knew Roberts understood the gravity of the situation.

Eventually, all the mussels were eaten and they ordered entrées. Their waiter, appearing less agitated, took their orders and headed to seat newly arrived patrons. Fisher continued to refine Roberts' understanding of the events until he was satisfied that no gaps in her knowledge existed.

Roberts stared down at her half-empty water goblet, running her finger around its base.

"How could they do this? Street people like Mattie don't know how to protect themselves. They're defenseless. And to kill to keep the operation silent. How could they do this?"

"Money and power, Natalie. It's about money and power. Human organs are a commodity, nothing more. If you control the source of human organs, you have both."

Fisher didn't take his eyes off Roberts as he spoke. "It's all becoming clear now. It's a window of opportunity, isn't it? Artificial prototypes of all human organs are in design phases in several labs now. They're a decade or maybe less away from successful application. The three dimensional printers capable of building an organ are increasingly successful. But until those studies are successful, someone inside Taggart Memorial saw the opportunity to make big dollars by keeping the organ supply flowing. A central clearing house for the organ you want. Just think about it. You're a rural hospital administrator or a transplant coordinator. You pick up the phone, it's there by FedEx the next day. Human organs on demand."

Roberts interrupted, "This is crazy. UNOS has tracked and enforced organ procurement in the United States for more than forty five years. That kind of black market can't hide."

"Not so," Fisher retorted. "Congress cut back UNOS funding earlier in the decade as severely as it did Medicaid and Medicare. UNOS is now a hospital-supported network. Any hospital with a transplant program is required to subscribe to UNOS services."

"And your point is?"

"My point is that the national organ procurement transplant network that UNOS administers is no different from any of the other healthcare programs that lost federal oversight. It's become a joke. More than a hundred thousand people are on waiting lists to receive organs in the United States alone. Believe me, a hospital like Taggart Memorial, with its underhanded business practices, will find a way to manipulate the system quietly."

Roberts looked down at the white table cloth. "Okay. What is it that you think I can do?"

"The night I came to the morgue, you said you work part time at Taggart Memorial as a Clinical Pathologist."

"That's right."

Fisher looked out across the crowded restaurant again. The mix of patrons had not changed substantially nor had the noise level.

"Darren Fitzpatrick told me I needed hard evidence of foul play before his agency could make a move. I intend to get him that evidence."

"You've got the email and the ledger. What more do you need?"

"Hard, irrefutable evidence," Fisher said. "Chip's email raised Questions, but didn't provide concrete evidence. The ledger could have come from anywhere."

"I can't provide you with anything better than what you already have. What is it you think I can do?"

Fisher dropped his gaze to the tabletop and inspected his left thumb. He had unconsciously dug through the outer layer of skin with his right thumbnail.

"You're on the inside at Taggart. There's something there. We've just got to look for it." Fisher could feel his frustration growing.

"I'm a part-time Pathologist at Taggart. I show up two days every other week to organize the tissue registry. That's all I do. I work my shift and leave. I'm not privy to any inside politics."

Alli had quietly listened to the entire conversation but she spoke up.

"Dr. Roberts, what is the tissue registry you spoke of?"

"In the late nineties, Congress passed a law requiring all hospitals performing organ transplantation in the United States to maintain a registry of human tissue. My job at Taggart Memorial is to maintain the registry."

"I don't mean to be naive, but what is it?" Alli asked again.

"The registry's nothing more than a storehouse of tissue, really. Every organ Taggart Memorial transplants is subjected to a small biopsy. The biopsy samples are placed in cryovials and snap frozen in liquid nitrogen. The vials are permanently maintained at minus eighty degrees centigrade in specially designated freezers in the Pathology Depart. . ."

Fisher and Alli smiled at each other and turned back to Roberts. As the conversation halted, they all three became aware of the restaurant's background noise once again.

Fisher broke the momentary spell by speaking first, a slight tremor in his voice. "You maintain the freezer logs?"

"Yes," Roberts too, sprouted an ear-to-ear grin.

"Uh, sorry ta interrupt yous again folks, but who gets the lasagna?"

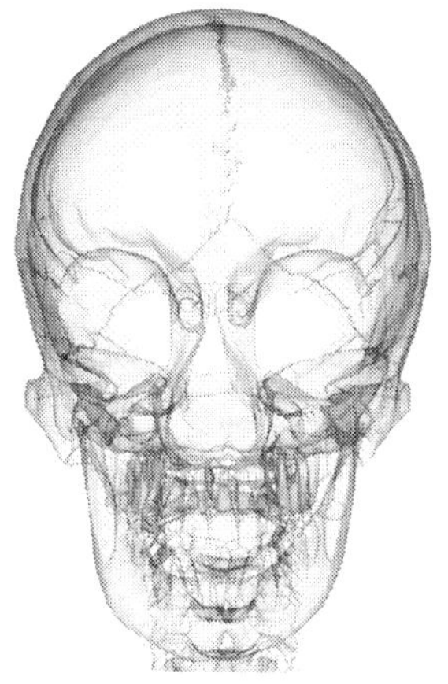

CHAPTER TWENTY-NINE

February 8, Over the North Atlantic

The Boeing 777 maintained its westerly heading, the sky at thirty-five thousand feet appearing blue-black. Radio chatter between Gander Oceanic Center and westbound aircraft intensified as they approached the North American coastline. Clearance out of the Shanwick Oceanic Transition Area had occurred four hours earlier, and despite strong westerly winds, their timing was near perfect. The ship would arrive at its destination on time.

Below the westbound craft, the North Atlantic was obscured by cloud cover. The jetliner's captain needed no view of the water below to know that it was churning. Prior updates of the surface weather from Shanwick and then Gander confirmed that gale warnings were still posted — the aftereffect of winter storms. There was no choice. The cargo had to be delivered.

To the captain's right, the co-pilot was busy with clearance matters, necessary for aircraft inbound from the Arabian Peninsula. "Yes, Gander," the co-pilot was saying in broken but understandable English. "We confirm a heading of two five zero degrees following OTS delta."

"Roger. This is Gander Oceanic Center. We confirm your transponder ident on OTS track delta heading two five zero degrees. You may continue at your current altitude. Please advise when you reach Teufel's intersection over the Newfoundland coastline."

Behind the captain, the ship's engineer studied navigation displays, continually replotting the flight path as the jet cruised over gray cloud cover.

Unnoticed by other members of the command crew, beads of sweat formed across the captain's upper lip as he watched the moving map portion of the global positioning display adjacent to the flight director. Digital readouts of latitude and longitude, visible below the moving map, ticked off as their airspeed remained constant in a west southwesterly heading.

The captain's body stiffened as the lat-long display indicated 47°00'N, 50°31'W.

It was time, he said to himself.

Slowly, the captain moved his left hand from the control yoke of the aircraft down to his thigh, where he rested it a moment. He glanced around casually. Nothing had changed. He was ready to continue. As slowly as before, he dropped his hand from his thigh down to the seat cushion. He gently massaged the foam padding of the captain's seat with his fingers.

A few moments passed. He could feel nothing. Panic began building.

Allah have mercy, he pleaded to himself as his fingers became moist from fear. Everything was so carefully planned. Where was that switch? He looked back up at the GPS digital display.

In a split moment, they had swept past the drop point and were positioned over 50°46'W longitude. His hands dripped sweat and his stomach cramped with fear. He probed up and down the seat.

It wasn't there! It wasn't there! he screamed to himself.

At last, he felt the round edges of the drop button protruding through the vinyl covering. With an awkward jerking motion, he pressed the circular protrusion. The sequence wasn't as subtle as he wanted, but with what seemed like a large black bear standing over him ready to attack, he had performed well.

For a moment, he reclined into the padded back of the captain's chair. He took a deep breath and exhaled quietly. His responsibilities were over, but he knew the delay would cause repercussions.

Below the emergency access door near the tail section of the aircraft, a three-foot-square panel opened as a low-energy radio impulse arrived. The door slid into a recessed pocket, revealing a small compartment on the under surface of the aircraft. Unknown to all passengers and crew, except the captain, a gray package dropped. Once it cleared the aircraft, the compartment panel closed.

As the package entered the stream of high speed air flowing across the fuselage, it tumbled violently. Soon, though, the effects of the turbulence passed, and the container decelerated, ceasing its tumbling. Once stabilized, it began its descent. About sixty seconds after beginning free fall, it entered the upper layers of dense cloud cover. Its color rendered it invisible to the naked eye and its absorptive plastic surfaces created no radar images. On the displays at Gander Oceanic Center, the trackers saw a single large signal on their screens — the Boeing 777.

The parcel continued its descent through layer upon layer of cloud cover. Sensitive instruments on board the package continuously monitored changes in atmospheric pressure as the free-fall progressed. Twenty-seven thousand — nineteen thousand — fourteen thousand — eight thousand — six thousand — four thousand — two thousand feet passed.

The container broke out below the dense gray ceiling above the churning black water of the North Atlantic. At fifteen hundred feet, a low frequency hum arose from the package. The sound, inaudible at first, intensified to a screech as the gray package sunk below one thousand feet. At nine hundred feet above the convulsive whitecaps, orange-red gas burst from its side. Behind the gas, a small gray parachute erupted, immediately slowing the velocity. The altimeter, nestled inside, had performed exactly as programmed and now continued to monitor the descent: four hundred — two hundred — one hundred — splash. The falling box had entered the frigid waters of the North Atlantic.

• • • • •

The Grand Banks (Zone 3L), East of St. Johns, Newfoundland

Sheets of icy salt spray crashed against the pilot's housing as the stern trawler *Mary Ruth* dug into another ten-foot swell. The one hundred-twenty foot trawler pitched rhythmically back and forth as it collided with one wall of water after another.

The man standing at the helm of the *Mary Ruth* took a deep drag off the cigarette clinched between his teeth and exhaled the smoke into a cabin that reeked of stale tobacco. His dense tar-stained fingers held the wheel, his feet firmly planted amid dozens of cigarette butts.

The captain of the lone trawler repeated his inspection of all four quadrants of water surrounding the pitching ship. Nothing had changed since his last check. The churning waters some ninety miles off the coast of Newfoundland were empty, as far as he could see.

That's right, he thought. He had experienced the same sinking feeling for months. The waters were empty. Empty of ships, and worst of all, they were empty of fish. He loosened his grip on the wheel and reached for the console, where he grabbed two large throttles. He hauled back on the *Mary Ruth's* engine speed. The swells had heightened, and he wanted smoother headway. He wanted no complaints of sickness from his crew that night. It would have to be a fast run to St. John's.

Although the captain's demeanor appeared outwardly tranquil, beneath his bearded face and weathered skin, he and other independent fishermen along the Canada's Atlantic coast suffered continually. All were soon to be relics, viewed in Canadian museums or elementary school history books. The water of the Grand Banks, once rich in ground fish like cod and halibut, was dead, the result of massive over-fishing in the nineties and two thousands. Ten years into a government-declared moratorium, there was little sign of recovery.

He knew the situation in his home waters wasn't unique. Spawning stock in the Donut Hole of the Bering Sea, the Challenger Plateau off New Zealand, and the Patagonian Shelf off Argentina were nonexistent as well. In every case, technological advances in taking fish from the ocean had killed the waters. However, all international authorities agreed — nowhere was it worse than the Atlantic Coast of Canada. Most of the independent fishermen he knew had folded, unwilling to fish the less desirable Hake and Redfish, the sole two species in Canadian waters to rebound during the moratorium.

The captain grasped the large wheel firmly as the ship nosed into another swell. Rain beat against the helm room windows diminishing visibility.

From the rear came a raspy voice, "Package is down, Captain. We're receiving its transmitter. It appears to be floating west of our coordinates. Looks like they've done it to us again."

"Shit," the captain uttered through locked teeth as he fought off an even larger swell of water. He swept his gaze down to the soft blue-white glow of the Sky Nav global positioning instrument. The digital read out blinked, indicating reacquisition of satellite signals. It read 47°00'N, 50°31'W. He was exactly where he was told to be.

The captain's face reddened as he looked back to the west. He knew the package could only be located by radio transmitter. Visual sighting was out of the question in these seas. "They think it's just a fucking pond down here, and they can drop their load anywhere they like, the sons-of-bitches."

He pulled back the wool cuff covering his left wrist and glanced at his watch. He had circled the GPS coordinates for two hours.

"Alert the crew," he screamed into a ragged microphone. "We're turning west."

The engines roared below the deck, vibrating the metal planks as the captain shoved the throttles forward. The crew below prepared as the ship lurched into a sharp turn to starboard.

"Transmitter signal is increasing in intensity, Captain. Turn back ten degrees to port."

The captain hit the alert horn as he came about. The horn broadcast a screech in the crew quarters. Two crewmen stood and began pulling on heavy foul weather gear. Without it, exposure to the North Atlantic's icy spray in February could produce hypothermia in less than a minute.

The *Mary Ruth* shuttered as the bow crashed ahead at increased speed, slamming into swell after swell. The captain assessed his westward progress. The GPS display showed 47°00'N, 50°40'W.

"Captain," the raspy voice called, "I've got a sighting."

The captain turned his head. His radio man pointed off the port bow. About a half a mile ahead, a gray box with a small amber beacon drifted on the rough waters.

On the rocking deck, two crew members, protected by foul weather gear, stood on the stern of the ship tied off by safety rope to the wench rigging. One crewman standing closest to the port side winced as the bow dug into a swell, sending icy spray over the entire length of the ship. The frigid water engulfed him.

"Shit!" the man yelled, his voice drowned out by the crashing water. The long, slender pole he held was almost lost as the over wash struck him. By grabbing the cabling that ran the length of the trawler's afterdeck, he retained control of the pole with the grappling hook attached. As the ship moved on to the next swell, he recovered, re-establishing his vigil out over the windswept Atlantic.

Within ten minutes, the roar of the engines lessened. The second crewman came up beside the port bow lookout. "There," the crewman shouted. Forty or fifty feet beyond the ship, the gray object bobbed in the water. He dropped the hook into the water beside the bobbing package. The hook quickly became entangled in the spaghetti-like parachute cords. Working together, the two men hauled the container aboard.

The crewmen worked fast, removing the parachute rigging. One of the crew then pressed a black switch beside the trawler's wench. The hold of the ship opened. There, stacked one upon another, were three packages identical to the one just brought onboard. One of the men affixed two orange-and-black adhesive labels that read "Fresh Fish" to the sides of the package. The newly labeled parcel, indistinguishable from the others, was neatly stacked and the hold closed. Less than thirty minutes' time had elapsed from high-altitude jettison to cold storage.

"High sign, aye, Captain," the raspy voice said as one of the crewmen waved from the stern deck.

"Fourth pickup's the charm," the captain said, lighting a fresh cigarette. He took a deep drag, pushing the throttles forward as he exhaled. "We'll be nonstop to St. John's."

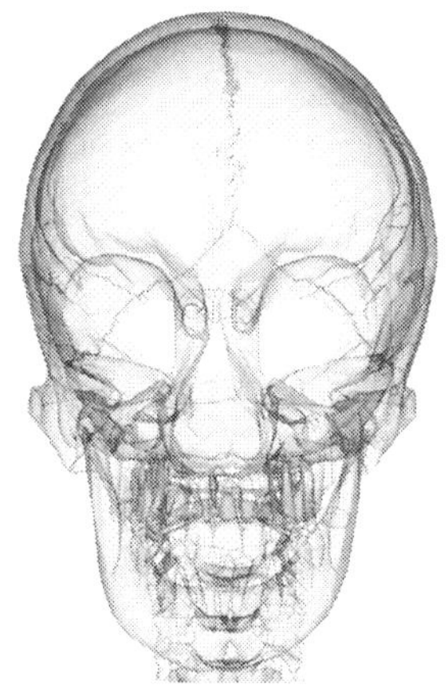

CHAPTER THIRTY

Natalie Roberts looked out from the interior of her car and scanned across the parking lot again. Though several persons had exited the building and driven off the small lot, the one car she recognized still remained.

"Damn," she hissed under her breath. "Why the hell is he here so late? This is a private hospital, not Medford University, for Christ's sake."

Roberts had carefully studied each person exiting the side door for the last half hour — Samuel Jacobson had not left the building. She recognized the Dodge Charger as Jacobson's, the moment she entered the physician's lot outside Taggart Memorial. When she saw the car, she drove to the farthest corner of the lot and parked between two larger automobiles. Once she felt well hidden, she switched off the ignition and simply waited.

As time passed, she began shivering. The cold penetrating the car's interior added to Roberts' uneasiness over the task she had set out to undertake, but she was determined to carry it out. Since her trip to Risarti's, she hadn't been able to clear her mind. She had lain awake until dawn thinking about the disturbing facts Fisher had uncovered.

Was Jane Doe really Mattie? She had obsessed over the Jane Doe puzzle for almost two weeks. She had spent hours online probing, questioning, and searching for clues. She had talked with colleagues, phoned researchers with queries, placed questions with the Pathology Usenet news group, but nothing. To a person, all experts agreed that her observations on the Jane Doe tissue were unique, but no one knew the significance. After that, the investigations had reached a dead end. She finally admitted defeat over the matter and was ready to set the puzzle aside — that is, until the night before. The meeting with Fisher and Alli rekindled her obsession. She had to find answers, and if Fisher was right, Taggart Memorial Hospital held those answers.

She lighted her watch face. It was almost ten o'clock. Jacobson's Charger still sat on the other side of the physician's lot, and she was growing doubtful that it would move. Roberts would have much preferred not seeing Jacobson on this particular trip to Taggart.

"This is crazy," she said finally, grabbing her white lab coat. She examined the front pocket to assure herself that her Taggart Memorial ID was clipped on. She stepped out of her car, zipped her winter coat and headed across the parking lot for the side entrance of the hospital.

As Roberts walked past Jacobson's parked car, a vexing question popped into her mind: Why had Jacobson resigned his position as head of Surgical Pathology at The Med? Two years had passed since he left, and it remained a mystery. She recalled the day he made a brief announcement to the department at their monthly faculty meeting. That was it. He never shared his reasons for leaving. A rumor spread through the department following Jacobson's departure that the Pathology Chairman was jealous of Jacobson's leadership.

The Chairman's jealousy was well deserved if it was true, Roberts thought. Under Jacobson's direction, Surgical Pathology ran smoother than all other Pathology Divisions. Rumor said Jacobson's leadership had caused friction between him and the Chairman for years. Most people guessed Jacobson resigned because he had his fill of the Chairman's childish behavior. No one knew for sure.

Roberts stopped and stood briefly in front of Jacobson's Charger. The whole affair with Jacobson's departure had troubled her from the beginning. During her years on the Medford Pathology faculty, Jacobson had acted as her mentor and friend — almost like a father. But before she knew it, he was gone. He had become the new Pathology director at Taggart Memorial Hospital. To her surprise, Jacobson had called her a year after he left, asking for help organizing Taggart's human tissue bank. She agreed to a part-time position working two weekend days every other week.

"Yep," she said softly as she patted the hood of Jacobson's car. "Strange stuff."

She turned and walked to the hospital's side entrance. Good thing he's got no family, she thought. They would definitely object to Jacobson's fondness for late nights.

Roberts crossed the street separating the physician's parking lot from the hospital and walked to the security door. To the left was a card slide with a numeric keypad. She unclipped the ID from her lab coat and dragged it through the slot. A low beep prompted her to enter her four-digit TMH doctor number. After she did, the door buzzed, indicating it would be unlocked for three seconds. She tugged the heavy door open and entered.

On the ground floor, a single long corridor ran the length of the building and intersected with a similar corridor spanning the building's width. Departments such as admissions, Emergency/Trauma, Pharmacy and Radiology were on that floor. The clinical laboratories, all under the direction of Pathology, were also on the ground floor. The remainder of the Pathology Department, which included Surgical Pathology, the morgue and the human tissue bank, were on the first basement level one floor below ground.

Roberts shed her winter coat and donned the knee-length lab jacket. She clipped her TMH ID to the front breast pocket and walked to the intersection of the two main corridors some fifty yards in the distance. As she walked, moisture mounted on the surfaces of her hands. That night was not her regularly scheduled work night. She was counting on being a face in the crowd, merely another hospital employee.

The ground floor corridors had heavy pedestrian traffic. Nurses in white uniforms and physicians in scrub suits swept down the corridor headed in their appointed directions. Self-propelled carts zipped along the sides of the corridors guided by onboard directional sensors. The carts, known as Smart Movers, transported cargo such as linen, sterile instruments, medication, and other consumable supplies to locations around the hospital. They were but one example of Taggart Memorial's obsession with technology. Everywhere, tasks formerly performed by humans, such as lighting, environmental control, medication administration and transportation, were automated. Roberts surmised Taggart was a hospital of the future.

At the intersection, Roberts waited for the Smart Mover to pass. She then entered the central stairwell and headed down one flight to the basement. Downstairs, she found a distinctly different atmosphere. The basement corridor was cloaked in near darkness. Light levels, controlled by a central computer, were reduced. One of every ten overhead fluorescent fixtures was lighted, leaving large patches of the subterranean corridor without illumination.

The hair on her neck bristled and a throbbing sensation filled her temples. She had not seen the corridor darkened to that extent. She listened.

There was complete silence. None of the traffic noise from the ground floor could be heard.

She was beginning to reconsider her visit to the tissue bank when the silence was broken. Roberts froze, her back pressed hard against the cold metal of the stairwell door. She wanted to move, but her body would not respond.

The noise grew louder. It sounded familiar, but she could not place it. She only knew it was headed straight for her, and she was frightened.

Out of her peripheral vision, she saw movement. Why couldn't she get her arms or legs to move? What can I do, she screamed to herself.

The sound intensified. She squeezed her eyes shut and awaited the inevitable.

Then, as quickly as it had come, the noise decreased in intensity. She opened her eyes in time to see the Smart Mover, assigned to Pathology, passing down the corridor to her left.

Roberts could feel beads of sweat roll down her temples. Her head throbbed, and she found herself hyperventilating. She was embarrassed and angry over her response.

Minutes passed. The sounds from the robotic cart were no longer audible. It had apparently entered an elevator some distance down the corridor. She released her grip on the stairwell doorknob and rubbed her hands together. They were sweaty and trembling. She adjusted her spectacles to their proper position and looked down the corridor.

"You have got to do this," she mumbled to herself, trying to bolster her courage.

Though Roberts was still shaky, she straightened her lab coat, turned right and headed to Surgical Pathology. As she walked, her gait was tentative and wary, with intentionally muffled heel strikes. She wanted to hear the slightest noise coming from the silent corridor.

At the turnoff into the Surgical Pathology suites, to Roberts delight, an overhead fixture lit the area. She fully expected to see the lights on in Jacobson's office, but it was dark. The office, small and cramped, was the first thing she had to pass, heading into Surgical Pathology, and she was prepared. She had cooked up a story to explain her unscheduled presence. The fib was going to be something about a trip to her mother's house for a visit, but it vaporized when she saw Jacobson's empty office.

"That's unusual," she whispered softly as she peered through the large pane of plate glass adjacent to Jacobson's office door. From the hallway, she could see Jacobson's briefcase sitting open. His desktop was cluttered with slips of paper as if someone had thrown them there. Maybe he's off in the hospital at some administrative meeting, she thought. Roberts looked down at her watch. It was after ten.

That's odd, she puzzled. In all the years she had known Jacobson, she couldn't recall him leaving for the day without a neat and orderly desk. Maybe he's in the middle of some large project, she thought, as she walked down the hallway to the tissue bank, but she was relieved to see his office vacant.

The tissue bank was the last laboratory at the end of the hallway. A single low wattage fluorescent fixture provided inadequate light, leaving much of the hallway dark, especially the door to the tissue bank. Roberts reached into the pocket of her lab coat as she arrived at the door and felt for her key ring. With minor trouble, she identified the key to the lab and unlocked the door. She stepped inside and locked it again.

The tissue bank at Taggart Memorial followed federal guidelines for its design. The rectangular space was small, containing only a single laboratory workbench. Directly behind that stood four ceiling-height cryochambers where tissues were kept frozen in extreme cold. On each chamber, a control panel monitored interior temperatures. Large liquid-nitrogen-filled tanks sat alongside each chamber. In the event of power failure, battery powered pumps would transfer liquid nitrogen into the chambers, preventing tissue-damaging fluctuations in temperature. She scanned the panels. Green digital displays indicated that all interior temperatures stood at minus eighty degrees centigrade.

As she examined the tissue freezers, Roberts reached into the side pocket of her lab coat and removed the cocktail napkin she had picked up at her meeting the night before. On the napkin, she had recorded the seven-digit number, 5046719, the number Fisher had taken directly from the final ledger entry.

The moisture returned to Roberts' hands as she refolded the napkin and placed it on the counter. Her pulse quickened as she walked to the second cryochamber from the left. On the small control panel keypad, she entered a five-digit security code. A soft beep indicated the door could be opened. She grasped the steel handle and pulled it. Super cooled air surged into the small laboratory with a noisy hiss as the door opened.

For a moment, the air became obscured by ice fog from the freezer. Roberts' heart raced as she waited for the fog to clear, which it did rapidly.

Then she studied the contents. The interior was divided into four rows of cryodrawers, three to a row. Roberts put on a pair of bulky gloves to protect her hands. "Five-zero-four-six-seven-one-nine," she said, her gaze jumping from cryodrawer to cryodrawer. The numeric index she had designed was clearly printed on the outside of each drawer. The index listed the highest and lowest sample numbers contained within a particular drawer. Her abdomen became heavy as her eyes stopped at the row of cryodrawers second from the top. Reaching up slightly higher than eye level Roberts pulled open the middle drawer.

She found it hard to control the tremor in her hands as she removed the drawer and placed it on the lab bench. An icy fog arose from the drawer. Roberts hauled out the contents. Each cryodrawer contained about two dozen white plastic boxes. In each box, one hundred tissue cores were stored deep frozen in specially designed plastic vials.

Within five minutes, Roberts had pulled virtually all the storage boxes from the cryodrawer. As successive boxes were removed, she examined the printed index taped on the exterior of each box. None of the numbers listed on the outside of the boxes matched the seven digits she had hurriedly scribbled on the napkin at Risarti's the night before.

"Damn," she said as she pulled the final box from the foggy drawer. "It's not here."

She repositioned her wire rims and blew a shock of blond hair away from her eyes. Her bun, always pulled tight, had worked its way loose, permitting several golden tendrils to fall forward across her face. She stroked at the remaining locks with a gloved hand.

For a moment, Roberts gazed at the cryodrawer as ice fog brimmed over its sides onto the bench top. Her spirits fell. She was angry at herself again for believing in Fisher's fantasy tale.

Stop this, she told herself. Steve Fisher was simply doing what he thought to be right. But how to explain the absence of a sample? Were Mattie's tissue cores taken from the cryochamber and disposed of? Or, did they simply go to another tissue bank?

"What to do now?" she muttered as she reached for two storage boxes to repack the cryodrawer before the tissues began to thaw.

The Question never required an answer. As Roberts lowered the two boxes into the drawer, the back of her right hand contacted a firmness not seen under the layer of ice fog that still filled the cryodrawer. She placed the two boxes on the bench top and pulled off her left glove. Her heart jumped as she dug her hand into the fog-filled drawer. In the far corner of the drawer, her hand contacted another storage box. Because of the dense fog, she had missed it as she unloaded the boxes the first time through.

She found it almost impossible to breathe as she hauled the last box from the cryodrawer. Nervously, she scanned the index, but a fine layer of frost obscured the numbers. With a glove-covered finger, she swiped across the label several times. As the printing of the index became visible, Roberts' legs grew weak and rubbery. Thirty-six entries down the list, she saw the digits 5046719.

For a few moments, she was paralyzed, her body in suspended animation, but her brain fired on all circuits. This is it, she said to herself. This is the proof of Mattie's identity. No, it isn't, another voice spoke from a far corner of her consciousness. It's the beginning of the proof of her identity. DNA fingerprint analysis is still required.

With an explosion of thoughts, Roberts placed the box on the bench top and removed its lid. Inside she could see the cryovials standing in place, each held vertically in its designated slot. She went directly to slot number thirty-six and pulled the vial from the box. She turned the vial and studied its white writing surface. The familiar seven digits were clearly visible.

The noisy cycling of the cryochamber thermostats behind her snapped Roberts out of her trance and into action. Knowing she had to act fast, she placed the vial containing the tissue cores into an empty tube rack on the bench top. She next unscrewed the vial to confirm that the cores were present. She then reached into the breast pocket of her lab coat, where she removed a similar-sized vial half-filled with a DNA preservative. She unscrewed the top of the vial and placed it into the tube rack beside the tissue cores. Next, she pulled open a narrow drawer under the bench top, reached in, removed a pair of long slender forceps and closed the drawer. She worked swiftly, using the forceps to remove one of the frozen thread-like tissue cores from the tissue bank vial and transferred it into the vial containing the blue liquid preservative. She recapped the vial and shook it gently to submerge the tissue core in the liquid.

Roberts redonned the gloves and reloaded all the tissue boxes back into the cryodrawer. She returned the drawer to its proper location and sealed the chamber. She then picked up the vial containing the blue liquid and shook it gently once again. The liquid would break down the tissue, freeing the DNA inside. The first step in the DNA fingerprint procedure had begun.

She placed the vial into her lab coat pocket, walked to the door leading to the hallway and stopped. She turned and glanced back at the area to ascertain that it looked untouched. From the door, she could clearly see the bench top. Satisfied that the laboratory looked undisturbed, she turned, unlocked the door, shut off the lights and entered the hallway. She locked the door and headed for the main corridor.

As she passed by Jacobson's office at the end of the hallway, Roberts' thoughts strayed back to Jacobson's car.

"Stop right there."

Roberts spun around, colliding with the wall as she sprawled backwards. Her chest heaved, her mouth parched instantly as she searched the hallway for the source of the voice.

She saw movement outside Jacobson's office. A large round frame emerged from the shadows and approached her. Roberts wanted to run, but she couldn't. She was cemented to the wall, her extremities stuck, unmoving. Her heart pounded, and her temples throbbed as the shadowy figure approached.

"Why are you here?" The voice was wheezy and curt.

She tried to respond, but her voice, like her arms and legs, would not respond. The odor of stale cigar smoke assaulted her nose, driving her to the brink of nausea as the man drew closer.

His right arm shot toward her. Roberts pressed herself against the wall, awaiting the worst. She could not escape.

Fat fingers yanked her TMH ID from its breast pocket location. He breathed heavily as he drew back and flipped the plastic ID card in his plump hand. "Dr. Roberts, eh," he taunted. "Do we not have a tongue in our head? I asked you a simple question. What are you doing here?"

Roberts could see the face redden, as the volume of his voice tripled. For a moment, she could only stare at the fleshy blob. Her mind raced as she weighed her next move. If he were an attacker, she told herself, he would have already dragged me away. She forced herself to relax as she stood mute and paralyzed.

"I'll ask you again."

"No . . . I . . . I . . .," she stuttered. "I'm finishing some work I started last week in the tissue bank."

The sweaty face drew closer. Roberts detected the odor of rotting eggs as his breath fell across her face.

He spoke again pulling to within inches from her face. "What's your authorization?" he asked, his eyes not breaking their penetrating stare.

Roberts looked hurriedly before she spoke, assuring herself that Jacobson's office was still vacant. She turned back to the blood-red face. "My boss," she said feeling a spark of life in her chest. "My boss is Dr. Samuel Jacobson, director of Pathology. He permits me to work after hours, if I don't complete my work." She said a silent prayer as she spoke. Please let this monster have no knowledge of my part-time schedule.

A few moments passed and the swollen face withdrew. Quietly, the man handed the identification badge to Roberts and pulled a small spiral bound pad from his pocket. He spoke as he jotted something down on the pad. "I will be speaking with Dr. Jacobson. If he doesn't corroborate your story, you'll be hearing from me. You may go."

Roberts burst through the security door that led to physician's parking. The severe temperature drop that occurred once she left the building went unnoticed as she struggled against the panic.

She had to reach her car, a voice screamed inside. She had to escape this place.

The tails of her lab coat flapped as she broke into a jog halfway to her car. Soon, though, Roberts gained a bit of control and slowed to a fast walk. The jingling in her coat pockets warned her she might lose important items. She reached for the pocket where she placed the vial containing the tissue core. It was right where she had left it. She breathed a sigh of relief. With another quick motion, she dug into the other side pocket and shuffled through it. The familiar shapes of her car keys and other items were present. But a sinking sensation hit her as she pulled the contents of the pocket into her hands. With awkward, clumsy movements, Roberts sorted quickly through the articles from the pocket.

"It isn't here, damnit!" Frantically, she searched every pocket, but nothing.

The cocktail napkin was gone.

She retraced her steps across the parking lot. There was no sign of the napkin.

Her hands shook as she realized what must have happened.

The Tissue Bank. The words echoed inside her mind as she eyed the side entrance to the hospital.

"Can't go back. Can't go back."

Roberts turned and sprinted to her car. Within seconds she pulled away, not seeming to notice the screeching tires as she pressed hard on the accelerator.

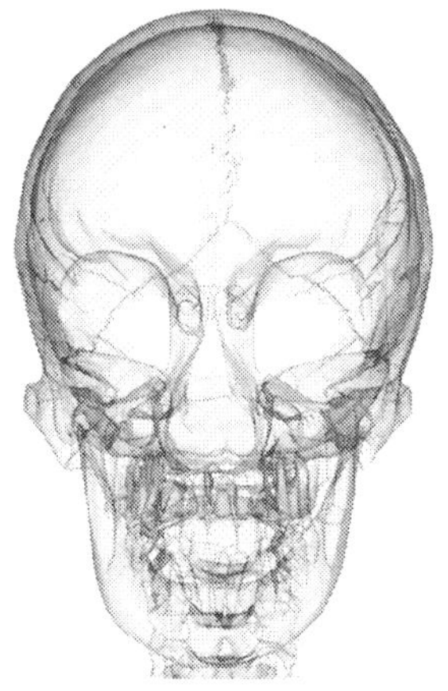

CHAPTER THIRTY-ONE

The wind that rushed off the Caton River stung all of Fisher's exposed body parts. He pulled a heavy collar over his face to lessen the bite and glanced at Alli as they walked. The night was moonless, but in the weak city light coming from across the river he could see she was having trouble too.

"Fifty bucks says the wind chill is subzero." Fisher strained to be heard above the stiff breeze.

"You'll win that bet, hands down," Alli quipped, her voice muffled by the shawl protecting her face.

The frozen surface of the access road crunched softly under their shoes as the emerging bridge superstructure shut off the meager light from the Richland skyline. They continued walking. Soon a low intensity rushing sound was heard above the wind, drowning out their footsteps. Although distant at first, the sound of the falls grew more pronounced as the road carried them toward the undersurface of the Ninth Street Bridge.

From the dirt roadway, Fisher saw a fleeting glimmer arise from an object lying ahead. He reached into the pocket of his coat for the flashlight he had used at the Chaparral and shined it directly on the object. The beam landed on a simple wire cart overturned in the center of the road. It lay on its side, one of its wheels frozen in the mud. Empty plastic bottles and pieces of tin foil lay inside the cart.

They gazed at the cart a few moments. As they started walking again, Fisher felt Alli grasp his hand. He held her hand tightly as they continued.

Within thirty yards, the frozen road turned, winding sharply under the massive bridge. Making the turn, they confronted a dense stand of short leafless trees and the end of the roadway. A continuous moan surrounded them as the icy wind coursed through the naked trunks.

Feeling a tug on his right arm, Fisher stopped. Alli spoke softly into his ear. "Are you certain this is the site where Mattie was found? It seems to be a dead end."

"It was definitely the Ninth Street Bridge. She was found unconscious in a corrugated box. The ambulance tech told me they saw appliance boxes scattered about the area where they found her. Let's follow on through the grove."

"Boxes?"

"Yes. They were probably dragged here for shelter."

Thoink, thoink. Thoink, thoink.

Fisher looked up at the bridge. He could hear the sounds of car tires striking the bridge's expansion joints. They continued through the head-high scrub grove.

The path narrowed as it left the roadway, but stayed wide enough for service vehicles to pass. From the looks of it, Fisher figured, it had been years since any city vehicle had passed that way. The city had neglected its bridges during the push for downtown renovations. The new downtown park across from the College Inn came to Fisher's mind.

After another forty yards, the roadway sloped upward sharply and the trees disappeared. Fisher and Alli had arrived on an elevated spot, a knoll of sorts, directly under the bridge. What they saw ahead brought them both to a stop.

In the shadows cast by aging concrete and rusted steel, six corrugated boxes were pulled together. The boxes were large, capable of holding a refrigerator or freezer.

Fisher scanned the area around the makeshift shelters. Empty food cans, beer bottles and liquor bottles were scattered about. Several articles of cast-off clothing trapped in the brushwood oscillated under the constant effects of the wind.

The ambient light was low, but not below that for eyes accustomed to near-dark conditions. From the far reaches of his peripheral vision, Fisher sensed movement. He reacted by turning his head sharply. The human figure approaching them in the twilight had just begun cocking back a long object, a club of sorts, to deliver a roundhouse swing. Fisher jerked around striking Alli's upper torso with enough force to send her reeling. Simultaneously, he arched his shoulders back, attempting to evade the object. His avoidance measures were not quite adequate, however, as the sting of cold metal grazed across his face.

Momentarily stunned, Fisher fell backwards landing on the frozen ground amid a pile of empty cans. He reached for his face to feel for the damage, but there was no time to assess injuries. The attacker advanced, the weapon held high in preparation for a second strike. Fisher rolled his body hard as the metal bar came down, striking a pile of cans. The attacker returned the bar to its overhead position. He turned and rushed to the spot where Fisher had ended his rolling maneuver.

He knew his best chance for defense was from a standing position. As he struggled to stand, his right foot slipped on another can causing him to fall again. The attacker approached hurriedly and stood ready to deliver another blow.

"Jáfo!" a voice boomed above the wind.

The attacker stopped and turned. The dark man hesitated, then retreated, bringing the bar to his side and stepping back.

"Jáfo, what the hell are you doing with that bar? Who are these people?" The voice came from a stout man standing in front of the closest corrugated box. He wore a ragged jacket that barely fit his large upper body. His face, framed by long black hair and beard, was barely visible.

"It is them, Mon. The men who come to take us," Jáfo said, his voice drenched in a thick Jamaican accent.

Fisher sat on the frozen ground, nursing his cheek where the bar had struck its glancing blow. Within moments Alli's arm went over his shoulder.

"Are you all right?" she asked softly as the two men continued their conversation.

Fisher nodded feeling his face for fractures. Finding none, he looked back as the two men approached them.

"What's your business here, mister?"

Fisher looked at the man who had saved his life. He had the appearance of a lumberjack with a heavily bearded face and broad shoulders. His belly poked out from under a barely visible flannel shirt and a dark blue coat that was in shambles. Fisher wondered how the coat provided any protection from the cold.

His head still spun from the blow, but it was improved. Fisher attempted to stand. The lumberjack reached down to help him.

"I'll ask you again, mister. What's your business around here this time of night?"

Fisher held a glove against the side of his face, slowly opening and closing his jaw. It was painful, but he was confident he had no fractures. He turned to the man. "I'm Dr. Steven Fisher from Medford University. This is Miss Shepard. We are here trying to find out any information on a woman named Mattie. She was found here under the Ninth Street Bridge by Richland Ambulance and taken to Medford Hospital about eight days ago."

The lumberjack looked at Jáfo, who came and stood alongside him. He pulled back the hood of his sweatshirt and revealed flowing dreadlocks.

The two men stared at each other for a fraction of a second before turning back to face Fisher.

"We ain't heard of the name Mattie, Mon." Jáfo cocked his head to pull the dreadlocks out of his face.

Fisher's instincts told him the two were lying. He was about to ask further questions, when he saw another figure emerge from one of the large boxes. He was an emaciated white man with a long shock of unkempt hair and a full beard. His gait was uncertain. He labored against the icy wind as he approached the group, an occasional cough rattling in his chest.

Slivers of light twinkled off tears that welled up in his eyes as he shuffled up even with the other two men. Fisher recognized him from the Richland Police Department. He had been the one searching for Mattie.

For a moment, the gaunt man stood silent, staring at Fisher and Alli.

"Jake." The lumberjack's voice snapped taught. "You don't need to be out in this wind. You've been sick and the cold wind'll just make it worse."

"I heard this man mention Mattie. Didn't you mention Mattie, mister? Do you know where my Mattie is?" His voice was weak and wavering.

Knife-like pains ran through Fisher as he stared at Jake, the same pains that had come a thousand times before, always making it a struggle to give bad news. A demon was at work inside him, swinging its white-hot branding iron, searing his guts and his heart.

Fisher reached over with his gloved left hand and placed it gently on the man's shoulder. "Mattie's dead, Jake."

Jake said nothing at first, but the effect of Fisher's news was visible. His tears abruptly increased, bursting over his lower lids and disappearing into his thick beard. His lips trembled as he turned his head toward the black wind sweeping across the knoll.

"She was the last thing I had left in the world." He spoke softly, his voice quivering. "Why did you do it, Mattie? Why did you do it? The money wasn't worth nothing like this. Not nothing."

The man sobbed as he sank to the frozen ground, his legs wilting beneath him. He reached out with his bare hands into the blackness as he slumped. Jáfo and the lumberjack grabbed his flailing arms, bringing him to a soft landing. He covered his face and wept.

"Jake, Mon, you've got to get back to your house." Jáfo knelt beside the man as he cried.

"Mattie, that money wasn't no good. You just took that money and bought whiskey with it. Why, Mattie? Why?" Jake coughed then hacked. The fit became so severe Fisher was convinced the man would fracture his ribs.

Jáfo and the lumberjack used force to pull Jake to his feet. With their ailing friend intermittently coughing, then sobbing, the two men escorted him back to his box.

The lumberjack turned and stomped back across the knoll to Fisher and Alli.

"Doctor, whoever you are, that's a cruel thing you done. Jake's a sick man. Don't know if he'll make it through the winter, him sick like that. And you come along telling him that Mattie's dead."

"She is." Fisher spoke softly to Jake's angry friend. "She died from cold exposure. She was taken to the Medford Emergency Department eight days ago."

"Doc, Mattie was her own person. She was stubborn. She didn't take suggestions from nobody. The night she disappeared, everybody up here went to the shelters in the city, 'cause of the freezing rain. When we left, we tried to take her with us, but she wouldn't come. She was more interested in drinking that wine. I guess what I'm saying is, it don't surprise me none."

Fisher looked at the man a moment, then spoke. "Would it surprise you to know that just before she died, someone removed Mattie's right kidney?"

The lumberjack was obviously caught off guard. In the half-light bathing the knoll, the face under the beard took on a mask of surprise. His eyes widened and his mouth dropped open. Fisher saw teeth covered with black spots as his mouth opened.

Fisher waited for him to speak, but he remained silent.

"I knew something was up with Mattie, Mon."

Fisher turned as the voice came over his shoulder.

Jáfo had returned. "Mattie was always in the food line at the shelter, just like the rest of us. Then all of a sudden Mattie not come to the shelter. Jake say she have money and spend it on wine and whiskey. She not care to come to the shelter for food no more."

"Where did she get the money?" Fisher searched for the dark man's facial features through the thick dreadlocks.

Jáfo looked down at the frozen garbage-strewn dirt. For a few moments, he looked about as if searching for something he could not find. He then looked back up at Fisher and Alli. "I come to America two years ago, Mon, from my home in Jamaica. I live in the city, because I think life would be fine. I have no money, so I live on the streets with these people. They also have no money. We all live here. The city take care of us. All of a sudden somebody like Mattie, they get money. Then they disappear."

A cold weight settled inside Fisher's chest. He glanced at Alli. In the twilight, he could see the shock of recognition crossing her face as well.

"Jáfo, did you report those missing people to the police?" Fisher restrained the urge to scream out the question.

"It don't do no good," the lumberjack said, speaking up. "We have all been to the police. They don't give a shit about us. Can't be bothered."

Fisher's hands oozed a cold sweat inside his heavy gloves. "How many have disappeared?"

Neither of the men was quick to respond. Finally Jáfo spoke, "Several people, Mon, several people from here, but there are others, Mon, from other camps."

"How . . . when . . . do your friends disappear? Do they walk out of this camp and never return, or do they just disappear from the street over in the city when no one is watching?"

"Both, Mon."

"Do you know who's taking your friends or where they're taking them?"

Jáfo and the lumberjack again turned their heads to glance at each other, as if speaking in a nonverbal language. They said nothing after that.

Fisher, realizing they had no intention of responding, said, "I know what you guys are thinking. If we don't mess with those people, they'll eventually just go away. They'll stop taking our friends and just leave us alone. Well, think again. These people taking your friends will stop at nothing. They want human organs. They specifically want your organs, because you're homeless. Nobody listens to a group of homeless people when they complain that one of their friends failed to return to the shelter. Jake was down at the Richland Police Department over a week ago, filing a missing persons report. What has resulted from it? Nothing. The first time Jake heard any news about Mattie was just a few minutes ago. That means they can get organs on the cheap without having to worry about the police." Fisher stopped, but the two men remained mute.

A few moments passed. The wind, the falls, the occasional car passing overhead provided the only noise.

Silently Fisher turned and looked at Alli. She looked back into Fisher's eyes. She nodded. Together, they turned to leave.

"It is the Mon with the snapping leg," Jáfo said, before Fisher and Alli had walked more than a few steps.

A blast of river wind smashed into the camp, particularly bad for those standing outside the boxes.

Fisher glanced at Alli again. She readjusted her coat, pulling the shawl tight across her face to lessen the sting of the frigid wind. They returned to the two men.

"How do we find this man? Where does he usually show up?" Fisher looked directly at Jáfo.

Jáfo pulled the hood of his ragged sweatshirt back up over the dreadlocks. He glanced at the lumberjack, as if looking for approval, but the lumberjack remained silent, simply staring at the frozen earth. He turned to face Fisher.

"Jáfo will take you."

"You know where the man is?"

"Yes, Mon. I see where the men take Mattie. The night she disappear, I was on the street. I see the mon with the snapping leg and several others pull Mattie out of a fancy car and take her into a warehouse down there."

Despite the freezing cold, Fisher's face flushed hot. His pulse raced with excitement and fear as Jáfo raised an arm clothed in rags and pointed in the direction of the river.

Jáfo walked back to Jake's box where intermittently, coughing and sobbing could be heard.

"Jake, mon," Jáfo said with a caring voice, "I will be back in a little while." Jáfo picked up the metal bar and returned.

"I will take you, Mon."

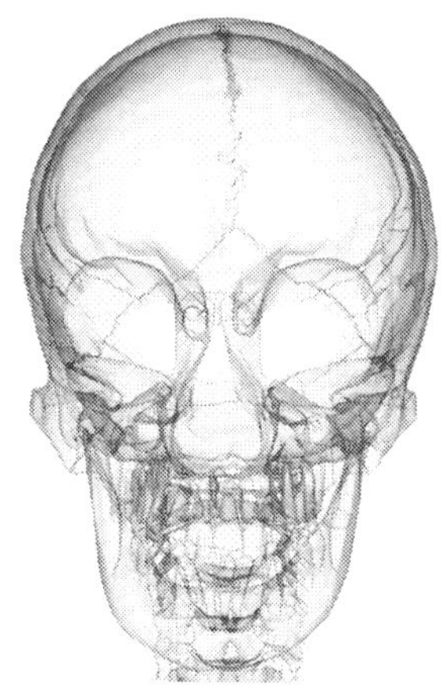

CHAPTER THIRTY-TWO

February 8, Pathology Building, Medford University

Roberts was lost in thought when she arrived in the lobby of the Pathology building.

The security guard looked Roberts over. "Surprised to see you again, Dr. Roberts," the kindly old guard said.

When he spoke, Roberts realized the trip marked her second after-hours entry into the building in two weeks.

She showed her identification and went straight to her laboratory. She knew exactly what she had to do. To prove the identity of the tissue core from the freezer at Taggart, she had to genetically match the core to the tissue taken from her Jane Doe autopsy. This could best be achieved by DNA fingerprint analysis.

Funny how things change, she thought, preparing a work area on her laboratory bench. Two months earlier she would have thought of her job at the Med as a bit boring; She took the part-time job with Jacobson at Taggart for that reason.

Roberts reached for the set of instructions she received from Melissa Greene, Richland's new Assistant Chief Medical Examiner.

Forensic DNA Fingerprinting — A Fast-track Method

By
Melissa Greene, MD
Assistant Chief Medical Examiner
City of Richland.

Under normal laboratory conditions, DNA fingerprinting took two weeks to complete, but Greene had devised a procedure that compressed the work into a matter of hours.

She began the fingerprint procedure by extracting the DNA from the two tissues. Within twenty minutes, raw DNA, a stringy material reminiscent of egg white, was present in the small plastic tubes on the bench. Roberts next cut the DNA into fragments using a specialized enzyme that attacked the molecules, at select locations along their immense length. If the autopsy tissue and the tissue core retrieved from Taggart originated from the same person, all the fragments of DNA would be identical.

Roberts struggled at first, still wrestling with the events at Taggart Memorial. She could not stop thinking about the missing cocktail napkin or the security guard who came out of the shadows in the pathology hallway. Once the enzyme step was completed, she had calmed a bit. You're just going to screw this up if you don't get your head on straight. There's too much riding on this, she told herself.

After the DNA was enzymatically cut, the fragments had to be arranged by size. To accomplish this, Roberts would rely on the driving force of electricity.

She carefully placed small amounts of each specimen into separate quarter-inch slots of a submerged flat rubbery gel. Commercially available DNA cut into known fragment sizes was placed in a third slot so the two specimens could be compared. She switched on the power sending current into the chamber holding the gel. Over the next two hours, the fragments would sort themselves by size. Larger fragments would localize closer to the slots where she pipetted the samples into the electrophoresis chamber while smaller fragments would travel further and further away from the slots.

Roberts next used a second electrical treatment to drive the DNA fragments out of the flat gel and onto nylon membrane. It was shortly after two o'clock when she laid the nylon membrane containing the genetic code from the two specimens on the laboratory bench. The DNA fragments on the membrane were still invisible.

She retrieved a vial from the refrigerator labeled with a series of letter-number combinations: D14S13, D16S85, D17S79, D1S7, D2S44, D4S139. Each represented a specialized form of marker DNA that attached to the genetic code of each specimen. If the Jane Doe tissue and the tissue core were from the same person, the marker DNA would attach to each at exactly the same point. Roberts withdrew the entire volume from the vial and squirted it onto the nylon membrane that sat submerged in a square plastic basin containing a chemical buffer.

After completing the procedure, she set her timer for two hours and walked into her office where she closed her eyes for a quick nap.

• • • • •

Beep-beep . . . beep-beep . . . beep-beep.

Roberts sat bolt upright, her breathing rapid and shallow, her pulse racing. She recognized the beeping sound, but for a few seconds, she was disoriented, unable to grasp its significance. Vivid images of Smart Movers lumbering down dark hallways filled her mind as she groped about the desktop where she had rested her head.

Beep-beep . . . beep-beep . . . beep-beep.

The thick vapor that fogged her mind loosened its grip as she wrestled free of her dream. Looking around the room, she recognized familiar objects — her microscope, her briefcase, the huge fig tree that continually shed leaves in the corner of her office.

Roberts stretched her arms and legs. She was groggy, but awake. The timer that still beeped sat exactly where she had placed it two hours earlier. As she reached down to her desk to shut it off, she glanced at the clock perched on the bookcase beside her. It was after four in the morning.

She returned to the laboratory where she took the plastic basin containing the membrane off the rocking platform where she had placed it earlier. In her right hand, she held a small brown vial containing a developer. Once poured onto the membrane, the familiar bar-code fingerprint of the two specimens should appear in twenty to thirty seconds.

She poured the contents of the vial into the basin, agitated it briefly, and waited.

Since arising from her nap, a low-back pain troubled her, no doubt the result of the awkward position she had assumed while asleep. Roberts stood erect stretching the cramp out of her spine. For a moment she became aware of the lab's familiar noises — the loud ventilation system, the cold-induced creaking of the half-century-old walls, the soft surging of the rocker platform which she had neglected to switch off.

"C'mon, damn it," Roberts said, stooping back over the membrane.

One sound Roberts failed to notice was the soft rhythmic snapping sound that made its way into the laboratory from the hallway.

As she studied the developing membrane, images of the fingerprint slowly emerged. She held her breath as she watched in amazement.

"Oh God," she said as the results became clear.

Roberts heard breathing behind her. She turned to face the sound, but lightening movement prevented her. Human arms as dense as iron gripped her upper chest and tightened around her. She struggled, but it was useless. Before she could scream, the cold grating feel of a wet gauze pad was slammed across her mouth and nose. She recognized the sweet odor of chloroform. Roberts held her breath and struggled harder, but she couldn't break the vice-like grip. As she fought, her chest burst with air hunger. She deeply inhaled, knowing full well the sweet anesthetizing fumes of chloroform would rush into her lungs. Her consciousness dulled slightly.

No, a voice inside her screamed. You can't give up! Don't make it easy for them!

Roberts opened her mouth to its full gaping extent, and two fingers of the intruder's hand fell inside her mouth. She bit down with all her might.

"*Itai Chikusho*," the intruder yelled as the grip was released.

Chloroform surged into Roberts' blood. She lurched forward to the work station where her DNA fingerprint was in the final stages of developing. At the same time, she looked at the intruder. A fuzzy green aura, formed around all things in her sight. Her head was light, her body off balance. The intruder came into view with a blackish green tint. No. He wore a black coat surrounded by a green aura. His Asian face, framed by straight black hair, writhed in pain as he held his hand. Roberts saw blood with a greenish red tint covering the middle two fingers of his left hand. She could hear mumbling as her head became lighter and her footing more uncertain.

Roberts grabbed the lab bench for support, struggling to keep the bleeding intruder in sight. The greenish tint promptly became pervasive, affecting her entire vision. The last thing she saw as her vision waned was another person. She looked at the second intruder — a man — as her vision went dark. His face was familiar. Sweating face . . ., trench coat . . ., obese . . .

Her mind attempted to reconstruct the elements, but it was — no, wait. Taggart Memorial, hours earlier.

With that last thought, Roberts lost consciousness still clinging to the lab bench. Her lower body collapsed. As she fell, she dragged the work station with her. Reagent bottles, the plastic basin containing the membrane, pipettes and, finally, the liquid-filled chamber, crashed onto the laboratory floor, landing in pieces all around her.

Roberts lay sprawled on the floor.

• • • • •

"Pick up the bitch," the man in the trench coat wheezed at the Asian bent over in pain. "We'll take the back stairs. I parked my car by the loading dock. And try not to screw this up, will you?"

The Asian stared after the obese man as he waddled out of the laboratory and into the hallway. Tears streamed down his face as he looked at the deep wounds inflicted by the tremendous force of Roberts' bite. He reached inside his black leather jacket and pulled out a handkerchief. He gently encircled the two fingers with the handkerchief. He held the hand closer to his face and flexed the fingers. A wincing grimace passed over his sharp features.

The intruder swept the remains of Roberts' fingerprint study away with his foot and reached down to pick up the unconscious woman. She weighed less than he had thought. He hauled her over his shoulders and walked to the laboratory entrance, his prosthetic leg emitting a soft snap with each stride. As he reached the door, he turned to shut off the lights, but he became distracted as he glanced down at the blood-soaked bandages. He turned and walked out, leaving the lab as it was.

Beside the lab bench, strewn across the space between the benches, sat the remains of the DNA fingerprint, intact.

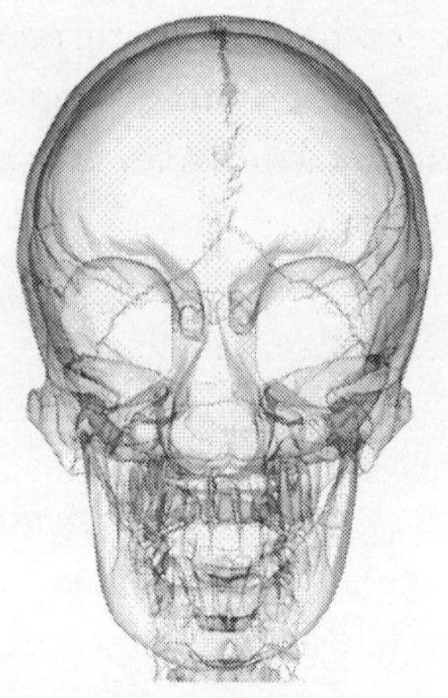

CHAPTER THIRTY-THREE

Fisher stumbled but did not fall, his foot entangled by an unseen obstruction. Each step was treacherous as he and Alli rushed in single file down a dark path by the Caton River. Icy winds screamed across the water, sucking the breath from their lungs when it struck their faces. Ten feet ahead, Jáfo's torso was barely visible as he plunged down the path into the gloom.

One second Fisher's trek down river was surreal, a floating effect with twinkling lights framed in darkness across the water. The next second he was starkly aware of frozen feet, airless lungs and the uncertainty of the charcoal blackness where he placed his feet. Each time they collided in Fisher's consciousness, he struggled to break his thoughts free, recalling their objective — to locate the site where Mattie was last seen.

The gap between them narrowed as Jáfo's pace slowed. When they came to a stop, the path sat amid a dense stand of leafless scrub.

"We are close to the place, Mon." Jáfo's low voice was scarcely audible above the roar of the falls. "This factory, burn in the fall. Many people killed."

Barely visible, the skeleton of a factory building loomed large above the river bank. Rectangular black holes indicated where windows had formerly existed. The hulk sat silent.

"The men, they brought Mattie there." Jáfo pointed toward the blackness beyond the factory building.

Before Fisher or Alli could ask, Jáfo turned and resumed his march down the black path that skirted the building some thirty yards away.

With Jáfo in the lead, they made their way off the path bordering the Caton River and moved carefully among stacks of large shipping crates as they edged alongside the first warehouse building beyond the burned out factory. As they moved through the crates, Fisher was grateful to be sheltered from the wintry blast that raged across the water. Soon, Jáfo stopped and signaled for Fisher and Alli to join him. He pointed to a lone door on the side of the dark warehouse.

Fisher was unfamiliar with the factory section down river from the Ninth Street Bridge. Since his arrival nine years earlier, he had never ventured to this section of Richland.

The carnage wrought in nearby drug wars has provided fodder for many a transplant surgeon, Fisher thought, as he stared at the warehouse entrance. A stark image of Rudy Smith's young body lying on a Medford OR table appeared fleetingly in his mind.

"Why would they have brought Mattie here?" Alli asked crouching with Fisher behind the crates.

"I'm not sure," Fisher whispered. "They obviously carried out the nephrectomy somewhere. The question is where? Maybe this is just a collection point, and from here she was taken to a secret operating room."

From their vantage point, Fisher and Alli looked at the door. It was poorly lighted by an overhead incandescent bulb. Its ribbed steel shade stood out in contrasting shadows producing a patchwork appearance.

Fisher reckoned the entry way to be about fifty percent larger than conventional size. Probably for hauling large items in and out of the building, he thought.

Suspended overhead was a ten-or fifteen-foot cement awning that shadowed the area from all other ambient light. The result was a doorway poorly visible from more than twenty or thirty yards away. To add to the obscurity, crates positioned at random about the building made the entrance invisible from the main road some fifty yards away.

"This is the place, Mon, the place where they take Mattie."

"You saw the men take Mattie into this building?"

"Yes, Mon," Jáfo said quickly. "I come up off the path on my way from the city. I walk by here and see four men pull Mattie out of the car. Jáfo hide here." He clunked the ground at his feet with the black pipe he still carried. "They not know I'm here. The men take Mattie through that door."

"It's pretty clear," Fisher said turning to Alli. "We're going to have to get into this building. You and Jáfo stay back. I'm going to have a quick look at that door."

Fisher stood from his crouched position and squeezed his way between the stacked crates. As he made his way to the entrance, he discovered containers of completely different construction. He glanced at them briefly, his attention drawn by the difference. They were small and gray, constructed of plastic, not flesh-toned plywood.

Fisher nudged past the odd stack. He had practically reached the open space surrounding the entry way, when he noticed the gray containers all bore bright orange labels that read, "Fresh Fish, St John's, Newfoundland, Canada."

Fisher stopped a moment and stared at the labeled crates, but then continued past the small containers.

The heavily constructed door had steel ribs across most of its surface. Nothing short of a jackhammer would open it. Fisher gripped the door's handle. It was worth a try, he thought, pulling the handle. Nothing budged.

There was no visible lock, but to the left, mounted adjacent to the door, roughly four feet above the walkway, was a small metal box some ten inches high and eight inches wide. The metal box was completely open. The bottom interior surface of the box was coated with a highly reflective black plastic material. On top of the box was a smooth, slanted surface. A card slide ran the length of the slanted surface. A small one-by-two inch screen sat beside the card slide.

Fisher reached inside the container. Instantly, a high intensity blue light illuminated the interior, as its laser processors studied the geometry and three-dimensional structure of Fisher's hand. The small screen on the top of the structure glowed pink displaying the words:

ACCESS DENIED

Within seconds, the blue light extinguished itself.

Fisher studied the device with dismay. The entrance was a dead end. By habit, the thumb of his right hand traced the bony ridges of his chin as he considered the problem. An old warehouse with a sophisticated access system. It was peculiar, he thought, as his mind raced to form an alternate entry plan.

Fisher stepped back lost in thought. He did not attach any significance to the soft rhythmic snapping sound bouncing off the wall of wooden crates near the corner of the warehouse. The sound grew in intensity, finally drawing Fisher's attention, but by then it was too late.

A small-framed man came into the dim light near the corner, his attention focused on his bandaged, blood-soaked hand.

Fisher, jerked from his thoughts, stared at the man. He was slender, his face Asian.

On noticing Fisher, the Asian crouched, his right hand disappearing into his coat.

Fisher froze as a pistol appeared from inside the Asian's jacket. The man stepped forward, brandishing the weapon.

A lead weight settled in Fisher's chest as the reality of his situation became clear. His breath quickened as the man approached. He glanced at the crates ten feet away. In a dash for cover, he would be an easy target. He stood still.

The light from overhead struck the Asian's face producing a demonic mask. Fisher's feelings of apprehension mounted when cocking sounds came from the pistol. His mind raced.

"Steve! Over here!"

Fisher's looked to the right. Alli had stepped out of hiding and was in clear view.

The Asian, surprised by the change of events, pointed the pistol at the crates.

Blackness flashed, and the Asian fell where he stood. Fisher looked up. Behind the fallen man stood Jáfo, his black pipe raised to deliver a second blow.

Fisher raced towards him. "Jáfo, don't!" Fisher screamed, catching the pipe before it began its death blow descent. "You can't kill him."

Jáfo stared at Fisher, the glowing whites of his eyes burning with fire for the kill. "This is one of the men I saw carry Mattie, Mon." Jáfo pointed to the crumpled heap lying at their feet.

"Okay." Fisher exhaled. "Okay, Jáfo."

"Steve, are you all right?" Alli asked, reaching the site where they stood.

"Alli," Fisher said heatedly, "I can't believe you did that. You could have been killed!"

"Hah, hah, hah, hah." Jáfo belly laughed. "You are funny, Mon. She is the one that thought up the scheme."

Fisher turned back to Alli and looked deeply into her eyes. "I'm sorry. Thanks for pulling me out of the fire."

"Good thing you brought me along." She grinned subtly.

Fisher turned back to the homeless Jamaican. "Jáfo, the door is secured. We'll have to search for another way into the building."

"Not so fast, Mon. Not so fast." Jáfo bent down and searched the unconscious Asian's pockets.

Fisher leaned down, picked up the small pistol and stuffed it into the pocket of his coat.

"Ahhh. This is what Jáfo looking for."

He stood. He held a credit card-sized piece of plastic.

"What's that?" Fisher asked.

"Help Jáfo drag this mon to the door."

Fisher and Alli both helped Jáfo haul the unconscious Asian to the door.

"Over this way, please."

When they had pulled the unconscious man past the door, Jáfo reached down and extended the man's limp arm to the metal box. He opened the Asian's hand and laid it flat onto the box's black reflective surface. An intense blue light shined down onto the hand.

Immediately, the small screen displayed the message:

Insert ID card now

Jáfo took the filched plastic card and pulled it through the card slide.

The access box emitted a hum for two to three seconds. When it ceased, the steel-ribbed door opened.

The looks on Fisher and Alli's faces sent Jáfo into another series of belly laughs.

"Okay, Jáfo, what's your secret?" Fisher asked when his laughter finally subsided.

Under the pale light from the overhead bulb, Jáfo grinned from ear to ear. For the first time, Fisher noticed Jáfo's gold eye-tooth.

"In Jamaica, all the hotels use systems to keep us out. To help feed my family, Jáfo had to know them all."

"That's incredible," Alli said.

"Yes, that's incredible," Fisher added.

"What do we do with this mon?" Jáfo asked.

"Let's drag him inside."

From the moment they dropped the unconscious Asian into a heap inside the door, all levity vaporized.

Fisher reacted first, recognizing the strong odors that permeated the air inside the warehouse.

"Disinfectants," he said, standing upright.

"It's unmistakable," Alli said.

Inside the doorway, they found themselves standing in a large open room, its ceiling rising to more than twenty feet. An enormous skylight brought in a remarkable amount of city light, even at night.

Fisher fished the flashlight out of his coat pocket and returned to the outer wall near the entry. He located a switch box and moved several switches into the on position.

All locations inside the strange room were bathed in subdued incandescent light. Soft machine like noises could be heard as he threw the last of the switches.

As Fisher turned back to the lighted interior of the warehouse, he saw it. Speechless, he returned to his two companions. All three were silent, their full attention taken by the object before them. Standing greater than ten feet high, occupying a third of the room's space, sat a large container reflecting the incandescent illumination overhead.

Fisher estimated its dimensions at some fifteen by thirty feet. Dozens of cables of varying thickness sprouted from the upper surface then traveled diagonally toward the ceiling. The droning sound that began once the switches were thrown came from atop the container.

Still surprised by what they were seeing, Fisher and Alli approached the container.

Jáfo called after them as they disappeared around the far side of the cube-like structure. "I stay with this mon. Keep watch at the door."

Jáfo's words fell on deaf ears as Fisher and Alli continued their inspection.

Alli finally broke the silence. "Okay, I give up. What the hell is it?"

"I'm not sure but . . . ."

Fisher halted mid-sentence as they reached the side opposite the warehouse entryway. Before them an opening led to the interior of the structure. At the left of the entry, to Fisher's disbelief, was a two-station surgical scrub sink.

"Oh, shit," Fisher whispered slowly under his breath.

Like Fisher, Alli needed no explanation of what they had stumbled upon. She was silent as they approached the entrance.

An infrared sensor activated as they approached and the door slid open, revealing an interior immersed in darkness. A flow of disinfectant-laden air rushed at them as the door opened.

"Positive pressure ventilation." Fisher reached for the panel of switches to the left of the entrance and flipped them upward.

The interior was immediately bathed with intense white light.

Fisher and Alli stood at the threshold, dumbfounded by what they saw. The continuous breeze of filtered air increased the strange reality they were experiencing.

In the center of the brightly lighted interior was a standard operating room table. Above the table, suspended by a counterweighted arm, was an enormous rectangular procedure light. At each of the corners of the light, two-foot-long metal shafts, oriented diagonally downward, supported small, high-resolution video cameras. Most chilling of all the items were two robotic arms on either side of the table. The arms were slender and easily extended the width of the operating table.

As they walked into the container, Fisher scanned the area, struggling to avoid sensory overload. At the head of the table, stood cardiac monitoring equipment combined with anesthesia instruments he had never seen before. All the devices that surrounded the operating table sprang wiring out the rear labeled fiber optic data transmission cabling. The trunks led first to a large gray column some five feet high and fifteen inches deep.

"This must be some form of data processor." Fisher ran his hand over the object. The wires from the column were thicker and fewer in number and extended to the ceiling. "Those probably connect to the cables we saw projecting out to the roof."

A row of cabinets with glass doors attracted Fisher's attention. A series of four elliptical frame-like devices sat enclosed under sterile plastic drapes. Projecting off each ellipse were additional small robotic arms, each bearing recognizable surgical instruments. Fisher scanned the frames. One label each, either "nephrectomy," "hepatectomy," "pancreatectomy," or "lobectomy," was present on the strange contrivances.

"Steve, what do you make of this?" Alli called from across the container room.

Fisher walked across to Alli.

"It's a medicine cabinet of sorts," she said as Fisher arrived. "Most of the drugs here are ones you'd expect. There are intravenous fluids, anesthetic agents, analgesics, and antibiotics. But I found this."

Alli turned to Fisher and handed him a multi-dose vial. Fisher rolled the vial in his hand until he could read its plain white label. It was imprinted KP-1049.

No other markings were visible on the label. As he held the vial, Fisher pressed his memory, attempting to attach significance to the printed code. He continued rotating the vial gently in the palm of his hand, searching his memory, but there was nothing.

"Let's take it with us," Fisher said finally, still staring at the vial. "Codes like that are ones pharmaceutical companies attach to drugs that haven't reached the open market. Maybe Gary can help us by searching the FDA's drug database."

Fisher handed the vial back to Alli, but the light reflected off the vial in a strange way. Fisher searched for the source of the reflection. Within a few seconds, he found it. On the vial's base, imprinted directly on the glass, two unusual markings were visible.

KΠ

Fisher's initial impulse was to ignore the scribbling, but as he stared at the two symbols he remarked, "There's something familiar about those two symbols." He pointed to the bottom of the vial. "I've seen this before, but I just can't recall where."

"Hey! this mon is waking up here."

Fisher and Alli turned in the direction of the voice. Jáfo was standing at the entrance to the container.

"Shall I put him back to sleep?"

Jáfo held up the body-length black pipe.

"No, we're ready to leave," Fisher said. "Keep this vial, Alli. I've seen that symbol before. Just can't remember where."

They hurriedly inspected the remaining parts of the structure. On the side opposite the entryway, they discovered a small room attached by a single door. The smaller room held a standard hospital bed and additional shelves with intravenous fluids. They also found more cardiac monitoring equipment.

"Post anesthesia recovery area, most likely," Fisher said as they looked around briefly.

They walked back to the sliding entry door, stopping at the threshold. "We've seen enough," Fisher said. "The video cameras, the robotic arms, the processing unit, those frames on the shelves — this is a remote operating theater. The surgeon probably operates by some form of video link, with the cameras serving as his eyes. The robotic arms are his hands." As Fisher stared into the room, the pieces gradually fit together.

"Those sons-of-bitches," Fisher said in a growl.

"What is it?" Alli asked, surprised by his change of voice.

"The ledger. It all makes such sense now. Chip found the control center for this place. Remember his email? He told us he was hunting for a rear exit out of the outpatient surgery center at Taggart and stumbled into a small room with a large console. There was some sort of chamber that held a pair of gloves and a hood connected to wires.

Fisher stopped a moment again, dipping deeply into his memory. "What was the word Chip used in that message?"

"Word?" Alli asked.

"Yes, there was a word he used." Fisher racked his brain. "What was that . . .? Uh. The word was telepresence."

"Telepresence?"

"Yes. In his message, Chip said the word teleprescence was printed on two rows of four buttons on the control panel. It all makes sense."

"I'm not quite with you on this."

"In the nineteen nineties, the Department of Defense sponsored the development of telepresence surgery. The idea was to create a way to perform major surgery on or near the battlefield without having a surgeon at the site. Using robotics and virtual reality technology, a surgeon could conduct an operation from a remote control center hundreds or even thousands of miles away."

"The concept sounds interesting. What happened to it?"

"It was never fully developed, as far as I'm aware. The largest program was axed in a congressional budget dispute, right at the beginning the century."

"Come now. This mon is waking."

Fisher and Alli followed Jáfo to the Asian.

"We're through here for now," Fisher said. "The proof that Fitzpatrick wants is building rapidly."

Fisher stepped to the switching panel and threw them all, sending the interior of the warehouse back into the twilight conditions they had found at entry. They dragged the man outside the warehouse and dropped him in a heap in front of the heavy door, once it was closed.

Fisher walked behind Jáfo to the crate stacks.

Alli shouted, "Wait just a minute!"

Fisher stopped and looked back at the warehouse door. Alli was kneeling beside the Asian.

"Are you okay?" Fisher returned to the spot where she knelt. The Jamaican followed.

Alli looked up. "We've got trouble."

"I don't understand." Cold air stung Fisher's face as he looked down at Alli.

"This fell out of his jacket when we pulled him back outside."

In the dim light from the single overhead bulb, Fisher could see that Alli held a small slip of paper. With a somber look on her face, she handed it to Fisher.

Taking the paper, Fisher was instantly struck by the paper's softness. "It's a small napkin," Fisher said, unfolding it.

"Flip it over," Alli's voice sounded weak and shaky.

"Oh, God," Fisher said as the reverse side of the small napkin became visible.

The light level was low, but Fisher had no trouble recognizing the logo of Risarti's Restaurant. Below the logo, the seven-digit number 5046719 was recorded.

Fisher's legs became rubbery, and a chill crawled through his body as he looked down at the napkin.

Fisher's first impulse was to kick the Asian out of his semi-conscious state, but he managed to retain control. They had no time to lose.

"Natalie's in trouble." Fisher struggled to keep his mind on a problem-solving track.

Fisher turned to the Jamaican standing close by. "Jáfo, you've got to get us back to the bridge where we parked. A friend is in danger."

"No problém, Mon," Jáfo said, leaning down to plunder through the Asian's pocket once again. Within moments, he stood holding a small leather case. Car keys jingled as he unsnapped the case. "Follow me, please," he said, his golden-toothed smile emerging.

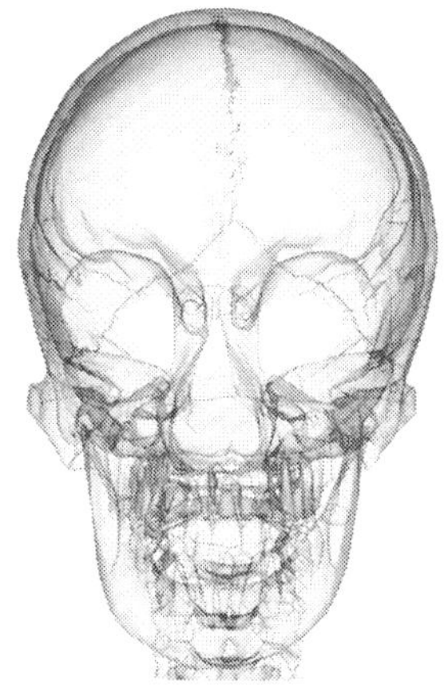

CHAPTER THIRTY-FOUR

Natalie Roberts awakened to darkness and the feel of intense vibration. She lay on her side, her wrists bound tightly behind her back, her ankles lashed together. She struggled to speak, but the cloth stuffed in her mouth caused her to gag each time she tried. With each heartbeat, her head pounded from the constricting band fastened tightly over her eyes.

The anesthetic agent slapped over her face earlier had begun to wear off. As she became more aware, her pulse rate increased and beads of sweat pushed to the skin surface across her forehead. For the next few minutes, terror filled her thoughts as she became fully aware of her situation.

Who has done this? Why have they done this? What will they do to me?

All Roberts' questions screamed across the recesses of her brain as she struggled against her bonds, vocalizing against the gag that shoved her tongue to the back of her throat.

Engine noise and the gag muffled her screams and prevented her from being heard. Only mumbling sounds transmitted into the rear cargo section of the executive jet.

Suddenly, she heard a noise above the vibration. It was the sound of a door knob turning. Roberts lay still as the door to the cargo sectioned opened.

"Listen, goddamnit. This is a bad idea," the voice said. "I would have killed her and plunked her butt on the bottom of the Caton. They would never have found her. It would have been nice and neat."

Terror crushed Roberts, but somehow she purposefully controlled her breathing, making it shallow and quiet.

A different voice spoke. It was closer to her and distinctly gruff. "Look, you talk to Graf yourself and tell him this is just crazy. But listen, the guy will kill you as soon as look at you. You cross him, and you'll end up gettin' popped just like that surgeon. That what you want?"

"Goddamn, I hate this," the first voice responded.

A foot landed hard against Roberts' thigh.

"Oomph," Roberts uttered in guttural surprise.

"Damn! The bitch is waking up. Get that stuff Domao gave you."

"Did he say how much to use?" the gruff voice questioned.

"Fun-eey boy. Does it fucking matter? Give her all of it."

Searing pain ripped through Roberts' thigh as the needle pierced through her clothing. She remained motionless and quiet as the liquid in the syringe was shoved into her muscle. These bastards won't get the pleasure of seeing me squirm, she told herself firmly.

"Let's get back up front," the gruff voice ordered. "Graf will be calling to check on our progress in about five minutes. He wants touchdown at Willowford."

The pain slowly lessened in Roberts' thigh. Soon, however, the injected chemical exerted its effects. At first she drifted, her senses at ease. Then, the vibration became severely acute — the floorboard noise rising in intensity. Then — blackness.

• • • • •

Roberts was vaguely aware of the icy cold as strong hands gripped her body. She floated, undulating in a head down position. Then, a brief free fall, but no impact.

"Goddamnit, you drop her, and you can kiss your ass good-bye," the gruff voice said as if transmitted through a tube.

"Don't goddamn me, these steps are icy. Open the door and stop bitchin'."

She couldn't see distinct images, but Roberts smelled leather as she was shoved forward.

"Take us to the big house," the gruff voice said with authority.

Roberts drifted off again.

"We're going down foot-first, this time. I'll lead the way," the gruff voice commanded. "If I leave it up to you, we'll all land in a heap down there."

"You keep up your shit," the first voice shot back, "and I'll have some hot lead for you soon."

Roberts' body floated in a diagonal position as the complaints and sarcasms continued. She could hear the sounds of feet landing on steps.

She didn't resist the hands that gripped her arms and legs. She remained limp.

"This is fine," the gruff voice said. "Get the ties off."

"You ain't my fuckin' boss," the first voice said, venom spewing.

"All right, all right. Cool off. You take down her wrists and I'll get her ankles. That soothe your tortured mind?" the gruff voice asked.

Roberts lay flaccid as the bonds were removed from her limbs. Finally the gag was ripped from her mouth and the blindfold removed.

She continued to lie unmoving.

The man with the gruff voice said, "I think you fucked up telling me to give her all that shit. She ain't looking so good."

"Just blame it on that asshole, Domao," the other man said, his voice already sounding far away. "Graf thinks he's an idiot anyway."

Roberts could hear footsteps retreating upwards into the distance. A door slammed shut.

Slowly and painfully Roberts pulled her arms forward. Her muscles ached; her hands were cool from hours of constricted circulation. She didn't sit at first. She simply rubbed the painful areas where her wrists had been banded. At the same time, she opened her eyes. She was in a room, the dimensions of which she couldn't determine. Her mouth was parched from the gag.

"Who's there?" a voice called.

Roberts froze in terror, her tormented mind incapable of dealing with another blow.

"I said, who's there?"

That voice, Roberts said to herself feeling her mind teetering on the brink of unconsciousness. It was familiar.

"I'm alone," Roberts called out, her words sounding scratchy.

"Natalie? Natalie Roberts? "Is that you?"

Weakened by hours of constraint and drug infusion, Roberts' head fell back against the floor where she lay. The inflection in the words she recognized, but she could not place it. How did the unknown man know her?

She slipped quickly toward sleep.

Roberts heard a distant rattling sound, but she couldn't gather the energy to investigate.

"Natalie, are you all right?"

Roberts opened her eyes as sleep descended upon her. She could barely make out the shadowy image of a man leaning over her.

Staring down at her was Samuel Jacobson.

"Natalie," he called. "Are you all right?"

The Question went unanswered.

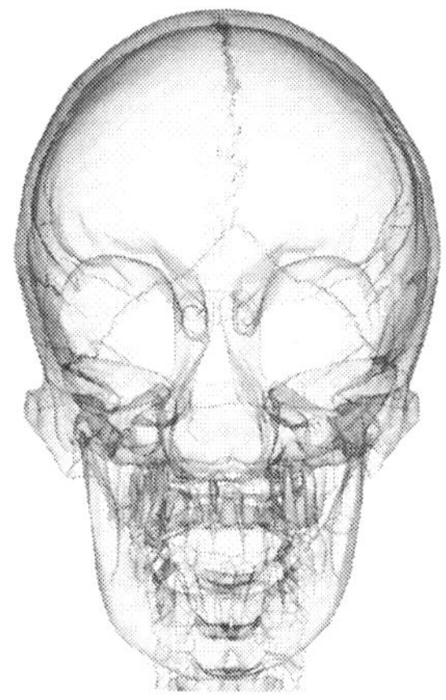

CHAPTER THIRTY-FIVE

"They've gotten to Natalie," Fisher said, pulling the cell phone away from his ear. "There's no answer at any of the numbers she gave us."

"Did you try her lab?" Alli asked, steering the cold Chevy Cavalier across the Ninth Street Bridge.

"The lab, the beeper, the apartment — nothing. They got to her. And I'm the stupid shit who recruited her."

Fisher slammed the cell phone down on the seat between them.

"Steve, don't blame yourself. Natalie would have found a way to get herself involved," Alli said, taking Fisher's hand. "I could see the determination in her eyes last night at Risarti's."

"We're damn powerless," Fisher said, feeling a surge of familiar emotion well up inside as they drove toward the city in early daybreak. His mind raced. That was it, he screamed to himself. Powerlessness. It was the emotion that knifed through him as he watched Danny Taylor fall on the battlefield in the gulf. Powerlessness. The feelings he failed to deal with as Sharon pulled further and further away from their marriage. Powerlessness. The dominant emotion he experienced as Chip Carlton's neck exploded in front of him eight days earlier. They all had driven him to escape — to drink, and it was bubbling to the surface again.

"Not this time," Fisher said, struggling to flush the demons from his mind.

"What are you talking about?" Alli asked.

"We're going to find out who's behind this. There's no turning back. Pull in over there by that pay phone." Fisher pointed to a convenience store parking lot.

"Your cell phone dead?" Alli asked, slightly bewildered.

"No, it's fine. It just struck me that using the cell phone is probably dangerous. We've got work to do, and getting hung up by Domao or his buddies will get us killed. I'm sure the Police Department tracks cell phone calls."

Alli stopped the car ten feet from the pay phone.

Fisher's face was stung by the cold when he opened the Cavalier's door and stood. As he shut the car door, he caught a glimpse of the vial they had taken from the mysterious operating room. It had rolled down into the seat. Fisher reached for the vial.

There it was again, he thought. The symbols on the bottom of the vial. Why were they so familiar? He turned the vial over, exposing the Greek symbols.

KΠ

The Cavalier's dome light barely lit up the marks, but Fisher could see them. He flipped the vial in his hand and looked at the printed label.

"KP-1049," he muttered.

Fisher went to drop the vial back onto the front seat when it hit him. He saw blue — scrub suit blue — an operating room — a ten-cc syringe filled with champagne-colored liquid. Holy shit, he yelled to himself.

"*Katsumi Pharmaceuticals*," Fisher said aloud.

"What are you talking about?" Alli asked, pulling her heavy coat around her chest. The cold air poured into the car through the opened the door.

"The Greek symbols on the bottom of the vial — it belongs to Katsumi Pharmaceuticals. The Greek kappa and pie symbols is their cute acronym for the company"

"Okay. But what's the significance?"

Fisher bent down and gazed into the car. "Katsumi Pharmaceuticals is the company that manufactures Myelopress."

Alli turned her head, her eyes focusing on a distant object in the early morning sky. A Heineken beer truck, completing an early delivery, lumbered out of the convenience store parking lot headed for downtown.

She turned her gaze back to Fisher. Their eyes met. Alli's voice was shaky as she spoke. "Steve, it's possible, then, there's a conspiracy here."

Fisher spoke without taking his eyes off her. "KP-1049 must be an investigational drug. Drug companies keep tight controls on investigational drugs. The only way the drug could have been in that warehouse is with the full knowledge and consent of Katsumi."

"Could it have been stolen?"

Fisher shook his head. "I seriously doubt it. I've heard tales about Katsumi. When Myelopress was investigational and undergoing multi-center trials across Europe and Asia, funny little stories from investigators at participating medical centers popped up." Fisher held up two fingers from each hand, mockingly showing quotation marks. "Two 'Katsumi employees' were stationed at each site. Most surgeons I spoke with, not so jokingly, indicated that they were really Japanese Mafia. One surgeon in Paris swore they carried concealed weapons to ensure the drug's security. The bottom line: KP-1049 wouldn't be in that warehouse, unless Katsumi Pharmaceuticals wanted it there."

"Jesus." Alli picked up the vial.

Fisher pulled his coat tight around his chest. "If this is a conspiracy involving Katsumi Pharmaceuticals, it's bigger than Taggart Memorial Hospital." He glanced at the pay phone, then turned back to Alli. "I'll be back in a minute."

Fisher dialed Alli's home in the east end. After five rings, Gary's voice came on the line.

"Gary, this is Steve Fisher."

"Oh, Dr. Fisher. I've been worried about you guys. Is my sister okay?"

"She's fine. We're still on the road. Did you have any luck accessing Taggart Memorial's mainframe?"

"No problémo, Dr. Fisher. Child's play. Wait 'til I lay this on you. Those guys must not think outside parties would have much interest in what they do."

"What do you mean?"

"Almost no one using the Taggart mainframe password protects their work. I was able to jump right to anyone's terminal. I had access to documents of all types."

"Is that unusual?"

"These days? Yeah. They're either stupid, macho or both. With all the hackers roving the internet not having a secure system is crazy."

"Before we go further," Fisher said, looking out across the convenience store parking lot, "is our conversation protected?"

"Oh yeah, Doc. The phone company installed scramblers on all the modem lines for the Richland Express. I got a voice scrambler thrown in for free with the deal. We're secure."

"Great." Falling temperature pricked Fisher's toes as he stood at the parking lot pay phone.

"I looked into that guy Cliff Stryker, the administrator. I sorted through all his electronic files. There's a considerable amount of communication between him and a Mr. Rupert Graf in New York City. Many of the memos concern routine things like patient census, patient length of stay and nursing matters. There were memos almost every week concerning a different Medford University doctor they were looking to hire."

"They're obsessed with Medford doctors. They've been hiring faculty away from Medford University for years. Rupert Graf is the CEO of Health Pursuit. He's the one who's taken Health Pursuit stomping across the planet, gobbling up every for-profit hospital in the U.S. and Europe. Health Pursuit owns Taggart."

"Oh, I see." Gary said. "There were a series of memos between Mr. Stryker and a company called American Robotics and another . . . ."

"Wait." Fisher said. "When were those memos dated?"

"About two years ago."

"Were there any purchases of robotic equipment?"

"Yes, more than two million dollars in robotics alone. They bought four Da Vinci Robots and other unspecified robotic equipment. What's this all about?"

"I'll tell you everything later. Did you find any memos between Stryker and Graf concerning the robotics?"

"Yes."

"Go on."

"Well, there's more. About that same time, Taggart and other Health Pursuit hospitals went on a capital equipment buying spree for computer hardware. They bought three Cray model-XJ Intermediate supercomputers."

"Is that unusual?"

"Very unusual. Companies as large as Wal-Mart are customers for Cray Intermediates. One Cray Intermediate would number crunch data for twenty-five hundred stores. Using a Cray Intermediate at a place like Taggart Memorial would be a waste."

"Unless they have a task for it we don't know about," Fisher mumbled into the receiver.

"There's one other thing about a Cray, Dr. Fisher — they start at around six million dollars."

Fisher visualized the equipment in the container OR.

"What do Cray computers look like?"

"They look weird, not what you would think. They sit up like huge vertical cylinders with a wedge cut down one side."

Fisher rapidly thought of the objects he'd seen. Nothing of that description was in the warehouse. Ahh, Fisher said to himself — the outpatient surgery center at Taggart. The room Chip discovered the night he found the ledger. It must be the control center for the container OR at the warehouse.

"Were you able to find a listing of transplants performed in Taggart Memorial operating rooms?"

"That was really the easiest," Gary said with a laugh. "The complete listing of all operations is kept on continuous download to the terminal in Cliff Stryker's office. I retrieved all those downloads from the last two years."

"What did you find?"

"Taggart Memorial Hospital performed one thousand four hundred and twenty transplants of all organ types in the past year."

Fisher gasped quietly.

"Dr. Fisher? You still there?"

"Yes," Fisher said finally. "That's an extraordinary number of transplants."

"That seemed like a lot. Does the Med do that many transplants in a year?"

"No. We perform less than a third of that number."

Fisher sorted through the information Gary had given him. "Gary, I need you to do some additional searching."

"Sure. What is it?"

"Can you access the databases at the Food and Drug Administration?"

As he stood shivering from the cold, Fisher was certain he heard snickering emanate from the icy receiver. "Gary, are you laughing?"

"Sorry, Dr. Fisher. The FDA's mainframe is part of elementary hacker field training. I've been all through their databases before. What do you need?"

"Try to find out any information you can on a drug designated KP-1049. If the FDA has the drug, it'll be found under investigational new drugs. I believe the parent company to be Katsumi, spelled K-a-t-s-u-m-i Pharmaceuticals."

"If I find anything, I'll download it to Alli's laptop," Gary said. "Tell her to be sure to have LapLink running."

"That would be great. Thanks."

Fisher cut off the call, fed the pay phone again and dialed Roberts' laboratory in the Pathology building at the Med.

No answer.

He hung up and looked at his watch. It was after five in the morning. Something's definitely happened to her, he thought, walking back to the idling Cavalier.

"Was Gary able to get into the Taggart mainframe?"

"Yes." Fisher returned to the passenger seat wearing a grim look. "That conspiracy theory's looking more definite."

"Yeah?" Alli said anxiously.

"I'll tell you on the way. We better head for Natalie's laboratory. I tried again, no answer."

• • • • •

"That's Natalie's car," Alli said pointing to the light-toned Honda.

"You're right," Fisher said. "She was driving it when we left Risarti's last night."

They continued toward the Pathology building.

The century-old gas lights flanking the front steps provided partial illumination in the winter morning darkness. Fisher and Alli climbed the steps to the building doors.

Fisher's mind was clear, but it was filled with a sense of dread.

They pulled open the door. At the end of the lobby, a desk was pulled across the hallway leading to the elevators.

The desk was vacant, no security guard present. The desk chair was overturned. Beside the chair, the admission log sat opened, face down on the floor.

Fisher picked up the log and scanned down the pages. Roberts had checked in, but no checkout time was listed.

"Steve, over there." Alli pointed to the darkened hall beyond the desk.

Just discernible on the floor lay a uniformed Medford security guard. They hurried to the motionless body. He was an elderly man. Blood stained the right side of his head contrasting sharply with his white hair. A large gash was evident just above his right ear.

"He's dead," Fisher said feeling no pulse.

"This looks bad."

"I know. We've got to hurry." Fisher sprinted for the stairwell. "Natalie's laboratory is on the fourth floor."

As they climbed the stairs, Terror clawed at Fisher's brain. Goddamn, he thought. How could I have brought her into this mess?

The hallway on the fourth floor was dark save for light pouring into it some fifteen yards in the distance.

"That's Natalie's laboratory." Fisher spoke softly as he and Alli, breathless from their climb, looked through a single glass pane in the heavy stairwell door.

"I don't see anyone."

"I don't either," Fisher said. "Stay behind me." For the first time since his encounter with the Asian at the warehouse, Fisher became aware of the pistol he had pocketed. He pulled the weapon from his jacket. It was a lightweight Glock nine millimeter pistol. He checked the clip. It was fully loaded.

Fisher pushed opened the stairwell door and walked quietly down the hallway. The fluorescent lighting poured into the space outside the lab. As he arrived at the threshold to the laboratory, he stopped and listened.

All was quiet.

He turned to Alli. She was pressed against the wall behind him. He gripped the Glock carefully and slipped into the doorway in a crouching position so as not to be seen over the tops of the laboratory benches.

His memory of the space was sketchy, but he recalled two benches that ran the length of the lab. There were three walkway spaces — the first between the bench and the wall closest to the hallway, a second between the benches, and a final walkway between the far bench and the outside wall that overlooked the courtyard.

The first walkway was clear. Fisher moved quietly to the end of the first bench and peered slowly around its back side. Paper and small equipment were strewn across the walkway. Seeing the rubble, Fisher paused and studied the area carefully. There was no one. He continued on. To complete his inspection, he moved to the end of the second bench and looked carefully down the walkway next to the courtyard wall. Again, no one. Using cat-like movements, he advanced down the walkway until he was directly outside Roberts' office. He looked in slowly, the pistol ready.

Nothing. The laboratory and the office were empty.

"There's no one here, Alli," Fisher called as he placed the pistol back in the pocket of his coat.

Alli came into view at the end of the center walkway. The two approached the scattered remains from opposite directions. She leaned down and picked up several typed sheets.

"What did you find?"

"It's a set of instructions for DNA fingerprinting by Dr. Melissa Greene."

Fisher looked up briefly but he said nothing. Alli would know what he was thinking. He proceeded with his survey of the center walkway area. There were reagent bottles, pipettes and small vials of various enzymes and buffers. An electrophoresis chamber, its buffer splattered across the floor, lay damaged by the fall. Next to the chamber, lying face down, was a square plastic basin.

The most distressing finding, though, was the blood scattered in dime- to half-dollar-sized droplets. Some had been stepped on and tracked down the center walkway.

They stared at the rubble.

Fisher's gaze was fixed on a large droplet of blood. He worked to fend off waves of terror. He pulled back from the brink. His pulse remained slow, his breathing rate controlled. "They caught her in the middle of her work."

Fisher stepped back calmly. As he did, the heel of his right shoe tapped the plastic basin, sending it skidding across the space between the two lab benches.

"Steve, look." Alli pointed to where Fisher had stood before kicking the basin.

There was a piece of white cloth, one of its corners partially folded back. Fisher carefully reached down.

As Fisher picked up the cloth and raised it from the floor, Alli saw its underside. "Oh God, Steve!"

"She did it," Fisher said, turning over the nylon cloth.

Fisher laid the white nylon cloth on the lab bench and flattened it. They both studied it.

Before them lay a piece of light-gauge nylon with three parallel columns consisting of stacks of quarter-inch hatch marks that traversed the entire length.

"Barcodes," Fisher finally commented "These columns of hatch marks look like extremely long barcodes."

Alli nodded. "The final images of a DNA fingerprint look like barcodes. Some of the hatch marks are thick and some thin. The key factor is whether all the bars across the two samples are of the same thickness and position."

"You've had experience with DNA fingerprinting?"

"No practical experience. Dr. Greene gave several lectures on forensic pathology right before Christmas."

"The labeling on the columns. What do you make of that?"

"In column one, the letters Mol W probably signify molecular weight. Dr. Greene mentioned that all DNA fingerprinting is performed with precise molecular weight markers. They're used to judge the weights of the various DNA fragments in the unknown samples."

They stared intently at the second and third columns. The letters TC and AUT were inscribed above those columns.

"Tissue core and autopsy," Fisher said finally. "This means . . . ."

"That Natalie found a tissue core at Taggart."

"Yes."

Together, they examined the DNA fingerprint Roberts had performed.

Fisher said, "If we are comparing two barcodes, then I'd say the tissue core and the sample from the autopsy are identical."

"I agree."

Fisher turned and disappeared into Roberts' office. After a few minutes he returned with a large envelope.

"Let's blot the fingerprint dry and place it in this envelope. I know someone who needs to see this."

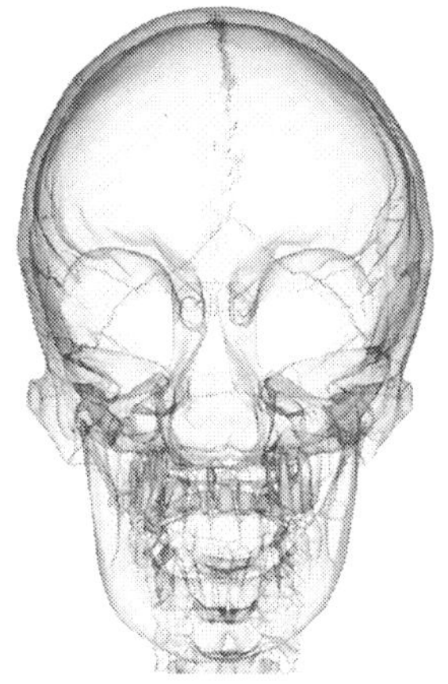

CHAPTER THIRTY-SIX

"Security's your responsibility, Domao."

"Some things just can't be anticipated, Dr. Talbott," the voice whistled into the phone. "How the hell did I know somebody would mug the stupid nip and steal his gun?"

"It's your fucking job to anticipate trouble, especially around that warehouse."

Wheezing was audible over the phone.

"I'll personally be using that operating room tonight for a procedure. Is he in good enough shape to assist?"

"Well. He uh . . ., also got a little injury to some fingers on his left hand, helping me with that Pathologist, but he'll be okay."

"Domao, you just make sure he's there and functional or Graf will hear about this!"

"Uh . . ., sure, Dr. Talbott," Domao said softly.

"Son-of-a-bitch," Harry Talbott uttered, slamming the telephone receiver down with great force. "Why in God's name did I let them talk me into using that warehouse?"

Talbott clenched his teeth as he leaned back in the plush leather-bound chair. The sinewy musculature of his jaws rippled as he seethed. A surgical scrub cap sat cocked back on the crown of his head. Shocks of silver hair, usually styled and fussed over, shot out in random directions from underneath. He gazed across the richly paneled office suite. Two large windows on the east wall framed the sunlit morning over downtown

Richland and the rushing waters of the Caton River. The office suite was one typically reserved for corporate CEOs, not cardiothoracic surgeons. But Talbott had become accustomed to rich surroundings. Transplant surgeons at Taggart Memorial floated in wealth — exclusive clubs, expensive cars, and large estates in exclusive neighborhoods. Their contribution to Taggart's bottom line was enormous, and Taggart rewarded them handsomely.

With his brain cooled somewhat, Talbott leaned forward in the chair and pressed the intercom on his desk. "Jane," he called impatiently. "Did Mr. Stryker return my call while I was in the OR?"

"No, Dr. Talbott. He didn't. I spoke with his office this morning after you left for the OR. His secretary informed me he had received the message that you called yesterday."

Talbott leaned back, resuming the backward tilt in the overstuffed chair, again deep in thought.

Finesse. Finesse and planning to provide that extra edge. Those were Harry Talbott's watch words for life. Stay fifty yards in front of disaster and always be prepared for the worst, he always said. Think of the worst thing that could happen and prepare for it. A ruptured left ventricle in a post-operative heart transplant. A stroke coming off cardiopulmonary bypass. Talbott simply hated surprises. Ninety-nine percent of the time, he was ready for the unexpected. Should the unexpected occur, his prime directive was to fall back on finesse. But the worst had occurred. No one had anticipated Chip Carlton's discovery of the ledger. Worse still, the matter had not been handled with finesse. He had stewed for more than a week thinking about it. Yes, Carlton had learned too much too quickly, and he had needed to be removed to keep the business operating smoothly. But a sniper-style assassination had lacked finesse.

Graf and Stryker, Talbott thought, gazing down on the city. They were idiots. Graf, with his power and connections, and Stryker the puppet, was humping to preserve a bottom line.

"Clumsy, stupid . . . ."

"Dr. Talbott, Mr. Stryker is on the line," the voice came over the intercom.

Talbott stopped mumbling mid-sentence and jerked forward. "It's about freaking time," he hissed softly as he picked up the receiver. "I've left three messages for you in the last day and a half, Stryker."

"Well, Harry, there have been continuing details to take care of since Dr. Carlton's death. You know, meetings with police detectives, the press, and concerned public awareness groups. Of course, proper seeds needed to be planted. The press needed to know all about the extremist anti-transplant group that picket in front of the hospital every month."

"What?" Talbott asked in disbelief.

"Sure," Stryker chuckled. "I simply posed the question to the media, could Dr. Carlton's assassination have been the work of a group like that? Of course reporters sprinted out of the room to blab the rumor to their respective news operations before I could finish my interview."

"Well," Talbott seethed over the line. "That's a result I bet you never thought would come out of this whole mess."

"Mess?" Stryker questioned, immediately changing to anger.

"Yes, mess," Talbott pushed. "There were a number of other ways the entire affair could have been handled, yet you and your goons decided to go in guns blazing, didn't you?"

"I'm not sure I understand exactly what you mean, Dr. Talbott." Stryker became suddenly formal.

For virtually all his calls, Talbott used the speakerphone. On this occasion, he held the phone in his hand. Without realizing it, his grip tightened on the receiver. "Don't play ignorant with me, Stryker." Talbott paused a beat.

"Even though this line's scrambled, I don't think the matter should be discussed over the phone," Stryker replied.

"Fine. But my input on this matter is that you or your representatives bungled this."

"Harry, I'm going to hang up now."

"No, you're not. I've got one more item to discuss."

"And what's that?"

"Security," Talbott said. "It stinks. This morning, one of the technicians was mugged outside the warehouse."

"Killed?"

"No," Talbott replied flatly.

"We can count our lucky stars for that."

"You just don't get it, do you?" Talbott almost screamed into the receiver. "We need protection. Our work can't proceed if the technicians aren't protected. You said burning that old factory would keep the vagrants away."

"I'll look into it," Stryker replied. "I'll just remind you, Dr. Talbott that burning that old paper mill was your idea. The only thing it really accomplished was killing thirty-six potential organ donors."

Talbott changed the subject. "I have a wealthy client who's going to put a transplant wing onto this hospital. He needs a heart for his son."

"Well, hearts are out for a while," Stryker quipped. "We can't pull another heart from New Delhi for quite some time. You remember the outrage the last two caused all across India. This heart will have to come from OrganLink."

Talbott retorted, "Waiting for OrganLink will take months. The kid can't wait that long. Besides, I've got the problem solved locally."

"I'll remind you that the robotics for taking hearts isn't perfected yet."

"I'm aware of that. Who do you think's designing the robotics? I'll be taking the heart in person."

"Fine," Stryker said coldly. "If you're foolish enough to do that, you take the risk. I'll be in New York for Health Pursuit's annual stockholder's meeting. Just remember to dispose of the remains properly."

After Stryker hung up Talbott still choked the receiver. His jaw was clenched tighter than ever as he gazed out the window.

• • • • •

In an equally plush office six corridors away, Cliff Stryker placed the phone on its cradle. He nervously tapped his finger on the marble-topped desk in front of him. Unlike Talbott's daylight-filled office, Stryker always kept his curtains drawn. For a few moments, his tapping intensified, then stopped. He reached for a pencil beside the phone and started thumping it against closed lips.

His position as Taggart's chief administrator was a high pressure job, and he knew it. But he could take it. He had clawed his way to the position, and no one was going to take it from him, especially not some smart-ass prima donna surgeon with a big mouth.

Stryker continued his nervous rapping. He was worried about the call. Talbott could be a loose cannon at times.

Finally, Stryker threw the pencil and reached for the phone. He pushed two buttons on the desk set similar to the one on Harry Talbott's desk.

He reached for the receiver. The sound of the phone's speed dial feature was in progress.

Moments passed. Finally, an answer on the other end. With humbleness uncommon for Cliff Stryker, he spoke into the receiver he held closely to his left ear. "Uh . . ., is he in, please?"

"Just a moment," was the unenthusiastic reply.

"Yes," a voice said, quietly filling the receiver.

Stryker spoke, his voice quivering slightly, "I'm uh . . . uh . . . sorry to bother you about another matter so soon, but I may have another problem that will need to be addressed in the near future."

The silence that followed brought small beads of sweat to Stryker's upper lip.

Then a subtle sound issued from the receiver Stryker gripped tightly. It was the click lips make as they part for speech. The noise was followed by a soft rush of air, an impatient hiss. "Do you perceive it as an acute problem?" the voice asked, obviously irritated.

Stryker struggled not to sound indecisive, realizing instantly that his call was premature. He started to proceed with his answer, but he stopped.

The skin under Stryker's starched collar became tight and uncomfortable as he waited for a reply. He reached quickly to place a finger inside it, to release the grip of the monster that choked him. Finally, he managed to squeak out a reply. "It's too soon to tell."

"Have you collected enough information on the situation to assess its urgency?"

Another painful pause.

Unconsciously, Stryker continued pulling at the collar. Fine moisture drenched his forehead. "No," his voice quivered.

A river of ice and scorn flowed from the receiver. "Don't ever call me like this without complete data."

"Yes but . . . ."

"Is the local talent holding operations secure?"

Stryker immediately thought of the mugging Talbott had mentioned moments earlier. "Yes," he lied, afraid of the consequences a truthful reply would bring. "There's been no breach of security."

Stryker's reply was cut short as he heard the unmistakable sound of a disconnect. He replaced the phone in its receiver. His finger furiously worked the intolerably tight collar as he stared at the phone.

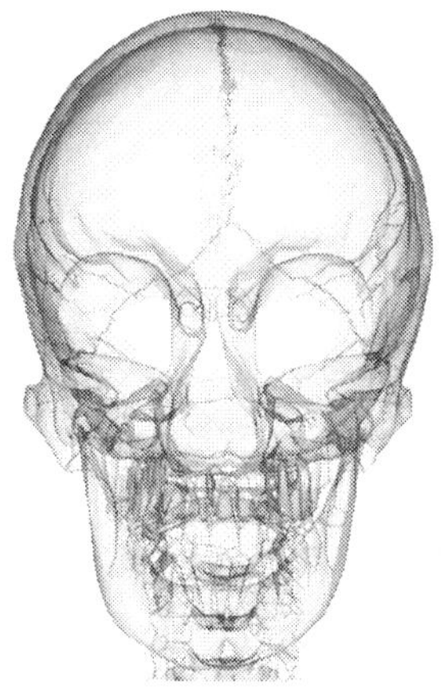

CHAPTER THIRTY-SEVEN

"Wha . . ., where?"

Natalie Roberts awakened disoriented, calling out involuntarily to dark, unfamiliar surroundings. She tried raising her body to a half-sitting position, supported by her elbows but stopped as both shoulders screamed with deep pain. Her sense of time was distorted initially, but within a few seconds, she remembered the lab, the DNA fingerprinting, the blindfold, her arms tightly bound, unfamiliar voices, a dark room. But there was something else, she told herself, rolling her body painfully to the left. The familiar voice, she recalled. It was here.

"Natalie. You're awake. Thank God you're okay. I've been worried sick these last few hours."

She felt the light touch of a hand on her left arm.

"Natalie, it's Sam. Sam Jacobson."

Roberts finished rolling from her back to her side and pulled to a sitting position without using her arms. She looked around her. Light from under the door at the top of the stairs produced half-light conditions. She could see partial details of the room. Jacobson was seated beside her on the cold cement. He reached out and placed his hand on her shoulder.

"Sam," Roberts said. Her shoulders screamed as she brought her hands to her face. "Where are we? Where is this place?"

"I . . . I don't know, Natalie."

His voice was drenched with despair, a tone Roberts had never associated with Jacobson. In those few words, Jacobson communicated volumes to her about their situation.

"How did you get here?" Roberts tried to work the soreness from her shoulders.

"I don't know," Jacobson said, his voice trembling. "It was late. I was at work preparing a report for a board meeting, and, suddenly, men rushed into my office. I heard a snapping sound, and then I was tackled. Someone shoved a cloth over my face, and that's the last thing I remembered until I found myself here. That was the second of February."

"That was six days ago."

Jacobson pulled his hand from her shoulder. "Was it?" Jacobson's voice was near breaking.

"There's only damn twilight down here — no day, no night."

Roberts could barely see her mentor and colleague look slowly around their prison. He lowered his head, resting his chin on his chest. She placed a hand on Jacobson's shoulder. "I was taken in the same way, from my lab at the Med."

Jacobson raised his head and looked at Roberts. "I suspect I know why I was taken, but why you?"

Roberts looked directly at Jacobson. She kept silent for a moment. He returned the gaze then broke away.

"It's no use keeping secrets," Jacobson said, a note of determination entering his voice as he looked out into the void of the dark room.

"What do you mean?"

He turned back to meet her gaze, staring silently at her. Roberts could make out his unshaven, sunken face.

"What is it, Sam?"

"Natalie, I discovered some things at Taggart Memorial I wasn't supposed to have discovered."

Roberts' pulse jumped as her breath quickened.

Jacobson lowered his voice to a near whisper. "I know they're listening. Some weeks ago I . . ., I found that Taggart Memorial was procuring organs for transplant from black market sources. I can't tell you how I found out. If I do, another person will end up either down here or dead."

"Like Chip Carlton," Roberts interrupted.

Jacobson stopped. He and Roberts stared at each.

"Then you know?"

"Yes."

"Then I'm not the only one who knows?"

"There are others," she said.

Though there was barely enough light to make out Jacobson's face, Roberts could see his facial features register astonishment.

"Sam," Roberts said, drawing closer to Jacobson, "I think I'm here for the same reasons you are."

Over the next few minutes, Roberts whispered directly into Jacobson's ear, telling him all that she knew. She ended with a description of the DNA fingerprint she had completed just before she had been taken from the laboratory. "I have virtually no experience with forensic pathology," Roberts whispered, "but the DNA fingerprint was definite. That biopsy core from the tissue bank was removed from my Jane Doe. It's proof that Taggart Memorial Hospital is running a black market for organs."

She saw a strange look come over Jacobson's face, a look she had never seen before. His face screwed into a grimace, taking on a ghoulish appearance. Jacobson stood up, but continued to stare at her.

"That's just too fucking bad. I told them they had it all wrong, that it was a case of mistaken identity. But you proved me wrong. I never should have doubted you for a minute, should I? You always were the grand inquisitor, Natalie. The one who asked, and eventually answered, the impossible questions. You're just too smart, aren't you?"

"Sam, what are you talking about? Are you feeling okay?"

"I'm feeling fine, Dr. Roberts. I'm just fine."

Jacobson spun around. "She knows," he said, speaking into the void. "Get me out of this hell hole."

Sounds arose from the across the prison-like space. Roberts could see a door opening at a considerable elevation. The light that flooded in fell on a short flight of steps.

"This way, Dr. Jacobson," a voice called from the top of the stairs.

Jacobson stepped toward the lighted stairway.

Roberts lunged forward from her sitting position, grabbing Jacobson's right leg.

"Sam, please," she said, holding onto his ankle despite the searing pain from both her shoulders. "You can't be involved in this."

With a strong jerk, he freed his leg and continued up the stairs.

"Get hold of Graf before he leaves the islands," Jacobson said. "I think he'll be interested to hear how Stryker has screwed this up."

"Sam, no," Roberts called again as the door at the top of the stairs closed.

The room went dark once again. Roberts rolled onto her back. She could feel tears forming under her closed eyelids.

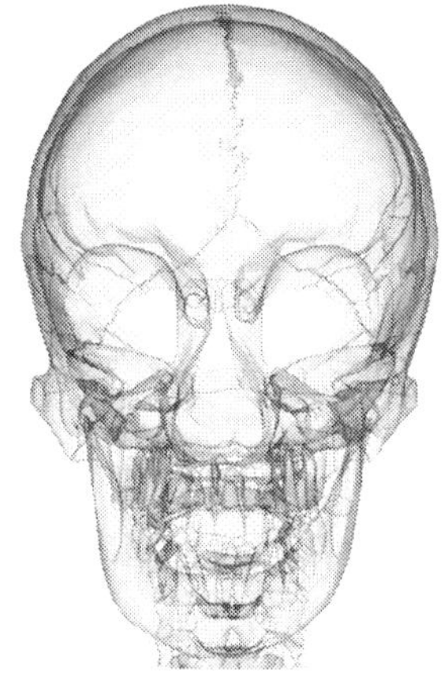

CHAPTER THIRTY-EIGHT

February 9

Fisher was thankful for the sunshine that warmed Alli's Cavalier. As they drove, Fisher rested his head against the headrest and closed his eyes. It had been a busy morning. Three Richland patrolmen had come to the Pathology building. Fisher had answered their questions as best as they could. Richland EMS arrived to remove the body. After leaving Roberts' laboratory and the Pathology building, he and Alli had stopped by the College Inn where Wallace Shaklein, excited to see his friend, had prepared them a filling breakfast. Shaklein's spirits were vastly improved since the last time Fisher had seen him. They chatted as Fisher and Alli consumed Belgian waffles. Fisher was relieved that no one mentioned Chip Carlton during their visit.

Following breakfast, they went straight to the Medical Examiner's office, where they caught Melissa Greene just as she arrived for the day. She examined the DNA fingerprint and confirmed for them that the autopsy and tissue bank specimens were identical. Fisher had diplomatically fended off Greene's questions regarding the nature of the DNA fingerprint, promising to inform her thoroughly at a later time. As they were leaving the medical examiner's building, the ambulance containing the Medford security guard was just arriving.

"We're here, Steve."

Fisher opened his eyes as Alli pulled up outside the regional offices of OrganLink.

"Why are we stopping here?" Alli asked.

"There's one last piece of information I need," Fisher said. He told her of Gary's discovery of Taggart's OR records inside Cliff Stryker's electronic files.

"Fourteen hundred and twenty transplants. That number seems high," Alli said.

"It's more than three times the number we performed at the Med during the same period."

Alli's eyes widened as the reality of Fisher's statement sunk in. She looked at Fisher, "How can OrganLink help?"

"An old friend and former Medford ICU nurse works here."

They entered OrganLink's modern building and walked to the reception desk.

"I'm hoping she'll tell us how many organs Taggart procured through OrganLink."

A few moments later, they were seated across from Valerie Thompson, OrganLink's procurement coordinator.

Fisher introduced Alli to Valarie. After a few moments of small talk, Fisher's expression turned serious. "Val, I would like to ask a favor."

"Small talk was never one of your virtues, Steven Fisher." Thompson smiled at Alli as if letting her in on a secret. "What can I do for you?"

"I need to know how many total procurements OrganLink arranged for Taggart last year."

Thompson's smile faded as she studied Fisher's face.

"You know I could lose my job if I revealed information like that. It's confidential."

The office went silent. Thompson's gaze stuck on Fisher. She expected a reply, but it did not come. Fisher merely stared back.

Thompson spoke first ending the momentary standoff. "But I never could say no to you, could I, Dr. Fisher?"

Fisher cracked a smile and glanced at Alli as Thompson pulled several file folders from her desk.

"A total of two hundred and twenty-one," Thompson said.

The ringing of Thompson's phone cut into the tension.

Thompson picked up the receiver, but continued to stare at Fisher. After a few moments she placed her hand over the phone. "I'm going to have to take this call."

Fisher leaned forward and took a slip of paper from Thompson's desk. He jotted the word "thanks" and placed it in front of her.

She waved at them as they left the office.

"That's a huge discrepancy," Alli commented as they returned to her car. If you take the number Taggart procured through OrganLink and add the one hundred eighty from the warehouse OR that leaves . . . ."

"One thousand and nineteen," Fisher said flatly.

"Where would those organs come from? Near-by cities?"

"No," Fisher said. "I don't think so. Every other hospital across the country is competing for organs, just like Taggart. No, those organs are being bought on the black-market and shipped in from outside the US. For years, there's been a black market for organs outside the US. It's operated mostly in the Middle and Far East, but reports filter in from Latin America and Russia as well. Transplant surgeons have whispered about worldwide commerce in organs for years, but it's never been proven."

"Transplant on demand," Alli said. "Just catch a plane to India or Pakistan, get an overnight transplant and fly out within two to three days."

"Precisely," Fisher responded. "But real horror stories have circulated. Apparently, huge problems existed with black-market organs implanted outside of American or European hospitals. Many people died from improper surgical care or post-operative infection. Poor implantation techniques frequently resulted in death of the organ or rejection. And worst of all, there was AIDS. Hundreds of patients receiving black market transplants in the India developed AIDS after implantation."

Alli started to pull out of OrganLink's parking area when a noise from the back seat stopped her.

Dong . . . dong . . . dong . . . dong.

"What's that?" Fisher asked

"It's my laptop's transmission-receive alert." She turned from her position behind the steering wheel and retrieved the chiming laptop.

Fisher saw a small red light flashing on the computer's plastic casing. The flashing ceased as Alli opened the notebook computer. Inside the cover, a thin, brilliantly colored screen flashed the message:

LAPLINK IS ACTIVE

Data transmission alert: This laptop is receiving a protected message via Transtar from:

—GARY SHEPARD—

Do You Wish To Receive?

Alli typed "yes" and the message appeared on the laptop's screen.

```
Data transmission time: 10:40 a.m.

  Hi, Sis

  Tell Dr. Fisher that my tour through the FDA's
mainframe was quite successful. FDA has condi-
tionally approved KP-1049 for release next year.
It will be marketed under the name GrowStimulin.
The drug is a potent, genetically altered, growth
factor capable of promoting accelerated wound re-
pair. Katsumi Pharmaceuticals has presented con-
vincing evidence to the FDA that normal tissue
subjected to surgical injury will repair itself in
less than eight hours without scar formation when
treated with KP-1049. Hope this helps. — Gary.
```

"So that's how they're doing it."

"What do you mean?" Alli asked, returning the laptop to the Cavalier's back seat.

"It's the perfect way of performing surgery. Do your cutting without having to worry about a surgical wound. First, Taggart gets some slime ball to circulate among the homeless offering them a pittance for their organs. Then, they wind up on the robotic operating table in that warehouse. After the surgery, the donor gets infused with KP-1049 and eight hours later, Voilà! No evidence of surgery."

"And that's precisely what Natalie found when she performed the autopsy on Mattie. A nephrectomy, but no surgical wound," Alli whispered.

"Exactly," Fisher said. "That way, homeless organ donors who complained or accidentally ended up dead like Mattie wouldn't draw undue attention. The problem they didn't foresee was Mattie dying of hypothermia the night they dropped her off under the bridge, and Natalie Roberts ending up as the Pathologist on call."

A wave of apprehension and dread rushed through Fisher's body as he uttered Roberts' name.

"We'll find her," Alli said, seeing his eyes turn sad. "Mr. Fitzpatrick will be able to help locate her."

"If he shows, that will certainly be top on the list of things we'll discuss. We better get going."

Alli pulled the Cavalier onto the interstate and headed north. The bright sunshine and a stark blue winter sky would make the drive a pleasure.

• • • • •

Fisher slumped in the front seat. He was fatigued, but his thoughts were clear and organized.

"Steve!"

Fisher's eyes snapped open.

"Is that him?"

Fisher looked toward the exit off the interstate. A late model sedan was pulling into the rest stop where they had waited for more than an hour.

"That's him." Fisher recognized the car that was always parked in Darren and Olivia Fitzpatrick's driveway when he and Sharon traveled to visit her parents.

The navy blue car pulled slowly into the deserted parking area about thirty yards from the Cavalier. Fisher recognized Agent Timmons from the agency office in Georgetown. Another male about Timmons' age occupied the front passenger seat. Both men wore dark sunglasses. Alone in the rear seat sat Fitzpatrick.

For a few seconds, there was no movement inside the automobile. Fitzpatrick then leaned forward and placed a hand on the shoulder of the young man sitting beside Timmons. Fisher could see Fitzpatrick's lips moving in conversation. The front door opened, and the young man got out and stood by the car. He was short in stature with broad muscular shoulders. Close-cropped blond hair sat atop a youthful face. Fisher judged his age at no more than twenty-five.

The young man slowly turned, looking carefully around the parking area. He gave no signs he intended to approach the Cavalier. He walked slowly to the small building across the parking area that housed the rest stop restrooms. Within a few seconds, Fisher could see the young man emerge from the building around its far side, still looking carefully at every corner of the rest stop. He walked back to Fitzpatrick's car and stood by its rear door. Fitzpatrick nodded. The young man turned and approached the Cavalier. Fisher opened the passenger's side window.

"Doctor Fisher?" the man asked, his voice age appropriate for his young facial features.

"Yes," Fisher replied.

"I'm Agent Wellesley. Mr. Fitzpatrick asks that you and your companion accompany me to his car."

Alli and Fisher left the Cavalier and followed him. Fisher could hear the quiet idling sounds of the car as they approached.

"Would you please be seated in the back with Mr. Fitzpatrick?" the youthful agent asked, pointing to the rear door.

"Thanks for coming, Darren," Fisher said, entering the back seat behind Alli.

Fitzpatrick cast a cold glance at Alli's beauty before moving his attention to Fisher.

"Darren, this is Alli Shepard. She's a fourth-year student at Medford University School of Medicine. She was on a medical school elective, when she became entangled in this, just as I did."

Fitzpatrick was visibly set at ease by the introduction, but his quiet resentment was palpable. Fisher knew Fitzpatrick blamed him for failing to maintain the marriage to his only daughter. "You said you had new information." Fitzpatrick turned slightly in his seat and gazed directly at Fisher.

A sense of urgency twisted its way into Fisher's brain as he recounted the events since their meeting in Georgetown. Nine days earlier, his single goal was to bring Chip Carlton's killer to justice. Now the stakes were higher. A friend's life hung in the balance, and the clock was ticking loudly, enunciating the passing seconds following Roberts' kidnapping.

Over the next few minutes, Fisher carefully told Fitzpatrick the details of his odyssey since meeting with him before. Fitzpatrick occasionally interjected questions, but for the most part, the information came as a monologue. He then painstakingly described the contents of the ledger, its significance and their meeting with Roberts.

"Good work, Steve," Fitzpatrick said softly.

Fisher glanced at the front seat where he noticed Agents Timmons and Wellesley turned to the rear seat, their gazes fixed on him. Finally, he continued. The details continued flowing as he described their trip to the Ninth Street Bridge, the discovery of the warehouse operating room and the vial of KP-1049. He told of Gary's hacking and the discovery of the correspondence between Graf and Stryker. He told the agents of the Taggart OR transplant records and the conversation with Valerie Thompson. Fisher next recounted the Jane Doe autopsy Roberts had performed, her flank tissue findings and how she had left their meeting at Risarti's to retrieve the tissue core from Taggart's human tissue bank.

"So where's Dr. Roberts?" Fitzpatrick asked, hanging on Fisher's every word.

"Kidnapped, or . . . dead we presume," Fisher stated hating to speak the words.

There was no immediate response and the car fell silent.

"But not before she provided us with important information." Pangs of apprehension again knifed through Fisher. He reached inside his tattered sport coat and withdrew the DNA fingerprint. He unfolded it and held it up, so that all in the car could see.

He pointed to the columns that contained the DNA in question. "The Richland ME told us this morning the tissues are identical," Fisher said, bringing his story to a close.

Agents Timmons and Wellesley quietly shifted in the front seat, rubbing their neck muscles, cramped from the awkward position they had maintained.

As the monologue stopped, Fitzpatrick's gaze moved past Fisher out across the parking area. He was obviously straining to grasp and digest the information Fisher had revealed. Within a few moments, he turned to look at Fisher. "Looks as if you've discovered the tip of a very large iceberg."

He turned his attention to the front seat, where both the young agents sat facing forward. "Gentlemen, sounds like we have some work to do."

"Yes, sir," Wellesley replied from the front passenger's seat.

"Timmons, get Barnett at FBI on the line. Tell him I'll need twenty-five agents. Wellesley, call Georgetown and tell them we won't be back today."

The two agents scrambled to reach for their cell phones, dialing within seconds.

Fitzpatrick turned to Fisher. "Seems the best place to start is that warehouse. Once the necessary forces are assembled, we'll pay it a visit tonight."

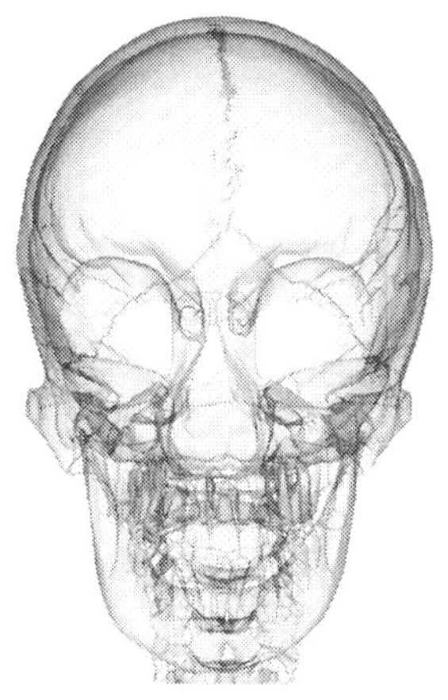

CHAPTER THIRTY-NINE

Harry Talbott was oblivious to the tears that had seeped from under the young Russian's eyelids before he administered the general anesthetic. He attributed Alexi Ibanov's glassy eyes to the heavy odor of alcohol that flowed out with each exhaled breath, not to a sign of remorse.

Talbott wouldn't have noticed the tears, anyway. He was angry. He, in fact, was on the fence as to whether he wanted Ibanov's heart.

"Shit," he hissed under his breath as he adjusted his sterile gown. "The last thing I need is an alcoholic heart. That fucking Stryker has double-crossed me for the last time."

"Sato," Talbott yelled across the warehouse OR. "What the hell are you doing? Get over here and start prepping the chest."

The Asian simply bowed his head and walked back to the OR table, his leg emitting the snapping sound as he walked. He struggled to get a sterile glove over the bandage covering his bite wounds.

"Time is of the essence, Sato," Talbott scolded, as the Asian swabbed iodine solution across Ibanov's chest. "I told you that before we started. Taggart's waiting to hear from me before the Winston kid's taken to the OR."

Airflow sounds were audible as Talbott stepped to the head of the table. He double-checked the concentration of isoflurane anesthetic gas that Ibanov was breathing. He wanted a smooth organ harvest under complete anesthesia. There would be no pain.

Talbott turned to the digital readouts that displayed the sleeping Russian's cardiac function. They were all normal.

The heart would have to do, he thought.

"Sato," Talbott snapped harshly at the Asian once again, "We'll use the modified Belzer's perfusate to preserve the heart. Do you have it prepared?"

"Yes sir," Sato said softly as he finished scrubbing the chest. "I have it ready."

Talbott then walked to the container entryway. The door opened as he approached.

"Domao," Talbott yelled out into the warehouse.

"Yeah, what do you want?"

"I don't want anything. Just checking to see that you are doing your job."

"You do your job, and I'll do mine," the wheezy voice rattled as Domao appeared from around the corner, a pall of cigar smoke wafting behind him.

"Hope it's better than your recent work," Talbott said, cracking a horizontal smile that wasn't intended for levity.

Domao's face turned a deep purplish red.

Talbott turned and walked back into the OR.

"Set the electrocautery on cut and have that sternal saw ready."

"Yes, Doctor," Sato said, glaring at Talbott's back.

• • • • •

"The steel ribs on that door are going to make it tough to get inside," Fitzpatrick said, crouching behind a chest-high stack of shipping crates.

"We were lucky the Asian came along when he did last night," Fisher whispered, "or we wouldn't have gained access."

Fitzpatrick turned to his right and spoke softly, "Timmons, pass the word to the other agents that we may have to set a charge to open that door."

"Yes Sir." The young agent disappeared into the darkness outside the warehouse.

"Optical recognition systems are hard to defeat," Fitzpatrick whispered.

"Wait a minute," Fisher said softly, turning his attention back to the warehouse door.

Around the corner, approaching from the same direction the Asian had come the night before, walked a familiar figure. The man held himself erect. He was gaunt and middle-aged with short, graying hair. Fisher instantly dug into his recent memory.

"I've seen that guy somewhere recently," Fisher whispered.

The man's look was distinctive. He wore dark pants and an undersized plaid sport coat.

"I'd say he's scantily dressed for the cold," Fitzpatrick whispered into Fisher's ear.

Fitzpatrick's comment sparked Fisher's memory. Scantily clad for such a cold day, he thought. Those were the same words Fisher had used to describe Hamilton Miller, the day Domao took him to inspect Carlton's house.

"Darren, he's a detective with Richland PD," Fisher whispered.

Miller fumbled through his pockets, beginning with his trousers. Not finding what he wanted, he launched into a search of the ill-fitting sport coat. Reaching the left inside pocket, he stopped. Moments later, he produced a credit-card-sized piece of plastic.

Fisher whispered, "That card's part of the entry procedure. First a hand scan followed by card recognition."

The whispered words hadn't been out of Fisher's mouth more than a second before Fitzpatrick leaned and spoke softly to a figure sitting in the shadows beside him. "Wellesley, take him quietly. Remember, I want him alive."

"Yes Sir."

"Steve, look at the door."

Fisher turned his head toward the whisper to see that Alli's gaze was fixed on the warehouse's entry door. He turned his attention back to Miller who stood in front of the optical device. The intense blue light ignited as he placed his hand on the bottom surface of the scanner. Miller was about to drag his plastic card through the slide.

A barely detectable movement distracted Fisher away from the door and toward a stack of shipping crates near the corner of the building. Although the crouching figure was not clearly defined at first, Fisher soon recognized Agent Wellesley making his way toward Miller. Wellesley's attention was focused, his movements rapid and cat-like, his black attire rendering him virtually invisible.

Miller was too engrossed in the entry process to know what was happening. Within seconds, the long barrel of Wellsley's pistol was nestled at the base of Miller's skull. The distinctive click that followed as Wellesley cocked his pistol was heard across the fifteen-foot distance to where Fisher, Alli and Fitzpatrick crouched.

"Federal agent, Sir," Wellesley said, reaching inside a surprised Hamilton Miller's jacket to remove his weapon. "Keep your hands where I can see them. All clear, Mr. Fitzpatrick."

Twenty-five shadowy figures descended on the spot where Agent Wellesley held Miller at gun point.

Miller didn't resist as Wellesley quickly frisked him. The search produced Miller's Richland Police Department badge.

"Working a case, Detective Miller?" Fitzpatrick asked, quietly inspecting the identification Wellesley had handed him.

"Who are . . .?" Miller stopped in the midst of his question when he caught sight of Fisher standing next to Fitzpatrick.

"You're that doctor — from the house."

Fisher remained expressionless as he stared at Miller.

"I told that stupid shit Domao he should have popped you when he had the chance."

"He tried, Mr. Miller," Fisher said, keeping his gaze trained on the man. "He tried."

"We'll need your hand for a moment, Mr. Miller," Fitzpatrick pointed to the optical device to the left of the door.

"Fuck you, you son-of-a-. . .," Miller struggled against the restraining grip of two agents. Before he could finish his expletive, he fell unconscious as the butt of Wellesley's pistol crashed down on his head.

Fitzpatrick said, "Timmons, Wellesley, we'll go in as two teams. Fan out right and left of the container. Does everyone recall the sketch of the interior Dr. Fisher provided?"

"Yes," was the quiet, corporate reply.

"Return fire only if you are directly threatened," Fitzpatrick commanded.

Fitzpatrick turned to Fisher and Alli, "Steve, I don't want you or Alli to enter until after the two teams. Are your vests secured?"

"Yes," Fisher replied, pulling at the bulky Kevlar cloth.

Fisher turned to Alli. "I'm okay." She tugged at her vest.

"Weapons ready," Fitzpatrick said as agent Wellesley placed the unconscious detective's hand into the scanner.

Fisher saw the familiar intense blue light, followed by the pink glow from atop the scanner. Wellesley dragged Miller's card through the slide, and the door opened. Quietly, Fitzpatrick and twenty-five agents passed through the entryway.

Fisher approached the opening and looked inside the warehouse as the last of the agents entered. All overhead lights were on, and he could hear the air-flow hiss on the top surface of the container. "Someone's using the OR," Fisher whispered to Alli as she crouched beside him at the warehouse entrance. "Let's go over there."

Fisher took Alli's hand and they moved behind one of the large supporting columns that ran around the periphery of the warehouse interior.

Federal agents dressed in black were crouched in random locations to the right and left of the container OR.

Benjamin Domao rounded the far right corner, obviously engrossed in thought, unaware of the environment around him.

"Federal agents," Timmons said, stepping from behind a column, his weapon aimed directly at Domao.

With speed surprising for his obese body, Domao drew his pistol and fired directly at Timmons.

The shot missed its mark striking the agent crouching to Timmons' right. As the agent fell, Timmons fired at Domao. The slug struck Domao in the chest. He went down.

Fitzpatrick's voice floated from somewhere to Fisher's left, "Wellesley, Timmons, take your men to the container entrance."

Immediately, the two groups of agents moved around the large cubicle.

Fisher and Alli moved to the downed agent who was pulling himself to a sitting position.

"I'll be okay, Doc," the young man said, wincing as he held his left shoulder.

Fisher inspected the wound. It was bloody, but the agent was right. The shot had simply grazed his shoulder.

"Alli, keep pressure on the wound," Fisher said as he turned and walked to the spot where Domao was lying.

Blood oozed from the exit wound in Domao's chest and was slowly puddling under his right arm. Fisher bent and probed for a pulse. There was none. Timmons' shot had killed Domao instantly.

"Steve, I need you."

Fisher walked toward Fitzpatrick's voice.

"Recognize these guys?" Fitzpatrick asked as Fisher appeared.

Four agents, weapons drawn, stood at the entrance to the OR. Fitzpatrick stood amid them pointing to the interior.

The surrealistic scene Fisher witnessed was one he would always remember clearly. Standing frozen under the high intensity lighting was the Asian Fisher had encountered the night before, wearing a sterile gown, gloves and mask. Although the second man was also masked, Fisher had no trouble recognizing the Chief of Cardiac Transplantation at Taggart. On the operating table lay a completely draped human figure. The operative field, a one-foot square area of skin on the sleeping figure's chest was blood-drenched — obvious signs of a hurried, careless incision. The victim's sternum lay open, and Talbott stood poised to place a sternal retractor.

"Step back away from the table and put your hands in the air," Fitzpatrick commanded.

The Asian immediately stepped back and lifted his hands. Talbott, however, remained still, seemingly weighing his options.

Without warning, Talbott launched the sternal retractor at the agent beside Fitzpatrick. The throw missed its mark, as the agent side-stepped the flying instrument. Talbott turned and sprinted to the recovery room.

"Wait!" Fisher yelled as two of the agents rushed to the small room. "It's a dead end. There's no way out."

A deafening pop arose from the adjoining room. All agents flattened themselves against the OR floor.

Timmons and another of Fitzpatrick's agents made their way to the small room's door, rounding the threshold with pistols drawn.

"You better come quickly, Sir." Timmons looked back to at Fitzpatrick and Fisher. This guy shot himself."

Fisher's heart raced. The pounding made his head feel as if it would explode.

"Nooooo," Fisher heard himself scream as he pushed past Timmons.

Talbott lay on the floor beside the drug cabinet Alli had discovered the night before. A gaping wound was visible on the right side of his chest. His breathing indicated he was still alive.

Fisher dropped to his knees as he reached the dying surgeon. "Talbott!" Fisher yelled.

Talbott stared at the ceiling, breathing rapidly, out of contact.

"Talbott!" Fisher screamed, grabbing the surgeon's bloody scrub gown. "Don't you die on me!"

Fisher shook Talbott's body until he screamed with pain.

"Who killed Chip Carlton, you shit? Who killed him?"

Talbott coughed, spraying bloody froth across Fisher's face. Slowly he turned to look at Fisher, attempting to form words with his mouth. "Stryker . . . Stryker and . . . Gra . . . Graf," he gasped through blood covered lips. "For hire . . . profess . . . professional hit."

Fisher jerked Talbott closer, "Where is Natalie Roberts?"

Talbott cried out in pain again as a staccato of rattling coughs brought renewed sprays of blood.

"Where, Talbott? Where is Natalie Roberts?"

Talbott's eyes closed.

Fisher shook the dying man violently until his eyes re-opened.

Talbott shrieked with pain. His breathing came shallowly in rapid breaths. "I . . . don't . . . know."

Fisher knew Talbot had only seconds remaining. "Where's Stryker?"

Talbott's head bobbed, his neck muscles weakening. "New . . ., New York," he whispered, his voice faint and barely audible. "Health Pursuit stockholders me . . . meeting."

Fisher pulled Talbott's bloody torso off the floor.

"Don't you die, Talbott! Where is Natalie Roberts? Where is she?"

Talbott didn't answer.

Fisher continued shaking Talbott's upper body.

"Where is she, Talbott?"

"He's dead, Steve."

Fisher could feel Fitzpatrick's hand on his shoulder.

"He's dead."

As Fisher released Talbott's blood-soaked gown, the room became silent, the white noise of positive pressure-ventilation flowing into the room was all he could hear.

• • • • •

Across the city of Richland, the call Spencer Winston had expected from Talbott never came.

Thomas Winston looked up at his father. "Dad, what time are they going to start the operation?" he asked, his breathing more labored as he lay in the hospital bed.

"I don't know, Son," Spencer Winston answered, staring out into the darkness from Taggart Memorial's fourth floor. "I don't know."

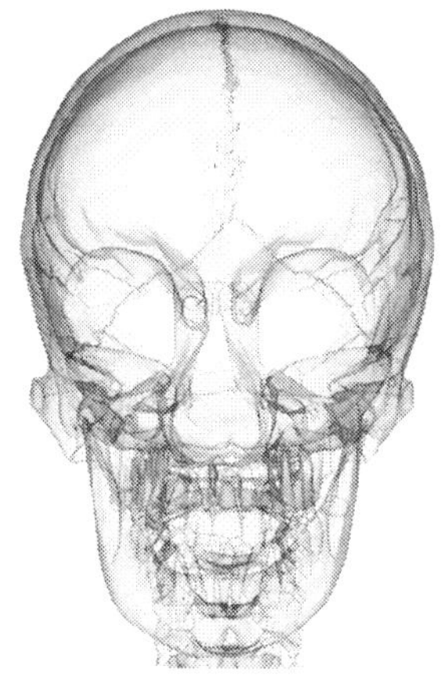

CHAPTER FORTY

Fisher sat on the floor aware only of the ventilation noise. His mind was spinning, yet he his thoughts came clearly: Stryker, Health Pursuit, New York.

"Steve," the soft voice came from behind. "We've got to do something with the man on the table."

Fisher turned.

Alli walked into the room and knelt beside him. "Are you okay?" she asked, seeing the blood that covered his hands and clothing.

"Yes. I'm okay. Let's see what we can do for this guy."

As Fitzpatrick and his men were securing the warehouse, Fisher moved to the scrub sink to wash up. He returned to the table where the man lay. The midline chest incision still oozed blood from several spots. Fisher took the cautery and electrocoagulated all visible bleeders. Within fifteen minutes, the wound was bloodless.

"I think we're ready," Fisher said, looking up from the surgical wound.

Alli turned and walked to the far end of the OR where the Asian stood handcuffed, an agent on either side. A look of complete surprise swept across his face when she removed a vial of KP-1049 from the OR cabinet.

Fisher signaled for the agents to bring their captive to the table. "I want to administer this agent exactly as it was given to all the other victims who have come through here."

The Asian momentarily engaged Fisher's icy stare, but then he broke off and stared at the floor. "As you wish," he said quietly.

Once he completed his task, the Asian was led away. Fisher then covered the chest wound with sterile towels.

"This man needs to be transported to the Med, Darren."

After the ambulance departed, Fitzpatrick rooted Richland Police Chief Ranson Williams out of bed and dragged him down to the warehouse.

When Williams arrived, he stayed calm listening to the news of his officers' complicity and the events that led to the death of one of his detectives and a prominent Richland surgeon. At first, he merely walked around the warehouse. He examined the bodies and studied the container OR carefully. He glared at Miller, who sat handcuffed and guarded by two agents. "Someone want to tell me what's really going on here?" he asked, finally.

Fitzpatrick recounted the highlights, calling on Fisher at intervals to fill in necessary details.

With a smile, Williams said, "Doc, you and Miss Shepard here can come to work for the Richland PD any time you decide medical stuff is too boring."

They all laughed.

Williams' expression changed rapidly as he stared at Domao's obese corpse. "I might have eventually suspected that Domao was dirty," he said. "But Miller here's a surprise."

Williams glared at Miller again, then turned to Fitzpatrick. "What can the RPD do to help you wrap this up?"

• • • • •

It was after three in the morning when Alli turned off Talton Avenue and drove through the back streets that led to Fisher's apartment.

The Cavalier's headlights shown on the bottom row of apartments as Alli nosed into the parking spot usually reserved for Fisher.

"Very interesting," Fisher said, gazing beyond the headlights.

"What do you see?"

"The door to my apartment. It's been replaced."

Of the three doors leading to downstairs apartments, number three clearly had a new coat of paint.

"The blast that struck that door would have left a hole at least six inches in diameter. Looks like my scumbag landlord did some work, for a change."

They got out into a pitch-black parking lot and ascended to the walkway.

Fisher whispered as they walked to number three. "Let's just hope he didn't change the lock."

As he had done four days earlier, Fisher extended his hand to the level of the dead bolt — key met lock and sunk in precisely. He turned the key — the dead bold opened.

Images of his last visit to the apartments were still fresh as he took the small pistol from his coat and reached inside to turn on the lights.

Fisher cautiously entered the apartment and searched it. There was no one.

"My God," Alli said as she entered.

All around them was chaos. Furniture was overturned. Sofa cushions were cut open, and their padding removed. Fisher's single bookshelf in the small living room had been emptied, and the books scattered. In the kitchen, all cabinets were open, and their contents dragged onto the floor. The kitchen table was overturned. Kitchen chair seat cushions were ripped open.

Fisher's small bedroom had not been spared. Dresser drawers were pulled out, and the contents strewn about.

Together, they stared at the ransacked bedroom, neither speaking.

The weight of recent events crashed down on Fisher's shoulders as his mind launched forward, reviewing events once again.

In the midst of his thoughts, the warmth of Alli's hand in his gently pulled him back. He turned to her encountering the deep blue of her eyes. Her heavy wool cap was gone, releasing long ringlets of light brown hair across her shoulders. For the first time, he became aware of the light scent of her perfume.

In the quiet of the wrecked apartment, their gazes intertwined. Fisher felt her softness as he touched her face.

An unseen force slowly moved Fisher closer to her beauty, her scent exploding in his senses as their lips met.

Time and its relentless pounding rhythm halted as he drew her closer. His shoulders relaxed as the weight of two weeks of terror lifted.

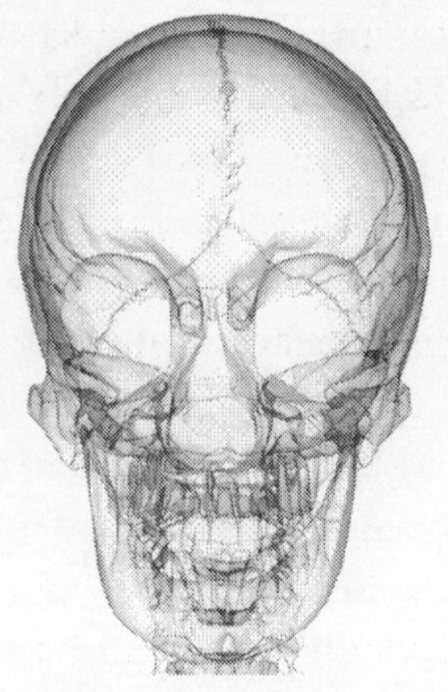

CHAPTER FORTY-ONE

February 10, Grand Ballroom, Plaza Hotel, New York City

Cliff Stryker picked nervously at the loose thread hanging off the lapel of the new Armani suit he wore. He was angry, especially after laying down twenty-one hundred dollars. He had waited patiently for Ramano's to finish the suit, and there was a fucking loose thread.

"Finest tailor in New York, bull shit," he whispered, tugging at the thread. He would have plenty to say about that before leaving New York. He looked up casually, trying not to draw attention, then stared down at the thread again.

The Question that consumed him was whether pulling the thread would damage the suit. Stryker had canceled two days of meetings at Taggart and flown to New York ahead of time to have the suit tailored. At his first Health Pursuit stockholder's meeting, he was damn well going for exemplary first impressions. Rupert Graf had made it clear that impeccable dress was expected of his administrators at all times.

"We have an immense reputation to uphold, Mr. Stryker," Graf had said during Stryker's promotion interview two and a half years earlier. "The world is watching our bold experiment in healthcare delivery. They are watching us every minute. Don't you forget that."

Stryker continued diddling with the lapel, but his thoughts were on Health Pursuit's CEO. He recalled the fire in Graf's eyes that day. He had stared at Stryker, his eyes searing hot like glowing coals. His face, eyes fiery, head and neck veins distended, had come forward until the festering cauldron bubbled six inches from Stryker's face. Graf's bronzed skin had reddened, contrasting sharply with his graying Germanic blond hair.

"Do you understand that, Mr. Stryker?" Graf asked following an uncomfortable quiet.

A few moments passed. Stryker had stayed motionless, unable to speak. "Uh . . ., well . . ., yes sir, I . . ., I will remember, Mr. Graf," Stryker had managed to squeak out.

Graf then stared at Stryker as if sizing him up, making his final judgment. Unexpectedly, he disengaged his stare, stood and walked across the vast penthouse office to a polished ebony cabinet. He pulled out two tumblers and a crystal decanter.

"Scotch, Mr. Stryker?"

Stryker hated Scotch, but knew he damn well he'd better not refuse. He accepted the glass.

"Mr. Stryker, I am offering you the position as Taggart Memorial's next chief administrative officer." Graf lofted his tumbler, proposing a toast.

Stryker recalled struggling for words. He had been taken by surprise.

"But Mr. Fenick . . . ."

"Mr. Fenick cleaned out his office today, Mr. Stryker. I should like you to accept the position and begin work tomorrow."

That brief meeting was Stryker's single personal contact with Graf. At that point, Stryker was a newcomer to Taggart Memorial, on the job just shy of a year, but his reputation was established. His peers recognized him as aggressive, someone who got what he wanted. Unfortunately, many of those peers became acquainted with Stryker's personality traits by feeling the weight of his shoe leather on their backs. Stryker's march to the top had left a trail of colleagues foundering in his wake. His interview with Graf heralded the fall of his last obstacle: Todd Fenick. Graf, perpetually aware of his organization's inner workings, had rewarded Stryker's aggressive achievement.

Stryker's thoughts vaporized as his eyes refocused on the annoying string. He would have to be as inconspicuous as possible, he thought, looking around at those seated beside him. Stryker yanked the thread from his lapel. It snapped neatly, leaving an unnoticeable stub. His knotted stomach relaxed a bit. He dropped the contentious thread on the floor.

At last he was undistracted. He looked around the Grand Ballroom of the Plaza Hotel. The room was flanked by imposing marble columns. Gold inlaid trim rose elegantly in a gentle slope intercepting a ceiling crowned by crystal chandeliers. A thousand people, seated or milling about, awaited the start of Health Pursuit's annual meeting.

From somewhere amid the massive chandeliers, a soft male voice announced, "Ladies and Gentlemen, please take your seats, the meeting is about to begin."

Conversations ended as meeting attendees moved promptly to their seats. Within minutes, a hush fell over the assembled body of Health Pursuit stockholders.

The ballroom darkened. Intensely colored laser lights crisscrossed the air, creating brilliant arrays of color. Deafening sounds of rocket boosters filled the room as light and sound flooded the senses. Beams of light clashed, melded and wavered, forming rapidly moving spectral images. Holographic images danced overhead. Each low swoop from the images provoked cheers and applause from the audience.

The laser light faded, as a large projection screen above the speaker's podium burst forth with new colors and images. The screen images, initially blurred, came into sharp focus as Health Pursuit's logo, a bronze shield and gleaming Excalibur, gradually became recognizable. The audience clapped a thunderous response. Music, aggressive and marching, filled the room as photographed scenes of dazzling Health Pursuit hospitals, construction sites and operating rooms; nurses in uniform, physicians standing over patients; smiling faces of adults and children paraded past in rapid succession. As the music began its crescendo, images flashed onto the screen with ever-increasing speed. The laser lights returned, creating a stunning cacophony of light and sound. Then, as suddenly as it had begun, it ended. The huge ballroom fell dark and silent.

The audience was hypnotized by the light show display.

Lengthy moments passed.

The room remained dark.

Stryker thought a malfunction had occurred, but then, a single beam of light pierced the tense atmosphere and struck the raised podium, bathing it with pure, white light. Out of the darkness of the rear stage area, Rupert Graf slowly ascended the steps to the podium. The powerful light ignited his bronzed features, and a thousand people stood in exuberant applause.

Graf stood board like and presidential. He rotated from side to side, raising one arm at a time greeting the cheering audience.

The applause rolled across the ballroom like waves. It would have continued well past five minutes, had Graf not raised both arms in an outstretched fashion to signal the beginning of his remarks.

"Ladies and gentleman," Graf began, his German accent unmistakable. "The organization and delivery of healthcare in the United States and the world is changing at a blinding pace. Legislation passed by the United States Congress and later deemed constitutional by the Supreme Court paved the way for strong healthcare industry leaders to compete and succeed. It cleared the way for a medical marketplace where the forces of supply and demand and head-to-head competition would rule. As healthcare price structures truly became subject to market forces, unique opportunities were created for those capable of capitalizing upon them. Health Pursuit is flourishing in the medical marketplace of the twenty-first century."

The audience flew to its feet, again roaring with applause.

Cliff Stryker, like all others in the ballroom, was mesmerized by the charismatic figure.

Graf continued, "It is with great pleasure that I bring exciting news from our acquisitions and holdings task force. Just two hours before the start of this meeting, final agreements were put in place for the acquisition of Hospital Consortium."

Once again the audience rose, cheering and applauding wildly. Stryker found himself cheering along with them. Next to him an old woman, not a day less than eighty, danced a jig in front of her chair. Everywhere he looked, handshakes and back slaps took place.

Graf extended his arms, signaling for quiet. The audience responded immediately by re-seating themselves.

"With the Hospital Consortium acquisition in Europe, Health Pursuit becomes the largest for-profit hospital corporation in the world with more than two thousand acute-care hospitals in the United States, Canada, and Europe."

Another round of exuberant applause.

Graf smiled, unable to hide the pleasure the frequent interruptions brought him. "Beyond the Hospital Consortium acquisition, there is additional exciting news. In October, Health Pursuit will open a chain of two hundred-twenty outpatient clinics in major airports, shopping malls and financial districts across the United States and Canada and Germany."

More thundering applause.

Although his seat on the third row placed him at a slight distance from the speaker, Stryker easily recognized the fiery redness as it crept up Graf's neck and onto his face. Stryker had seen it before. The expression was one of glee.

"Ladies and Gentlemen," Graf continued, gently pounding the lectern with a closed fist in cadence with his speech. "Health Pursuit will soon finalize its vision of vertically integrated healthcare delivery. Acquisition talks are now under way with one of the largest health insurance carriers in the United States."

Again the audience came to its feet in ovation.

Graf continued his presentation, giving data on Health Pursuit's gross and net revenue for the year. Despite the Hospital Consortium acquisition, the bottom line for Health Pursuit was one of strength. Before concluding his remarks, he announced a one-dollar-and-seventy-five-cent-per-share earnings.

As Graf concluded his remarks, the audience delivered its most enthusiastic and prolonged applause.

A smile broke out on Graf's face as he continued. "Ladies and Gentlemen, as you know, Health Pursuit annually presents to one of its facilities an award of recognition for areas of excellence. The Health Pursuit Board of Directors serve as judges for this coveted annual prize," He lifted a large plaque from the lectern. "All our facilities in the Health Pursuit family are considered in the judging," he continued. "I am proud to announce that this year's award is presented to Taggart Memorial Hospital for excellence in organ transplantation. Mr. Cliff Stryker, administrator of Taggart Memorial, please come to the podium."

Cheers and applause broke out from all parts of the Plaza's Grand Ballroom.

Stryker's stomach knotted and the collar of his stiff new shirt grew tight. His legs were mushy as he walked to the steps. As the applause continued, Stryker climbed weakly up the stairs, the weight of one thousand sets of eyes bearing down on him. He shook hands briefly with Graf, took the heavy plaque, and turned toward the audience. He lifted his arm and gave a sweeping wave of acknowledgment.

I've arrived, Stryker thought, smiling out across the ballroom. It's my just reward for carrying out Graf's dirty business, for dealing with stinking shit like Harry Talbott and the other assholes in transplant. Stryker's chest inflated as the applause persisted. He continued waving a few seconds longer.

Finally, the applause settled. Stryker prepared for his return to the steps, but caught sight of Graf's burning stare. During that fleeting moment, scorn and loathing flowed from Graf's eyes. A heaviness filled Stryker's chest as he returned to his seat.

What's up with Graf, he thought, placing the plaque across the Armani pinstripe fabric of his lap.

• • • • •

Stryker splashed cold water across his face. The stockholder's meeting had ended two hours earlier, and he had returned to his suite for an afternoon nap. He had closed his eyes, but sleep did not come. He was worried. He could not flush the image of Graf's face from his mind.

The guy was giving me an award for outstanding performance, Stryker thought, staring at his reflection in the gold-leafed mirror, yet he looked like he wanted me stuffed into a shredder. I've done his dirty work faithfully for three years and this is the treatment I get.

Stryker pulled back from the mirror. He couldn't understand the mystery. As he returned to the sitting room, he tightened the belt on the fresh terry cloth robe he'd discovered in the marble bathroom.

When he passed the large window, Stryker stopped. He looked out onto a snow-covered Central Park. Darkness was descending on the city, but winter activities in the park were proceeding. Beyond the row of trees lining Central Park South, hundreds of skaters carved circles into the frozen pond next to Wollman Rink. His gaze swept away from the park and closer to the Plaza. Twelve floors below, a line of horse-drawn carriages lined Central Park South waiting to whisk tourists away on frostbite tours through the snowy park. Everywhere Stryker looked, the city had cleared the streets of the recent heavy snowfall.

Stryker left the window and settled into an overstuffed wingback chair. He glanced around the room attempting to relax. The Plaza's high ceilings, gold trim, original art work and hand-turned furniture were its trademark. And, on any other occasion, he could have enjoyed them. But not today, he thought, his gut grinding into another twisting cramp.

What was it, he asked himself again. The whole episode in the Grand Ballroom haunted him.

He reached for the large fruit basket and wrestled through its bright purple cellophane. Maybe an apple would help.

The suite's doorbell rang, startling Stryker. His mind was as tense as a trip wire, still electrified by images of Rupert Graf.

Ring ring. Ring ring. "Bellman with a message, Mr. Stryker."

The voice drifted across the suite, its volume muted by the thick wooden door.

Stryker stood, went to the door and gazed into the peephole. Ordinarily he wasn't skittish, opening the door for visitors, but the whole thing with Graf worried him. As Stryker inspected the hallway, he could see the Plaza bellhop and his familiar uniform. The young man held a silver tray that bore an envelope Stryker couldn't make out. His pulse increased as he continued looking through the peephole.

Finally, he summoned his courage and opened the door. He received the small envelope and tipped the friendly bellhop.

He returned to the overstuffed chair and studied the envelope for a moment, his insides churning more.

The cream-colored envelope bore his name, handwritten across the front. He tore it open and pulled out the contents. Stryker held his breath as he read:

Mr. Rupert Graf
And the
Health Pursuit
Board of Directors
Cordially Invite You
To A Celebration

In Your Honor

¥¥¥

Tavern on The Green Restaurant
Seven-Thirty p.m.

For a moment, Stryker simply stared at the invitation, confused. Slowly, confusion faded as a wide grin spread across his face.

He lapsed into loud, almost uncontrolled, laughter as he stood and walked back to the huge window. He looked out over the darkening park a second time.

"That son-of-a-bitch," he said as he belly laughed. "Did he make a fool out of me or what? I thought the old fart was angry. Shit. You can't trust those Germans."

Stryker dropped the invitation onto the credenza, turned and headed for the bathroom. He had work to do, he thought. Things had to be perfect.

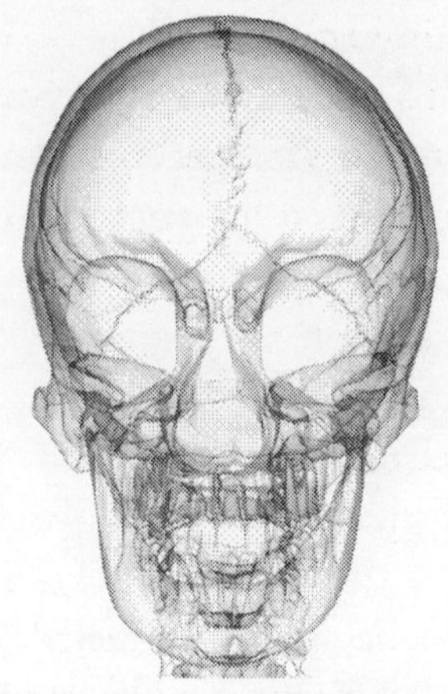

CHAPTER FORTY-TWO

"Well?"

The one-word Question hung lead-like over the phone line for a few moments.

"Your . . . uh . . . Your men questioned her very thoroughly, Mr. Graf."

"And, what else did she tell you?"

"Uh . . . we . . . we weren't able to get anything further from her, I'm afraid."

"Jacobson, you and the whole lot. You're all idiots, just idiots!"

"But Mr. Gra —"

"Shut up!"

Rupert Graf lowered his voice, bringing his lips close to the phone before speaking. "I can see that trusting you imbeciles at Taggart will be the costliest mistake I have ever made."

"No . . . please don't think . . . ."

"I said, shut up," Graf snapped.

Venom flowed over the phone line. "I want answers, not excuses."

Graf awaited a reply from Samuel Jacobson.

"There isn't much more than what you know already," Jacobson said, a tremor in his voice. "After she met with a transplant surgeon from Medford University, a Dr. Steven Fisher, and his medical student friend Alli Shepard, she took a tissue core from the tissue bank and matched it to a specimen she removed from an autopsy. There's no doubt she knows."

"Imbeciles! You're all imbeciles!"

"Forgive me for saying so, Mr. Graf," Jacobson said, gathering his courage to speak. "This was a security issue, and those matters were left strictly to Mr. Stryker and that idiot police detective."

"Goddamn! You're all to blame!"

"Please let me . . . ."

"Shut up!" Graf yelled into the phone.

A heavy silence ensued.

Finally Graf spoke, "Kill her."

"And the others?" Jacobson tried to inject calm into his question.

"They will be taken care of. All of them, including Stryker." Graf slammed the phone loudly onto its receiver, shaking as he stared at it. Quietly, he rocked back in the massive chair and looked out on a snowy New York landscape forty floors below. He tapped his index fingers against his lips for a moment then he turned back to face his vast penthouse office.

"Update me."

Quietly, a man arose from the shadows of the far corner. He spoke softly. "The mainframe computer servers at Taggart were entered from the outside. Files were opened, memos were read."

Graf said nothing, but his plethoric face and fiery eyes disclosed his state of mind.

"The mainframe's security trapped digital shadows left in many places by the intruder," the soft-spoken man continued. "They were traced to a residence on the east side of Richland."

"You know who lives there?"

"Yes," the reply came almost as a whisper.

"And," Graf said, a look of glee entering his eyes.

"The name is Shepard."

Behind the index fingers that still danced across Graf's lips, a smile cracked as he spoke. "You will make arrangements?"

"It's already being taken care of."

"And this Dr. Fisher?"

"He's dropped out of sight, but he'll resurface. We'll be ready."

"Like you were ready for him last time?"

The soft-spoken man hesitated, then commented, "No excuses. He will be taken out."

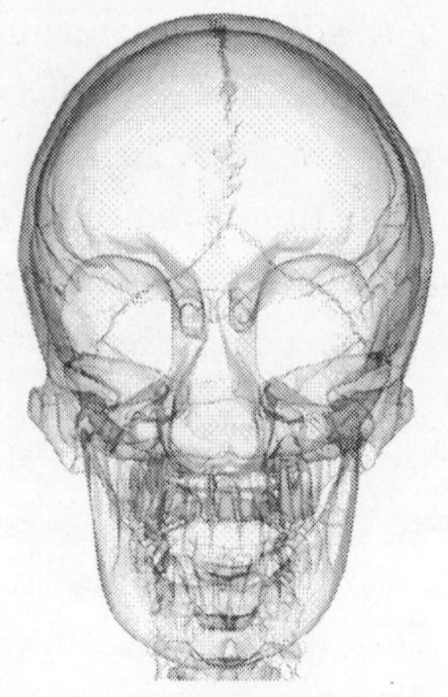

CHAPTER FORTY-THREE

Icy air surged into the Plaza foyer as Cliff Stryker gazed at the frozen fountain across the street. The fountain, a part of Grand Army Plaza, slightly short of Fifth Avenue, had produced a flowing ice sculpture as water trickled from its topmost spout during the freezing cold.

Stryker looked at his watch, then back into the night. It was seven fifteen, and midwinter New York City pulsated with activity. Hotel guests and visitors rushed past Stryker out of the Plaza's Fifth Avenue entrance, melding into the mass of humanity that pressed its way forward on the sidewalks. Stryker pulled the collar of his overcoat tighter around his neck. The temperature of the foyer had fallen fast, as a crowd of a dozen or so had left the hotel.

Cliff Stryker did not stand out particularly, except for the wide grin pasted on his face. He still wore the new Armani, not having expected an evening affair. Thoughts of the invitation and the reception in his honor filled his mind as he waited.

"Your limousine's here, Mr. Stryker," the doorman called.

When Stryker broke free of his spell, he looked at the doorman. He was pointing down the steps to a sleek, black limousine pulled up to the curb.

"This way, Mr. Stryker," the doorman said, preparing to accompany Stryker to the limousine.

Stryker seated himself in the rear of the automobile and gazed back briefly at the brilliantly lighted hotel. He worked hard to control his grinning as he became lost in thought again.

Moments ticked by as the limousine simply sat. Stryker came up for air as a voice came from the front. "The taxis are all over me, Mr. Stryker," the driver said. "This may take a minute or two."

Stryker gave a passing glance at the sea of yellow cabs blocking their departure, but quickly returned his thoughts to the dinner in his honor. Finally, the area in front of the Plaza cleared and they pulled away from the curb.

"Mr. Stryker, would yous care for a ride through Central Park? It's beautiful this time of year."

"Sure," Stryker replied, not really caring how he arrived at the celebration in his honor.

"I think we'll just enter the park at East Drive here. You been to New York before, Mr. Stryker?" the chatty limousine driver asked.

"Once," Stryker spoke flatly, aware that the driver was looking back at him through his rear view mirror.

"This is just a great city, Mr. Stryker. I've lived here twenty years. Oh! Look over there to the left. That's the pond where all the skatas come. The cops don't like it, because someone always breaks through the ice, but they do it anyways. To your right is the Central Park Zoo. They've probably got the animals all tucked in for the night by now."

Stryker snorted his disapproval at the driver's persistent babble.

"Now, we'll just swing left here at Rumsey Playfield," he went on. "Of course you can't see the Playfield this time of year, because of the snow, but that's New York. You take the good with the not-so-good, ya know?"

Stryker had no intention of striking up a conversation with the imbecile on what should have been a five-minute ride to the Tavern on the Green.

"Now I want yous to take a look at that," the driver continued. "As we come up the hill by the Sheep Meadow, I want yous to look up at those lights. Ain't they gorgeous?"

Stryker looked out over an open meadow on the left side of the limousine. Through the trees of Central Park, he could see thousands of twinkling lights peeking above the leafless canopy.

"Ain't that beautiful?"

Despite his total disgust at the driver's endless chatter, he could readily appreciate the thousands of lights that ignited the trees inside the Tavern on the Green.

The driver continued across the park using one of the cross-park roads that led by the snow-covered bowling greens. They turned left onto West Drive and, within a quarter of a mile, arrived at the drive leading to the magnificently illuminated restaurant.

A doorman dressed in a gray overcoat stepped out to greet the limousine as it arrived under the covered drive.

"Welcome to the Tavern on the Green," the young doorman said, opening the limousine's right rear door. He moved stiffly in the heavy tan overcoat. The doorman's top hat made him appear more than six and half feet tall. "Watch your step, Sir. We tried to get the walkways clear, but they're still a bit slippery after last night's snow."

Stryker emerged from the limousine, glad to escape the chatty driver.

"You're right," Stryker replied. "Tonight would not be the night I need to fall."

• • • • •

The limousine pulled away from the restaurant, exited the park on West Sixty-seventh and turned left onto Central Park West. It drove a half block south before it turned into a small, unlighted, delivery area to the rear of the restaurant. There, the driver shut off the limousine and buttoned his black overcoat. The trunk release sounded with a thud as he pressed the button. He walked to the rear, stopped and inspected the small parking area carefully. Satisfied there was no one else, he raised the trunk lid and removed a two-foot-long carrying case. He closed the trunk and headed for the sidewalk running along Central Park West, stepping carefully on the icy surface. Within twenty yards, he left the sidewalk and made his way up a small flight of stairs. Reaching the top of the stairs, he studied the cobblestone walk that traveled along the backside of the tavern.

The sidewalk was about thirty yards long and was dimly lighted by lampposts stationed at ten-foot intervals. Dense, snow-covered shrubbery and trees ran along the side of the cobblestone path obscuring the rear of the restaurant. To the left of the walkway sat a dark valet parking area that was full. The driver walked quietly into the darkness of the parking area, making his way through the rows of parked vehicles. Reaching the far side, he turned and moved slowly in the direction of the restaurant's entrance. He reached a point where he could view the drive and the rear walkway, then stopped and crouched. Working swiftly, he opened the small case and removed the two halves of a high-powered rifle. Within seconds, the weapon was assembled, night scope mounted and silencer attached. With his task completed, he sank back into the shadows of the dense stand of trees that lined the far side of the parking area.

• • • • •

"Atta boy, Cliff," the fat-faced gentleman said with a grunt. He wrapped his fleshy hand around Stryker's. "We're proud of you, old boy."

"Thank you, Mr. Chapel." Stryker hoped he had blushed appropriately for one of the members of Health Pursuit's board.

Preston Chapel was a cheerful, obese philanthropist who had inherited a position on the board from his mother, a long time believer in the medical marketplace. She had died leaving son Preston to carry the banner in her name. Stryker knew Chapel from the pictures published of him in the Health Pursuit annual report.

He's even fatter than his pictures look, Stryker thought as he pasted the plastic grin on his face again.

From behind Stryker in the crowded room came a female voice, "Mr. Stryker, you must be extremely proud of your accomplishments and those of your hospital."

Stryker turned to confront a tall, slender woman, probably in her forties wearing an attractive, black evening gown decorated with sequins.

"I'm sorry. I don't think we've met," Stryker said, feeling his chest puff out further than before.

"Oh . . . oh!" Chapel said, sounding embarrassed. "Please forgive me. Cynthia Burke, this is Cliff Stryker, administrator of the Taggart Memorial Hospital. Cliff, Cynthia is an administrator of a Health Pursuit Hospital in southern Illinois."

"It's a pleasure, Mr. Stryker," Burke said, offering her black-gloved hand.

"The pleasure is all mine, Ms. Burke," Stryker said.

"Okay, Cynthia, you'll have to excuse us," Chapel said, interrupting the two administrators. "Cliff, I want to introduce you to several people. Why don't we move into the Crystal Room where the main reception is going on?"

Stryker squeezed away, and he and Chapel inched their way along the semi-circular hallway past various dining rooms, all of which were packed with Health Pursuit stockholders and personnel. Stryker continued receiving back slaps and handshakes. The pair pushed on toward the glass-enclosed room in the center of the tavern's horse-shoe shaped building.

As they pressed into the Crystal Room, the crowd became denser and conversational noise rose. Tuxedo-clad waiters and their captains scurried about the crowd carrying silver trays of brimming champagne flutes. The aroma of seafood and roast beef wafted up from numerous tables of food. Outside the room, leafless sycamore trees bore thousands of small white lights.

In the Crystal Room, Chapel continued dragging nameless faces over to offer congratulations, making Stryker the center of attention. Though uncomfortable with the crush of back slaps at first, two hurriedly consumed champagne flutes relaxed and emboldened him.

In the midst of the jocularity and handshakes, Stryker let his gaze sweep the room, casually sipping from a third champagne flute. Off to his left, he caught sight of Graf, next to the Crystal Room's transparent wall. He was engaged in conversation with two unfamiliar faces. In a frightening moment, Graf slowly turned a subtle but scornful stare on Stryker almost as if he had sensed the weight of Stryker's gaze.

Stryker's blood chilled. Preston Chapel tugged at his sleeve, attempting to redirect his attention, but it was no use. Stryker was paralyzed by Graf's scathing stare.

Graf placed his drink on a waiter's tray and moved in Stryker's direction, never withdrawing his gaze. As revelers inched out of Graf's way, the subtle look of hatred that radiated from his face went unnoticed. Stryker recognized it, though.

Graf swung his head back and forced a mechanical smile as he approached. "Ah, Mr. Stryker, you appear as if you are having the time of your life."

"There you are, Rupert," Chapel swung around and patted Stryker on the back. "Aren't you proud of our boy Stryker here?"

"Yes, Mr. Chapel, very proud, very proud indeed." The cadence of Graf's speech decelerated as he spoke. He drew his face to within eight inches of Stryker's. "Mr. Chapel, you will have to excuse us. Mr. Stryker and I have a few things to discuss. Mr. Stryker, would you come with me?"

Stryker's head was pleasantly spinning from the champagne, but he was gripped by fear. A pounding fullness crept into his consciousness as the pleasant champagne stupor rapidly gave way to pain and dread. Graf turned and moved between densely packed bodies as he made his way out of the Crystal Room. Stryker was terrified, but he was helpless to resist.

No one noticed as the two men progressed through the packed hallways to a section of the Tavern where the crowd had thinned out. At last they walked into an unused dining room.

Graf stopped abruptly. He turned to face Stryker, revealing facial features on fire with anger. Stryker tried to control his fear as he looked upon the face of hell.

Graf sprayed spittle as he spoke. "Why did I ever think you could be trusted?"

A mixture of fear and confusion gnawed at Stryker as he looked at Graf. "I . . . I'm not sure I know what you . . ."

"Shut up!" Graf yelled.

Stryker dropped his head down as if he were being beaten.

"Because of your ineptness and stupidity, mainframe security at Taggart Memorial was breached."

Stryker was unable to command his vocal cords to function. He then squeaked out the remnant of a question. "But how?"

"Because of your lax security," Graf boomed. "I can see it now. The whole fucking place was a pushover. To goddamn think, I let you talk me into hiring that slob from the Richland Police Department to handle security. He was a joke."

"Please, Sir," Stryker implored Graf. "What happened?"

Graf stared at his quivering administrator. Stryker tugged at his dress shirt collar.

Blood filled Graf's face. Finally he spoke. "You just don't get it do you? You idiot! First, your fat friend detective botches hospital security by letting a part-time pathologist break into the tissue bank and remove a tissue core."

"What?" Stryker shrieked. "I know nothing of this."

"Of course you don't, and that speaks volumes for your sloppy operation, Mr. Stryker. Now I've got the messy little task of having to dispose of her. You've cost me money and caused me trouble, Mr. Stryker," Graf said in a menacing whisper. "I had to bring her here to dispose of her."

Virtually all of the blood drained from Stryker's face as hundreds of sweat droplets popped out across his forehead. He looked as though he would faint.

Graf drew back and rubbed his chin as if deep in thought, his eyes aimed at the ceiling. "And let me see, what's next in your long line of screw ups, Mr. Stryker? Oh yes, there's the mainframe computer server that was breached by a hacker yesterday. Oh, and you'll be happy to know that all your personal email memos were read. Isn't it funny, Mr. Stryker? The contact who called me today says you didn't even have your network files password-protected. That is strictly against Health Pursuit regulations."

"You imbecile!" Graf roared. "The single most sensitive project we have is in jeopardy because of your stupidity."

Stryker's head spun. His worst nightmare was coming true. He struggled to hold the urine in his bladder as he looked at Graf's fiery eyes.

Then Graf's face cleared as he looked across the empty dining room. He took a moment to straighten his jacket and adjust his tie.

Graf turned back to look at Stryker, who was leaning against one of the sturdy oak tables, struggling to stay upright.

A thin smile made its way across Graf's face as his eyes settled on Stryker again. "Enjoy yourself, Mr. Stryker. As they say, eat, drink and be merry."

Stryker's consciousness began to slip as Graf disappeared from the room. The cream-colored light from the glass fixtures overhead became brown toned as Stryker struggled to stay alert. His chest heaved, his pulse raced and his entire body shook.

The significance of Graf's words sunk in all too quickly as he jumped, almost falling over the table, when a waiter entered the room.

"Sir, are you all right?" the waiter asked, seeing the difficulty Stryker was having.

Stryker didn't answer. His face was cold, his eyes burning from the droplets of cold sweat raining down from his forehead. His palms were clammy. He tried commanding his brain to think rationally, but all he could think of was the brutal slaying of Dr. Charles Carlton ten days earlier. He had seen the grisly photos. As Taggart's point person with the news media, Stryker had relived the killing over and over, hundreds of times. Every wire service that came to town had to have the story all over again. His position was awkward because he knew Graf had let the contract on Carlton's life. He would carry the horrible burden with him for a long time.

"Sir, may I bring you some water, a drink perhaps? You look dreadful."

Stryker never made eye contact with the waiter. His mind was consumed by fear as he pushed away from the table and stumbled, struggling to get to the entrance of the deserted dining room.

"Sir, I can call a doctor, if you wish."

The voice chased after him, but Stryker never heard it. He reached the hallway, the spine of the restaurant, and headed to the Tavern's entrance. He bumped and shoved as the party goers increased in density, making the hallway a series of roadblocks.

Unkind words flew at Stryker as he pushed and shoved his way along through the crowd of intoxicated merry makers. He recognized the face of Cynthia Burke, the administrator from southern Illinois, as he pushed his way by.

"Mr. Stryker, you aren't leaving so soon, are you?" She reached for his sleeve. "Wouldn't you like to have another drink?"

"Maybe another time. I . . . I . . . need to leave," Stryker said, not really understanding the words he had spoken. The siren of fear gripped his mind and drove his actions.

Stryker struggled past the Crystal Room where a knot of people had formed around Rupert Graf. He didn't pause. A killer would likely be near Graf, he thought, his brain managing to put together two pieces of information for the first time in a half hour. I must get away from him. I must.

Stryker pushed on, looking right and left for someone approaching in a hurried fashion, someone who would be carrying a weapon. That's right, a concealed weapon. That's how Graf would do it, he thought.

Terror gripped Stryker's mind as he burst into the Tavern's small entrance lobby. The hostess looked up from her desk as Stryker appeared.

"Sir, are you okay?" the hostess asked.

Stryker walked around the small lobby liked a caged animal, looking for a path of escape.

"Is there some way I can help you?" the persistent young receptionist asked.

"No, no, no," Stryker said, his voice weakened and confused.

The entrance to the Tavern opened as more guests arrived, gelling things in Stryker's mind. He spun around. Without another word, he disappeared out the front of the Tavern, his unbuttoned Armani flapping as he ran.

The doorman wearing the top hat was assisting arriving guests. Stryker was oblivious to it all as he rushed out from under the covered drive. He shivered as he glanced in the direction of Central Park. He had come that way two hours earlier. He knew nothing of Central Park, and his primitive instincts, working in lieu of his logical mind, told him he would probably get lost.

Those primitive instincts drove Stryker to turn toward the valet parking area and the dimly lighted walkway running along the side of the restaurant out to Central Park West.

That's it, Stryker thought, conversing with himself as he pulled the Armani jacket tight around his rapidly cooling chest. Get to Central Park West, get a cab and get to the Plaza.

Stryker moved rapidly down the walk, but the Tavern doorman had been correct. They had cleared the snow, but the walkway surface was treacherous. His pace slowed as he struggled to stay upright. To his left sat a dense line of snow-covered shrubbery bordering the icy path, and to the right was a dark parking area. Gas lights provided soft cream-like illumination. The sounds of traffic on the thoroughfare that bordered the west side of Central Park grew more distinct as Stryker shuffled along.

The trunk of a nearby Sycamore tree suddenly exploded, sending wood fragments flying. Instantly, sharp, stabbing pain burned across the side of Stryker's face as shrapnel from the tree struck him. The impact sent him reeling backwards. He spun to the right, stunned. Blood from the shrapnel was wet as his hand reached his face.

In the best of circumstances, Cliff Stryker should have flattened himself against the walk or in some way reduced the size of his silhouette in expectation of a second shot, but Stryker was dazed, preoccupied by the searing pain cutting into his face. He simply stood, gripping his face, moaning in pain, completely unaware of what was taking place behind him.

At that moment a shadowy figure moved out of the snow-covered hedge and crouched. He was invisible to anyone in the valet parking area. An arm reached up, gathered the cloth of the Armani jacket and jerked the unsuspecting Stryker into the hedge along the side of the Tavern. Stryker disappeared without a trace.

The limousine driver slowly lowered his rifle as he prepared for a second shot. For the second time in ten days, his first shot had missed Its target.

"Goddamn," he muttered. In Richland, he had been tricked by the afternoon shadows as he sighted across Midtown Park at that surgeon Graf had wanted taken out. This night, it was a darkened tree trunk. He had wanted a clean shot at Stryker, but perhaps all wasn't lost. His target had disappeared from view. Probably killed by the shrapnel exploding off that tree.

He waited, watching the frozen sidewalk. Stryker did not reappear. Then the driver crouched beside the case and disassembled the rifle. He would have to double time it to reach the limousine before Graf did.

Cliff Stryker's world was in free fall, yanked by some unseen force into the blackness. With a painful thump, he landed on his back on snow-covered earth behind the dense shrubbery. Searing pain throbbed across his face, blurring his vision. Within seconds, though, his eyesight corrected. Slowly, the figure kneeling beside him changed from a blur to a sharpened image. At first, he didn't recognize the face looking down at him. But then his memory surged back. Stryker never forgot a face.

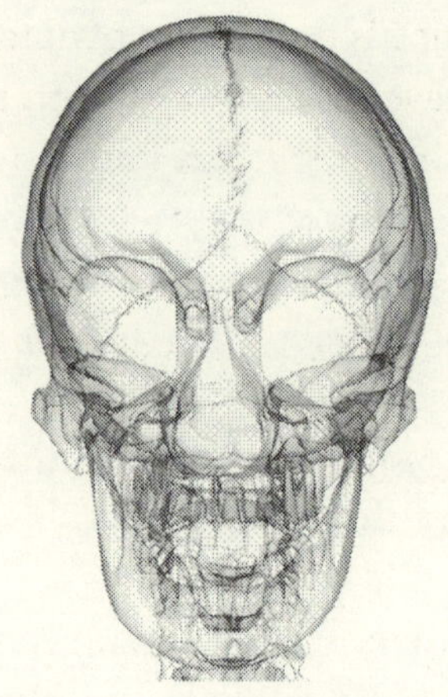

CHAPTER FORTY-FOUR

Stryker lay on his back, the look of terror on his face made worse by the sounds of hyperventilation. He blinked as he tried to remove blood spatters from his eye.

For a few moments, Stryker was motionless, seemingly out of contact. Soon, however, his breathing slowed and he turned his gaze toward the dark figure above him. Recognition crossed his face.

"You're . . . Dr. Carlton's friend from . . . ."

"Keep quiet, Stryker," Fisher ordered in a whisper, jamming the small Glock pistol against Stryker's jaw, "This pistol will kill you quicker than your limousine driver out there will."

A look of renewed horror crossed Stryker's features.

"Yes, your limo driver, Stryker. He just tried to put a bullet in your head from across that parking area."

"How did you know it was . . . .?"

"Well, let's see," Fisher quipped. "Seems like you were preoccupied with being famous. Your driver, on the other hand, was too busy figuring out how he was going to pop you. Neither of you noticed the taxi that pulled out behind the limo at the Plaza. I followed you here, but got out on West Drive in the Park. After you were let out, I watched as your driver parked his limo and took up a position over there." Fisher pointed to the far side of the parking area.

Fisher glanced at the rear area behind the snow-covered shrubbery. For two hours, he had hidden there. He was chilled to the bone, but he didn't notice it. He swept his gaze down behind the dense row of shrubbery to the back of the Tavern. A snow-covered bank led down to the rear wall, where it formed a swale that emptied into a small delivery area in back. Several cars were parked there.

Fisher looked down at Stryker, who was struggling to sit up. He reached inside his overcoat and pulled out a handkerchief. As he handed the cloth to Stryker, Fisher's attention was distracted. The lights had come on inside the black limousine. A figure standing by the rear was closing the trunk.

At the same time, Fisher heard voices on the other side of the shrubbery. Two men, engaged in conversation, walked down the sidewalk where Stryker had stood earlier. The voices moved in the direction of Central Park West.

"That sounded like Graf," Stryker said in a shivering whisper, holding the handkerchief against his face.

Fisher grabbed the front of Stryker's jacket and yanked the man to a wobbly standing position.

"C'mon, Stryker, we've got some traveling to do," Fisher whispered, pushing the pistol into Stryker's ribs.

The two men made their way down the embankment to the rear wall of the Tavern then inched their way toward the small parking area. Fisher saw two men approach the side of the limousine.

"Who is that?" Fisher whispered, pressing the pistol into Stryker's chest again.

"It's Graf."

Fisher and Stryker flattened themselves against the rear wall, no more than thirty feet from the limousine. Evergreens drenched them in total darkness, making them invisible. Fisher's mind traveled at the speed of light, quickly weighing his options. He had quietly slipped out of Richland and come to New York alone. There he had one mission — to render justice to Chip Carlton's killers. At that precise moment, he was two easy pistol shots away from accomplishing that task, but killing Graf meant Natalie would never be seen alive again.

The loud thump that sounded as the driver slammed the back door pulled Fisher away from his strategy session, before it could really begin. The lights came on as the limo prepared to pull out onto the cross park roadway that intersected Central Park West at the parking area behind the Tavern. I'm helpless, Fisher thought. Without running down and putting a shot into the rear seat of the limo, I'm going to lose that son-of-a-bitch.

Car horns blared and rubber screeched. The limousine had pulled in front of traffic coming up off Sixty-fifth Transverse from Central Park. For a moment, all cars came to a halt.

It was the break Fisher needed. Still holding the pistol to Stryker's chest and pulling him by the collar, Fisher rapidly made his way to the intersection where the column of cars had stopped. As they arrived, chaos was everywhere. The limousine driver had persisted, pulling farther into the intersection to make the turn onto Central Park West. As far as Fisher could see cars were halted, blaring their horns in objection.

Fisher surveyed the situation at the intersection. The limousine was completing its turn out of the parking area. He saw thwarted traffic as a column of headlights. The glare from the lights obscured the drivers of all cars, except for the lead two cars. One, a Mercedes, was driven by a white-haired elderly woman and the other, a New York taxicab, was driven by a dark-skinned young man. At first glance, the young man appeared to be wearing a hat, but further study revealed it to be a turban.

In the one or two seconds Fisher had to make his decision, the choice was easy. He pulled Stryker hard toward the intersection and stepped out in front of the taxicab, the small Glock aimed at the young driver. Taking his hands off the steering wheel, he clasped them in front of his face, as if in prayer, closed his eyes and moved forward and backward in the seat.

The driver's momentary distraction was the second break Fisher needed. He jerked Stryker around the side of the cab, opened the back door and shoved him in.

"Please, Allah, please, Allah, please, Allah, please, Allah, please . . . ."

Fisher tapped the pistol's barrel on the Plexiglas that divided the front and back seats. "Follow that black limousine," Fisher commanded. "There'll be a triple fare for you. I promise you, you won't be harmed."

The young man unclasped his hands, stopped his swaying, and threw the cab in gear. The car surged out of the intersection and raced north on Central Park West. The black limo was a block and a half ahead.

Fisher tapped on the plastic again. "Please don't let them know they're being followed."

The driver's turban nodded, as the cab surged to within one half block of the black limousine. Fisher, for the first time, noticed the license plate. It was a New York plate that read simply: HP 1. Fisher branded the plate into his brain as he watched the young driver weave skillfully through traffic to stay a comfortable distance from Graf's car. At West Seventy-second, the limo turned left and accelerated west. The cab driver followed in pursuit.

Fisher glanced at west side New York as they rushed down Seventy-second. Snow had been cleared from the walkways, nighttime pedestrian traffic was heavy. Shops passed as a blur, pizzerias, espresso dives, night clubs with bouncers slapping their arms for warmth, small walk-up hotels, and a bagel shop.

Satisfied that the cabby would follow, Fisher turned his attention to Stryker, wet and shivering, his plush suit damp and smeared with blood. He had balled up for warmth and was holding Fisher's handkerchief to his face.

Fisher jammed the pistol into Stryker's chest. Stryker winced and cried out in pain.

"That get your attention, Stryker? You murdering shit."

"I . . . I . . . haven't killed anyone."

"That's a lie," Fisher roared.

The cab driver looked up.

"It's okay, keep following the black limo," Fisher said to the driver's eyes in the rearview mirror.

"Yes, Sir," the cabby responded, "but it looks as if they will be heading north onto the Hudson Parkway."

"That's okay," Fisher said, "Keep following that limousine."

Fisher jerked his head toward Stryker, "I'll have no regrets over pulling the trigger, Stryker. I took this pistol off that little Asian snot who's been running your organ-stealing center in Richland's factory section."

Stryker's complexion, which had been recovering inside the taxi's warmth, visibly paled as light from the street bathed his face.

"Yes, I know a great deal, Stryker," Fisher said, a dangerous note in his voice. "And if you don't tell me everything, you're going to feel hot lead carve a path through your right lung and into that putrid heart of yours."

Stryker's hand trembled as the two men stared at each other.

A thin smile crossed Stryker's face. With unexpected swiftness Fisher had not anticipated, Stryker grabbed for the pistol. Fisher's reflexes, however, were faster, not slowed by champagne.

Stryker's quick movement was followed by a deafening pop as Fisher discharged the Glock into the rear half of Stryker's right thigh. Stryker screamed in pain as his handkerchief-clad hand grabbed the point where his flesh had exploded.

"Please, Allah, please, Allah, not to kill, not to kill," the cabby screeched.

Fisher tapped the pistol on the Plexiglas. "Everything's okay. Everything's okay."

Fisher turned back to look at Stryker. His face was screwed into a tight grimace as he grabbed his leg.

"There aren't any vital structures back there, Mr. Stryker, but it hurts just the same, doesn't it? I guess I didn't have a chance to share with you all the lovely things I learned from my tour in Iraq a few years back. The Iraqis had some sweet ways of making GIs talk. Saw men alive with ten maybe fifteen non-fatal bullet holes. They all talked eventually; that is, if they didn't take a bullet to the brain first." Fisher cocked the Glock and held it up to Stryker's right temple.

"No," he screamed. "No, I'll tell you what you want to know!"

"Then get started, old boy."

"First," Stryker said hyperventilating with pain, "I didn't kill anyone. Dr. Carlton was killed by contract, and I didn't learn about it until he was dead."

"Who put out the contract?"

"Graf."

"Why?"

"He discovered the . . . ."

"The what, Stryker?" Fisher dug the pistol into Stryker's temple.

"All right, all right. Carlton discovered the telepresence center. He stumbled onto it, somehow. But he pressed Talbott about it and then me. I told Graf what was going on and the next thing I knew, Carlton was dead."

"Tell me about the telepresence center," Fisher ordered, knowing the answer.

Stryker grimaced and whined. Fisher dug the pistol in deeper.

"It was Talbott's idea. Surgery by remote operator. He had friends in the Army where remote robotics surgery had been developed. Graf went crazy over the idea and pulled strings inside the Defense Department. Before I knew it, they had sold Health Pursuit a functioning model and all the software. The rest is history. Talbott and two of the renal transplant guys handled the remote surgery from a secret location at Taggart."

"The Outpatient Surgery Center." Fisher stared at Stryker.

Stryker turned his head quickly in Fisher's direction, for a moment forgetting the pistol jammed into his right temple.

"Ugh," he screamed again. "How did you know that?"

Fisher ignored the question. "Well, your boy Talbott won't be signing off in that little green ledger anymore."

"What do you mean?" Stryker asked, gazing out into the dense traffic ahead of the cab as it crawled slowly north on the Henry Hudson Parkway.

"He didn't take too well to a few Federal agents busting into your scummy little operating theater last night. Seems he was so distraught, he put a pistol to his chest and pumped a slug into his heart. Didn't take long for him to die, watched it myself. Oh, and your buddy Domao's out of action too. He went down when he charged a Federal agent. Kind of stupid, don't you think?"

Stryker continued staring ahead.

"So, how does it work, Stryker? You hire some trash to go out and shake down the homeless neighborhoods, offer them a pittance for their organs, then cover up your tracks with hefty infusions of a powerful wound-healing agent?"

Stryker's eyes widened in disbelief.

"Please, Sir," came a call from the front seat of the cab. "The limousine is getting too far ahead. May I take the appropriate steps to follow?"

"Do whatever you have to do, driver," Fisher said, not taking his eyes off Stryker.

The cab lurched wildly to the right as the driver spun over to the emergency shoulder and accelerated. He squeezed around the far side of the construction site that had slowed traffic. Within a minute, the limousine was comfortably in sight again.

"So, that's not all of it, Stryker. Isn't there more?" Fisher asked, thinking back to the huge numbers of organs transplanted by the surgeons at Taggart Memorial in the past year.

"Why, no. There's no more. You've figured out the whole scheme," he said, his voice quivering.

"You're lying." Fisher seethed, moving the pistol to Stryker's thigh where he pressed the barrel hard against the fresh wound.

"No!" Stryker yelled, a pitiful weakness in his voice. "Please, no. There's more. I'll tell you the rest. Just don't shoot me again."

"Then let's hear it, or the next slug will let a little life blood flow."

"Graf," Stryker struggled, terror drenching his voice. "It was Mr. Graf. Oh please, Dr. Fisher. Mr. Graf will kill me if this gets out."

Fisher looked at Stryker, "Get your head together, Stryker. What do you think that shot in the parking lot was all about, a little slap on the wrist? As far as Rupert Graf is concerned, you're already dead."

Stryker took the bloody handkerchief away from his thigh and wiped tears from his eyes as he sobbed. "I'm so sorry, Dr. Fisher. I never planned to be a part of this. I never meant to hurt anyone. Things just progressed, and the deeper I got, the harder it was to pull back."

"Stop whining, Stryker," Fisher yelled.

"Okay, okay," he sobbed, his face buried in the bloody handkerchief. "Graf entered into a secret agreement with the CEO of Katsumi Pharmaceuticals, a Toshima Kamatsu. Together they crafted a sort of global approach to organ procurement. Sites were set up at several locations in Russia, Pakistan and along the Arabian peninsula."

Rage began building inside Fisher. He knew it would take extreme control not to finish the job Graf had started. "Go on," he commanded.

"Using a secret Internet access code with high security software, Taggart Memorial notified the sites of which organs the hospital needed. The organs were procured, preserved and smuggled into the States by open ocean air drop through St. John's, Newfoundland. Taggart or some other designated Health Pursuit hospital then received the cargo coming down from Canada, and distributions were made."

Immediately, Fisher saw an image of the stack of unusual gray cartons outside the warehouse, the ones with orange labels that read "Fresh Fish, St. John's, Newfoundland, Canada."

A sardonic smile crossed Stryker's face as he lost contact with reality. "It's funny," he said with a sickening chuckle. "The best service came from our Russian contacts. The unofficial word was that the Russian Mafia ensured our supply. Isn't that funny, Dr. Fisher?"

Stryker's sick humor and callous attitude caused Fisher to lose control. He drew back the pistol and struck Stryker's face, sending him reeling against the left rear window of the cab.

Stryker covered the right side of his face but continued his mournful laughter.

The taxi cab accelerated. Fisher looked up from the back seat. The cab was still more than one hundred yards behind the limousine, but traffic had thinned out and cars in all lanes had picked up speed.

In a flash of speed, the left rear door of the cab opened, and Cliff Stryker hurled himself out.

Fisher looked on in horror as Stryker rolled briefly across one lane of the Hudson Parkway into the path of a gasoline transport. Nine of its eighteen wheels crushed Stryker in an instant.

Fisher's heart pounded. A sickening nausea rose from inside as he pulled the door closed. The cabby briefly looked up, but was apparently unaware of what had taken place. Off to the left of the cab, the lights of the George Washington Bridge were almost upon them.

The limousine turned onto the Cross Bronx Expressway, and the cabby followed, while Fisher still struggled with waves of nausea. After a few minutes, they stopped coming. He glanced at his watch. It was twelve forty-five. He reached inside his jacket and took out the cell phone. He retrieved the same tattered slip, dialed Darren Fitzpatrick's number and waited.

After a few rings, an unfamiliar voice came on the line. "Yes, this is Mr. Fitzpatrick's secured line," the voice said matter-of-factly.

"My name is Steven Fisher. I need to talk with Mr. Fitzpatrick. It's urgent."

"Hold the line, please."

While holding Fisher thought for a few moments. He realized he had no clue to Natalie Roberts' whereabouts. The occupant in the back seat of the black limousine ahead was his last hope.

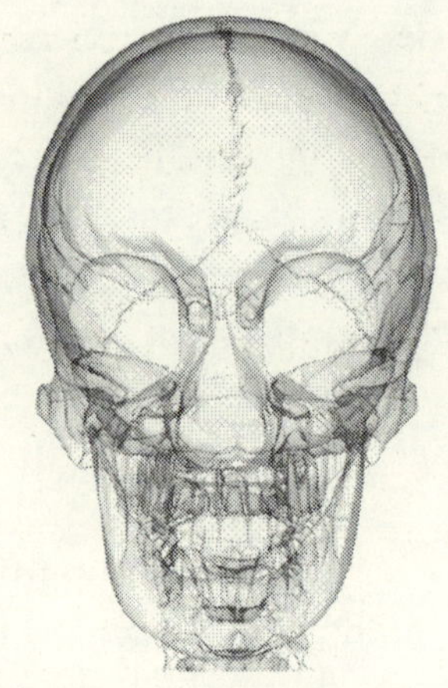

CHAPTER FORTY-FIVE

February 11, Shepard Residence, East End Richland

Alli Shepard stood up from the easy chair in her living room and walked to the hearth. The fire, started a couple of hours earlier, had begun fading. She wanted to continue reading next to its warmth, but the temperature in her living room had fallen noticeably. She leaned down, retrieved a slab of seasoned oak and planted it firmly on top of the dying fire, hoping to rescue it a while longer. She picked up the heavy wool cardigan off the sofa, pulled it on, and stared at the fire, thinking. Her day had started at six with a trip to the Richland Municipal Airport. She drove Fisher there to catch the first flight out to New York. Although she had tried to talk him out of his plans, he politely refused. He had not mentioned her going along.

They kissed before he left the Cavalier. "Please come back alive," Alli told him as they clung to each other for a few seconds.

"Don't worry about me. I'll be back," Fisher said, kissing her again. He then pulled away from her lips and looked deeply into her eyes. "There's a very important graduation coming up in a couple of months that I've gotta attend."

After leaving the airport, Alli spent a great deal of the day at the Med trying to extract data from the medical records for her Myelopress project. The month was nearly half over, and she had been sidetracked for ten days. However, by mid-afternoon, she found concentrating difficult. She worried about Fisher. She ultimately quit, closing the fifteenth medical record she had reviewed and left Fisher's office, bidding good-bye to Mary Walker as she departed.

After brief stops at the laundry and the grocery store, she returned home to await any word from Steve. He had promised to call if he had a chance.

She looked at the fire for a moment, Fisher still filling her thoughts. Then she returned to the chair across the room and closed her eyes. The mantel clock showed that it was just before midnight.

"Sis, I'm getting something to eat. You hungry?"

Alli opened her eyes and looked at the kitchen. A shallow grin spread across her face. She would never understand how Gary could eat around the clock and never gain an ounce of weight. "No thanks. I'm just going to close my eyes a moment and then probably go to bed."

"Ah, c'mon, Sis, how's about a salami on rye?"

"Pass, Gary," she said, already drifting off, despite the noises of silverware and plates clanging in the kitchen.

• • • • •

"It doesn't matter whether they are awake or asleep," the gangly, figure whispered, grasping the small brick-like objects. "We will make no noise," he smiled in the cold darkness. "And we'll be miles away from here at the time of detonation."

The silent man standing beside him was short and stocky, his black overcoat at least two sizes too large for him. He said nothing, nodding his understanding as he cradled two identical bricks.

"Show me the fuses," the tall man commanded softly.

His short partner fumbled through his pockets, finally producing two shiny cylinders the size and length of half a pencil. They were connected to about twelve inches of narrow-gauge wire.

"Good," the tall man said. "And finally, the receiver connect."

From the other pocket, the man's partner produced a small, hard-plastic case.

"Are the connects free of obstructions?"

"Yes."

"Very well," the other whispered. "We will split up. I will go to the front, and you will go to the back. Press the bricks into the siding just above the foundation. Once you're sure they stick nicely, place the fuses and attach the receiver."

The shorter of the two grunted softly his understanding as the two turned to the house. They silently approached from the side, repeatedly scanning the neighborhood for signs of activity.

They split up. The larger of the two headed to the front, the barely visible shorter man headed to the rear.

The lanky man studied the area where the plastique explosive would be molded into the brick siding of the Shepard residence. He stepped quietly onto the front porch. Through the gauzy drapes to the left of the front door, he saw a young woman asleep in a chair. Across the room, a fire intermittently gave off flashes of subdued light.

She'll never feel this, he thought, smiling to himself. He knelt in front of the porch window. Quietly, he removed the two clay-like objects from his pocket. One by one, he pressed the soft plastique into the brick, molding them slightly into large cigar shapes. He then pushed cylindrical fuses into the explosives. Finally, he took the loose wires leading from the fuses and inserted them into a box identical to the one his partner had shown him moments earlier.

In total silence, the tall figure rose from a crouching position. He glanced into the front room again. The young woman was motionless, except for the subtle movement of her sweater-covered chest. Happy she was still sleeping; he made his way off the porch. He was out of the yard and waiting at the rendezvous site one block away in just under a minute.

He glanced up and down the dark street as he waited for his partner to return. He hated the work, but the money made it hard to turn down. For a couple of years, he had only worked two to three days a year. He snorted quietly, thinking about the money Graf had thrown in his direction.

"Easy money," he whispered softly, searching the direction from which his partner would be coming. He actuated the dial light on his watch. "Shit," he hissed, allowing the final sound to whisper through his teeth. "I should have done the whole fucking thing myself."

After three more minutes, he uttered further obscenities, and then walked back to the house.

His eyes were fully accustomed to the dark, so he went directly to the back yard. He stepped up off the sidewalk and easily vaulted the three-foot picket fence. He skirted around two leafless fruit trees, his feet quietly squeaking as the pressure of his weight pressed the newly fallen snow.

As he approached the house, he stopped and gasped.

His partner lay motionless in a crumpled heap on the ground, a leg hanging part way onto a cement stairway that descended to the basement. Around his lifeless head, the snow was stained dark with blood. White matter oozed from his face.

The lanky man had trained endlessly in Iranian terrorist camps across the Middle East, but he couldn't fight the sickening sensation that welled up from inside as he looked down at his dead partner. Shaking it off, he dropped his well-trained frame onto the ground. He looked around the small yard for signs of movement.

There were none.

The lanky man slowly retraced his steps to the picket fence.

Before he had moved three full steps, soft thumps sounded off to the man's left. He immediately knew the significance of the sound, but after the first slug struck his head, the significance wasn't important.

Half of the man's head exploded. He fell lifeless as additional slugs were pumped into his body.

Silently, black-clad figures appeared from several directions. One figure rounded the side of the house coming from the front. He held the plastique bricks with fuses he had removed. Another man was gently removing plastique from the rear of the house. Four other men quietly lifted the lifeless bodies and headed to the side yard.

A black van rolled to a stop by the side of the Shepard residence. As the men approached, a lone figure opened the side door. The dome light momentarily cast a subtle beam across Agent Wellesley's face.

"Good work, guys," Wellesley said quietly, sliding the van door shut. "I'll communicate this to Mr. Fitzpatrick."

Alli awakened with a start. Something had aroused her, but she had no idea what it was. She looked at the fireplace where the new logs were burning brightly. The antique clock read twelve fifty-five. Normally she rose to check the house, but that night she was too tired. She leaned back again in the deep chair. Her eyes closed, and she fell back to sleep.

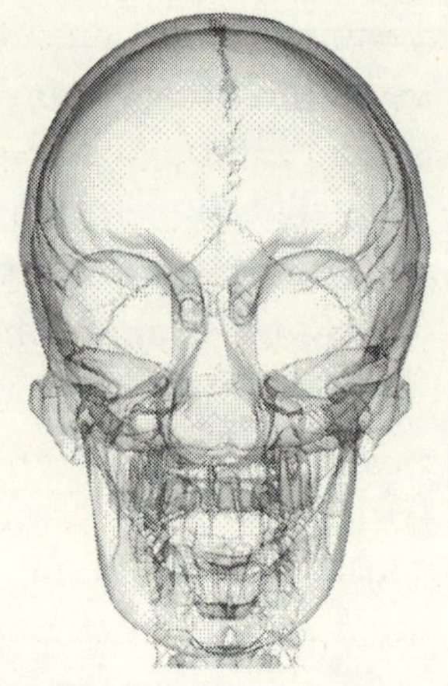

CHAPTER FORTY-SIX

Graf Estate, Mamaroneck, New York

The sumptuous study was quiet. Intense incandescent light shone down from the dark-shaded brass lamp onto the rich leather chairs in the center of the room. Samuel Jacobson sat in one of the two chairs, nervously picking at his thumbnail. Five hours had passed since his conversation with Graf, and he was troubled by a mounting sense of dread. In fact, since his arrival at the Graf estate five days earlier, a battle had raged inside — a battle for Samuel Jacobson's soul. Where had he gone off track in his life? That was the question he struggled to answer. Two years earlier the decisions had seemed clear. When Graf approached him with a lucrative offer to coordinate the flow of organs into Health Pursuit transplant centers, he resigned his appointment at the Med. There had been too many years of low wages and kowtowing to an idiot Pathology Chairman for him not to jump at the opportunity. Graf had assured him that over time, their approach to increasing the organ supply in the US would emerge from secrecy into public daylight; that it would be a model for other governments to use to equitably distribute the scarce commodity.

It simply hadn't happened. Graf had seen how easily the money flowed, and he wanted more, as the potential for growth seemed limitless. Graf had assured Jacobson that, in every situation, donors would be treated humanely and compensated fairly. Then came the secret alliance with Katsumi Pharmaceuticals and the choice of "source centers," as Graf called them, in Russia and Pakistan. Jacobson began receiving secret Internet messages from an agent in Russia detailing kidnappings, murders and multiple organ harvests from single donors. In the beginning, Graf had assured him that no hearts would be procured from live donors. His Internet reports had told him differently.

Up until recently, Jacobson managed to ignore those incidents, what he referred to as the "business end" of the organization, choosing to think of the problems as the price to be paid for start-up of a new enterprise. With the assassination of Chip Carlton, everything changed. He strongly suspected Graf had engineered Carlton's murder, but he had said nothing. Finally, out of nowhere, Roberts had landed in his lap, saying she had proof that organs were being illegally taken from the homeless of Richland. Graf's way of dealing with Natalie: kill her.

His edict had been terse and emotionless.

Jacobson stared down at his thumb. Unintentionally, he had whittled the nail down to the quick. He kept glancing at the cordless phone on the small table beside him. Graf had told him to expect a call between twelve and one. He looked at his watch. It was just before one. He planned to tell Graf he would rather pull out of the business than be responsible for the death of Natalie Roberts.

The door to the study opened, and the two henchmen who had brought Roberts from Richland entered the study. He knew them solely by their first names. Rupio, the smarter of the two, wore richly tailored suits over a tanning-bed tan. An ever-present stubble of a toothpick bounced from side to side as he worked a succession of new gum sticks, always emitting a Juicy Fruit odor. His partner, Don, was Rupio's exact antithesis, seemingly unable to obtain a satisfactory fit for any of his articles of clothing. He was paunchy, his movements unrefined and clumsy, his protuberant belly straining an over-stretched dress shirt.

The ringing of the cordless phone jolted Jacobson's frayed nerves as he reached down and took the instrument off the small table.

"Hello . . .Rupert?" he said. His voice was timid and strained, and he shifted his body nervously in the deep red leather chair.

"No, Rupert, I . . . I did not tell them to proceed. I cannot be a part of this, and I cannot allow it. She's done nothing to deserve that."

Jacobson's hand shook as he strained to hold the phone to his ear.

"I'm sorry," Jacobson said, his voice quivering. "Okay, we can talk it over when you arrive, but my decision must stand."

Jacobson clicked off the portable phone and set it back in its cradle. He looked up at the two men. His face was drained of color.

Within seconds, he heard a subtle chirping. Rupio reached for the inside pocket of his jacket and produced a cell phone.

"Yes Sir," was his sole reply.

Holding the phone to his ear, Rupio quietly let himself out of the study. Jacobson went back to his nervous whittling, clearly distracted by what he had heard. Intermittently, he glanced up at Don, who stood off in the shadows, beyond the intense light bathing the chairs in the study.

The door opened, and Rupio quietly reentered.

"Doctor, you look like you could use a little drink to relax you," Rupio said, a concerned tone in his voice. "Mr. Graf has some very fine imported port."

"I think that would go well about right now," Jacobson said, the quivering in his voice unmistakable.

"Let's all have some," Rupio said. What do you say, Don?"

"Uhhh, sure," came the confused reply.

On the far side of the study, Rupio opened a richly appointed cabinet, removing a heavy crystalline decanter. In short order, three glasses were filled.

In the shadows beyond the light, Jacobson could hear the high-pitched tinkle of crystal as Rupio distributed a glass to Don. Within moments, a glass filled with rich amber liquid appeared under the incandescent beam.

Jacobson reached for the glass, his hand still tremulous. He knew a long night was ahead, once Graf arrived, but his mind was made up. Things had gone too far. He pulled a long draw of air in through his nose, smelling the port's sweet fragrance. It was rich and luxurious. He knew of Graf's tastes, and his own senses confirmed its quality. He drank deeply from the glass, hoping the burning, sweet liquid would calm his frayed nerves. If anything, the alcohol would embolden him for the confrontation to come.

Jacobson reclined onto the rich leather of the high-back chair, closed his eyes and exhaled gently through his nose, searching for a second wave of the port's fragrance as it entered his circulation. Instead of relaxation, however, Jacobson sat bolt upright. His olfactory senses weren't transmitting wine fragrance to his brain. It was the unmistakable odor of bitter almonds.

Cyanide, Jacobson screamed to himself, unable to speak. His chest became heavy and his breathing labored as the poison was instantly absorbed from his stomach.

Unable to avoid a primal human reflex, Jacobson gripped the clothing over his chest as his breathing became more labored. He struggled to hold his head upright, to pull in air through his mouth, but it was no use. He tried to stand, but his legs never reached full extension. He fell to a kneeling position.

From his rapidly diminishing peripheral vision, he saw Rupio approach, his jaw bouncing, his Cheshire-cat smile three inches away. "Doc, you having some kinda problem here? Huh?"

The volume of Rupio's voice was decreased, but its taunting tone was clearly transmitted.

Jacobson saw the blackness coming, but he fought it. His chest was bursting, but he channeled his last threads of consciousness to the arm that gripped his chest as he fell flat. Rupio's face and taunting smile followed Jacobson down to the floor.

Jacobson's hand reached inside his coat feeling for the pistol he had purchased before going to the Graf estate. His hand closed around the weapon. But the paralysis of his arms was virtually complete, the pistol wouldn't budge. Using all his strength, he rotated the weapon slightly in his jacket pocket and pulled the trigger.

The pistol discharged with a deafening pop through the front of Jacobson's jacket, entering Rupio's chest about one inch to the left of his sternum.

In Jacobson's final moments, he witnessed the beginning of Rupio's death. Rupio jerked away from Jacobson's face, his right hand over the site where the small slug had torn into his chest. He stayed upright for a few seconds as his chest filled with blood. Then he fell forward with a thump. Rupio turned pale as he exsanguinated. After three coughs of bloody froth, he lay still.

Next to Rupio, Jacobson's eyes rolled back, a small slit of white all that remained. He arched his back involuntarily as a violent seizure began. Cyanide had robbed the final vestiges of oxygen from his brain.

From the shadows across the study, a crystal glass smashed on the floor as Don struggled to deal with what he had seen. Within moments, the chaos was over. He walked slowly to the two men. Rupio lay face down, a slowly enlarging pool of blood beside him. Jacobson lay on his side, a soft hiss of air exiting his lungs as his soul departed.

For a few moments, he was paralyzed. Then the words came out. "Oh, God; oh, God," he said softly.

He rubbed his sweaty hands on his cheap, ill-fitting suit. As he stroked down the cloth, he came across the hardness of the automatic weapon in its shoulder holster. He stopped as the shape of the gun brought him back from the brink, back from the panic that gripped him.

He stopped. He had become reoriented. He had business to attend to. A last bit of work to do for Mr. Graf. He turned and walked to the door of the study. From the threshold, he looked back at the two men lying beside each other and smiled. He was the boss now. He disappeared from the study, headed for the kitchen and the basement entrance.

• • • • •

Roberts wasn't sleeping when the sound of Jacobson's pistol shot surged down into her basement prison.

Who had they just killed, those cruel men? What did it mean? Would she be next, she wondered? Dozens of other questions raced through her mind.

Roberts' pulse raced as she jumped to her feet, wobbling as she stood, weakened by inactivity and hunger. She almost fell back onto the cold cement, but was able to bring her hand against the wall for support.

Fright and terror had been constant during her three-day captivity, and they had had extreme effects on her. During the first day, she had cried until her eyes were swollen, her tears seemingly limitless. Her role model in life, her inspiration and compass, had betrayed all that was good and right. How could she have been so naive, so easily deceived? As time passed, however, sorrow evolved into resentment as the full impact of Jacobson's deceit became apparent. By day two, she pulled herself together, attempting to form a plan for her escape.

"It'll be a cold day in hell when I give up without a fight," she whispered over and over, twenty-four hours into her imprisonment. At that point, she spent her lonely hours creating an exact mental image of her world. She walked the length and width of the large basement repeatedly, logging its dimensions into her brain, fully developing her sense of the area. With darkness practically complete, she explored her prison with her hands, searching for anything, anything she could use as a weapon against her captors. There was precious little, though. After hours of searching, she came up with a ball of twine she found under the steps that led out of the basement. Her captors had done a thorough job of cleaning the area, obviously knowing their intentions for its use.

When the pistol shot sounded, she had been exploring the far side of the dark basement. An old burned out furnace sat off to the right of the area. It had obviously not seen use for years. She tried lifting the old fire door, hoping to find something inside she could use as a weapon, but it wouldn't budge. Try though she might, she was unable to move it. She continued to touch and probe around the far side of the furnace, back against the cold cinder block wall. She found simply small piles of what she presumed to be soot. It caused her to sneeze when she kicked it up into the air around the furnace.

She was about to give up, when her heart jumped. In the darkness, her hands moved across a long smooth object around the far side of the furnace, a heavy-gauge metal bar about three feet long. It was wedged between the furnace and the wall. She yanked several times before it pulled free.

When the shot rang out, she hurried as fast as she could in her weakened state back to the stairs, where she had hidden the twine. She grabbed it and returned to the soot. She knelt beside the furnace feeling for the piles. Once she found the one, she unrolled the twine, pressing the soot into the cord.

She had blackened about twenty feet of twine when she heard footsteps and fumbling with the locks at the top of the steps.

"This is no time to back down," she muttered softly. She hurried to the side wall, where she had left her lab coat. During her captivity, it had provided a modest degree of warmth in the cold basement.

As someone turned the lock her pulse raced. She arranged her lab coat on the floor about fifteen feet from the stairs and hurriedly tied the blackened cord to the sleeve. She had just completed the task when the door at the top of the steps began to crack open.

She wasn't going to make it, she told herself as she hurried to the stairs, letting out the string. She had only covered half the space when the door opened fully. A diffused light flowed into her prison. Roberts squinted. The frame of a rounded man was silhouetted in the doorway. She froze, holding her breath. Something was different. A slender man had made all prior entries, always switching on a stairway light, flooding the area around the steps with illumination. This time, the stairway light had not been switched on, and there was limited visibility into the basement.

"Where are ya?" a voice called.

Roberts realized he couldn't see her with only the light from the room above the basement. She needed five additional feet to reach the steps. Continuing to hold her breath, she slowly moved the remaining distance. Once there, she nestled quietly under the steps, not knowing what the man would do next.

"Come into the light where I can see yous, bitch."

Terror cut deeply into Roberts as she squeezed herself under the wooden staircase.

"I said, come inta da light, goddamnit."

Roberts' hands trembled as she gripped the metal bar.

The steps squeaked as the man's heavy weight landed on the second step. He still had not turned on the light over the stairs. Did he not know it was there?

The man stopped.

"I'm not going to tell yous again. Come out inta da light."

The man descended seven additional steps. She could hear his labored breathing in the dead silence of her basement prison.

The man stood three steps up from the cement floor. Though almost paralyzed with fear, she had to initiate her plan.

She peered out from under the stairs. In the shadowy light, she could see her lab coat spread out as if she were sleeping. Holding her breath, she said a silent prayer and joggled the twine.

"Goddamn, there you are," the man yelled. A deafening bang followed as the man fired at Roberts' lab coat.

With her ears ringing, Roberts stood and swung the metal bar with all her might.

The fat man screamed as the bar struck him squarely at midback. He tumbled face first into the basement. Roberts stepped forward and delivered another blow to the same area, as the man sprawled onto the dark cement floor.

Roberts turned and struggled up the stairs to the first floor. She was weakened and slow.

"Come back here, ya bitch," the man yelled.

Another shot rang out from the where the man lay on the basement floor, but it went wild, striking the door molding ahead of her. She didn't look back.

As she reached the first floor, she could hear the squeak of the man's weight on the first step. She grabbed the door, slammed it shut and turned the deadbolt. A slug ripped through the door as she moved her hand away.

Roberts didn't wait to see whether the killer had breached the door. She looked around, squinting in the bright light of the first floor. She was in a luxuriously appointed kitchen. A long corridor ran off into the house's interior. She moved slowly down the corridor. A door on the left was open. Something caught her eye as she passed it. To her horror, Roberts saw a lifeless Jacobson lying next to her other captor, both men surrounded by a large pool of blood. On the floor next to Jacobson lay a white portable phone.

Roberts rushed into the room, stepped around the blood, grabbed the phone and switched it on. Before she could dial, however, she heard a muted crash. Returning quickly to the corridor, Roberts saw the basement door splinter as the man threw his weight against it. She turned and ran down the corridor. About forty feet farther, she passed an atrium, an entrance to the house. She turned as another shot rang out behind her. A mirror crashed at the end of the corridor.

Roberts ran through the atrium and opened the door. She was immediately stung by the cold. Although her clothing was light, she charged out into the black winter night.

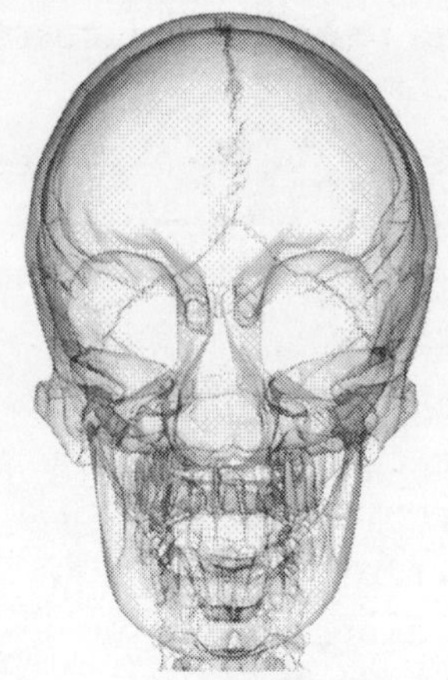

CHAPTER FORTY-SEVEN

Mamaroneck, New York, 1:15 a.m.

Minutes dragged by like hours while Fisher held the cellular phone to his ear. Fitzpatrick finally came on the line.

"Steve, it's good to hear your voice," Fitzpatrick said first, without stopping to permit a reciprocal greeting. "That's been quite a long cab ride you've taken. I can't imagine what the fare's going to come to."

"Darren, how do you know I'm . . .?"

Fitzpatrick's voice was easily audible, but a loud hum in the background made the conversation distracting. "Check your airline ticket," Fitzpatrick said, his snickering clearly heard above the machine noise.

"My what?"

"The airline ticket you purchased in Richland. I suppose you have a return trip planned."

Fisher reached into the inside pocket of his suit and retrieved the ticket. "Got it," Fisher said.

"Now pull out the advertising insert for the city of New York."

Totally confused, Fisher complied.

"Now hold the slip of paper up to the light."

Fisher switched on the dome light inside the cab and held up the colorful rectangular sheet. In the center, he could see a quarter-sized, lacy object.

"If you've managed to transilluminate that card, you're looking at a GPS tracker."

"Darren, you're telling me I've been followed."

"Sorry, Steve. We figured no matter what we said, you'd be going after Graf and Stryker."

"But how did you know about my cab ride?"

Fisher could hear voices engaged in laughter. "Look out the window."

Fisher looked out of the cab at the traffic on Interstate-95. He saw nothing unusual. Then a strobe caught his eye. Fisher cocked his head. No more than one hundred feet off the interstate, Fisher could see the body of a black helicopter.

"That's you up there?"

"It's us. Why don't you instruct your cabby to pull over at the next rest stop? I think it'll be faster if you ride with us."

"But the limousine."

"Steve, don't worry about the limo. We've already run the plates. We know where it's going."

The Bell helicopter surged into the winter sky. Fisher watched as the blast from the rotors drove the recently fallen snow into a blizzard. The cabby continued to wave, despite the near-blinding conditions the helicopter produced as it took off. Fisher had thanked him profusely and emptied his wallet. The cabby had smiled and said nothing.

Fisher's momentary spell was broken as Fitzpatrick spoke. "NYPD has removed Stryker's body from the Henry Hudson Parkway."

Fisher turned to look at Fitzpatrick seated beside him. In addition to Fitzpatrick, Agent Timmons and five others he recognized from the warehouse raid filled the small quarters.

"We saw Stryker come out of the cab. He was crushed instantly."

"He leaped before I could stop him, Darren."

"Timmons captured the whole thing on infrared video. There's no Question Stryker leaped."

After a few moments Fisher spoke again, "He told me everything. It was just as we suspected."

"Save it. Others will want to be involved with your debriefing."

"He jumped before I could get any information out of him concerning Natalie's whereabouts."

"We're okay. The Asian confessed to being an accessory to her kidnapping. He told us she was taken to Rupert Graf's estate three days ago for 'questioning.'"

Twinges of nausea bubbled up inside Fisher. "She's dead. There's no way they would have held her in captivity for three days. She's dead. I should never have gotten her involved in this fucking mess."

"Not so fast." Fitzpatrick looked at his watch. "Mamaroneck police reported a 911 call from the Graf estate about eight minutes ago. They have units responding now, and they know we're in pursuit of Rupert Graf."

Fisher still couldn't relax.

The pilot interrupted, "We're approaching the estate now, Mr. Fitzpatrick. Units are on the scene."

All eyes looked down on the immense estate. The front entrance of the manor house, at the apex of a mile-long drive, was brightly lighted. Blue strobe lights flashed atop law enforcement vehicles. An ambulance and a fire truck were parked in the drive. Fisher spotted the black limousine he had followed earlier.

Agent Timmons spoke from the co-pilot's position. "Mr. Fitzpatrick, wide-angle infrared scanning has detected several images outside the structure."

"Location, please, Timmons," Fitzpatrick said.

"Right, Sir." Timmons studied the softly glowing screen in front of him. "Laying a grid down now, Sir."

Moments passed as the helicopter hovered.

"Okay, you can set her down. I've got my fix," Timmons said to the pilot. He turned and spoke to Fitzpatrick. "Sir, we have a single image detectable fifty yards up the north limb of the drive, and three separate human image profiles about two hundred yards behind the large structure. But there's also a complex image with very high heat scatter in the immediate vicinity of the human images. It's an aircraft signature. They're making a run for it, Sir."

"Weapons ready," Fitzpatrick ordered as the descending helicopter created a snowstorm in the center of the drive. Two agents plunged into the cyclone of snow surrounding the helicopter's blade blast. Fitzpatrick's final command trailed after them. "I want two agents, night vision equipped, to pursue the single human image. Do not fire unless fired upon."

Fisher saw two uniformed policemen trotting to the helicopter, shielding their eyes. As they arrived, the pilot opened the door, letting in a blast of frigid air and snow.

"Mr. Fitzpatrick?" the lead officer yelled above the chaos.

"That's me." Fitzpatrick offered his hand.

"Good to have you, Sir. The house is vacant, except for two bodies. One's a doctor, the other's a male named Rupio Cerreti. Cerreti's wanted in three states for murder and extortion."

Fisher tensed as the officer spoke, but he remained silent.

"The doctor, a Samuel Jacobson, is from out of state."

Fisher breathed a sigh of relief.

Fitzpatrick interrupted. "Look, officer, our heat sensing equipment shows that all the action's behind the house. Two of my men have headed to check out a signal about fifty yards up the drive, but it looks like the real action is about two hundred yards to the rear of the mansion. We detected three human images immediately adjacent to an aircraft signature. Send your men straight back behind the structure. We'll hop back there in the chopper."

"'Nuff said, Mr. Fitzpatrick." The officer spoke briefly into a wireless communicator then sprinted back to the front entrance.

Fisher felt his weight double as the helicopter surged off the ground and jumped over the mansion into the blackness beyond.

Timmons spoke as the helicopter cleared the roof line. "Problems, Sir. Our three human images are gone, and the aircraft signature is pegging out on the intensity scale. I'm afraid it's on the move."

The pilot, who had been silent, said, "Permission to let them know we're here, Sir."

"Proceed."

The pilot switched on the row of high-intensity lights on the craft's undercarriage.

Captured in the intense beams a small white jet turned onto a paved runway.

"We are heat-seeking-equipped for tonight's flight, Mr. Fitzpatrick," the pilot said.

"No, no missiles" Fitzpatrick responded. "We have no idea who's in that jet. We only have suspicions."

The small jet accelerated down the runway and disappeared into the black winter sky.

"Timmons, any remaining thermal activity?"

"Negative, Sir."

"Okay. Set us down in front of the big house."

"Scout One, reporting," came the soft radio transmission.

"Go ahead, Scout One," Timmons responded as the helicopter settled on the snow-covered lawn.

"We have a Dr. Roberts here, Mr. Fitzpatrick. She's cold and shivering, but she's fine."

Agent Timmons turned to the rear seat of the helicopter where Fitzpatrick and Fisher sat. He wore an ear-to-ear grin.

"Tell Scout One to escort Dr. Roberts to the manor house," Fitzpatrick said.

Fisher relaxed a bit for the first time in almost two weeks, but he knew one last item needed attention.

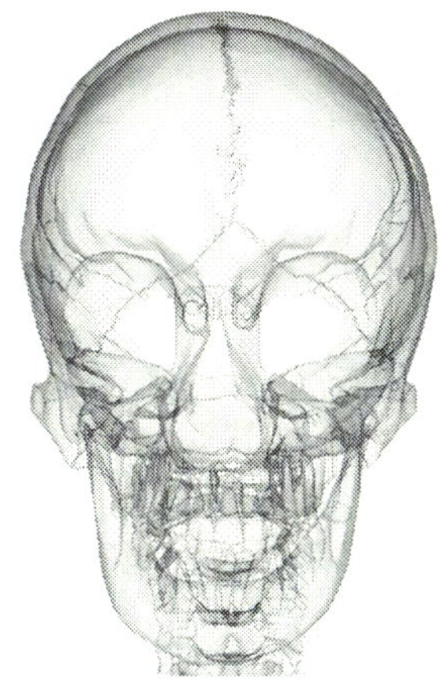

CHAPTER FORTY-EIGHT

Parc de Bruxelles, Brussels, Belgium, February 14

Winter wind pinched Fisher's face as a gust danced past him on its journey down a crowded Hertogs Straat. The afternoon traffic rush had begun, but Fisher would take his time crossing the busy avenue. He checked his watch. He was early, but he had combed every inch of the downtown park, and he knew precisely where he had to be. He wanted no surprises.

An electric trolley loaded with commuters lumbered quietly along, followed by flocks of BMWs and Mercedes.

Fisher's mind raced as he stuck his hands down into his heavy overcoat. The afternoon was clear and cold, the sunshine bright. He closed his eyes and leaned back against the massive stone wall that surrounded the Palais des Académies, Brussels' renowned conservatory of music. Since his arrival in the city twenty four-hours earlier, he had struggled to stay focused, but his mind had only partially cooperated. At intervals, he still replayed the events of the previous two weeks. The treachery, the deceit, the violence — it was all a spinning, seething, whirling, nightmare. Unfortunately, the center of the conspiracy, the one responsible, the creator of the vortex of horror, had escaped. After the FBI's debriefing, an agent informed Fisher that operatives had fanned out across the Caribbean basin searching for Graf. There was no sign of him.

"The jet that raced off that runway in Mamaroneck was seemingly swallowed up, vanished. He could be hiding anywhere, Dr. Fisher," the debriefing agent had told him as he left FBI headquarters in Washington, DC.

Before Fisher's departure, Fitzpatrick informed him that arrests had quietly begun at Taggart Memorial and at many other Health Pursuit hospitals across the US. Administrators, surgeons and low-level operatives had been taken quietly and — not surprisingly — they were talking. "It'll be weeks before we'll know the true size of the operation," Fitzpatrick said. "One thing's for sure, though, you guys found the mother lode." Fitzpatrick's agency had placed a total news blackout on the arrests until Fisher's mission to Brussels could be completed. A remaining principal in the intrigue had yet to be reined in.

Alli's face bubbled up into Fisher's thoughts as he studied the columns of traffic funneling into the avenues that skirted the Park. He smiled, recalling their night together before his departure. He and Alli had stopped by Roberts' apartment to see how she was recovering from her ordeal. After a night in the hospital, the doctors sent her home to convalesce. "I'm a little fatigued," she said during their visit. "Nothing that some rest won't cure." After the brief visit, they departed, their destination, Fisher's favorite restaurant on the cliffs of the Caton River. They shared an intimate meal and later ended up at his apartment. His memories of that night, her satin skin, her gentle weight lying on him, remained fresh in his thoughts.

The sounds of skidding tires pulled Fisher from his daydream. He glanced at his watch. It was time.

He waited for the traffic signal to change, then walked to a corner entrance at the confluence of Rue Ducale and Hertogs Straat.

The Parc de Bruxelles was practically square, measuring roughly half a kilometer on each side. It was dotted with towering oak, ash and sycamore, its lawns and gardens neatly manicured. For the most part, the Parc was flat, with minor hills providing excellent vistas during warmer months. On the west face, the side adjacent to Belgium's Royal Palace, the landscape dropped off sharply some forty feet below street level. The depression, running the entire distance of the west face, was heavily wooded and artistically landscaped. Dense vegetation in the hollow made it a favorite place for privacy and solitude among Brussels' residents. Fisher had chosen the west face for an important meeting.

The icy wind stiffened, lifting sand and dust into the air as Fisher entered the Park. Pedestrians traveling ahead of him pulled their coats up tightly and rushed to shelter. Fisher walked for a short distance fighting the cold wind while he studied the half-mile columns of leafless ash trees. Their branches were woven together into two continuous grids ten feet above the ground. Eventually, he presumed, long sashes of green would form in the spring.

After walking about two hundred yards, Fisher turned and passed between the rusting iron pickets of an aging gate and began his descent into the sunken gardens. He followed the steep trail, soon coming to the garden floor. Almost immediately, both the traffic noise and gusty winter winds were gone. Upon reaching the center of the garden, Fisher seated himself on a stone bench. His watch showed the time at almost three thirty. He took a breath and slowly exhaled, trying to remain calm.

"Dr. Fisher?" a voice from behind came unexpectedly.

Slightly startled, Fisher stood and turned.

The man before him was at least a head taller. His wiry blond hair was cut short; his physique, athletic with wide shoulders. Over most of his kind, but powerful face, his skin was scarlet red, as if stung by the icy air that cut through the city. Fisher estimated his age at thirty-five.

"I'm Dr. Timothy Thornley, Dr. Fisher. I hope you don't mind, but I came at the end of my run."

He wore a brightly colored jogging suit. His breathing was still rapid.

"No, not at all." Fisher offered his hand.

"Nice to make your acquaintance," Thornely said.

"Thank you for coming on such short notice, Dr. Thornley," Fisher said, recalling his uncertainty about the phone call the night before.

"Please, call me Tim."

Fisher smiled at the man who had discovered Myelopress. Within twenty-four hours, he would receive the World Transplant Congress Medal of Achievement. He wondered how he would respond to the news Fisher had to convey.

"Sit down, Tim." Fisher pointed to the long stone bench. "I've got a story to tell you."

• • • • •

The afternoon sun was about to drop behind the Royal Palace, when Fisher completed his detailed account. Timothy Thornley's face showed shock, disbelief and pain. His robust scarlet coloring from an hour earlier had long since been supplanted by pallor.

"Dr. Fisher, I . . . I don't know what to say to you," Thornley said. "There's just no way I can believe this. Why should I believe it or you? It's too fantastic, especially the part about Katsumi's involvement."

Fisher had anticipated Thornley's response. He pulled an envelope from his coat. "Tim, this is a sworn, sealed affidavit from Darren Fitzpatrick, Director of Domestic US Intelligence for the FBI, detailing the involvement of his agency over the past several days. I think you'll find my account and Fitzpatrick's identical."

Thornley examined the raised, Department of Justice seal and looked back up at Fisher. He opened the envelope and read. For the next few minutes, he scanned the document carefully, then lowered it to his lap.

"I'm sorry, Dr. Fisher. It's just too unbelievable. I mean, Katsumi's involvement. It's just too far out. I know the head of the company, Mr. Kamatsu. He's totally honest. Look, if you don't mind," Thornley returned the affidavit to Fisher, "I think I'll be leaving now. There's a dinner in my honor tonight, and I certainly can't be late."

Thornley had already headed for one of the paths out of the sunken garden when Fisher called after him.

"Think again, Tim."

Thornley stopped at the edge of the clearing and turned to face Fisher.

Fisher rose from the bench walked a few steps away then turned back to face Thornley.

From the pocket of his bulky overcoat, Fisher pulled out a small glass object. "Have a look at this." Fisher pitched the object to Thornley.

Thornley caught the multidose vial. He examined the vial, first noting the Katsumi Pharmaceuticals corporate logo. He continued his inspection, turning it ninety degrees to read its small rectangular label. Thornley froze.

After a few moments, he looked up at Fisher from across the clearing, the color again lost from his face. "Where did you get this? This is one of our most secret projects."

"Tim, that vial was taken from the outpost OR I told you about. And thanks to an enterprising young friend of mine, I know that KP-1049, set to be released next year by Katsumi, will be brand-named GrowStimulin. I can also tell you exactly what it does to wounded human tissue. I've seen it with my own eyes. A pathologist at Medford University is preparing a detailed report of its molecular effects, as we speak. I also know that on receiving FDA approval, Katsumi Pharmaceuticals will market the agent for wound repair."

"You can't know that!" Thornley shouted as he stomped across the clearing to where Fisher stood. "This has been Katsumi's most secret project."

"And, who at Katsumi was directly responsible for the security of KP-1049 before its release, Tim?"

"Mr. Kamatsu. Only Mr. Kamatsu." The volume of Thornley's voice decreased as realization set in.

Fisher stared into Thornley's eyes. "So, could I assume that finding more than one hundred vials of KP-1049 in an unauthorized outpost operating room where homeless victims were subjected to illegal organ removal would be a breach of security?"

"Yes," Thornley stared at the ground between his running shoes, "Yes."

"The FBI lab at Quantico analyzed the chemical in the vial you're holding. It was compared to the FDA's chemical structure data on KP-1049 supplied by Katsumi Pharmaceuticals. It's identical."

Fisher pulled another envelope from his pocket and handed it to Thornley, who looked more distressed.

Thornley returned to the bench, ripping into the sealed envelope as he reseated himself.

"Oh, God," Thornley whispered as he studied the results of the mass spectrometry studies. The first page of the FBI report detailed the analysis of the substance removed from the outpost OR vial labeled KP-1049; the second was an analysis of a sample of KP-1049 provided by the FDA. The two reports had been certified and notarized February twelfth.

They were identical.

After a long pause, he grabbed the zipper of his jogging suit and pulled it to his neck. He stared through the trees at the shades of peach and teal forming in the clouds above the Royal Palace. "I suppose you're here to ask me to refuse the medal at tomorrow's award ceremony."

"Yes," came Fisher's quiet reply.

Tears dropped down Thornley's cheeks.

"Tim, the conspiracy will eventually become public knowledge. When it does, it'll spread across the globe like wildfire. Toshima Kamatsu will be arrested and prosecuted."

Thornley turned back to Fisher, his eyes reddened. "And this scum bag, Graf. What about him?"

"There's a manhunt on. That's all I can tell you. My contacts at the FBI feel certain he'll eventually be caught and brought to justice."

"Why did you come here, seek me out like this, demand this secret meeting? Why?"

Fisher stared at the small gravel stones that lined the clearing. "For many reasons, I guess," Fisher finally said, his chin on his chest. "I lost a friend, and I became aware of the significant loss of life that was occurring. And," Fisher hesitated a moment, "I saw how the greed of a few threatened to forever change an important human enterprise."

Fisher looked down at Thornley. "I know the sacrifices you and your close personal colleagues made to bring Myelopress into clinical use. Those motives shouldn't ever be threatened. By refusing the award tomorrow and exposing the conspiracy before your peers and the world, your work won't be jeopardized. Yes, there'll be an outcry. But you will have risen above the greed and dishonesty. The true understanding of your contribution to science will be delayed awhile, but in the end, you'll be vindicated. My sources at the FBI have assured me you'll have immunity from prosecution. Tim, public condemnation of the conspiracy between Graf and Kamatsu is crucial for the continued evolution of organ transplantation."

In the gathering darkness, Thornley stood. "I must go now, Dr. Fisher."

Fisher watched as the young man disappeared up the gravel path. He pulled his overcoat tight around his chest and walked slowly out of the sunken garden.

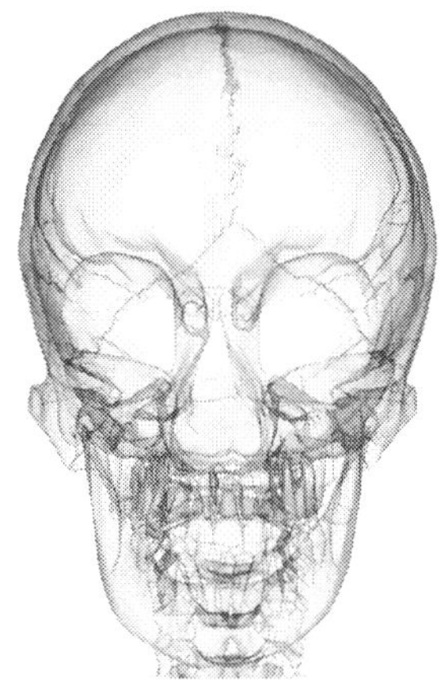

CHAPTER FORTY-NINE

Palais des Congres, Brussels, February 15, Awards Colloquium, World Transplant Congress

Fisher slept restlessly, plagued by nightmares of fiendish faces and blood-drenched torsos. At three in the morning, he had awakened, startled and sweating, as he once again witnessed Stryker's violent death on the Parkway. Unable to sleep after that, he arose, showered and left his small hotel to walk the streets of old town Brussels. For hours, he wandered aimlessly, able to concentrate on little else but his meeting the afternoon before. One central question kept plaguing him as he walked the pre-dawn avenues of the sleeping town: Did Thornley share Fisher's values and vision, the ones that had driven Fisher halfway around the world to seek out the meeting with Thornley in the first place? He was unable to sound the depths of Thornley's mind from such a short meeting. In the end, he realized he hadn't a clue to Thornley's innermost thoughts.

With a sense of dread, Fisher finally landed in the expansive assembly hall of the Congress Center. The hall teemed with activity as constituents of the world's governing body for transplant medicine streamed in. People engaged in conversations stood in random groups around the hall. Fragments of Dutch, French and German floated softly into earshot as Fisher scanned the large hall. He had entered the hall early and chosen a seat along the left side, near a series of glass booths elevated eight or ten feet off the main floor. Inside, an army of translators milled about making preparations for the address. Fisher glanced at his watch. It was time for the proceedings to begin.

At that moment, a barrage of strobe lights flashed from the cordoned international press corps area. More than a thousand heads turned to the rear of the hall as a group of five Japanese men made their way down the center aisle, their bright green identification tags signifying they were guests of the Congress.

"Katsumi," Fisher muttered under his breath.

Portions of the audience seated to the right and left of the center aisle stood and broke into spontaneous applause as the group approached the front of the hall. Within moments, applause came from all parts of the room.

Fisher studied the delegation. All were dressed in conservative suits. Three of the men displayed toothy smiles and took short bows as the applause continued. One member of the group, however, remained stone-faced and emotionless.

"Toshima Kamatsu," the crowd whispered. The CEO of Katsumi Pharmaceuticals walked behind the others, seemingly disconnected from the events. Fisher's chest pounded reflexively. He tightened his grip on the arms of his chair. He had seen photographs of Kamatsu, in the lay and scientific press. Although Fisher was separated from Kamatsu by thirty yards or more, he could clearly see the man's face, brooding and cruel.

The group's final member traveled closely behind Kamatsu casting menacing glances, his eyes lingering no more than a second in any direction. He stood a head taller than the Katsumi chief, and filled his suit coat with muscular arms and shoulders.

The Katsumi delegation took reserved seats at the front of the hall. From Fisher's position, he could see that one of the reserved seats was not occupied.

Fisher gasped, looking first at the vacant seat, then madly around the assembly hall.

Timothy Thornley was absent.

Fisher continued searching the gathering for any sign of Thornley. He was nowhere to be found. What did his absence mean, Fisher asked himself, his mind racing again. Did Thornley, in a pursuit to be forthright and honest, confront Kamatsu the evening before? Had he been injured, perhaps killed?

On schedule, the lights dimmed, signifying the start of the proceedings. A hush fell over the massive audience as all eyes turned toward the stage, which was elevated three to four feet above the audience. A small lectern was positioned to the left of center. A large multicolor flower arrangement to the right and left added the proper accent.

From behind the curtain, at stage left, emerged Louis Bâsteau, the president of the World Transplant Congress and a giant in the field of transplantation. His contributions during three decades as a professor of surgery at the University of Paris ranked him with Debakey, Shumway, and Starzel.

Fisher anxiously searched the lecture hall for Thornley as Bâsteau began his introductory remarks.

"Mesdames e Messieurs."

Fisher hurriedly picked up the plastic earphones off the translator station in front of him. They fit easily into his ear canals.

"We are gathered here on the occasion of these grand proceedings," Bâsteau continued, "to honor the extraordinary contribution of a young scientist. Through his keen observation and power of intellect, you, I and the world have stepped into a new era. An era where the horizons of organ transplantation will have no boundaries. An age where the frontiers of disease will be pushed back further than our wildest dreams. We, the citizens of the world, owe Dr. Timothy Thornley a huge debt that can never be repaid. Ladies and Gentlemen, it gives me great honor to present the World Transplant Congress' highest honor, the Award of Achievement, to Dr. Timothy Thornley. Dr. Thornley, would you please come forward?"

During Bâsteau's remarks, Fisher had continued looking around the hall for signs of Thornley. There were none — Thornley was not present.

The gathering rose to its feet, erupting into thunderous applause. From all corners, cheering, whistling and yelling were deafening. Strobe flashes again winked as the press corps anticipated Thornley's approach to the podium.

In less than a minute, the applause dropped in volume. Some audience members turned and peered down the aisles while others watched the podium and Bâsteau. Slowly, people returned to their seats as whispers and murmurs raged on every row.

Où est-ceque Thornley?

Donde está Thornley?

Where is Thornley?

Bâsteau finally broke free of his board-like stance and paced to stage left, where he conferred with two officials. Within seconds, gestures flew as the conversation became heated.

Suddenly, heads snapped around. Conversations became clearly audible everywhere. Strobe flashes resumed their barrage as everyone turned toward the center aisle. By standing on his toes, Fisher could see a disheveled Timothy Thornley slowly making his way to the stage. He wore the same jogging suit from the day before. Scattered applause broke out as he continued his slow approach. He was unaware of any intended congratulations, however. He stared straight ahead, detached, his face a mask of despair.

Fisher had seen that expression many times before. It was the one patients wore when struggling with a terminal prognosis, the emptiness easily visible in the eyes as family members dealt with the forthcoming death of a loved one. It was the same tight-lipped pallor one drew from an emotional free-fall into the bottomless pit of human despair.

Bâsteau looked down the center aisle. He turned back to the two men he had moments earlier engaged in argument, then returned to the lectern. One of the men hurried off stage and approached Thornley, while the other placed a walkie-talkie to his mouth and disappeared behind the curtain.

Thornley showed no reaction to the official's approach. The man simply fell in step beside him, gently grasping his arm. As Thornley passed the front row, he showed no signs of recognition of the Japanese delegation.

At first, Fisher worried that Thornley had been injured. Brussels, like every major city across the globe, had become increasingly violent. Fisher saw no signs of injury, however.

Applause picked up momentum as Thornley mounted the steps, the meeting official still at his side. As the two men arrived at the podium, Bâsteau broke into a nervous smile and offered his hand. Thornley greeted Bâsteau, but did not shed his look of despair. Thornley conversed briefly with Bâsteau, at first shaking his head, then nodding, in response — Fisher presumed — to Questions concerning his health.

The applause continued as Bâsteau led Thornley to the lectern. The instant Thornley faced the audience Fisher saw the deep flush of his face, the glimmer of his eyes as the stage lights reflected off tears.

An unexpected sound from the rear of the auditorium momentarily diverted Fisher's attention. Several of the double doors to the right of the press corps opened, and uniformed Brussels Police officers filed into the assembly hall. Then, Darren Fitzpatrick entered the hall, accompanied by at least ten men dressed in plain clothes, who were unmistakably government agents. Belgian, Fisher presumed.

"Ladies and Gentlemen," Thornley started, his voice frail and soft. "It is with deepest and profound . . . ." Thornley's voice broke. He lowered his chin to his chest and stepped back from the podium, attempting to collect himself. Murmuring spread throughout the hall that had become pin-drop quiet.

Fisher's cold, sweaty hands trembled as he stared at Thornley. The actions he was about to take were gratifying, yet truly terrifying as they would likely produce new uncertainty in the field of organ transplantation.

Appearing emboldened after a few moments of reflection, Thornley re-approached the rostrum. "Ladies and Gentlemen, your confidence in my work and that of my colleagues has been gratifying. Myelopress has far exceeded my wildest dreams." Thornley hesitated, looking briefly at his hands. "But," he continued, "it is with deep and profound regret that I cannot accept this award."

Fisher saw heads move erratically in all directions as the audience again burst forth in hushed conversation. On stage, Louis Bâsteau appeared shaken by Thornley's announcement. He started to approach, when Thornley began speaking again.

"Within the past twenty-four hours," Thornley said, his voice strengthening, "I have learned of a conspiracy to traffic human organs from Europe and the Middle East into the United States. In these countries and in the United States, the perpetrators secretly hunted their prey among the poor and the homeless, strong-arming their victims to give up their organs. In many cases multiple organs, including hearts, were taken from a single individual."

People all around Fisher became boisterous and disorderly. Brussels Police moved into the aisles, exerting an immediate calming influence.

"I refuse this award, because I've learned the conspirators included my employer, Katsumi Pharmaceuticals, and the American for-profit hospital corporation, Health Pursuit."

Meeting officials hurried to escort Thornley from the podium as individuals rose and shouted. Multi-lingual jeers and threats directed at the Japanese spewed from every corner of the hall.

Fisher glanced at the stage. Bâsteau had returned to the podium and was preparing to speak. Suddenly, movement caught his eye as an agitated group left their seats and charged down the aisle at the Japanese. Before the Brussels' police could react, two men vaulted over the rows toward Kamatsu.

With lightening quickness, the burly Asian, who earlier trailed the Katsumi delegation, dived in front of Kamatsu and confronted the mob. Hysteria ruled as the rabble, undeterred by the bodyguard's defense, crushed forward.

Fisher saw a pistol appear in the brawny Asian's hand, and a struggle for the weapon ensued. Moments later the pistol discharged, echoing across the open space. Partial quiet fell over the congress hall as one of the members wrestling with the Asian fell back, wounded by the shot.

Brussels Police and Belgian Secret Service rushed the swarm of rioters and began pulling bodies away from the Japanese. Before long, calm returned and the injured Congress member was removed by an emergency team. As Toshima Kamatsu was partially dragged, partially carried from the hall, he never broke from his cruel stare at Thornley.

In the hour that followed the hurried adjournment, the assembly hall emptied. Fisher finally made his way over to Fitzpatrick as the crowd cleared.

"I'd say your plan worked exactly as intended, Steve." Fitzpatrick shook hands with Fisher. "Kamatsu's in custody."

Seeming to ignore Fitzpatrick's comment, Fisher asked, "Did you . . .?"

"No, I'm sorry, Steve," Fitzpatrick interrupted, guessing the content of Fisher's question. "Graf's still out there somewhere. An assault team made a run on his island estate last night, but he slipped through their fingers."

"You guys have got to find him, Darren." Fisher could feel anger building inside as he stared across the vacant assembly hall.

"We'll find him. It's only a matter of time. NSA and CIA agreed to re-task a satellite over the Caribbean basin, and Interpol's got all the details by now. There aren't many places Graf can hide without us knowing."

Fisher calmed as Fitzpatrick spoke.

"Besides," Fitzpatrick grinned, "maybe you didn't get Graf, but you shut down the Katsumi connection."

Fisher smiled.

"How about an espresso?" Fitzpatrick said, patting Fisher's back.

"Sounds good."

Both men smiled as they turned and headed out of the assembly hall.

As the two men left the sprawling room, a member of Congress security emerged from the shadows and moved to the rear of the hall. He glanced about carefully, studying the room to affirm he was alone. The hall, for the most part, had emptied. The only visible movement came from the elevated translation booth where a single individual appeared preoccupied with final clean up.

Satisfied, the man extracted a small phone from his coat pocket, punched a set of digits, and waited. The conversation that ensued was brief, lasting less than a minute. With the cell phone back in his pocket, he made his way to the front of the Congress Center.

• • • • •

Rupert Graf gazed at the massive snow-covered peaks as he lowered the antenna of his cell phone. A mirthless laughter soon flowed from his mouth as the vessels across his head and neck engorged. The wind off the mountains stiffened, transporting the continuing laughter to the valley below.

THE END

Author Biography

Doctor Fowler has been engaged in the practice of medicine and in biomedical research for over 35 years. He has published more than 300 medical research publications. His laboratory continues to delve into the mysteries of acute lung injury.

Made in the USA
Middletown, DE
04 March 2023